Elaine DeBohun

The Starlight Menagerie

with original poetry by

Rory Sidney

The Starlight Menagerie
Ballads of the Starlight Menagerie
Copyright © 2025 by Elaine DeBohun and Rory Sidney

Cover art and dust jacket by Sarah Anne Bachman, hardcover laminate by Shelby Schena, woodcut fairy tale illustrations by Laura Craig, digitized Renaissance emblems by Nitisia Roland of Urania Press

This is a work of fiction. Names, characters, places and incidents either are the product of the author's imagination or are used fictitiously, and any resemblance to actual persons, living or dead, businesses, companies, events, or locales is entirely coincidental.

This story includes themes on page that some readers may find disturbing, including: murder, murder of a pregnant woman, sexual violence, suicidal ideation, spirit possession and psychosis.

First Edition: November 2025
ISBN:
979-8-218-60006-8 (paperback)
979-8-218-59421-3 (hardcover)

Printed in the United States of America

Dedicated to the plot twist

"I know your voice. I've been hearing it inside myself for decades."
— *Walter Russell upon meeting his wife, Lao*

AUTHOR'S NOTE

There are many ghosts who reside within the pages of this novel that deserve their due. While the story of Troilo and Philippa is of a fictitious nature, the tragedies that inspired it are not. You will recognize the names of many of these characters, some quite well-known, whose lives and deaths were truly stranger than fiction. I have tried to portray these figures as accurately as possible according to historical accounts, while still affording myself creative liberty to tell a completely unique story.

The dragon lore found within Philippa's story trickles down from my own ancestry. It is spoken of orally in the most remote Balkan villages, so much about the *zmaj* remains unknown without being privy to that corner of the world. To my knowledge, at the date of publication, this is the first time it has ever been fictionalized in the English language.

Just as well, I should mention that *The Starlight Menagerie* is a book that walks a blurry line between mental illness and the notion of spirit-induced phenomena, so if psychosis is a sensitive topic for you, please take caution.

I hope you enjoy this haunting blend of history and fantasy.

And most of all, I hope you struggle to parse the two apart. The bold letters are **not** a typo, by the way.

Visconti

Bernabò Visconti
Lord of Milan
(1280 – 1327)

Troilo Visconti
(unknown)

Elisabetta Visconti
(1297 – 1335)

Matthias von Habsburg
Duke of Pazin
(1315 – 1362)

House of
Wittelsbach

Habsburg
Lorraine

King Ludwig II
of Bavaria
(1845 – 1886)

Empress Elizabeth
(1837 – 1898)

Emperor
Franz Joseph
(1830 –   )

Archduke
Karl Ludwig
(1833 – 1896)

Crown Prince
Rudolf
(1858 – 1889)

Archduchess
Philippa
(1876 –   )

Archduke
Franz Ferdinand
(1863 –   )

Archduchess
Erzsi
(1883 –   )

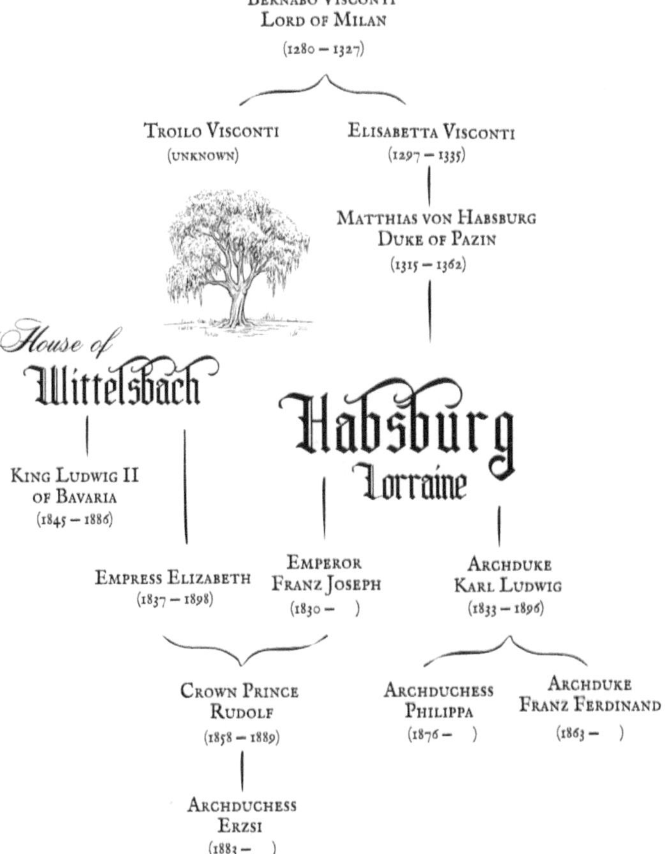

The Starlight Menagerie

ONE

June 21, 1900 — *present day*
9:45 A.M.

Inspector Ziegler took a knee next to the corpse of the duke, which lay within a partially laced body bag. With the added variable of heat making everything more perishable, summertime investigations were difficult enough without the body having been submerged in water all night.

"Duke Sixten's assailant attacked him from behind, here, delivering five blows between his neck and shoulder. Then two more blows just below the clavicle." The inspector dabbed his perspiring hairline, which seemed to recede more by the day. "Then they used the pocketknife to finish the job, right here across the throat."

"Chief Inspector, are we certain the original puncture wounds were made by a knife?"

Ziegler glanced up at his curly-headed understudy, twenty-year-old Rudolf Kaspar, who was gazing toward the glass pond, pregnant with midsummer lilies. The son of a dead merchant, he'd been thrown into Ziegler's office as a potential replacement earlier that year, and had shadowed him on every investigation since.

"What are you suggesting, Herr Kaspar?"

Ziegler tried his best to taper his despairing tone. Despite being a creative thinker and well-read university drop out, the boy was still an unseasoned policeman with very few field hours.

"See..." Rudolf knelt, pointing to the torn fabric of the duke's tunic. "The punctures are so blunt that if they were made by a knife, it must have been incredibly dull."

"A dull knife, perhaps, lad," said Ziegler. "But a knife all the same."

The boy's chiseled cheeks softened. "Yes, sir," he replied, smiling deferentially. "It was only a suggestion."

"On to business then." Ziegler felt his knees crack as he rose slowly to his feet. "We will question Archduchess Erzsi, and then her governess, Fräulein Coudenhove, in that order. Has there been any word from Zürich?"

"The Burghölzli sent a telegram. The hospital claims it has not received any correspondence from the doctor since the eighth of June."

"Then request the departure records of every train that has left Vienna in the last forty-eight hours," Ziegler ordered.

"Do you believe the doctor may be guilty of something, Chief Inspector?"

"*Something*, yes."

According to the testimonies of multiple servants, he was at the Kaiservilla, in the presence of Archduke Franz when the murder took place. Still...

"An innocent man has no reason to flee." Ziegler pulled out his pocket watch, then tapped the glass so that the minute hand would reset. "But worry not," he added. "We will find him."

"And her?"

Ziegler looked over at Rudolf, whose expression had grown cloudy and sentimental.

"Archduchess Philippa," he clarified.

Ah yes, the royal of the hour, who, like her foreign doctor, had vanished without a trace.

"Do you believe she is dead?"

Ziegler glanced briefly over his shoulder, where, nestled seductively against the green slopes of the Salzkammergut mountains, the unpolished, pink marble of the empress' tea house blushed like a garden rose after a rain shower.

Archduchess Erzsi and her governess—who had both resided within the cottage with Philippa and her doctor—awaited questioning inside. And while it was true that Habsburgs always seemed to perish in the most opulent of places, until Ziegler could cross examine them, any statement on the missing archduchess' whereabouts would be pure speculation.

"As it stands, we are investigating only one death, Herr Kaspar." Ziegler motioned to Duke Sixten, lying face up in the grass. "The lovely archduchess is missing unless determined otherwise."

"Yes, sir."

"Time is working against us, lad," he added. "We mustn't keep them waiting."

Hung with European oil paintings and stuffed to the brim with ornate sculptures, the cottage built for Empress Elisabeth seemed the very pinnacle of opulence. Ironic, it was, that she had been no happier for it. Some sources claimed that she'd appeared *relieved* to die—nearly leaning into the blade of her Italian assassin. Everyone knew that she had died with her son nearly a decade before, when he'd put the barrel of a pistol to his temple.

Past the assembled constabulary in the window-lit foyer, Archduchess Erzsi—Elisabeth's granddaughter and namesake—waited to be received in the crimson parlor. Seven years younger than Philippa, she resembled her in all but the eyes, which belonged to her late father. Her fingers moved in calculated circles as she stroked the miniature terrier on her lap with one hand, and held a mauve book with the other.

"Your Imperial and Royal Highness."

Lifting her gaze from the open pages, Archduchess Erzsi met Ziegler's eye as he closed the parlor door behind him, enveloping the room in an awkward pause.

"I am Chief Inspector Alois Ziegler."

"We have met before," she replied, lowering her book.

"Yes, of course."

The archduchess had been only a fraction of herself, then. A little girl with bottomless moon eyes the color of an ice pond. *Erzsi's saucers,* her family had called them.

"You were just a child," Ziegler added. "I did not think you remembered."

Erzsi felt her cheeks lift in a half-smile as the inspector took the seat directly across from her. As if she could have ever forgotten the day that her father had shot himself.

"Do you still have that silver pocket watch I used to play with?" she asked.

Inspector Ziegler nodded, opening his coat to reveal the watch chain attached to his vest. "Your Highness," he said, closing his coat, "may I ask you a few questions?"

"I have told your men all I know."

"I am afraid further questioning is necessary for the investigation," he replied. "It is standard procedure."

Closing her book, Erzsi tucked the spine between her thigh and the armrest, then motioned for the inspector to continue.

"I understand that you were the last person to see Her Highness, Archduchess Philippa?"

"That is correct," she said, resetting her long, sandy braid to one side.

"Can you tell me a bit about the last time you saw her?"

"Pippa and I talked in her bedroom, as we often do in the evenings."

"What was her demeanor like?"

"She was still reeling from an upsetting encounter with Duke Sixten the previous night."

"Did you know Duke Sixten Siegfried well?"

Erzsi's stomach curdled at the thought of him. "Too well for my liking," she replied, combing her fingers through Blitz's fur.

"May I ask the nature of this encounter you speak of?"

"Perhaps it would be better explained by my cousin, Archduke Franz."

"I do not plan to question His Highness until he arrives this afternoon, so if you would be so kind," Inspector Ziegler replied. "Time is of the essence."

Erzsi straightened up in her chair. "Franz banished Duke Sixten from the premises the previous night for violence against Philippa."

"According to His Majesty, The Emperor," the inspector countered, "Duke Sixten left early due to business."

"Franz was too embarrassed to repeat what he had seen," said Erzsi. "After all, it was *he* who brought Duke Sixten to Kaiservilla. It would have reflected horribly on his character, and relations between my grandfather and Franz are already tense."

Inspector Ziegler cleared his throat, filled with what she could only assume was summer phlegm. "Archduchess Philippa's doctor, he was new here, yes?"

Erzsi nodded.

"All the way from Italy. An interesting choice on His Majesty's part."

"He was from Istria, not Italy," she corrected. "And he was supposed to be the best of the best."

"Did he have anything against Duke Sixten?"

"It was *Duke Sixten* who insisted on making enemies, Chief Inspector. Surely you are aware of his record."

"The Munich incident, yes," he replied, lowering his voice. "His Grace was cleared of all charges."

"Do you believe it is a coincidence then, that the crime is one and the same?" Erzsi asked. "Violence against a woman? Philippa was still awake when I went to bed, so he must have lured her outside."

"Did you *see* Duke Sixten lure your cousin outside, Your Highness?"

Erzsi blinked, remembering how she'd watched the duke wander drunkenly along the path next to the pond.

"I was in bed, asleep," she said. "If I had only indulged her company a bit longer, she might still be alive."

"As it stands, there has been no evidence to confirm she is anything other than missing."

"Keep looking, Chief Inspector." Erzsi felt her eyes glaze over him like a wall of frost. "You will find it."

The gaze of the inspector seemed to narrow on her, as though she were an insect beneath his looking glass.

"You must forgive my insensitivity," Erzsi added. "I am a veteran of tragedy, as you know."

His nod was subtle as he laced his fingers over his lap. "I understand that you were first to discover Duke Sixten dead."

Erzsi recalled watching the sunrise ripple across the pond, where the body had floated freely among the pair of swans on the other side. Knowing that every tragedy that had ever befallen her had been for that moment alone, Erzsi had gripped the railing and inhaled deeply, filling her chest with the sweet dewy air of the June morning. Then, she had expelled a scream so convincing—so *bloodcurdling*—that every songbird in the Salzkammergut went silent.

"That is correct, Chief Inspector."

"Did you see the body up close, Your Highness?"

Erzsi shook away the thought of the duke's slit neck. "Only from where I stood on the veranda," she replied.

"I will not share the gruesome details." Inspector Ziegler spoke with a low rasp. "Only that he was attacked from behind."

Erzsi felt her chest heave up, then down. "She would have fought him, Inspector," she whispered. "To the very end, she would have fought him. It was her doctor that she loved."

That seemed to grab the inspector's attention.

"It is why Duke Sixten despised him so," Erzsi explained, feeling Blitz's fur dampen with the sweat of her palms. "They planned to marry."

"Archduchess Philippa and her doctor planned to marry?"

"Yes, Chief Inspector. That is why he was at the villa speaking with Franz last night."

Inspector Ziegler sat back in his chair, pulling a handkerchief from his vest pocket.

"I know what you are thinking," Erzsi said, watching him wipe his forehead. "You want to ask me if he loved Pippa enough to kill a man for her—and I will tell you that he would have done anything to keep her safe."

The inspector lowered his handkerchief.

"But he is innocent." Her gaze slipped past Inspector Ziegler to the turning parlor doorknob behind him. "He was at the villa all hours of the night. Franz will tell you the same thing."

"Did the doctor say anything to you before he left, Your Highness?"

Erzsi thought back to how Troilo had knelt before her, covered in bloody handprints. "I fear the details of our last conversation are lost to me," she replied.

"With a memory such as yours, I find that surprising."

Erzsi blinked. "Do you?" she poked, motioning to the young man with dark curls peeking through the cracked door.

The stranger met Erzsi's gaze from where she sat in the chair. "Chief Inspector?"

"*Herr Kaspar,*" Inspector Ziegler said sternly over his shoulder. "Just a moment more."

Like a chastised child, the young man redirected his attention to his boss. "Uh—yes sir," he replied.

Erzsi grinned down at her lap, listening to the parlor door shut behind them.

"I apologize for the interruption," said the inspector as he shifted back to her. "That is Herr Kaspar."

"Your understudy?" Erzsi guessed.

"Nothing slips past you, Highness."

"Things always hide in plain sight, Chief Inspector. If only one has the eyes to see them." Erzsi glanced down at the mauve book, wedged between her leg and the armrest. "Am I free to go, then?"

"Yes," Inspector Ziegler replied. "Thank you for speaking with me."

Rounding her dog in her arms, Erzsi jumped from her seat and grabbed her book. The parlor door opened for her on command, as if Herr Kaspar had sensed her on the other side, but the moment was short-lived. Next to him stood Mellie, her face still whiter than the waterlogged corpse of the duke.

She'd been the first to come to Erzsi's aid that morning, and, together, they had searched the upstairs of the tea house to find Philippa and Troilo both missing.

"Fräulein Coudenhove, please come in."

Erzsi nodded to her governess as they slipped past each other in the doorway.

"Herr Kaspar," called Inspector Ziegler. "Stay."

Nodding to Erzsi, the young man obeyed. "Your Highness," he said, leaving her in the ruby hall.

Lowering Blitz to the floor, she gripped the book with slippery fingers. Most of the constabulary were still outside by the pond, and the maids and servants had gravitated to the second floor. When Erzsi was certain she was alone, she stepped closer to the parlor door, determined to listen in.

"I am Chief Inspector Alois Ziegler, and this is my apprentice, Herr Kaspar."

"Have you found him?" Mellie asked.

Erzsi rolled her eyes at the thought of her sitting across from the inspector, shoulders hunched. Unable to make out her soft-spoken voice, she pressed her ear to the wood.

"We are working to locate the doctor and Her Highness both."

"I shall not sleep until they are both found."

"I understand," said Inspector Ziegler. "But be assured, we are doing our due diligence to make sure they are found in a timely manner."

"I do not think you understand, Chief Inspector. *No one* will be safe with the two of them running loose," Mellie added, somewhat frankly. "She only needs to ask him to kill someone else."

Erzsi scoffed under her breath.

"It would seem you and Her Highness, Archduchess Erzsi, have conflicting opinions, Fräulein."

"Her Highness lacks a father figure, as you know, Inspector."

Erzsi felt her pulse erupt like a volcano, clouding her vision in red—

"Liar!" Bursting full force into the parlor, she hurled her book at Mellie's head, missing by a hair. "How could you say such a thing?"

"Your Highness," hushed Herr Kaspar, "This is a cross examination. *You cannot—!"*

"Troilo has nothing to do with this, and *you know it.*"

"Nothing to do with it?" Mellie shot to her feet, her fists balled at her side. "He has done nothing but bring trouble since the day he arrived," she whispered tearfully.

"And did you tell them of your personal quarrel with him?" Erzsi demanded.

"Herr Kaspar! Please see Her Highness out."

Erzsi turned her baleful gaze on Inspector Ziegler. *"Did she, Chief Inspector?"*

Herr Kaspar was at her side now, trying to gently commandeer her.

"Did she tell you that she wants revenge because he loved Philippa and not her?" Erzsi demanded, refusing Herr Kaspar's arm. "Did she?"

"Your Highness!" shouted the inspector. "If you do not leave this room, I will be forced to—!"

"As if the love of your beloved cousin means anything more than nightly visits to her quarters," Mellie spat.

Erzsi lunged at her, but was caught by Herr Kaspar. "Let go of me—!" Trying to leap from his grasp, she aimed a finger at her governess. "Your envy is unbecoming," she warned.

"And you are as devious as they are."

Only yesterday Erzsi had Mellie believing she was on her side. But contrary to her prudish governess, Erzsi could admit *her* deceitful nature.

"I am sorry, Your Highness," Herr Kaspar whispered, urging her toward the door, "you must leave."

Shoving him away, Erzsi rolled her shoulders back, casting a cold glance at Mellie. "Then you are relieved of me, Fräulein Coudenhove." Her tone did not falter, as though the last decade they'd spent together had evaporated into thin air. "The housemaid will see to it that your bags are packed at once."

Leaving Mellie stunned to silence, Erzsi at last allowed Herr Kaspar to guide her out the parlor door and into the crowded hall, where the boots of the constabulary had dirtied the parquet floors.

"I am sorry," he said again, leading her through the tangle of police who had just come in from outside. "Cross examinations are confidential, Highness," he went on. "You cannot just barge in—"

"Let go of me!"

Rudolf's hand was only lightly touching her back.

"I do not need a *chaperone,*" Archduchess Erzsi hissed over her shoulder.

"I apolo—"

Whipping around to face him, she pursed her lips together, and widened her eyes. "And stop apologizing when you are *not* sorry!"

"Yes, Your Highness."

"If you were sorry, you would not have *dragged* me from the parlor like a common peasant! Have you forgotten that my father was the Crown Prince?"

So starstruck was Rudolf by Archduchess Erzsi, he didn't even flinch as she berated him. Having little experience with women as it was, he had even less with the royal variety.

"My grandfather—His Majesty, *The Emperor*—will be hearing about this," she added.

"Your Highness. If I may speak."

Her giant eyes snapped to Rudolf's face, then back down to his feet, as though she'd only just realized the considerable height difference between them. *"What?"*

"You must excuse me," he said. "I need to get back."

Archduchess Erzsi pulled her long, blonde braid around front. "You would do well to remember, Herr Kaspar," she said, readjusting it, "that women with broken hearts are quick to villanize. Fräulein Coudenhove is no different."

Rudolf bowed. "Your Highness," he said, taking his leave.

Already having taken too long, Rudolf knocked twice on the parlor door before reentering. Inspector Ziegler only motioned to him to close the door. Across from him, the governess sat with red-rimmed eyes.

"And your relationship with the doctor, Fräulein?"

Rudolf sidelined himself to the corner of the room, pocketing both of his hands.

"I certainly did not meet him in the corridors." Governess

Coudenhove's tone was as sour as a hot lemon. "Nor did I receive his love letters."

"Love letters, you say?" asked the inspector.

"He wrote her a whole journal of poems," she whimpered. "They are in Archduchess Erzsi's possession if she has not burned them already."

Inspector Ziegler nodded to himself in that way he did when he was unsatisfied. "Thank you, Fräulein. That will be all for now," he said, glancing at Rudolf. "Herr Kaspar, the door."

The governess, too, seemed unsatisfied as she rose to her feet, arms crossed tightly over her chest.

Rudolf nodded as he opened the door for her. "Fräulein Coudenhove."

Nose held high, she refused to look at him. Out of self preservation, he could only guess.

As he shut them back in the parlor, Rudolf looked across the room to see Inspector Ziegler swiping the mauve book Erzsi had thrown from the floor.

"Did you see to it that Her Highness understands she cannot barge into a cross examination?" he asked, sliding it onto a nearby table.

"She understands, sir," Rudolf replied. "Though, I believe I only provoked her further."

"You mustn't ever be afraid to provoke," he replied, finding the double windows that faced the veranda with hands clasped behind his back. "Understood?"

"Yes, Inspector."

"Never in my days have I witnessed such a spectacle," Inspector Ziegler scoffed. "Archduchess Erzsi claims it is a case of double murder, though there is no body. Her governess claims it was premeditated execution, carried out for Philippa by her lover."

"What seems most likely to you, sir?"

"Neither."

Finding the side of his superior, Rudolf's attention floated just outside the window, to the wrap-around veranda and its accompanying chairs, where Archduchess Erzsi sat paging through a book. The mere sight of her made Rudolf feel that bees were buzzing about in his stomach.

"Fräulein Coudenhove believes what she is telling us. But *she*..." Inspector Ziegler motioned to Archduchess Erzsi. "She is hiding something."

Rudolf tracked his gaze to the pond, glistening with sunshine. From that distance, you could not see that the water was reddened with blood.

"We should have a look at these poems Fräulein Coudenhove speaks of in case there is anything to be gleaned from them. At the very least, they are proof that an affair took place."

"Yes, sir," Rudolf murmured warily.

"I would like you to speak to Archduchess Erzsi privately on this matter." Inspector Ziegler met his gaze with bulging eyes, the color of a brewing thunderstorm. "And lad," he added. "Stay objective."

"Yes, Chief Inspector," Rudolf said, slinking away.

Ziegler held the sizzling match steady as he lowered it into his pipe, puffing once, then twice before snuffing out the flame with a wave of his hand. At the ripe age of sixty-two, no number of disapproving stares of the servants would deter him from his ritual.

He paced from one side of the parlor to the other, then halted again in front of the window where Archduchess Erzsi sat. Clenching the bone pipe between his teeth, Ziegler lifted back the curtain, shifting his attention to the sunny reflection of the pond.

Not so long ago the body of the empress' cousin, King Ludwig II of Bavaria, had been found floating in Lake Würm with that of his own Zürich psychiatrist. Though Ziegler had not investigated that case, he was no stranger to the disposition of Philippa's family. Royal minds riddled with visions and voices.

Ziegler had seen it firsthand that cold winter's day, when he'd arrived at the Mayerling Hunting Lodge to find the bedroom door barricaded shut. He knew what they would find when they pried it open, but the scene of Crown Prince Rudolf—Erzsi's father and the sole heir to the Habsburg dynasty—slumped against the wall with blood gushing from his mouth would follow Ziegler to his grave.

The people's prince was dead, and on the bed next to him, the body of his seventeen-year-old mistress already lay in a state of decay.

Erzsi von Habsburg had been only five years old then, and already in the care of her grandparents. That's how Ziegler had come to meet her at the Hofburg, when he'd let her play with his pocket watch. She had even sat on his knee at the Crown Prince's funeral, neither of them aware that they would cross paths again one day. The archduchess sitting outside on the veranda resembled little of that girl, but who among those touched by death had not been hardened?

Turning his attention back to the smoky inside of the parlor, Ziegler was met by Archduchess Erzsi's gray terrier, who seemed almost cognizant as it watched him with its beady, all-knowing eyes from the hall.

Then, Ziegler remembered the book she had launched at Governess Coudenhove. Situating the pipe in his mouth, he reached for it on the table, opening to a pen and ink sketch. *The Sky Flower's Bride,* he read silently. *By Philippa von Habsburg.*

The penmanship was messy, as though she'd scribbled it down while half asleep. Ravings of a madwoman, certainly. Over the years, Ziegler had read of Philippa—*the Archduchess of Attention,* he liked to call her—while sipping his morning coffee. Accounts of her losing control of her limbs in the middle of a ball, or spouting nonsense in an angry rage were commonplace. But it was the claims of spirit possession and family curses that sold papers. Poppycock.

With a string of unsuccessful doctors and failed treatments, the real story of this young woman was much grimmer. So plagued by these hysterical fits, she'd long withdrawn from Vienna society, which only fueled the public's fascination more.

Shutting the book, Ziegler moved to slide it back onto the table, but something in him hesitated and he reopened it.

"Everyone remembered the night he fell from the heavens." Lowering his pipe, he read out loud from the first page. *"The most radiant star flower."*

TWO

June 17, 1900 — *three days before the murder*

9:15 A.M.

"Promise me," Philippa whispered, waking herself from her trance state. "Promise me that you will return."

As the cacophony of voices in her mind faded, her green eyes circled the Bavarian hunt that stretched across the walls. This *room*—it was her bedroom. One of them, anyway. Less decadent than her room at the Hofburg or the Schönbrunn. But that was the point of Kaiservilla, part of what made it a sanctuary.

Now she looked around and saw with horror that it was far from its normal state. Open books with shredded pages covered the made bed and scattered the hardwood floor in heaps of star-cut patterns.

"Did I do this?" Philippa asked, noting the melted candlesticks next to her.

The last thing she remembered was Erzsi chasing after Troilo as he walked back to the cottage in the dark of night. Had she carried the books upstairs from the library while everyone slept?

How much time had passed since she had spoken with Troilo? How many hours or days had passed?

In this state, time felt like an ocean. And like the water, Philippa's memories lapped and peaked like waves, losing their linear order. The ache of her ink-stained hand was evidence that she had been sitting there channeling for quite some time, though Philippa could recall none of it. The words wrote themselves, her quill moved by an invisible force.

With the sudden awareness of the smooth glass quill between her fingers, she turned her attention back to her vanity. The familiar trinkets it housed were anchoring reminders of her identity, or at least that she had one that was completely her own.

Dropping her gaze to her open diary, Philippa immediately averted her eyes.

There is one more condition, Highness, Troilo had warned her. *You must not read back what you have written.*

He had not given a reason as to *why* she should not read her channeled messages, and Philippa—trusting in his unconventional methods—hadn't pressured him for one. Sitting before her vanity each morning for the past four days, a ready vessel, she'd never been tempted enough to peek.

Yet, never before had Philippa woken mid-trance.

Swallowing hard, she dropped her lashes to the last sentence she'd written.

"'I have seen the face of Death...'"

Letting go of the quill, Philippa shot back in her chair across the wooden floor. As though the phrase had reached into her ribcage and pulled a thread that might unravel her completely, she sat paralyzed while a vision bled into her mind. A vision of her, sitting in the chair. Philippa watched her hands grip the carved armrests as she turned slowly toward the vanity mirror that faced her.

Something—or *someone*—was peering out at her from the glass.

Philippa watched in her mind's eye as she leaned closer to her reflection, where her irises darkened to a shade of hazel until they were no longer her eyes at all. Another face overlapped with Philippa's likeness in the mirror. Full cheeks of a young woman with a button nose and heart-shaped chin.

"Costanza," she whispered.

The ghost did not speak, and Philippa felt the air empty from her lungs. "I know you drowned," she gasped. "I know you and your baby—!"

The lips of the apparition did not move, but still, she spoke as blood ran from her eyes. *Come with me and you will feel no pain.*

Feeling frantically across the vanity's top, Philippa grabbed hold of her silver sewing shears, then threw their point into the mirror, smashing her reflection to pieces. Her ears rang as the glass fell to the floor and shattered, leaving only one piece remaining in the frame.

Philippa glanced down with a sense of detachment at her hand and the cuts that covered it. Then, she reached again for her glass quill.

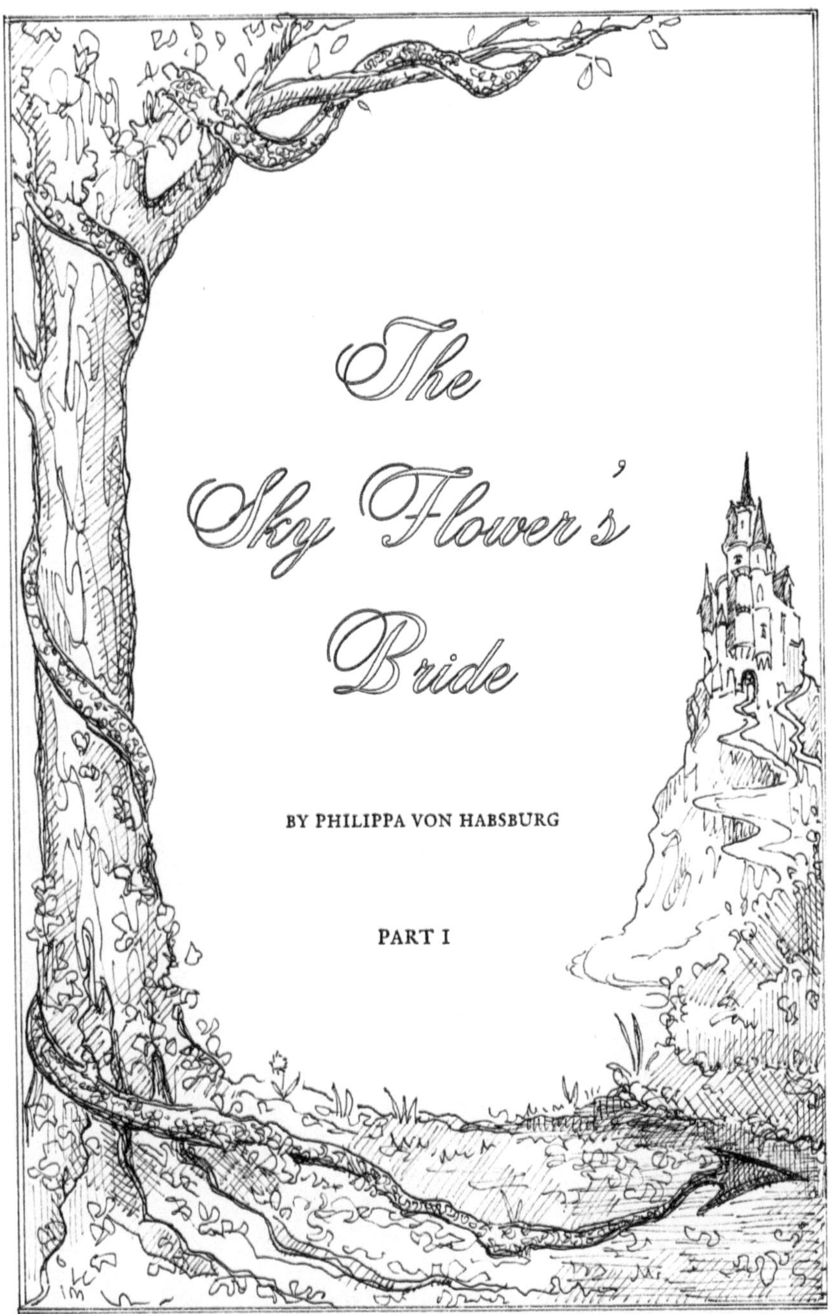

The
Sky Flower's
Bride

BY PHILIPPA VON HABSBURG

PART I

Everyone remembered the night he fell from the heavens, the most radiant star flower. It was the year 1432, and the eve of Costanza Indrigo's nineteenth birthday, under a midsummer new moon.

Unaware that her life was about to change forever, the young shepherdess sat under the starlit blossoms of the pear tree, picking at a piece of long grass with her fingernails. The dirt beneath them seemed a permanent fixture, a sign of a long day of herding in the fields. Most nights, while her village slept with only an occasional hearthstone flicker, Costanza found herself perched on the hill, crafting stars out of grass. It was only there, beneath the endless sky and its graveyard of flickering eyes, did God ever speak to her.

She had been only a child when the visions began, an unfortunate side effect of her father's lineage. At least, that is what her grandmother had always told her. Costanza had learned early on never to speak of the glimpses she saw, no matter how inconsequential they seemed. *Such a curse, if people knew,* her grandmother had told her, *will destine her for a life of martyrdom.* Still, when she was alone, Costanza received her visions willingly, just like the saints that her grandmother prayed to.

Costanza leaned her head back onto the bark of the tree trunk with a smile, forfeiting the grass star to the soft nose that nuzzled her hand. But the baby goat resting in her lap only lifted his head to the white blooms above them.

"You are good to remind me, Orlo," she said, running her hand over his soft ears. "Baka will be waiting up for—"

A fierce wind blew Costanza's hair from behind, rustling the sea of grass around them in a symphony of zephyrs. She sat upright among the swaying stalks, which brushed against each other in hypnotizing sighs, as though the wind itself might be speaking to her. Words entered her mind that she had heard as a girl from the village elders.

"Where spirits are, the winds blow," she whispered.

As it dissipated, she considered that she might have imagined the strange gust. Then, a loud fizzle sounded overhead, turning the night sky to day within an instant. Costanza stumbled to her feet, just in time to see a fiery, green tail stretch across the celestial plains overhead. Stunned in its wake, darkness again enveloped her.

When her grandmother found her wandering down from the hill, Costanza was searching the sky in a daze. "Out here without any good sense!" Gripping her with a sturdy hold, her grandmother led her to the door. "Come inside *right away!*"

Costanza's gaze clung to the horizon line even as she was pulled through the doorway.

"Your father would have my ear!" her grandmother scolded, shutting them inside.

Costanza walked over to the dwindling fire.

"Costanza! Are you listening to me?"

She turned toward her grandmother, having not heard a word.

"You must not speak of what you saw tonight."

Costanza clutched Orlo to her chest, slipping her fingers beneath his brindle coat. "You saw it, too? The zm—"

"Not a word, girl!" The eyes of her grandmother were hard and full of fear. "Take the goat to his pen and think of it no more."

Knowing better than to test her, Costanza did as she was told. Her grandmother knew as well as she did what they had seen. Her family rarely spoke of their ancestral legends, despite how deeply the old lore ran through the bloodlines of Pićan. The sighting of the fallen star would spread through the streets of her village like wildfire.

Unlatching the door, Costanza envisioned the brightness of the flaming tail, but the dark skies held no trace of the star. It had flown north toward Pazin, where her father worked as the royal goldsmith, and likely fallen somewhere near the Sopat waterfall.

"Hello?" she asked suddenly.

The distance from her back door to the little wooden pen

seemed a long way as Costanza stood paralyzed on the stone step, overcome by a feeling of being watched. Her eyes felt strange, too, as if someone might be looking through them.

Gathering her courage, she scurried across the dark grass to the barn. "Good night, dear Orlo," she said, dropping him in.

Then, the strange feeling vanished, just like the spirited wind.

Her grandmother must have known, too, that the village would wake that Sunday morning abuzz, because she was quick to remind Costanza that gossip was sinful as they approached the half-moon archway of Pićan's fortified walls.

On their way to church, her grandmother pretended not to see how the women reached for the hands of their husbands when Costanza passed by. The lack of effort she put into her appearance did little to deter sharp, envious tongues, or the gawking of young village boys. Having not only inherited her Vlasi mother's slender figure, but also her father's pale hair and hazel eyes, Costanza was one of the loveliest girls in Pićan. With some tumbling and polishing, she would make an exceptional ring to be worn, and rumor had it she already had an interested buyer. But for all her beauty, the only daughter of Luka Indrigo was known for being solitary and peculiar. Living on the village outskirts, she was usually seen from the top of the wall in the happy company of sheep and goats. The church of Saint **M**ichael was the only place the townsfolk could get a good look at her, and each Sunday, they seized the opportunity to do so.

Costanza looked up at the tiny stone church, set atop the highest point on the highest hill, overlooking miles of rolling Istrian landscape, and, taking her grandmother's arm, she helped the old woman climb the embedded stone stairs. Costanza had been baptized there only two days after her mother's death. The sturdy walls of Saint Michael had witnessed her blossom from an infant to a woman and its stale, musty smell was one she had grown accustomed to. The services, however, rarely kept her interest, and she would often find herself counting the silver strands in the braid that hung over the pew in front of them, only to be chastised by her grandmother later for having a head full of wool.

Never had she celebrated the ending of a service more than she did that morning, knowing that her grandmother's friends would be congregating under the shade of the olive tree outside with plenty to talk about.

Costanza nodded to the three elderly women—Zita, Borna and Guila—who seemed as much of a staple in her life as the masonry of the church.

"Good morning, Lucija," said Guila to her grandmother. "Have you heard the news?"

"No shame, the lot of you! Gossiping just outside the church walls."

Costanza's lips upturned in a grin, which she quickly wiped away.

"It is not gossip, Lucija. There is a *zmaj* among us."

"He will be seeking a bride," Guila added, turning her attention to Costanza.

"Lucija, is today not Costanza's nineteenth year?"

"It is," Costanza chimed in.

They all fell silent.

"Be wary of handsome strangers in your dreams, dear," said Zita to Costanza.

"Enough!" her grandmother demanded. "If there *is* a zmaj, where is he?"

"The Sopat waterfall." Costanza shrunk as their collective attention fell on her. "The tail flew right overhead of me. It is the direction my father and I..."

"Speaking of her father," her grandmother scolded, pulling her away, "*Costanza* has plans to visit Pazin this week with Luka. You must excuse us."

"Baka!" Costanza snatched her arm back. "Why must you chastise me for simple curiosity?"

"You are a foolish girl," her grandmother muttered. "Always looking up instead of at what is right in front of you."

"Why can they speak of the zmaj, but I am forbidden to do the same?"

"Your father is on his way home, lest you forget. I will not have him thinking I filled your head with superstition in his absence."

Costanza bit her tongue as the stories from her childhood floated to the surface. Cautionary tales of the *zmajevi*—the celestial serpents that fell from the heavens—and their bonded *zmajeve nesteve*, the unlucky women who share their birthday.

The lore varied from village to village. Sometimes, the zmaj would court his bride in a dream, then come down the chimney to claim her. It was important to always keep a lit hearth to deter him. The woman chosen by the zmaj would share his powers of sight and lead the life of an oracle. She would give birth to dragon-men that led conquests in wars, or daughters that would become seers. In the case of a bad match, the lust of her zmaj might exhaust her. In the case of a *good* match, the bride had even been known to wither away and die of lovesickness if ever they were separated.

No matter the variation of the prophecy, they all agreed that to wed a dragon destined a woman for an unfortunate fate.

"The duke is quite taken with you," her grandmother reminded. "You must think of your family."

It was true the Duke of Pazin had expressed his interest since Costanza came of age, showering her with small tokens of affection when she accompanied her father to the castle, while requesting her father's attendance more and more. It did not seem to matter to her family that the duke was already married, so long as they could delight in his Habsburg wealth.

"*Costanza,*" her grandmother said again, her eyes a soft ebony. "You must forget this."

"Yes, Baka," she replied, nodding an empty promise.

· · ·

With four hours to sunrise the next day, Costanza set off, tugging Orlo alongside her as he trailed the length of her skirt. Having stopped at the Sopot with her father while traveling home from the castle, she knew the way by heart, and if ever her heart-memory failed her, she could find her way by sky. The waterfall could be found by following Draco, home to the old polestar, which hung directly above it. But Costanza knew not what she would find, nor what it was she was looking for as she sifted through the tangled weeds, chasing the imaginary embers over the sleeping, blue hills.

The path to the waterfall was as rough and rocky as she remembered, with tree limbs blocking any semblance of a clear trail. Gathering Orlo in her arms, Costanza listened for the sound of the pattering water, hopping from stone to stone with only the light of approaching dusk. If it had been any darker, she might have tripped over the twelve-foot snakeskin that stretched across the woody terrain.

Her mouth turned to sand at the sight of it. "Come, Orlo," she called, willing herself over the dry scales.

Cedars lined the top of the Sopot's cliffs, where fresh water spilled into a grotto from about thirty meters high, and if she had not felt watched, Costanza would have thought she was alone.

"Show yourself!" she called out. "I command you to show—"

A pair of curious, green eyes emerged from the aquamarine grotto, sending Costanza backward in fright. "Ah! Who are—?"

The boy bobbed innocently in the water as he pushed his hair from his forehead. Hair that was as dark as a night without stars.

"What is your business here?" she demanded. "It is dangerous to be wandering out here alone!"

Costanza could see that the lustrous stranger was likely not much older than she as he swam to the edge. Feeling the hypocrisy of her words as he peered up at her, she pinched her lips together tight. "I am seeking the zmaj. Have you come seeking him, too?"

Staring intently under arched brows, the boy only dipped his chin below the water line.

"I wanted to see if the old legends were true," she mumbled, more to herself than to him. "Why do you not speak, boy?"

His jaw flexed, then loosened, as beads of water dripped from his lashes down his cheekbones. His eyes seemed confused, as though he did not understand her German tongue.

"Oh..." she said, steadying Orlo on his hooves. "You are a foreigner."

Orlo took a step forward, lowering his mouth to the water for a drink. The boy grinned, reaching up to pet the tufts of fur on his cheek.

"Stop! He does not take to—"

Seemingly unbothered by the touch, Orlo did not so much as flinch.

"...people."

Costanza watched as the goat lifted his head and, as though under an enchantment, nuzzled the boy's wet hand with his nose.

"*Orlo,*" he said suddenly, sounding out the name.

Now, it was Costanza who struggled for her words. "I did not tell you his name."

The boy only smiled up at her awestruck expression.

"It is *Orlo* who told you?"

Surely this peculiar boy could not be the lusty and powerful zmaj, ally of saints and hero of men! Speaker of the Language of All Things!

"*Costanza,*" he whispered, clutching onto the rock's edge.

"That is my name," she stuttered. "How do you know *my* name?"

He grinned an omniscient grin, and deciding that she would rather not know, Costanza abruptly shot to her feet. Coaxing Orlo to follow with a click of her tongue, she looped his rope around the branch of a fallen tree trunk before reaching into her knapsack and breaking off a piece of bread.

The boy gripped the edge of the quarry as she brought it to her mouth.

Costanza had lived through enough of the Venetian wars to know hunger when she saw it. "Would you like some?" she asked, extending the bread. "Here."

As the boy leveraged himself out of the water, Costanza was confronted with a body that was very much a man's. She had only ever seen such parts on animals, and the sight of him was enough to make her mouth go dry a second time. He was tall and muscular, yet lean, and seemed to have no shame with his nakedness as he stood before her, which made it all the more difficult not to stare. Water dripped down the center of his abdominals to the indentations at his waist, pooling in a puddle at his feet.

Dropping her lashes, Costanza tore her shawl from her shoulders. "You need clothing..." Finding his eyes and managing to avoid the rest, she wrapped the cloth around his waist, then turned back to the bread, which she had left on the edge of the tree trunk. "Would you like something to eat?" she asked, holding it out to him.

Once the bread found his hands, he seemed unsure of what to do with it. Costanza motioned to her mouth, and he lifted the bread to his lips, finally taking a bite.

"There you are," she said, doing the same. "Not too much at once."

A tender feeling overcame Costanza as she watched him eat, as if this boy were someone she had known all her life. She knew not what to make of the mute, naked stranger, ravenously devouring her bread, but the sun was rising, and she needed to head home.

"You keep the rest," she said, setting the remaining bread next to him. "I shall return tomorrow and bring you clothing."

The look in his eyes seemed to Costanza like sadness as she reached for Orlo's leash.

"Do not leave this place," she instructed, praying that he understood her. "I shall return."

Costanza resisted the urge to look back as she followed the path of stones. What she had found at the end of her quest was not the zmaj she imagined, but a young man who hardly knew how to eat or speak, which meant only one thing. She would need to find a place for him before someone else did.

As promised, Costanza set off before sunrise the next day, disappearing into the shadows of fading night with a bundle of her father's old clothes. She had not slept particularly well, haunted by visions of the boy in the quarry each time she closed her eyes. It was a thought which made her uneasy. He could enchant Costanza as easily as he had Orlo if he *were* truly the zmaj, and if he intended to seduce her, he certainly would. The carnal appetite of these beings was legendary, and for that reason, they were vilified as much as they were hailed, at least by the likes of human men. Nothing would stop a zmaj from pursuing another man's wife if he wanted her.

The boy in the quarry could have any woman he wanted by a mere glance in her direction. Costanza shook the thought out of her head, feeling foolish for thinking she had any real reason for concern.

Water rushed from the dizzying heights of the cliffs, hung with overgrown vines as she walked to the edge of the water, which gleamed with muted hues of twilight. The boy was nowhere to be found. Feeling a twinge of disappointment, Costanza readjusted her knapsack and turned to leave, but an unexpected grip on her shoulder stopped her in her tracks.

Ripping herself away, she aimed a finger in warning at the bright eyes and beaming smile. *"Do not touch me!"* she shrieked, cursing in her grandmother's Slavic tongue.

The enthusiasm melted from the boy, who was still wearing only her shawl from the previous day.

Costanza lowered her finger; her lips seared shut. "You startled me," she muttered, reverting back to German.

He eyed her knapsack as she dug her hand inside, hardly having time to pull out the half-loaf before he snatched it from her fingers. Barely chewing, he seemed to swallow it whole, even dropping to the ground to pick up the crumbs. He would need more than bread to eat.

Costanza handed him the clothing she brought, which he unfolded clumsily. Reaching for the tunic, she motioned for him to lift his arms. "Here you are," she said, standing on her toes to guide the neckline over his silky hair and broad shoulders. One arm emerged from a sleeve, followed closely by the second, and then a smile.

"You must dress in these yourself," she added, handing him the pair of pants. "One leg through each hole, just as the tunic."

He moved to untie her shawl around his waist.

"Not here," she choked, motioning to the fallen tree trunk. "Behind the tree!"

Costanza ran one nail under the other, picking away the dirt as she waited for him to dress. Admittedly, she would have liked to have another look at him, just for the sheer fascination of it. One day she would need to perform her *duty* as a woman, a thought that often nauseated her. But looking upon the boy, she felt a sort of hunger.

When he at last emerged from his hiding place, his thin physique was swallowed by the oversized tunic, but by some miracle, her father's old pants seemed to fit. Costanza covered her laughter as he lifted his billowing sleeves with a playful, lopsided grin. In that moment he could have passed as any handsome village boy, but the faint conversation of men close by was quick to remind her otherwise.

The interest in the falling star had surpassed far more than Costanza's curiosity. Men from all provinces would seek a zmaj for their military, by will or force. Their only aid in escaping such men would be the remaining darkness.

"We must go." Swiping her knapsack from the ground, Costanza ran over to the snakeskin. "Help me!" she urged, shoving fistfuls of scales into her open bag.

Finding her side, the boy moved to do the same, but sparks flew from his fingertips as he touched it.

"You cannot..." Costanza gaped with wide eyes as he retracted. "You will change into your—!"

Glancing at the quarry's entry, he reached for the skin again.

"Do not!" Costanza cursed in Slavic. "They will know it is you!"

As though he understood her, the boy snapped back.

Costanza paused to look at him, then asked, "Do you understand the old tongue?"

The voices grew louder before he could answer, and Costanza scanned the quarry for another means of exit, deciding quickly on a shallow cliff. Dragging the boy by the sleeve, she halted in front of it, moving her hands in a way that imitated climbing. He knelt with an open palm, hoisting her up with the full knapsack, then grabbed onto the jagged rock. Once she reached the top, Costanza extended her hand, pulling her new friend over the edge and out of sight just as the hunters poured into the clearing. Breathlessly, she peered over the rocky ledge as a group of ten armored men came into view, their allegiances not immediately clear.

Realizing it was him they had come for, the boy watched with eyes just as wary until Costanza's touch seized his attention. Motioning gently to stay quiet with a finger over her lips, she coaxed him to follow her as she backed away from the ledge and into the woods.

Daylight was fast approaching. *If* she could manage to navigate the unfamiliar forest, Costanza knew there was little chance she would make it home in time before her grandmother awoke, and when she *did* return...

What had she done, taking responsibility for this boy who could hardly look after himself?

So focused on her grandmother's wrath, Costanza did not hear the crunch of leaves nearby. She did not see the white she-wolf until she stepped into view, bearing sharp, milky teeth.

"Stay behind me," Costanza ordered the boy over her shoulder. Cautiously lowering her knapsack, she reached inside, pulling out the dried fish she carried for just such occasions. But the snarling wolf paid no mind to the fish tossed her way, and Costanza knew at once that this was no ordinary wolf. "A Spirit of the Forest," she said, keeping her eyes forward. "We have offended her."

As the wolf prowled closer, saliva dripping from the unforgiving fangs, Costanza stumbled backward, nearly blown off her feet by a breeze that whipped at the bottom of her skirt. Leaves on the ground began to tumble toward her, picked up by an invisible current. The golden eyes of the wolf tracked upward as a cold wind began to cycle around Costanza with a whirling ferocity, swallowing everything in sight. With pinned ears, the wolf cowered as the cyclone grew higher, brushing the tops of the trees, and suspending the leaves in mid-air.

Then, a fierce *hiss* erupted with such force that Costanza was thrown to the ground. Scrambling away, she threw her head back to the sky. There, amongst a tempest of swirling leaves and twigs, rose a creature unlike anything she had ever seen. With the scaled body of a serpent and feathered wings of an angel, it stood fifteen feet or more in height, wearing a crown of ram's horns.

Ally of saints, hero of men!

"*Zmaj,*" she breathed, deaf to everything but the blood pounding in her ears.

Another hiss sent Costanza crawling to the nearest tree for shelter. From the safety of its trunk, she watched as the wind began to calm, and the dragon erected himself. The white she-wolf, whose coat was pure as snow, looked up at the celestial prince, then bent one of her front legs. Deepening the bow, the Lady of the Forest paid her respects before at last turning around and disappearing into the sunrise.

Steadying herself with the tree, Costanza rose timidly to her feet as the zmaj turned his gaze on her, sending a warm breeze through her hair.

It is I, said the gentle wind.

Costanza stepped forward, miraculously unafraid as his serpent form began to collapse into a sea of leaves. Rushing to his side, she fell to her knees, sliding into an embrace with the boy, who had again lost his clothes. He shivered as she tried to collect the snakeskin around him. Cupping his hot cheek in her hand, Costanza lifted his electric eyes to hers. "It is you," she whispered. "*You* who has sent me visions all these years? For all my life?"

The boy did not seem to know how to respond. He only reached up to touch her hand, pressing her palm against his cheek.

She only let it lay for a moment. "Your clothing," she reminded him, standing up. "We must keep moving."

From the sun's placement, Costanza estimated it was around eight in the morning when they finally reached the worn road that would lead them back to Pićan. What she did not expect to see when they stepped out of the woods was her father on his way home from the castle.

"You!" In full speed, he galloped toward them on horseback with a shiny white stallion in tow.

"*Tata?*" Costanza gasped.

"Step away from my daughter!"

"It is all right, Tata!" she yelled back. "Please!"

The hooves of her father's horse skidded to a halt, and the tall, burly man slid from his mount, eyeing the twigs caught in Costanza's pale waves, and the earthy stains across her clothes.

Knowing what he must be thinking, Costanza blurted out the first lie that came to mind. "One of the sheep ran off this morning and I went to look for it, but I lost my way, and was cornered by a she-wolf," she huffed, out of breath. "This boy came to my aid and fended her off!"

The goldsmith's chocolate eyes sizzled from beneath his thick, unkempt brows. "What is your name?" he asked the boy.

"He does not have one," Costanza replied.

"All men have a name."

"Not this one," she said, suddenly remembering what filled her knapsack. "He does not speak."

Costanza's father stepped forward to inspect the young man, and she thought it a miracle that he did not recognize the threads from his own wardrobe, though they had stopped fitting long ago.

"I thought I would bring him back to Pićan to repay my debt," she added awkwardly. "I think he is hungry."

The boy, unaware that his fate was being discussed, seemed only to care about the white horse her father had brought along. The stallion lifted his nose, nuzzling the boy's hand with a snort.

"He is yours, Costanza," said her father, motioning to the stark white coat.

Her smile fell, but she did not let her father see. "A most unexpected and generous gift," she murmured.

"His Grace hopes that he might encourage you to visit more often."

Costanza stepped closer, sliding her fingers across the horse's glossy cheek. "I shall call him *Mjesec*," she said, turning to her father. "For he is as white as a full moon."

The stallion's attention seemed focused purely on the boy, as though he might be speaking to him mind-to-mind. Then, as if he had been riding all his life, he mounted up before offering Costanza a hand to do the same.

"He is someone," her father mused, watching him closely. "A Venetian captive broken free, perhaps..."

Seated atop the horse with the boy at her back, Costanza could focus on little but his breath over her shoulder, and the faint thump of his heart against her shoulder blade. Her father's words seemed to disappear between its beats.

"He will join us in Pazin."

Costanza snapped to, clutching the sack full of snake skin in her lap. "Pazin!"

"I will find him work at the castle," he went on. "It is my debt to repay, not yours."

"But he cannot speak!"

Her father reached for the reins of his horse, climbing up. "He will learn."

When they returned to the village about an hour later, Costanza was glad to be riding alongside her father. The stranger on the white horse drew more attention than she had anticipated, turning the head of every man, woman and child they passed by. Some held their breath, others shook their heads at the handsome outlander and the village beauty that rode with him, picking debris from her hair. Among the faces Costanza met with red cheeks, Guila stood at her fence as they rode by. Glancing over her shoulder, Costanza met the knowing gaze of her grandmother's friend until she shrunk into the distance.

Outside the stone house, her grandmother greeted them with a taut expression. "*You* rotten girl! I have been..." Her face paled at the sight of the young man seated behind her on the stallion. "Dear child," she whispered under her breath, "what have you done..."

"Costanza ran off after one of the sheep and found herself in trouble," said her father, dismounting his horse. "I found them by the Sopat wood."

The old woman's glare was unflinching as the boy helped Costanza down.

"Mama, come. Do not be cross with the girl."

"Do not be cross? She is out all hours of the night rolling around in the woods with...Lord only knows, and you ask me not to be cross?"

Costanza's stare hardened as she wiped her hands across her skirt in a weak attempt to brush the stains away.

"We owe this young man a great deal," her father added.

"Man?"

Their eyes met briefly, then her grandmother conceded, knowing her father had long ago abandoned the superstitions of the old ways.

"A Venetian prisoner," he said at last. "I have seen enough soldiers in my day to know how one rides."

"His silence disturbs me."

Her father held back at the door. "It is only until tomorrow," he added on his way inside. "He will ride with Costanza and me to Pazin."

Costanza clutched her knapsack to her chest as her father disappeared into the house, leaving them at the mercy of her grandmother.

The dark eyes of the elderly woman, constellated with crow's feet and a permanent scorn, found the boy. *"I know what you are,"* she warned in Slavic, eliciting a subtle flinch. "He sleeps in the barn!"

The boy's lack of table manners did little to hide his true nature, and so focused on dissecting him from across the table, Costanza's grandmother hardly touched her stew. It was by mere luck that her father excused his behavior for that of a hungry prisoner, but what would happen when they took him to the castle? Oh, the castle with its etiquette! Courts with rules, and unforgiving nobles. What would happen to him there?

The thought troubled Costanza as she led him to the barn after dinner to make his bed among the sheep.

"You must choose a name for yourself." She glanced over her

shoulder to see the boy trailing behind. *"Name,"* she repeated in Slavic.

He would need something strong, beautiful, and knightly. Something like...

"Orlo."

She turned on her heel with an unexpected laugh. "You cannot name yourself Orlo!"

It seemed for a moment that he might be jesting as he grinned back at her. "Name," he murmured, pointing to her.

"You want *me* to choose your name?" Costanza thought to herself, only needing a minute. "Troilo," she said. "It is the name my mother wanted to give me if I had been born a son."

The tender innocence of the boy hugged her shoulders like a soft wool, and she wondered what heavens might produce such a creature. But much like a human at birth, zmajevi, too, forgot their origins upon the fall. Tilting her chin to the head of Draco, Costanza searched for the old polestar, following the starry tail of the serpent until her eyes landed on Thuban, burning bright.

"She gave her life for mine," she added.

The tip of Troilo's finger brushed across Costanza's cheek, catching a single tear on the end. Inspecting it, he then looked at her.

"It is a mortal affliction," she whispered with a smile.

Yet another reminder that the young man sleeping in their barn was no *man* at all, but a celestial dragon with a second skin, which Costanza had hidden away in the cellar for the night.

"Come, Troilo," she said softly.

Opening the barn doors, Costanza saw that for all her grandmother's begrudging, she had still left some blankets for him by the hay. "This is where Orlo sleeps," she said, spreading one of them across the crunchy straw. Brushing her hands over her skirt, she rose to her feet in the musty, concealed barn, where their aloneness was particularly apparent.

"We will not be seeing much of each other after tonight," she said in the old tongue. Her palm opened flat, revealing a grass star in the center. "I was weaving this when I saw you. I thought…"

Holding it in both hands, Troilo studied the token intently.

"Each star is but a flower of the sky, and the night, a heavenly garden." Costanza stepped back, rounding the splintered wood of the barn. "A gift to remember me by," she said.

Still reeling, she did not immediately notice her grandmother spreading the coals of the hearth in a smoldering annoyance when she walked back inside.

"You are a foolish girl," the old woman muttered.

"Troilo is not dangerous. He has been nothing but gentle, I swear it."

"Troilo?" Her grandmother narrowed her eyes on Costanza in a way that made her feel small. "You come inside red as a beet and tell me he is not dangerous?"

Costanza's hand found her flushed cheek. "Would not any girl blush in front of a soldier?" she stuttered.

"You are not any girl," her grandmother warned in a low rasp. "And he—*he is no soldier.*" With a shake of her head, she turned back to the hearth. "Your father might have been born blind, but I have lived a thousand years, and I know his kind when I see them."

Costanza had to remind herself to breathe. Troilo was only a boy—zmaj or not—and if his identity were revealed, what would become of him? Would he be hunted by men like those who had sought him at the quarry? She tried to picture him out in the barn, lying in the hay, having done no wrong to anyone.

"He has shown himself to you, then," her grandmother said at last. "His true form."

"In the forest," Costanza answered shakily. "There was a wolf, and he—"

"*I told you to forget!*"

Something stirred in the back room of the house, silencing

them both. When the old woman was certain they were alone, she turned back to her granddaughter.

"Do you have any idea what harm you have done by seeking him out?"

"Baka, I..." Costanza shook her head, losing her words in a panicked breath. "I know not why I did it! I know not what brought me—!"

"It was your bond that called you to him."

Costanza stepped toward her grandmother, whose face had hardened in the shadows of the hearth cinders.

"I have dreaded this day all your life," she added. "The day when he would come for you."

"Come for me..." Costanza fought for her gaze as her grandmother stared silently into the coals.

Motioning for her to take a seat on a nearby wooden chair, the old woman reached for the broom. "A great star flower appeared three days before you were born, and stayed for two days afterward," she began, sweeping the cinders. "I prayed that you would be a boy, that the omen would be an auspicious one..." She paused, then leaned onto the broom. "For a girl to be born while one is visible indicates she will be Other. That she is *bonded* to something Other."

Costanza's voice cracked, regardless of her attempts to hold it steady. "Other."

"My child, zmajeve nesteve are not chosen at random. The pact is made in the Otherworld, long before birth." She pursed her lips, again glancing to the back of the house. "The day you had your first vision, I knew."

Dropping her gaze to her lap, Costanza again thought of Troilo in the barn, and what the wind had told her.

"I thought perhaps I could hide you from your fate," her grandmother admitted. "But your souls shimmer to one another."

"And what of my say? Do I have none?" Costanza argued. "Can he not choose another?"

"You may refuse him, yes." Her grandmother reached for a blanket, then wrapped it around the girl's trembling shoulders. "He cannot take you as his earthly bride against your will."

"Mama."

Costanza turned toward her father's voice as he hovered in the doorway.

"That is enough storytelling for tonight," he said gently, eyeing his daughter. "Come, now. To bed with you. You must be fresh for the journey tomorrow."

With a simple kiss goodnight, Costanza left her grandmother by the hearth.

The next day she found herself again seated in front of Troilo, her nervous heart hidden beneath layers of her nicest garments. Even he was decorated for a visit to the castle, thanks to her father. She had imagined the warmth of this boy—his steady breathing against her spine—all night as he slept curled up next to Orlo in the barn. Not even the frightening words of her grandmother could stop the blushing of her cheeks, or the wanting to be near him. Already, she had forgotten what Troilo *really* was.

"Costanza, are you listening to me?"

She glanced over at her father, riding next to them. "Yes, Tata."

"It is of the utmost importance that you find a way to show your gratitude for such a generous gift."

"A copy of the *Nibelungenlied* would have been more than enough. I told His Grace how much I would love to read it."

"The duke thought this more appropriate. You must..."

"Be a gracious receiver, Mjesec," she teased, running her fingers through the horse's white mane. "I know."

Heavily fortified and with only one tower, the stone walls resembled more of a guard's prison than a castle. Over Costanza's shoulder, Troilo stared in awe at the stone-carved heraldries above the gate. There were a variety of noble crests, though he seemed most enticed by the serpent with a human in its mouth.

Costanza glanced down at her knapsack, filled with the scaly skin of a zmaj, strapped to Mjesec's side. "Are you certain, Tata? About bringing him along?"

"I have long been in need of an apprentice," her father replied confidently, nodding to the approaching guards. "You mean so much to His Grace, I see no reason why he would not wish to repay this young man as well."

A few ladies-in-waiting eyed Costanza sharply from the sidelines. Loyal to the Duchess of Pazin, the ladies of the castle already believed her to be a spoiled, uneducated peasant girl, knowing the duke tucked her away in a lavish room in the South Wing when she came to stay. Mjesec would do little to help her win their favor, or anyone else's.

"Here you are, my dear," said her father, offering his hand.

Troilo dismounted behind Costanza, petting Mjesec's nose as two grooms found their side. Her father motioned for Troilo to give up the reins. The remaining guard moved to unpack the horse, throwing Costanza's knapsack over his shoulder.

"Carefully!" she scolded. "You must not be so rough with my things!"

"Yes, Mistress."

Sweet giggles erupted from the group of women watching nearby, their attention no longer on Costanza. Lady Melisande, the most beautiful of the three, held up a hand that stopped Troilo in his tracks.

Costanza halted alongside him, feeling at once invisible. "Come now," she snapped. "There is no time for play!"

Troilo smiled at his female admirers, then stepped forward.

A fire roared in the entrance hall, hung with all its colorful banners, and Costanza looked to Troilo as the door slammed behind them. His eyes, a soft green, followed the stone walls to the ceiling, studying every structural inch.

"If all goes to plan," her father added, watching him with equal interest, "this will be your new home."

No sooner had he spoken the words than the Duke of Pazin appeared, followed by a few servants.

"Ah!" Clapping his hands joyously, he eyed Costanza with a big, jovial smile. "Joyous day." Dressed head to toe in blue, satin garb, he reached for her hand. "I cannot tell you what happiness your presence brings me."

"I as well, Your Grace," she replied, glancing at her father. "Thank you for your most gracious gift."

He found her eye, his blue irises bright. With his sandy colored hair and straight smile, Matthias von Habsburg, Duke of Pazin, was a handsome man indeed, and village girls and noble women alike would have fallen over each other to be in Costanza's position.

"He is much more impressive than a manuscript, is he not?"

Costanza forced a smile, then a nod.

"I do hope he rode well for her," the duke said to her father.

"A fine stallion, indeed, Your Grace."

The duke gave a satisfactory nod, then turned his attention to Troilo. "What have you brought me, Indrigo? A stable boy?"

"My father is in need of an apprentice," Costanza interjected.

"I see." He eyed Troilo in a predatory manner. "And who is this...goldsmith's apprentice?"

"Costanza and I found him wandering the woods without a name or a voice," her father replied.

Rivaling him in height, the duke stepped up to Troilo. "This man is no peasant," said the duke. "What is your name?"

"He is a good rider and seems to learn quickly, but he does not speak, Your Grace," said her father. "A Venetian captive, perhaps."

The duke held up his hand, tracing Troilo's face with a luke-warm regard. "Who are your people?"

Troilo found the banner of serpent heraldry he had seen outside, and with a single point, sealed his destiny.

"Visconti of Milan, you say?"

Troilo stepped past him to the hanging threads of the blue biscione. *"Visconti,"* he said.

Costanza nervously exhaled as the duke found his side. "Bernabò Visconti is my mother's father," he said.

Troilo turned to him like he understood. Perhaps he was beginning to.

"What is your name?" the duke asked again.

He looked at Costanza. "Troilo."

"He speaks," her father gasped.

The duke pivoted toward him. "This man claims to be my mother's kin. Do you believe him to be honorable?"

"The most honorable, Your Grace," Costanza replied, stepping forward in her father's place. "He risked his life to rescue me."

"Rescue you? From whom?"

"From a she-wolf." She met Troilo's eye for a brief second. "I stumbled upon one in the woods while searching for a sheep."

"While searching for a sheep!" The duke forced a laugh. "Is this true?"

"Yes, Your Grace," said her father.

The duke at first was unreadable, a quality that often made Costanza nervous. "Then he has my sincerest gratitude," he said at last, turning back to Troilo. "Call my mother! She must come at once and meet this lost relative."

The duke's mother, Lady Elisabetta Visconti, appeared promptly. Costanza had only ever seen her once before, in the chapel of the castle. She lifted the black veil she wore for her late husband, revealing a beautifully aging woman, with eyes so blue they were almost violet.

"Mother," said the duke, taking her by the arm, "this man—this, Venetian captive—claims his name is Troilo Visconti."

The woman stepped toward Troilo and grabbed his chin, pivoting him to the left, then the right. "He certainly has the face of a Visconti," she said, turning back to her son. "No doubt the offspring of my father's many liaisons."

"A bastard."

Costanza cast a smile to the floor, unaware that she could know such relief.

"I have granted him permission to stay and work under Indrigo," the duke added.

Lady Elisabetta looked to the goldsmith, then to Costanza next to him, the village plaything of her son. "We must repay the sins of the father," she said. "Will you see to it that he is comfortable, Matthias?"

The duke cleared his throat, then turned to a servant. "Collect his belongings and have a room made up for him in the South Wing," he said.

"He has no belongings, Your Grace," said Costanza's father. "Nothing at all."

"Then he will be needing clothing. Mother?"

Lady Elisabetta extended her hand to Troilo, which Costanza urged him to accept.

"Blessings are aplenty today!" the duke exclaimed.

Costanza felt a hint of sadness as she watched Troilo disappear down the hall, where a better life awaited him. By some miracle or, perhaps, enchantment, Lady Elisabetta had accepted him as her brother. But with a secret like Troilo's, falling into an identity of noble blood was dangerous. Not to mention Costanza's father, who would likely be killed alongside Troilo if he were found to be an imposter.

And so, vowing to protect the truth at all costs, Costanza untied her knapsack when she found it waiting undisturbed in her room. Reaching inside, she pulled the snakeskin out in handfuls, kneeling before the crackling fireplace. Its thousands of scales shone in the firelight as she laid them over the flame, watching as they turned to ash.

.   .   .

With Troilo in Pazin, Costanza's life resumed its normal rhythm. Having been commandeered by the duke, she had seen little of him during her short stay at the castle, and when she did manage to catch a glimpse of him, she found him occupied. Soon enough it was time for her to return to Pićan, and so they parted ways without goodbye.

At first, Costanza was eager to hear news from her father, but as the months went by, it became clear that Troilo had built himself a life in Pazin. A life of excess and flattery, of courtly dances and leisure. The duke, having found a brother in him, insisted on his near constant company. Whether they were hunting chamois or sword fighting in the courtyard, her father rarely saw them apart. The last she had heard, Troilo had been inducted into the Order of the Dragon and he had left with the duke to fight the Venetians.

Zmajevi *were* hailed as heroes of men, after all. Equally fierce as they were intelligent. It was no wonder Troilo had taken to his new role like a fish to water.

In the day, Costanza told herself he had long forgotten her. But each night as she laid her head down to sleep, she imagined Troilo doing the same in the South Wing of the castle or on some foreign battlefield. She imagined him imagining *her,* and the more she focused on it, the clearer the vision became, until it was as though he were sleeping beside her.

When Costanza finally saw Troilo again, it was November.

She was in the pastures when she spotted him on horseback, galloping toward her home in glinting armor. Dropping her staff, she ran to meet him, her feet hardly touching the ground.

Troilo pulled at the reins of his black stallion, inciting a swirl of dust.

Her grandmother glanced up at the knight, hands deep in the dirt. "Good sir, do you bring us news from my son in Pazin?" she asked, wiping her brow.

Removing his helmet, Troilo shook his hair free before slipping down from his mount.

"You," the woman grumbled. "What business have you here?"

"I have come for—"

"Dear Troilo, you speak!" Costanza interjected, appearing around the corner.

"Mistress," he greeted. "I can do a good many things since you saw me last."

In mere months he had matured so much, suddenly seeming so much taller, and stronger.

"His Grace, The Duke of Pazin, requests your presence at the castle," said Troilo.

"I am unprepared," Costanza replied. "Mjesec is..."

"I will ready him for you," he replied, glancing at the barn. "Gather your things."

Once inside, Costanza leaned her back against the wall and inhaled deeply. The visit was unexpected, and she, so untidy. Even Troilo was different now, so formal, and chivalrous. Was there nothing left of that boy at the quarry?

"You will leave with him?" Her grandmother's voice was uncharacteristically soft, yet forlorn, as she hovered in the doorway.

"His Grace has requested my presence," Costanza sighed, brushing off one of her nicer gowns. "I have never before refused him."

With fearful eyes, the old woman nodded knowingly, leaving her to dress.

Troilo studied the length of Costanza's emerald gown as she emerged, ready for reception. "Mistress," he said, offering her a hand up.

She tried her best not to look him in the eye as she accepted. "Your horse," she said, fixating on the black steed. "What is his name?"

Troilo ruffled his mane, running his palm across the silky coat. *"Noć,"* he replied, mounting up. "For he is as dark as night."

Taking a last look at her grandmother, who watched from the door, Costanza kicked her heel and followed Troilo onto the road. They rode silently, neither willing to speak first, until Costanza at last succumbed to her curiosity.

"Why did His Grace ask you to fetch me instead of my father?" she asked.

Troilo turned over his shoulder with a grin so cheeky, she felt her face warm. "I volunteered."

"You had nothing better to do?"

"I had plenty of things to do," he replied. "But none were better than this."

Costanza turned forward, pulling her long hair aside.

"Though," he added in between hoof steps, "you do not seem so glad."

"We have yet to have a proper introduction, Sir Troilo," she said. "You are a stranger to me."

"I would argue that it is you who is the stranger." He spoke directly, but his tone was amused. "For you have seen much more of *me* than I have of you."

Costanza's words dried up. For all her imagined conversations they might have had, she had not foreseen he would be so...

"'Tis a jest," he added.

She looked down at the rocky ground, dispersed with patches of grass. "My father told me that you had gone off to fight the Venetians."

"Did you worry for me, Stanzi?"

Costanza snapped her neck to look at him. "Why would you address me in such a way?"

He only laughed. "You did not answer the question."

"Should I worry for you?" she countered. "You are immortal, are you not?"

"Only in comparison to man." Troilo lifted his chin to the

rustling leaves of the woods, as if he were listening for something. "You have done me no favors by roasting my skin over a fire. I can no longer wield the wind."

Tensing her shoulders, Costanza shied away. How had he known?

"I looked through your sight and saw you kneeling by the fire," he added.

"I only wanted to protect you. To protect my father."

"I can only be killed while in my true form, so you have succeeded." Troilo reached forward to pet his horse. "Though, you have condemned me to an awfully long life in the process."

"Condemned you?"

Her discomfort must have been palpable, because he turned to her, adding suddenly, "I like this form. It is like yours, after all."

Costanza fell quiet, regretful in her decision to burn the snakeskin.

"I know you meant well," said Troilo. "I feel your heart as though it is my own."

"My heart..."

"Yes." His eyes glimmered back at her. "Your heart and all its reasonings."

The pair again rode without speaking for a long while, down the windy road and past the Sopat woods, guarded by forest spirits.

"They know not what you...*are*, then," Costanza said finally. "At the castle."

Troilo laughed, swerving his horse. "They believe me only to be a bastard of many talents."

"So I have heard," she said.

"Your father has told you of my accomplishments?"

Costanza nodded.

"Good," he replied with a smile.

Silence again took the reins, and Troilo cleared his throat. "You will find the *Nibelungenlied* waiting for you in your room."

"Oh!" Costanza replied cheerily. "It has been nearly half a year since I asked His Grace for a copy. I had relinquished all hope of reading it."

"Your father told me that he had taught you...I have learned to read as well," said Troilo. "I spend much of my time in the castle library."

"I am envious of you," Costanza murmured. "The library is the only room in the castle that I am barred from."

Troilo nodded to himself, facing forward. "Matthias tells me you will be his mistress. He makes no secret of it."

Feeling both ashamed and embarrassed, Costanza picked up her pace.

"But he does not know that your heart belongs to another," Troilo added.

She slowed, seeing the Pazin gate up ahead. "He does not, no."

"Does the keeper of your heart reside within the walls of the castle?"

"He may," she replied.

"A lucky man, indeed." Troilo swerved closer to her. "And does he return your affections?"

Costanza met his eye, uncertain. "I cannot say."

"Perhaps he should make his intentions known."

"Well, I should hope to see him. If he can manage the time away."

"If he knew where to find you, I am certain he would..."

A cool breeze blew at Costanza's neck as she looked up at the stone-carved Visconti heraldry. "He could find me in the court-yard, just before midnight," she replied, trotting ahead to the gate.

The wooden door within it opened, but instead of guards coming to retrieve her, the duke stepped into the sunshine, glistening in gold threads.

"My most precious treasure." Nodding to Troilo, he helped

Costanza down from Mjesec. "Thank you for seeing that she arrived safely."

"It was my pleasure, Your Grace." Troilo glanced at Costanza, slipping from his mount. "I am pleased to be of service to you in any way I can."

Led away on the arm of the duke, Costanza watched him disappear around the stone wall with Noć at his side. The promise of seeing him that night made the duke's touch tolerable as he toted her through the halls like an embroidered accessory.

"Thank you for indulging my request, Your Grace," she said. "The thought of reading the *Nibelungenlied* brings me much joy."

"The *Nibelungenlied?*"

"Yes, I..." Costanza blinked, confused. "Sir Troilo told me that a copy awaited me in my room?"

"Ah, yes. How forgetful I am!" The duke laughed under his breath. "You know all things of the castle are at your disposal, Costanza."

Holding onto his arm, she did not meet the eye of the ladies that passed by.

"Troilo has cleaned up quite well since you saw him last, has he not?" The duke paused, long enough for Costanza to tell that he, too, was under the zmaj's spell. "He learned German in less than a month and is already fluent in French! I was rightfully skeptical when he arrived, but he is as clever as a fox and is a better swordsman than my most skilled mercenary. There is no doubt he is my kin."

Costanza and the duke floated over to a window overlooking the courtyard where, below, Troilo laughed with Lady Melisande.

"Of course," the duke added, "when we are not hunting or fencing, he is enjoying the spoils of his new rank."

The words rolled off his tongue with a laugh, constricting around Costanza's chest. Troilo was aware of his beauty, that much was clear from where she stood.

"This view has grown tiresome," Costanza said suddenly, tearing herself away. "May we walk elsewhere?"

"Of course." The duke extended his arm, which she adamantly grabbed hold of as she met Troilo's eye over her shoulder.

Costanza retired early from the banquet hall that night, having lost her appetite at the sight of Troilo's flirtations. For all the flattery earlier, he had not so much as glanced in her direction all evening, too distracted by the sultry Lady Melisande at his side. He was likely *enjoying his spoils* right then, in the very same wing of the castle, while Costanza sat like a child, having never so much as kissed a man.

Gazing into the fire, she wrapped a strand of grass around her finger, tying a tight knot. Even the beautifully painted copy of the *Nibelungenlied* at her side could not lift her spirits. Perhaps Troilo had only been toying with her.

Costanza threw the unfinished star into the flame, and as she watched it burn, a vision of a window bled into her mind, its insides flickering with a lit hearth. It took her only a moment to realize it was the view of *her window,* as seen from the courtyard. Jolting to its stone ledge, she peered down to find Troilo standing below, presumably waiting for her.

Costanza knelt out of sight, watching as he took a seat on the mantel shelf, powdered with white, nocturnal petals. She wondered if Troilo could see himself through her sight as she studied him from her perch, like she had somehow seen through his.

He waited for almost an hour until her eyes grew heavy, and he grew hopeless.

For all their talk on the way to the castle, Costanza and Troilo did not again cross paths until it was time for her to return to Pićan.

With a nervous stomach, Costanza squinted into the stark overcast sky as the guards opened the gate, where Troilo waited with Mjesec.

"I find these walls brighter when you are within them," said the duke, handing her off. "I should like to see you again, soon."

"Yes, Your Grace." She offered a curtsy. "As always I thank you for your generosity."

"Sir Troilo," the duke added playfully. "The lady has been glum all morning, dreading her departure. A scenic route may do well to cheer her."

Troilo's eyes glazed over Costanza as she accepted the duke's hand up. "It would be my pleasure to cheer her, Your Grace," he replied.

Costanza grabbed her reins, willing herself forward. It was true she had spent the morning sulking, but only because *he* had ignored her!

"Did you enjoy the *Nibelungenlied*?" Troilo asked, not even twenty yards away from the castle gate.

Costanza glanced over at him coolly, refusing to answer.

"I had hoped that your reading of it was the reason you chose to leave me waiting in a dark courtyard," he replied. "Surely you know it was *I* who left it in your room?"

Her lips pinched together, despite the flutter in her chest. It did not matter that he was the one who left it. Not after how he had treated her.

"I would like to know what sin I committed to offend you so," he went on. "To make you think so ill of me."

"I would prefer if you would stop invading my mind," Costanza snapped at last.

"Invade!" Troilo let out a flustered laugh, swerving closer to her. "You hardly treat me as an intruder."

"You are a trickster with your gifts and your flattery," she spat angrily. "His Grace has told me of all your *conquests!*"

"It is an act!" Troilo exclaimed. "Can you say the same for Matthias, or was the hearth lit in your room because you were performing your duties?"

Racing past him in a fit of madness, Costanza galloped in full speed over the green hills, hair flying ferociously behind her. Troilo took off after her, catching up at lightning speed.

"Costanza!"

Pulling on the reins with all her might, Mjesec skidded to an abrupt halt. With her windblown hair framing her face like a lion's mane, Costanza turned to Troilo with misty eyes.

"*It is an act,*" he said, breathless.

She only scowled, unconvinced.

"What is it you want from me? My soul? It is yours! I lay it at your feet!"

"I much preferred you as a mute!" Jumping from her mount, Costanza stormed off into the field, leaving Mjesec in the shade of an oak tree. "I will not be like the ladies at the castle, fawning and falling all over you!"

"You are a tempest of a girl!" Troilo shouted after her. "I have never forgotten you. Not in the presence of any noblewoman, not as I lay in a field of dying men—*not once!*"

Costanza turned to face him, losing her breath at the sight of her grass star in his hand.

"You humor me in believing I think any one of those women fairer than my mate."

"Why would I want a mate who insults my honor?" she raged. "You act as though you own me, exactly as he does! Well, I am *not* your bride, Troilo. I do not have time to help you see your destiny —I have my own!"

"Oh?"

"Yes! Just because I cannot see it clearly does not mean I do not have one!"

"If you cannot see it," Troilo taunted, "how are you *so* certain it does not involve me?"

Costanza took off on foot through the tall stalks of grass, and, as Troilo found her waist, they tumbled to the ground.

"Unhand me," she ordered, struggling to squirm out from under him.

Tracing her face with a gentle regard, Troilo loosened his grip on her pinned wrists. A breeze sifted through the grass, and through his hair as Costanza lay docilely beneath him.

"We are from different worlds," she said softly, gazing up at him.

"Right now, we are in the *same* world."

"Still, we are held hostage by our fates. You, to be something great, and I…"

Troilo closed his eyes and leaned into her palm that had found his cheek. As Costanza drew away, he followed, teasing her lips with a delicate kiss.

"I am not like Matthias," he said softly, lifting himself off of her. "I will not force you to love me."

Costanza shot to her feet, picking the bits of grass from her hair as she watched Troilo walk through the clearing, back to the horses. Could he feel her heart now, spitting fire? This coquettish knight, prince of starlight, not of this world?

Troilo accumulated his usual stares from the village folk as they trotted toward Costanza's home that afternoon. They had talked little on their ride back during which, if it were not for Troilo's occasional glimpse and grin, she might have thought him angry with her.

"I will leave you here with Mjesec," he said at last.

Costanza glanced back at him from over her shoulder.

"I do not want His Grace to think I lost my way," he added, reading her mind.

"Oh…yes. I see." Slipping down from her mount, she nodded to him. "I bid you farewell, then, Sir Troilo."

Troilo offered a faint smile, then turned back to his horse. "Mistress."

Costanza watched as he guided Noć back onto the road, not knowing when—or *if*—she would see him again. Biting her tongue, she tried to resist it, but the words burned like fire in her throat.

"Troilo!"

His eyes begged her to speak as she rushed to his side.

"Promise me that I shall see you again," she begged. "You must promise."

"Tonight," he promised, urging Noć forward. "In your dreams tonight."

If it were not for the roaring fireplace in the hearth, Costanza would have thought her home vacant as she closed the front door behind her. Her grandmother clutched her skirt in a way that told her she had seen their interaction outside.

"Baka, what will I do?"

"Dear child..."

Costanza could not remember the last time her grandmother had embraced her, but now, she held her in a maternal grip. "I love him," she cried, unleashing a fury of tears. "What shall I do with this unspoken love! How can I die at peace with a heart so full?"

"Come," her grandmother hushed, holding her around her shoulders. "Come and sit by the fire. There is a chill in the air."

Costanza took a seat on the wooden chair, then reached down to pet Orlo.

"It is not him that is the danger, child. It is what you *become* by being with him. Once you lie together, you will never be the same. He will bestow his gifts of prophecy and language upon you."

"Are zmajevi not revered for their benevolence?"

"In times past, marriage to a zmaj was known to bring prosperity to a village, blessing its inhabitants with a seeress, and storms to water their crops." The old woman's voice was low and husky. "The alliance between these beings and humans has been largely forgotten by our people, having been touted as silly superstition, or worse. The people of Pazin may not believe the whispers about your Troilo, but if ever he makes an enemy..."

Costanza gazed into the flames, and the red-hot cinders they carried.

"Women have burned for much less."

Persecuted and killed were the women deemed as witches. At last, Costanza understood her grandmother's fear.

"He can no longer change, Baka," she admitted. "I...I disposed of his skin."

Her grandmother's face wrinkled with worry.

"I believed I was protecting him."

"Without his skin he can no longer protect *you*," the old woman hushed.

"If Troilo cannot change, then who will ever know he is the zmaj? We will lead a humble life together. No one will ever need know."

Her grandmother turned away from the firelight in clear disagreement, but she would not speak it aloud.

"He is the warmth of my shadow," Costanza said at last. "If to love him is wrong, let it be my sin."

Her grandmother reached for her hand, bringing it to her lips. "Then you have made your choice, *zmajeva nesteva*," she said, kissing it.

THREE

June 7, 1900 — *3 weeks prior to the murder*
11:04 A.M.

"Doctor Visconti, welcome to Marmorschlossl."

Troilo nodded at the young woman standing at the top of the veranda stairs in a simple, beige button-up blouse and skirt. "Fräulein Coudenhove." He motioned to his colleague—who, with his thinning hair and permanent pucker, looked much older than he, despite being nearly ten years his junior. "I would like you to meet my assistant, Herr Carl Jung. He will be helping me settle in."

"It is a pleasure, Herr Jung."

"Likewise, Fräulein."

"I cannot tell you what a joy it is to finally meet you, Doctor." The governess hugged her elbows with a friendly, albeit shy smile. "We have heard so many wonderful things."

Troilo's gaze slid past her, to the lush interior of the teahouse, where he imagined Archduchess Philippa might be waiting for him. Having meditated on her picture in the newspaper, he'd memorized her features by heart, though her smile was still a mystery to him.

A disarming grin twinkled beneath Troilo's mustache as he turned his attention back to the governess. "Tall tales, surely," he murmured.

"How is the climate suiting you gentlemen so far?" she asked.

"It is admittedly warmer than I expected," said Jung.

"All the more reason to visit the springs." She split a smile between them. "If you can make the time."

"Herr Jung is only here until tomorrow," Troilo added. "He is needed back in Zürich."

"Of course." The governess stepped toward the glass doors of the cottage. "I will notify Her Highness of your arrival."

Troilo cleared his throat, noting the flies that buzzed over a nearby table, a result of untouched tea cakes that had been left out. "I defer to your discretion," he said.

"You are welcome to wait in the parlor, if you like."

Troilo motioned to the veranda. "If I may?"

"Please," she replied. "Enjoy the scenery. I will send someone when she is ready to receive you."

"Thank you."

The governess pursed her lips in a smile, disappearing beyond the cottage door.

Resigning himself against the veranda's railing, Jung removed his glasses and began to clean them. "Fräulein Coudenhove is the governess to the Crown Prince's daughter?"

"Yes." Troilo reached up to touch the cottage's pink stone. "She has been with Archduchess Erzsi for nearly a decade," he replied, running his fingers over the cool marble.

Aside from a few wrinkles around her eyes, Governess Coudenhove herself looked quite young. Close in age to Philippa, if Troilo had to guess.

The crow began to caw again as he walked the veranda's perimeter.

"And what do we know of her?" asked Jung, following behind him. "Archduchess Erzsi."

"Much like Philippa's, her life has been an unhappy one," Troilo replied, assessing the iron rods that stretched high over the corner portico, forming geometric flowers across its concave roof. "Though, she shows no signs of the same condition."

"Some are more inured to life's hardships than others," said Jung, returning his glasses. "But perhaps Archduchess Erzsi can assist you. If they truly live as sisters, she will know her better than any doctor."

Beckoned by a glint of high noon sun across the pond, Troilo lifted his gaze. "Perhaps," he said, making his way to the portico's iron railing for a better look.

A woman in a white nightgown, with a waterfall of champagne hair flowing down her back, stood quiescently at the water's edge. Glistening like an opalescent mirage, she was framed perfectly by the half-heart of a corkscrew willow that curved over the shallow embankment. So lost in the vision, Troilo nearly forgot where he was when Jung spoke.

"It would seem we have found your patient."

It was a meeting Troilo had imagined a thousand times, over countless hours. An untouchable phantasm that had come to life.

"Herr Visconti, Her Highness has gone" —Governess Coudenhove shut the cottage door behind him— "for a walk..."

Troilo turned his cheek, sensing her approach. "Do you often find Her Highness outdoors in her nightgown?"

"She does not care to be confined," the governess replied, finding his other side.

"By the likes of corsets?" Jung asked.

"By the likes of anything."

Troilo watched the governess tuck a stray brunette hair back into its proper place. She was a curious creature. A plain beauty: timid and unassured, with a sweet-natured amiability, though he was under the impression that his presence made her nervous.

Loosening his damp cravat, he turned his attention back to the pond. "Might you introduce us?"

"Of course. Come with me."

Leaving Jung on the veranda, Troilo trailed his chaperone down the stairs. The slope that led to the pond was populated with flowers and pollinators of all kinds, and Troilo's heart quickened faster than the wings of a hummingbird.

At long last he would speak to this woman, whose soul he had been connected to all these years.

But would she know his face?

Slowing his step, Troilo inhaled sharply, casting a last glance over his shoulder. On the second floor of the cottage, the face of a young girl peered down from the window, then vanished just as quickly.

"Your Highness," said the governess ahead.

Troilo followed the length of Philippa's nightgown, which glowed against the glistening lily pads as she stood in front of the pond. The bottom of the fabric was wet, as if she'd waded in only to her ankles.

In no hurry to turn around, her voice was soft and trance-like. "Good morning, Mellie."

"The doctor from Zürich has arrived," added Governess Coudenhove.

"Doctor Visconti—"

Troilo braced himself as Philippa sprung to life and whipped around. She was as tantalizing as her picture, with muted green eyes. But her expansive pupils, full of feline hunger, held little recognition for the man who stood before her.

A strand of blonde hair blew across the beguiling, upturned corners of her mouth. "The Italian traveler," she said, inspecting him from top to bottom.

"Your Royal and Imperial Highness," Troilo said with rehearsed composure. "It is an honor to finally meet you."

"Hm." Philippa angled her cheek to Governess Coudenhove. "I trust Fräulein has shown you the cottage?"

"I have only just arrived," said Troilo.

Philippa lifted her wet gown, revealing her bare feet as she stepped forward onto the grass. "Then I shall give you the tour myself," she declared, hooking him by the arm. "It would be my pleasure."

Upon first impression, her personality seemed as fanciful and aberrant as the headlines Troilo had read about her.

"Highness, do you often swim in the mornings?" he asked.

"Oh, I do not *swim*." Philippa pulled him along with a wry laugh. "I am dreadfully afraid of water—unless it is contained in a bathtub, of course. It is *bodies of water* that make me nervous."

Up on the veranda, servants swarmed the breakfast table, replacing the melted cakes with stacks of finger sandwiches. Troilo nodded to Jung as Philippa pulled him around front, where a girl was seated in one of the white wicker chairs.

"Look who I have sequestered, Erzsi," she said.

Troilo met the eye of the younger archduchess who'd watched him from the window. With her dirty blonde hair and pouted lips, she could have been Philippa's blood-sister.

"*Easy on the eyes, with olive skin and a lily pad gaze,*" Philippa whispered playfully. "Just as they said."

The terrier she mindlessly petted in her lap seemed more impressed than Erzsi. "Yes, yes, *lily pad gaze,*" she mumbled, fanning them away. "As long as he can see properly."

"You are the talk of Kaiservilla, you know," Philippa teased, yanking Troilo toward the cottage doors. "Come! You will have lunch with us, won't you? Do you like pastries?"

"I—"

"Mellie!" Philippa held the glass door open as she called back. "Would you have them bring out the puff pastries with cream?" She did not wait for confirmation before turning back to Troilo.

"My great aunt—*Her Majesty, The Empress*—had an entire kitchen built here just for pastries."

Something as trivial as cream puffs was not among the things Troilo thought he might discuss with Philippa, though he'd seen them through her gaze plenty of times. The bond between them was wildly unpredictable in that way.

"They are my favorite. I would eat them for breakfast, lunch, and dinner if they would allow it," she added, releasing him.

Sunlight poured through the grand windows as she walked to the center of the mahogany parquet floors, as if even the sun itself wanted to warm her skin. From where Troilo stood, he saw little of the hysteria he'd been briefed on.

"Tell me, Doctor, were you born in Italy?" she asked, twirling to face him.

"The Istrian Peninsula."

Philippa combed the ends of her tangled, yard length hair with a smile. "Is it beautiful there?"

"Incredibly."

An awkward pause settled between them, and Troilo dropped his gaze to the carved wooden table by his side.

"It is a figure from the *Nibelungenlied,*" she said. "There are sixteen of them here at Marmorschlossl."

Turning away, Troilo found his reflection in a mirror hanging above a carved chestnut panel. Was it fate or mere coincidence that even the *Nibelungenlied* had found its way back to her through a set of sculpted furniture?

"It is an epic poem from the Middle Ages," Philippa added.

"Yes..." Troilo kept his eyes on the Hungarian turul perched atop the golden mirror frame. "Perhaps the first ever recorded in High German."

Philippa spoke behind him. "You have read it?"

Knowing she did not remember that it had been *he* who had introduced her to it, Troilo glanced at her through the mirror, wary.

"Long ago," he said, studying the tarnished edges of the mirror. "Do you like poetry, Your Highness?"

"I suppose, in a way, it is an inherited passion."

When he looked up again, Philippa seemed to be studying his reflection. "Her Majesty adored poetry," she said. "It was one of the many things she shared with her beloved cousin, Ludwig."

"Ludwig II of Bavaria."

The Swan King, whose madness was still spoken of in the halls of the Burghölzli.

"Ludwig believed that my aunt was his soulmate," she said. "The only human who truly understood him."

At last, Troilo pivoted toward her. "Is that what you believe? That they were soulmates?"

Philippa stared for a moment, and through her sight, Troilo saw the translucent overlay of his own sunlit irises.

Was she admiring his eyes?

"Come," she urged.

Away from the foyer windows, the cottage was intimate and sumptuous. Its halls, wallpapered in a crimson floral, gave the indication of a great many secrets sealed beneath.

Philippa led the way, briefly introducing each room they passed. "You come highly regarded from my aunt Valerie Marie," she said over her shoulder. "How long have you lived in Zürich?"

"Almost five years."

"You are not at all what I expected," she admitted. "When I was told a specialist from the Burghölzli was coming."

"You expected me to be Swiss."

"I expected you to be *old.*" Philippa halted outside the parlor, turning to face him with a childish grin. "You are young." Voice dimmed, she leaned closer, her eyes a soft, sea foam glass. "I was certain you would not be as lovely as the maids claimed, yet..."

Bewildered by her forwardness, but equally bewitched, Troilo did not move as Philippa placed a finger over his lips, hushing any objection.

"Perhaps, Doctor," she whispered. "You may study me more efficiently in my bedroom."

"I think the library would be better—"

Her kiss was forcefully ardent upon his lips, a gesture with little meaning.

"...suited," Troilo finished, gently distancing himself from her.

This shallow girl with a lecherous appetite, as strange to herself as she was to him. Could one really be so disconnected from one's own soul?

"It is bad form, you know," Philippa said. "To let a woman make a fool of herself."

"I do not believe I gave you any indication of—?"

"I am well acquainted with the male gaze, in recognizing desiring eyes when I see them," she said. "And *you*, Doctor Visconti, well..."

Troilo could feel his face turning hot. "Do you know who I am?" he demanded softly.

She blinked, as though she'd walked into a room and forgotten why. "No."

With a stern eye, he prodded further. "You have never met me before this day?"

"No. Well, not unless it was in some otherworldly manner."

"Otherworldly manner—you mean to say, a fantasy?"

Philippa angled her chin as if she may kiss him a second time. "Certainly, if we had met in a fantasy, it would have been *yours.*"

Now it was Troilo who wanted to give way to temptation, to lock mouths with this familiar stranger. "Are you so certain, Highness?" he whispered back.

"Your Highness? Doctor Visconti!"

Troilo followed the call of Governess Coudenhove over his shoulder.

"Coming Mellie!"

Philippa leaned in closer with a feathery laugh as Troilo turned back to her. "The moment has passed, Doctor," she teased, sliding by.

The warmth of the room went with her, leaving Troilo to compose himself in the hall. His collar was damp to the touch as he reached up to loosen it, replaying the interaction in his mind. He had hoped for attraction, of course, but hadn't anticipated she would be so forthcoming. Worse yet was how *easily* she could have swayed him.

There was too much at stake to engage in reckless passion—Troilo knew that better than anyone.

He would need to reevaluate.

Philippa plucked a cream puff from the top of a three-tier stand, piled high with sardine and cucumber sandwiches, savory tarts and cranberry scones as Troilo walked out onto the veranda to see a table set for a party double their size.

"There you are, Doctor," she said, taking a generous bite. "We were beginning to think you lost your way."

Troilo exchanged a quick glance with Jung, who assessed his frazzled aura with the instinct of a bloodhound. He was often too clever for his own good, his intuitive muscle whittled like a blade. A similar, though less enthused, look came from Archduchess Erzsi, who was picking at the crusts of an uneaten sandwich.

"Tea, Herr Visconti?"

Troilo nodded across the table to Governess Coudenhove as he took his seat. "Please."

"Will you try one?"

To his left, Philippa offered him a cream puff with a coy smile.

"No thank you, Your Highness," he replied. "I am not hungry."

"Very well," she said, biting into it. Wiping the buttercream from her smirk, she licked her finger clean. "I for one have worked up an appetite."

Erzsi's terrier coughed, having gobbled too hastily the crust she'd dropped into his ravenous jaws.

"Tea would be lovely, Fräulein," said Troilo, extending his teacup.

"How do you like it?"

"No sugar," he murmured. "Thank you."

Jung cleared his throat. "We were just discussing how invaluable you are to the Burghölzli."

"Herr Jung claims your work on hypnosis is unparalleled by any in the field," said Philippa. "How very lucky for me."

Troilo sipped his tea, relaxing into the wicker chair. "Herr Jung is very kind," he said, keeping his attention straight ahead.

"What is it you are doing at the Burghölzli, Herr Jung?" asked Governess Coudenhove.

"I am working toward my medical degree, interning under Doctor Bleuler at the hospital."

"And working on a remarkable dissertation," Troilo added.

"Oh, well you must not tease us," said the governess. "What is it about?"

Jung turned his teacup on its saucer. "The psychology and pathology of so-called occult phenomena."

"You are studying occult phenomena?" Philippa leaned forward with visible interest. "How?"

"I am conducting séances with my cousin and logging my reports."

"Because you believe it to be real?"

"Because I believe it is injudicious to dismiss the things we do not understand, simply because we don't understand them."

Troilo peered into the rings of his lukewarm tea, imagining the bridge between Philippa's mind and his, only to be met with a riddling fog.

"What is it you specialize in, exactly?"

Troilo glanced upward at Archduchess Erzsi across the table. "I am a neurologist," he replied. "I specialize in psychoanalytic hypnosis."

"So, are you an occultist or a doctor?"

"Oh, Erzsi," Philippa scolded.

"Did Aunt Valerie not find him *on stage* demonstrating mesmerism?"

"You will have to excuse her." Philippa shot her cousin a visible dagger across the table. "You see, Her Majesty was wild about mediums and the like."

"And it seems grandfather has learned very little," Archduchess Erzsi went on. "As he will apparently call upon *anyone* to treat you. He is no better than Doctor Bohm!"

Troilo set his sights on the teenager. "You are quick to dismiss me, Your Highness."

"Erzsi believes people who entertain such ideas are charlatans," Philippa added.

"I believe they prey on the heartbroken and desperate."

It was clear from the way Archduchess Erzsi held Troilo's stare that her opinion of him was not subject to change. She couldn't possibly have known that he had once been among them. The heartbroken and desperate.

"What say you about charlatans, Doctor?" Erzsi asked.

"My apologies, Your Highness," Troilo replied, clinking the edge of his teacup with his spoon. "In my profession, I have learned that it is never wise to share one's opinions."

"But on the contrary," Jung interjected, "there is still much we do not know. If mediums like Eusponia Palladino, whom Doctor Visconti sat with in Milan, *are* indeed charlatans, then they have fooled some of the most brilliant minds in all of Europe. And that alone is a reason to study them."

The tension of the table was broken only by a handsome, young footman shutting the cottage door behind him.

Philippa called him over as she fanned herself, slouched back in her chair. "Felix?"

"Yes, Your Highness?" he asked, finding her side.

"I am so warm. Would you bring me a fan?"

Entranced by the same spell that had befallen Troilo inside,

Felix nodded with a sheepish grin.

"Are you sure you would not like something to eat, Doctor?" asked Governess Coudenhove. "There is always more food than we know what to do with."

Troilo averted his eyes to his tea, unable to focus on her words. He had felt *them* before—Philippa's lovers—like an aching cold sweat in the night. A cruel coincidence it was that this boy with dark hair and hazel eyes resembled him so much.

"I am afraid we must make our way," Troilo said suddenly. "Herr Jung and I have an audience with His Majesty at four."

"Then we mustn't hold you up," said the governess.

"You must leave right now?" Philippa asked, redirecting her attention from Felix. "I have yet to show you the library."

"You may show me tomorrow," Troilo replied. "Thank you for the tea, Fräulein."

Catching the sharpness of his tone, Erzsi's attention snapped upward just as a sudden wind swept through the veranda, rustling the leaves of the hanging creepers. Philippa's face had flattened, and her new doctor looked nothing short of flustered. What had she done, now?

The Hungarian china on the table shook as the men stood in unison, returning their chairs.

"Your Royal and Imperial Highnesses," said Doctor Visconti, splitting a nod between Erzsi and Philippa. "Until we meet again."

The stagnant air returned as they descended the stairs, and, aside from the panting of the dog, the tea table fell silent. Truly odd men, they were.

"Come, Blitz." Mellie snapped to her feet, scooping the dog from Erzsi's lap. "Erzsi, it is time for your French lesson."

"I will be right up."

Mellie glanced back at her, unconvinced as she opened the cottage door and headed inside.

Expelling a rattling sigh, Erzsi assessed the leftover food on the table. Both the cream cheese in the sandwiches and the filling of the pastries had already turned lukewarm. Why did she need to learn French anyway? She had little desire to visit France.

"Your Highness, would you still like your fan?"

Erzsi looked over at Felix. So distracted by her new interest, Philippa had forgotten the poor sap standing there, waiting on her beck and call.

"Not after all," Philippa replied quietly. "You may go."

Erzsi held her tongue long enough for Felix to leave the table-side. "He is married, you know," she said, swatting a fly from the last remaining cream puff. "Doctor Visconti."

"Married?" Philippa countered. "I did not see a wedding band on his finger."

"That is because it is hanging from a chain around his neck."

"How do you know?"

"The same way you heard of his *lily pad gaze.*" Erzsi rotated the oozing cream puff in her fingers before dropping it onto her left-over sandwich crusts. "One of the maids at the villa saw him fiddling with it."

"She must be dead," Philippa said, a little too nonchalantly.

"Perhaps she is. But in any case, he wears it, so I do not suggest trying to *comfort* him."

Philippa watched the two men disappear slowly beneath the shade of the trees. "We have a connection," she said. "I can feel it."

A connection.

Erzsi couldn't help but roll her eyes.

"You do not believe me?"

Swatting away another fly, Erzsi leaned onto the table with both elbows. Having long mastered the art of listening, she knew everything there was to know about Philippa's new doctor.

"You know they say he has *ink* on his arms?"

Philippa turned to her, surprised. "Ink?"

Erzsi smirked, as though she might just withhold this scandalous nugget.

"Her Majesty got ink of an anchor in Greece," Philippa reminded. "It is the mark of someone who has traveled the world."

"Doctor Visconti has much more ink than a puny anchor." Widening her eyes for dramatic effect, Erzsi rolled up the sleeves of her white sundress. "They say he has *serpents* branded around both of his forearms."

"Then I shall like to see them."

Erzsi's expression drooped in annoyance, seeing that if anything, she had probably just inflamed Philippa's interest even more.

"Well, if he *is* a real doctor, you would do well to remember why he is here," she chastised.

Philippa tossed her a smirk as she sunk further into her chair. "He shall be my cure, then."

"You are an impossible creature—always going on about *connections*. Charlatan or not, I pity him."

"I will prove it," Philippa whispered, running her thumb over her bottom lip. "He will look back."

Erzsi stood up, then leaned over the table for a better view of the oak path, where Doctor Visconti and his assistant had been reduced to tiny, distant figures.

She couldn't help but laugh. "He will not look..."

The words hardly escaped Erzsi's mouth before the prophecy rang true, and the doctor glanced over his shoulder.

Philippa only grinned ear-to-ear in a gloating victory.

"Oh, I do hate when you do that," Erzsi sighed, ignoring her.

Troilo snapped his attention forward, past the pine branches bending to the breeze, to the canary columns and neoclassical splendor of the villa beckoning them up ahead. Like Orpheus, he couldn't resist turning back to see that she was still there—this woman of his dreams.

Next to him, Jung lifted his glasses to wipe the perspiration from his nose. "Archduchess Philippa seems to have taken a liking to you."

"Such behavior is not uncommon with her condition," Troilo replied. "And it is not the first time I have dealt with it."

"This is true, however...forgive me if this is too personal, but from the little you have told me about your wife, I cannot help but wonder if you find the archduchess in her likeness."

"You forget nothing, Herr Jung." His fingers habitually found the rounded indent of her wedding band beneath his clothes. "But any likeness between her and Stanzi is coincidental."

"Since I have known you, you have been alone."

Troilo avoided Jung's gaze in favor of the yellow villa ahead. He'd confided in him once about the death of his wife, albeit changing the timeline to better suit his backstory.

"Perhaps you might consider seeking a companion one day soon...only so much healing occurs in solitude," he added. "The real healing happens within partnership."

Loose pebbles crunched under their feet as they approached the courtyard fountain, where marble children frolicked with mythical catfish. The men slowed their steps until the only sound was the pitter patter of the fountain droplets.

"Do you feel we will be met with pushback this evening?" asked Jung.

"My impression is that Doctor Kerzl will interfere very little," Troilo replied as he studied the frieze carving of a deer herd across the villa's peak. "I have spoken with him about using the Talking Cure to accompany her hypnosis in our correspondence."

"What of the psychiatrist? Archduchess Erzsi does not seem to care for him."

"Something tells me she does not care for *anyone.*" Troilo stepped forward, coaxing Jung to come along. "Though, for what it's worth, Freud does not endear himself to Bohm either."

"He warned you of him?"

"Only that he is an anti-Semite," Troilo replied. "But if a man is narrow minded in one aspect of his life, it will surely bleed into the others."

Under the foliage of the villa's veranda, the butler waited to greet them. "Welcome back, Doctor," he said. "Perhaps you both would like to see your lodgings and freshen up?"

"Please."

The interior of the Kaiservilla was a modest eggshell and resembled nothing of the cottage, shy of the matching wrought iron and creepers outside. Taxidermy and antique weapons stood in place of silken red wallpaper and specialty carvings, making each corridor indistinguishable from the last. But despite its maze of antlers and horns, the villa felt somehow *lighter*—its only residual energies being that of mundane, everyday happenings.

A younger footman waited at the top of the bifurcated staircase to greet them. "Herr Jung, please follow me," he said.

Parting with a nod, Troilo began his walk down the long hall, whose bustling housemaids seemed to quiet at the sight of him and his *lily pad gaze*. But whether they'd deemed him a charming savior or dangerous outsider, it was too soon to tell.

"Your luggage has already been brought up," assured the butler.

"Where will Herr Jung be staying?"

"His room is at the end of the innermost corridor, sir."

As his chaperone slowed his step, Troilo looked to the end of the hall, where the portrait of a child hung alone in a gold-leaf frame.

"His Highness, Crown Prince Rudolf," said the butler. "When he was a boy."

There was a sad finality in his statement, as though within the walls of this now-crumbling dynasty, hope lived only in the past. Perhaps that's why the portrait of the young prince had been hidden away.

Troilo was torn from the thought only by the turning lock of the door next to him.

"Here you are, Doctor."

Surprisingly lavish quarters awaited on the other side, stacked floor to ceiling with scenic landscapes, and gold accents in all directions. Lace curtains framed the towering window, which spilled evening hues over Troilo's suitcases that waited patiently at the foot of the bed.

Relieved to see his hand-painted oriental box among the luggage, Troilo sauntered over to the window and lifted back the lace.

"His Majesty thought you may enjoy a view of the courtyard," the butler added, glancing at his watch. "There are a little over two hours until your audience with him in the parlor. Shall the footman bring Herr Jung when he comes to retrieve you?"

Troilo untied his cravat, peering through the waved glass to the marble fountain. "Please," he murmured. "That will be all."

Holding his gaze steady on the pines beyond the courtyard, Troilo fell backward onto the bed as the door closed behind him. Pulling his tiny, green confidant from his trouser pocket, he fanned the journal's pages, landing at last on a cursive passage he'd scribbled that morning on the train.

> *The time will come,*
> *Our time will come!*
> *When we will break from our bondage,*
> *Free of our debts,*
> *And take flight.*
> *Where shall we go, my love?*
> *What is your fancy?*
> *What paradise awaits us?*
> *O what heaven awaits me,*
> *In your eyes, and in your arms*
> *At long last*

Slipping the sweat-soaked cravat through his collar, Troilo

stretched the length of his arm over his head. He couldn't help but feel foolish as he stared at the poem, having written it for a woman whose affections seemed as fickle as a summer rain. Pages on pages he had filled in her name, year after lonely year.

Perhaps it had been presumptuous for Troilo to assume he'd imprinted himself on her soul with the same intensity that she had his.

Willing himself upright, Troilo reached for the decorative box, embellished with a red Chinese dragon. Having toted it all across various continents, it would have been much wiser to have burned the contents inside. But in a world where evidence was every-thing, it was the closest thing he had to proof of who—and *what* —he was.

Troilo reached into his jacket lining for the miniature key, then, placing its head in the iron lock, he turned it counterclock-wise and lifted the lid.

3:55 P.M.

Under the watchful glass eyes of deer and chamois, Troilo and Jung trailed behind their escort, walking through clouds of old conversation that hung in the air. Again, a pair of maids seemed to halt their route to watch from afar. The male servants were less friendly, and quick to avert their eyes.

Jung glanced at Troilo, then lowered his voice to a murmur. "I must ask," he said to the footman leading them, "are the workers of the villa always so entranced by visitors?"

"There are rumors..."

"That I am a progressive," Troilo guessed, finding the face of Empress Elisabeth, who hung immortalized in another oil painting above them. "An anarchist that cannot be trusted."

"There are rumors that you are a *conjurer,* sir." The footman's shoulders tensed as he turned his cheek. "That the spirits of the dead speak through your patients."

Troilo nodded intently, fixated on the diamond stars that adorned the late empress' chestnut hair.

"But just as well, Doctor Visconti," murmured the footman, motioning toward the parlor entryway. "They believe in your miracles."

The pair of doctors in the room quieted, and as if they'd just been discussing the very same gossip, an uneasy mood lingered, shrouding the lamps in an ambiguous haze.

"Doctor Troilo Visconti and Herr Carl Jung," the footman announced.

Troilo recognized the signature white mustache of the emperor's personal physician as he puffed on a cigar in front of the mantle, having seen his photograph in a medical journal.

"Doctor Visconti, at last we meet," he greeted with a ready smile.

"Likewise, Doctor Kerzl. This is Herr Jung, my assistant from Zürich."

"You should know Doctor Bleuler speaks very highly of you as a hypnotist," Kerzl went on, ushering him in. "He has told me of your studies in Paris—he claims you have the makings of Charcot himself."

"That is kind of him."

"I do regret that I never went to see Charcot's hysterics at the Salpêtrière." The second doctor, a middle-aged man with curly hair and broad shoulders, glanced up at Troilo from his seat on the velvet sofa. "Do forgive my lack of manners," he added. "I am Doctor Wilhelm Bohm, Archduchess Philippa's psychiatrist."

"Pleased to make your acquaintance," Troilo replied.

Bohm's chuckle was dubious, as though he knew better to believe him.

"May I ask how old you are, Doctor Visconti?"

Troilo turned back to Kerzl. "I am thirty-four."

"By God, you do not look a day over twenty-five." He laughed under his breath. "The youthful skin of the Peninsula, I presume. Drink?"

"No, thank you."

Kerzl nodded, retracting his hand from the crystal decanter.

A pause blanketed the room, then Bohm spoke. "Your credentials are impressive, Herr Visconti. I am curious to know what you make of Her Highness' condition?"

"I have not studied her long enough to hypothesize."

"Certain acquaintances of yours, Charles Richet for example..." Bohm rose from his seat and walked over to the mirrored tray, generously helping himself to a pour from the decanter. "These acquaintances might claim that her affliction is of a *supernatural* origin, would they not?"

Troilo willed a polite smile. It was always a relief when the opposition presented themselves so early.

"It depends on one's definition of supernatural," he replied.

"Define it for me, if you do not mind."

"Charles is a Theosophist." Troilo paced the length of the mantle. "Contrary to Spiritualists, Theosophists believe a medium to be accessing a higher level of the *self* during a séance, as opposed to speaking with spirits who are present."

"I have only asked for a simple definition..."

"One cannot be asked to define the undefinable, as the answer will always be relative. And as doctors" —Troilo smiled again— "we must be willing to work outside of definitions as much as we create them."

Bohm brushed something from the cuff of his sleeve, then looked up. "I understand you lost your wife and child, is that correct?"

"There is no need, Herr Bohm," Kerzl scolded.

"I am *only* pointing out that Herr Visconti holds a personal bias toward such ideas—"

"You cannot assume to know my beliefs, Herr Bohm, because

they are a mystery even to me," Troilo interjected. "I know only that Her Highness is suffering from a fractured mind, and that whatever conventional methods you have implemented to help her are not working."

"His Royal and Imperial Majesty, Emperor Franz Josef."

The commanding figure in the parlor entryway stood at only about five-foot-five compared to Troilo's five-ten, and was dressed rather casually in a brown suit. His brow, seared with the permanent worry lines of a fellow griever, softened as a welcoming smile grew beneath his snowy handlebar mustache.

A kind ruler, admired by his people. At least that's what Troilo had always heard about him.

"Good evening, Your Majesty," said the doctors, each taking their turn to bow as the emperor walked in.

Taking his seat in a wingback chair, the emperor motioned for the party to settle themselves on the velvet sofas. A valet walked over, filling a glass of brandy for him.

"Doctor Visconti," the emperor began. "I do hope you have found your lodging comfortable?"

"I have, Your Majesty. Thank you."

The emperor nodded to Kerzl and Bohm, sitting on the adjacent sofa. "We are deeply grateful to you—and to you, Herr Jung—for your expertise, and willingness to join us here in Bad Ischl."

Troilo offered a humble nod, knowing his presence at Kaiservilla was merely the successful result of an image he'd spent years meticulously crafting.

There is a doctor at the Burghölzli who treats unusual cases like Philippa's. He'd imagined what Archduchess Valerie Marie, the emperor's daughter, might have said to her father after meeting Troilo briefly at one of his hypnosis demonstrations in Vienna. *Visconti is his name.*

"The gratitude is mine and mine alone, Your Majesty," said Troilo.

"It is my hope that Herr Kerzl and Herr Bohm may offer up their own knowledge to assist you in Philippa's treatment."

"Of course, Majesty," Bohm replied, sipping from his crystal glass. "We are eager to hear all about Doctor Visconti's treatment plan for Her Highness."

The emperor centered his attention back on Troilo. "I was told that you met earlier this afternoon?"

The sight of Philippa at the edge of the sunlit, sparkling pond—he would never forget it—not if he lived a century more.

"We did, yes," Troilo replied.

"How did you find her demeanor?" asked Kerzl.

"Her Highness was polite, albeit a bit...uncouth."

The old physician didn't seem the slightest bit surprised, nodding to himself with a humored grin.

"Whenever you are ready, Doctor."

Troilo turned to Bohm, and, knowing full well there wasn't anything they could tell him that he didn't already know, he readied his pen and paper anyway. "Let us begin with her symptoms. When was her last episode?"

"Her last was at Schonbrünn on the second of May," Kerzl answered. "It was her worst yet."

"This was the incident in the bathtub, correct?"

"Not an ounce of water remained in the tub," he said. "She was in bed for several days."

"The emptied bathtub was from her *thrashing*," Bohm cut in.

Troilo envisioned the flooded tile floors of the Schonbrünn—details he'd received mentally while sitting at his desk one Tuesday afternoon, nearly three hundred miles away.

"Aside from thrashing, what else do her fits normally consist of?" Troilo asked.

"Intense anger, involuntary convulsions, confused behavior," said Kerzl.

Troilo scribbled in his notebook, mostly for show. "Any short-term paralysis?"

"No, but she does have lapses in time."

"Are her convulsions ever of a sexual nature?"

"Sometimes."

Troilo pressed his pen into the paper. "When was her last menstrual cycle?"

"Four months ago," Kerzl replied. "It is wildly irregular."

"Did anything significant happen the day of her last fit?"

"Her Highness' fits come at random."

"Nothing is random, Herr Kerzl."

"As neurologists, we look for patterns in the mind, Your Majesty," Jung added, turning to the emperor. "Stimuli that may remind the patient of a traumatic event."

"It can be something as minuscule as the change of the weather—hours or even days before the patient experiences a fit," Troilo added. "In our field of study, what we've come to know as *hysteria* originates somewhere in the unconscious."

The emperor motioned for him to continue.

"In the event of a fit, the mind of a hysteric reverts to another time and place when they felt helpless. Often, they cannot tell the difference between past and present."

"We understand that Her Highness' father, your brother, passed away four years ago from typhoid," said Jung. "Is that correct?"

"Yes, he had just returned from Palestine." The emperor paused to stroke his whiskers. "There has been...a string of tragedies in our family."

"Your Majesty." Troilo tapered his voice. "Might I ask the exact relation between Her Highness and your son, the Crown Prince?"

The pulse of the room dropped, measured only by the ticking hand of the mantle clock. No one would dare mention the madness of the late Crown Prince Rudolf, at least not out loud. The boy in the gold frame—though a sore reminder—was far too beloved.

The emperor readjusted in his chair. "They are first cousins," he said finally.

Troilo examined the way Kerzl's face fell, knowing he'd been the first doctor on the scene at Mayerling. Troilo had seen that same expression, or rather lack of one, on the faces of countless haunted men.

"I am afraid I do not see the relevance." Bohm's tone was growing impatient. "I am much more interested in hearing of the methodology and technique you plan to apply."

Troilo's gaze slid to him. "I plan to use hypnosis in tandem with talk sessions to gain a better understanding of what may be troubling her unconscious."

"You plan to *talk* to her."

"That is correct, Herr Bohm. It is called the Talking Cure."

"Did this magical Talking Cure come out of the Burghölzli?"

"Josef Breuer and Sigmund Freud coined the term in *Studies in Hysteria*," Jung added. "Some of the leading pioneers of our field."

"Yes, I am aware of Freud."

"Then you have surely read it." Troilo raised a taunting brow. "And know that the Talking Cure has proved effective in symptom relief, as well as accessing any memories, thoughts, or dreams that come up for the patient."

"Dream analysis," Bohm said patronizingly. "One's dreams are purely anecdotal."

"On the contrary, Herr Bohm. The imagination is the most accurate representation of a person's unconscious. Now—is Her Highness currently on any medications?"

"Laudanum," Kerzl replied.

"We will need to halt her dosage immediately. I need her to be coherent."

The emperor nodded. "I trust your discretion."

"Ah, yes, always trust an Italian."

"What was that, Doctor Bohm?"

"I said *very well*, Your Majesty."

"Does anyone else have any concerns they wish to voice?"

Troilo watched Bohm reach for his drink on the table, only to find it empty. This psychiatrist, likely bitter over being demoted, was a snagged bobbin Troilo had not foreseen.

"Please make yourselves available to Doctor Visconti for any assistance he may require."

Bohm and Kerzl answered in unison. "Yes, Your Majesty."

"Gentlemen, you are dismissed," the emperor concluded. "I would like to speak with Doctor Visconti privately."

Bohm was the first to stand, followed by Kerzl, who rose at a snail's pace by comparison. Jung collected the empty glasses, returning them to the decanter's tray.

The valet walked over to refill the emperor's glass with brandy as he motioned for the footman to close the parlor doors.

Now, the *real* interrogation would begin.

"I have heard a great deal about you," the emperor said at last. "From the Italian Alps to the streets of Paris, tales of intrigue seem to follow you."

"They are only tales, Majesty."

"You spent time in the Orient, did you not?"

"I did, Your Majesty. Tangier."

"You seem very young for such a reputation, Doctor Visconti." The emperor clutched the arm of the chair, pushing himself to his feet. "But you are here because the director of the Burghölzli says you are the best of the best," he said, making his way to the double French doors. "He says your medical instinct is so sharp that he himself has questioned the nature of it."

"The Greeks believed in treating the mind and soul as much as the body," Troilo replied. "The ideas I draw on are not unique. They were practiced in Asclepion temples for hundreds of years with highly effective results."

The emperor sipped on his brandy, eyes fixated on the hazy summer sky. "My Sisi believed that the veil between the living and dead was akin to a curtain." He looked to Troilo with an inquisitive brow. "That from time to time, we could pull it back."

"Her Majesty would not be alone in that belief."

"She held séances here at Marmorschlossl for her cousin Ludwig, and for our Rudolf."

"In the cottage?"

The emperor nodded.

Of course, Troilo had long known about the empress' interest in spiritualism and séances. Such news traveled fast, even over borders.

"I must admit, I expected more outward eccentricity from a man of your character," the emperor added.

"A certain reticence is a necessary requirement in my line of work," Troilo replied. "At least, if one is to be taken seriously."

"Very well, Doctor Visconti. You may don your mask, if it makes you more comfortable here. But you should know that in the presence of my niece, strange things occur. As though the world is at the whimsy of her moods."

Troilo stood and walked over, joining the emperor in front of the dark French doors. "Would you share with me how she came to live with you at the Hofburg?"

"Her fits began when she was Erzsi's age but seemed to worsen when my brother passed. Philippa's mother brought her to court in Vienna, hoping she would find a suitor."

"I understand there was a short engagement."

"Until she called it off, yes."

"But she did not return home to Bohemia with her mother. Why?"

"She is my niece," he replied. "When my wife was killed, Erzsi was all I had left, and she adored Philippa." The emperor walked to the mantle, setting his glass on its top. "I thought I could look after her better if she stayed in Vienna with us. But none of the four doctors she has seen so far can explain…"

"What happens to her?"

"Precisely." He paused long and hard, seemingly wrestling with himself. "Some say she is spirit-bothered," he admitted. "That she is their instrument."

"Is that your belief?"

The corners of the emperor's blue eyes crinkled beneath his thick, unruly brows. "Perhaps it is my selfish hope," he admitted.

"I, too, have lost a wife and a child," Troilo admitted. "Such hopes are human instinct. But with all due respect, Majesty, we can be haunted by more than ghosts."

The emperor seemed to shed his persona, leaving only the palpable loneliness of an elderly man. "Do you believe you can help her?" he asked at last.

"Yes," Troilo replied without a beat. "I am certain of it."

"Certain?"

Anyone with his credentials could have landed on the doorstep of the Kaiservilla, but Troilo had an advantage over every doctor that had come before him, and any that could come after. A card he would reveal to no one. That the *true* origin of Philippa's hysteria—the trauma that had taken root in her body— had grown from the same seed as his own grief.

"Yes, Your Majesty," Troilo answered. "I am certain."

The emperor crossed in front of him, resting his palm on the back of the wingback. "You must be tired, Doctor Visconti."

Mirroring the same faint smile, Troilo thought of the moonlit room that awaited him, where beneath the blankets of another foreign bed, in another foreign country, he would close his eyes and find *her* there. "Quite," he said.

FOUR

June 8, 1900
4:37 A.M.

It was a static sensation that woke him, prickling the hair on his arms with the electric intensity of a dry winter's day. Propping himself up on his elbow, Troilo lifted his head from the pillow, which had only hours ago carried the tempo of Philippa's steady, rhythmic heartbeat.

The nightly picture charades had started as usual, with Troilo summoning a cream puff doused in powdered sugar to the forefront of his consciousness. As it dissipated, a curious swan slid down the stream of his own thoughts, pausing to look at him as though to ask, *Is that you? Are you here with me?* To that, Troilo answered in the way he often announced his presence—by envisioning the fiery tail of a comet as it shot across an imaginal sky. And, as if its light had vanquished any of her doubts, he'd sensed a smile in return.

Troilo rubbed the twin dragons coiling his arms with a shiver. Since Philippa's birth, his body would tingle and burn with the need to *change* when danger was near her, perceived or otherwise.

Jumping from bed, he fought to shove his arms through the holes of his paisley dressing gown as a frantic fist clamored against the wooden door.

"My friend, you must make haste!"

Jung did not look remotely surprised to see that Troilo was already awake. "I will give you a moment to dress," he said with worn breath.

"There is no time," Troilo replied, lunging for his medical bag on the floor. "How long ago was her fit?"

"Fräulein Coudenhove rang the house about ten minutes ago."

Pushing his dark, unkempt hair from his forehead, Troilo glanced up at Jung. "The others have been alerted?"

"Kerzl has gone to wake His Majesty," he said, allowing Troilo to squeeze past him in the doorway. "Bohm has called a carriage and will meet us outside."

Unaffected by the ogling stares of the servants, Troilo hustled at the fore, leading himself and Jung through the maze of the villa until they at last reached the staircase. Greeted only by an empty entrance hall, there was no sign of a carriage waiting.

Troilo turned to the footman standing at the door. "Where is Doctor Bohm?" he demanded, so harshly it made the boy flinch.

"He went ahead to the cottage, sir," he blubbered. "I can call anoth—"

Troilo swiftly pushed the doors open, but as he stepped out into the courtyard, he was seeing red. "How did he ready himself so quickly? Unless..." He turned to Jung, who nodded. "He was already awake."

"The decanter in the parlor was nearly emptied."

Troilo lifted his gaze to the wrought iron steeples of Marmorschossl that pierced the fog. The static sensation on his skin began to fade, leaving only the impression of a calm blackness. A deep sleep.

"What?" Jung asked. "What is it?"

"He has given her a sedative."

Opting to cut through the meadow, Troilo led the way across the pebbled courtyard, toting his leather bag at his side. An opaque mist hugged the mountain slopes, shrouding the cottage in a haunting mystique as they traipsed through the dewy grass toward the rising sun.

Inside, the walls spoke with lackluster quietude.

Governess Coudenhove snapped to attention, using the mahogany staircase to pull herself to her feet as they entered. "Doctor Visconti." Her eyes trailed the sliver of bare chest peeking through his housecoat.

"Fräulein Coudenhove," Jung greeted.

Troilo readjusted his collar awkwardly, tucking his wife's ring further behind its folds. "Please take me to her," he directed.

"Of course," she hiccupped, pivoting toward the stairs. "This way."

A soft, morning light trickled into the hallway of the second floor, where Felix, the servant boy, sat slouched on a sofa. The bloody cloth he held to his temple was a bright red, vibrant even against the ruby wallpaper. He could have been a painting, this dejected man with downcast eyes.

"What happened here?" Troilo asked.

"Her Highness attacked one of our footmen while in a rage."

Troilo caught a glimpse of Archduchess Erzsi peering out through her cracked bedroom door as he walked by. *"Attacked,"* he said. "Would you care to elaborate, Fräulein?"

"She threw a glass of water at his face."

"What was a footman doing in her room?" Jung asked. "And so early in the morning?"

Resigning herself to the wall outside of Philippa's room, Governess Coudenhove only pressed her lips together, confirming Troilo's suspicion from yesterday.

They were lovers.

"Doctor Visconti." Bohm emerged from the bedroom; his

reddened, oily face crinkled in amusement at the sight of Troilo in his bed clothes. "Terribly sorry about the carriage."

Still wearing the same clothes from their roundtable, Bohm's breath smelled of alcohol.

Troilo nudged past him without a word, turning back only to address Governess Coudenhove. "Please have some water brought up."

The crunch of glass shards beneath his feet was the only indication of bloodshed as Troilo walked into the bedroom, where men on horseback stretched across the walls in various shades of green. The Bavarian fox hunt coincided just above Philippa's head, where she sat slouched against her wooden headboard like a unicorn in captivity.

Troilo had seen too much of this in Paris—human beings bound in jackets, strapped to hospital beds. Patients deemed lost causes, *unable to be helped* by the likes of modern medicine.

Dropping his bag with a thud, he walked over to the side of the bed, where Philippa's shimmering hair ran over its edge like a golden river. "Your Highness, it is Doctor Visconti," he said, unbuckling the belt around her shoulders.

"You should be thanking me, you know," Bohm remarked, standing aimlessly in the doorway. "You get to keep your eyes."

"Can you hear me?" Troilo asked, freeing Philippa's wrists.

Her eyelids twitched, but could not lift her heavy lashes.

"It is doubtful," Bohm replied. "Her Highness is in a deep, restful sleep."

Troilo lifted his glare to see a maid slipping past him in the doorway, prescribed water in hand.

"Do be mindful of the glass," Bohm warned as she crossed the room.

"Doctor Visconti," she said.

"You may leave it on the nightstand—thank you." Troilo motioned Jung over as he shifted Philippa more upright against her headboard. "There is nothing restful about a patient being so drugged she cannot respond," Troilo murmured, offering the glass of water.

But her eyes did not open, and her lips did not move. Even her breathing seemed to still.

Troilo lifted her head, pressing his fingers to her neck. "I can hardly feel her pulse—how much did you give her?"

"The same as always. I..."

"Which is *how much*, Doctor Bohm?"

If he answered, Troilo did not hear him. As Philippa's pulse faded further, he found himself thrown into the past, steering Mesjec in the pouring rain through the streets of Pićan. "No," he whispered to himself, looking down to see his fingers tangled in Costanza's wet, bloodied hair. *"No!"*

Another goodbye was a fate far worse than any death!

Troilo blinked, trying to banish the way her grandmother had looked upon him at the sight of Costanza limp in his arms—like *he* had brought this upon them.

"Look there—what is she saying?"

Tearing Troilo from his flashback, Jung motioned to Philippa, whose lips had parted as though she might be trying to speak.

Troilo leaned in, only for the sound of cracking glass to overpower her whisper.

"My knight," Philippa gasped, shooting upright.

Uncertain of whose eyes he was looking into, Troilo found he could not speak, *nor* could he look away from her disoriented gaze, so adamantly locked on his.

"Doctor..."

Troilo's voice trembled. "Yes, Herr Jung?"

Jung only tapped his shoulder, bringing his attention to the bedside table, where the glass of water had been split down the center, its contents slowly seeping across the wood surface.

Troilo turned back to Philippa in his arms, gripping his sleeves with white knuckles.

What Otherworldly pact had bestowed this young princess with the tendency to *move water?*

"Highness," Troilo whispered. "Do you know who I am?"

Philippa's bejeweled eyes seemed to glimmer with recognition. But in place of words, a frothy liquid erupted from her mouth all over his dressing gown. It was only as she heaved the rest onto the floor that Troilo noticed the spectators watching from the hall. The episode had attracted a crowd, though he was unsure if it had lasted two or twenty minutes. He often lost track of time when he was thrown back into the past, back to that terrible day.

Standing among the tangle of servants in the doorway, Archduchess Erzsi retracted to let Doctor Kerzl through.

"Herr Visconti, do you need to take a seat?"

Troilo had not noticed Governess Coudenhove standing there. She always seemed to appear out of nowhere.

"You are as white as a ghost," she added.

Troilo wiped the sweat from his forehead as he scanned the crowd for Bohm. "Thank you, Fräulein, but I am fine."

From her seat on the sofa, Erzsi watched Doctor Bohm like a bird of prey as he pleaded his case with the emperor at the end of the hall. She had only caught the end of the scene, but it wasn't hard to see that he was somehow at fault, especially since he'd taken it upon *himself* to telephone the villa, meanwhile leaving Doctor Visconti and his assistant to remedy his mistake.

"I assure Your Majesty everything is under control," Bohm insisted.

Erzsi could almost smell the brandy on him from where she sat. "Rotten liar, he is, Blitz," she mumbled to the dog on her lap.

Blitz's ears perked up as the remaining servants scattered, making way for Doctor Visconti in his vomit-covered dressing gown. "Herr Bohm thought it appropriate to take the carriage without us, Your Majesty," he interjected.

"Time was of the essence," Doctor Bohm replied. "And it would seem Herr Visconti has a hard time getting out of bed."

"Yes—and Doctor Bohm never went to bed in the first place."

"Gentlemen." The emperor cast a glance toward Erzsi across the hall as she stroked her dog's ears. "This is a discussion for behind closed doors."

Doctor Bohm motioned to the entrance of the dressing room, where Erzsi took her French lessons. "Let us discuss, then."

Erzsi slipped down from the velvet cushion as her grandfather shut the door, eclipsing the hallway in darkness. Strange and foreign as Doctor Visconti was, she would not stand by and allow him to take the fall for a drunken pervert, charlatan or not.

Closing one eye, she peered through the keyhole until she could see the side of Doctor Bohm's pant leg.

"Her Highness needed to be sedated for her own safety," he began. "Majesty, she—"

"It was enough laudanum to tranquilize a horse!"

Erzsi steadied her breathing.

"It is irresponsible practice to employ opiates so carelessly," added Doctor Visconti.

"If you believe you can calm her without any—*be my guest,* Herr Visconti. Her Highness is known to act violently in this state, I was thinking only of her comfort!"

"You were thinking of *your* comfort," Doctor Visconti snapped. "You could have killed her with a dosage that high."

"I will not be lectured on the subject of medicine. Least not by a man who claims his cures in dreams and—!"

"Enough."

The room filled with a pregnant pause as the emperor lifted his hand.

Erzsi's fingertips hovered on the wooden door as her lashes brushed against the metal lock. She knew all about opium, and how generously Doctor Bohm implemented it.

But enough to *tranquilize a horse?*

"Majesty." Doctor Bohm's voice was almost too low to make

out when he at last spoke. "I cannot do my work properly under the direction of this man."

"Then he shall not work under me at all," Doctor Visconti cut in. "I will not accept responsibility of Her Highness' care without Doctor Bohm's immediate resignation."

"No!" Erzsi gasped.

Doctor Visconti's gaze snapped to the door, and Erzsi stumbled back just as her grandfather opened it.

"*Erzsébet*," he scolded.

"You mustn't let him go!" she begged.

"What on earth?"

"You yourself said that he is our only hope!"

Erzsi's stern gaze found Troilo as she hugged onto the emperor's arm.

Their only hope?

It seemed his reputation had preceded him. But what could've possessed the moody Archduchess Erzsi to jump to his aid, and with such righteousness?

"He cannot leave," she added.

The emperor nodded, slow and thoughtful. Then his eyes came alight with an idea. "Doctor Visconti will stay here, at Marmorschlossl," he announced.

Archduchess Erzsi frowned in obvious protest. Vouching for him was one thing, but sharing her quarters with him was another.

"*Here,* Your Majesty?" Troilo asked.

"In the event that Philippa has another fit, you will be close by."

Close by, he would be. But could Troilo really trust himself to sleep just down the hall from her? The thought alone was enough to rouse him.

"It is decided, then."

Troilo turned to the losing party, who, knowing he was about to be dismissed, wore his annoyance plainly.

"Doctor Bohm."

"Yes, Majesty," he grumbled. "I will take my leave."

Archduchess Erzsi scrunched against the doorframe, allowing the scorned psychiatrist to shuffle past.

"Doctor Visconti, I will have your luggage brought over at once," the emperor added. "I believe you will find the cottage most comfortable."

"I am certain I will, Your Majesty. Thank you."

Faced again with Archduchess Erzsi's frosty stare, Troilo wiped the smirk from his face.

"Come, Erzsébet."

Her gaze tracked Troilo as the emperor led her out with one hand on her back. An unlikely ally, but an ally all the same.

Governess Coudenhove was standing by the staircase bannister when Troilo emerged from the room, and the clean, folded clothes she held were a sure indication she'd been waiting for him. "I had the housekeeper send for them," she said, handing him the laundry. "I thought you might be wanting something fresh."

"You are too kind."

Smiling, she looked away. "It is my pleasure, Herr Visconti."

It wasn't the first time a woman had been nervous in Troilo's presence, and the governess would not be the last, but he had yet to learn how to navigate these one-sided infatuations.

"If there is anything else I can do for you," she went on, "please do not hesitate."

"Thank you, again, Fräulein," Troilo said, spotting Felix at the bottom of the stairwell.

"Mellie—please, call me Mellie."

He nodded politely. Innocently. "Please see that Her Highness gets some rest, Fräulein."

"I will."

Maids cleared the bottom of the staircase as Troilo began his descent to the first floor. But the wounded footman at first paid him no mind, only removing the cloth to access his bleeding.

"Felix, may I speak with you?"

The boy grimaced as he looked up, reminding Troilo of the stench wafting from his chest.

"You are the doctor from Italy," said Felix.

"Istria," Troilo corrected.

Felix didn't seem to care either way.

"If it is not too much trouble, I would like to hear your version of what happened this morning."

"I cannot tell you because I do not know," Felix replied, bringing the cloth back to his temple. "I hardly understand what happened myself."

"What were you doing in Her Highness' quarters so early?"

Felix's lips parted in a near tremble, a damning silence.

"Are you lovers?"

"What does it matter why I was there?"

His tone was agitated, distrustful. He couldn't be more than twenty years old, which was enough reason to pity him.

"People will be asking questions," Troilo warned. "It is for your own benefit that you rehearse how to answer them."

"I did not pursue her—I swear it."

If Philippa's behavior with *Troilo* was any indication, he had no reason to doubt Felix's word.

"You did not try to force her against her will, then?"

Felix sat up straight, visibly appalled.

"You are bleeding," Troilo reminded him.

"I did not do anything wrong!" he protested, lowering the cloth. "It had not even reached that point when—" He locked his jaw.

"When *what?*" Troilo interrogated.

Felix looked up at him with a palpable tension. "What they say about her is true," he whispered.

Troilo recalled what the emperor had told him. *In the presence of my niece, strange things occur, as though the world is at the whimsy of her moods.*

"She did not throw the glass," Troilo murmured.

"I realize how it sounds."

To most, *yes,* such a claim would be enough to question someone's sanity. But not Troilo—least of all when he had witnessed the same chaos of a lesser magnitude only moments ago. He knew from personal experience that manifestations of the Otherworld, unless controlled, were reflections of the vessel's emotional state. So what had *triggered* this volatility within Philippa?

"Tell me, please." Troilo cleared his throat. "Do you visit her often?"

"I visit when she asks," Felix admitted.

"Did you notice anything different about last night?"

"Different in what way?"

"Just anything out of the ordinary," said Troilo. "No matter how small."

Felix perked up as a thought washed over him. "Her mirror," he said. "Her vanity mirror was uncovered when I walked in."

"Uncovered."

"She usually keeps a handkerchief over it."

"Do you know why?"

"She does not like her reflection, I suppose."

Troilo's thoughts slid back to when they were conversing about the *Nibelungenlied* in front of the gold mirror. Even then, she'd avoided her reflection.

"One last question." Troilo lowered his voice. "Are you in love with her?"

Of course, he was asking for himself. And Felix squirmed in his seat, as though he could sense it, somehow.

"Truthfully, sir, I do not know," he replied. "She is like a siren. It is such a sweet song, but I cannot say if..."

Between the thoughts of Felix with Philippa and the staunch odor of her vomit, Troilo was nauseous.

"Sir."

Turning back to Felix, Troilo saw that his attention had caught on something—or *someone*—lingering behind him.

"You did the right thing, checking on the commotion in her room," said Troilo, keeping his focus on the conversation at hand. "I will pass the details along to the butler."

Felix strangled the bloody cloth, looking a little surprised. "Thank you, sir."

"A word, Doctor Visconti?"

Shifting the pile of clothing in his arms, Troilo turned around. "Herr Bohm," he said, motioning to his robe. "I would very much like to change my clothes."

"Then we shall talk outside by the pond when you are finished."

"I am afraid I have nothing more to say to you," Troilo replied, intent to walk around him.

"Perhaps not." Bohm held out his hand, stopping him in place. "But I have much to say to you."

The words left Troilo uneasy as he stood in the vacant entryway. Thanks in part to Bohm's negligence, he'd secured quarters in the heart of Philippa's dwelling, but such an advantageous position would come at a cost, and something told him that Bohm wouldn't be shy about naming it.

Freshly changed, Troilo readied himself for confrontation as he stepped off the veranda beneath the blanket of an overcast sky. It was not the first time someone had excavated his past to find that the numbers didn't quite add up. But how serious the threat would depend entirely on Bohm—who Troilo found waiting by the pond as promised.

"Herr Visconti," he greeted. "It is unwise for a man with secrets to make enemies so willingly."

"Please make this quick, Herr Bohm." Troilo pocketed both hands in his trousers. "I have business to attend to."

Bohm smiled, his teeth rather yellowed. "You said you were

born in Istria, yes?"

Troilo did not stammer. "That is correct."

"Tell me why, then, there is not a *single* birth record for a Troilo Visconti in the whole peninsula," Bohm said, stepping closer. "Not a marriage certificate, nor a death certificate for your wife, Costanza. She was long dead by the time you got to the Salpêtrière, was she not?"

Life had been much easier back when people had taken Troilo's word at face value. But lucky for him, even *with* the evidence that could be found rolled within his oriental box, his real origin was inconceivable.

It was exactly this that kept him safe.

"You are accusing me of what, exactly, Herr Bohm?"

"I do not know your true business here," Bohm went on. "But I know that you are not who you claim."

"It seems you have forgotten my references."

"And *you* seem to have forgotten that you are a foreigner."

Bohm was right to remind him of that much. That Austria-Hungary had not forgotten the Italian anarchist who had driven a knife deep into the heart of their empress.

"What is it you want?" Troilo asked.

"I would like you to tell His Majesty that we have reconciled our differences, and you have reconsidered my resignation."

Troilo turned his cheek to the corkscrew willow next to them, to its slender arms swaying in the breeze. Near its roots, the tail of a viper twitched in the grass.

"And if I refuse?"

"If you refuse, I will tell them you have come here to wreak havoc. And Herr Visconti..." He lowered his voice. "The royal family will not take kindly to a spy."

There were worse terms. Far worse terms. And Troilo hadn't come all this way to be outed by a vindictive psychiatrist, desperate to keep his job.

"I will reconsider your resignation but let me be clear," he said. "If I catch even a whiff of brandy on you, I will pack my bags."

Archduchess Erzsi had given him enough power to bluff, but Bohm's lips parted from their thin line in a way that told Troilo he was unconvinced.

"We will see," he said, taking his leave. "Expect me tomorrow morning."

Jung met Bohm's eye briefly on his way down to the water, and, glancing back over his shoulder, he adjusted his spectacles as though he'd seen a mirage. "I fear you do not know what you have walked into," he said.

"Oh, I fear I know it all too well."

"There is still time to turn down the case and come back with me to Zürich," Jung floated. "Doctor Bleuler would not fault you for it, given the circumstances."

A gentle reminder that the last doctor from the Burghölzli who'd treated a member of this family had been found floating belly up.

"Take comfort when I say I am a good swimmer," Troilo said, dropping his gaze to the watery grass beneath his feet.

"So was Ludwig II of Bavaria," Jung countered. "Allegedly."

"History does not always repeat, Herr Jung."

"That may be true," he replied. "But you cannot deny how it rhymes."

Troilo turned into the breeze, ripe with the smell of lilies and pond water. Jung could not know that him ending up in this ominous Eden was no accident.

"Did you speak with the footman who was injured?"

"I did," said Troilo. "It would appear to be a classic example of being in the wrong place at the wrong time."

"I think we both know what he was doing in her bedroom."

Troilo watched his assistant's eyes drift to the ground, where the viper lay coiled beneath the willow, listening to them. Had Jung known how venomous it was, he might have done more than place his hand on Troilo's back and gently lure him away.

"Drop the case," said Jung. "This *place*—it is a place of ill omen."

"And that is why I have been called here." Troilo scanned the empty windows of the cottage, then found the emperor, finally loading into his carriage. "You witnessed what happened just now with the glass," he said quietly. "The servant boy claims she never threw anything at him, that it happened all on its own."

Jung met his eye with a reluctant sigh.

"If I cannot be counted on to help her, who will? Certainly not Doctor Bohm."

"If you truly intend to take your residence here at Marmoschossl as Fräulein says, I feel *Bohm* will be the least of your worries."

Having made it this far, there was only one thing Troilo knew for certain.

He would not be returning to Zürich.

"You must go," he said. "I will not have you missing your train because of me."

"If there is anything I can do to assist you from the Burghölzli, please." Jung extended his hand to shake. "Do not hesitate to write."

"Safe travels, and give my regards to Doctor Bleuler."

As Jung pivoted back toward the cottage, Troilo knew that he would not have another chance to say it.

"Carl—?"

His assistant paused among the wildflowers to look back.

"You have been the only friend I have had in many years," he added.

Jung nodded, then sparked a smile. "Take good care, Troilo," he said. "Until we meet again."

As the sound of footsteps in the grass grew distant behind him, Troilo stared sightlessly across the pond. A shy breeze whipped at the water's surface, sending a cascade of ripples across his reflection as he looked down at it.

You stand on the shore...

He could still remember the thin, papery skin of the old Hungarian reader as she shuffled her cards, and flipped a couple over.

She is one with the water.

Troilo reached for the wedding band, and as he relaxed his gaze, a familiar image appeared in his mind's eye—a woodcut of a shooting star, printed on white paper. An emblem of his past.

Why was he seeing it right now, of all times?

The image dissolved within the ripples of the pond as a twig snapped beside him. Realizing he wasn't alone, Troilo whipped around to see a pair of icy eyes watching him through the rustling branches of the curly willow.

Erzsi tried to duck, but it was too late.

"Do you *often* make a habit of listening to others' conversations?" the doctor demanded, finding her around the back of the tree.

"I did not hear a thing!" She stumbled to her feet with a strangled expression. "I was only—!"

"I suggest you channel your curiosity elsewhere."

Erzsi held the stare of the foreigner with his disquieting beauty. "I am the daughter of the late Crown Prince Rudolf," she declared. "I shall take my curiosity where I please. Did it not benefit you just now, inside?"

The muscle in Doctor Visconti's jaw twitched as he tried to hold back a smile—a sight which brought Erzsi an unexpected flicker of gratification.

"Are you going to thank me?" she taunted.

"You have yet to tell me how it benefits *you,* Your Highness."

"An enemy of my enemy is a friend," said Erzsi. "Wilhelm Bohm only has his place here at the villa because his father and the emperor grew up together. He cares nothing for Pippa aside from the pleasure it gives him to feel up her dressings in the name of…" Erzsi gulped her words, seized by the movement of something quite large slithering over her foot. *"Medicine!!"* she screamed. *"Snaaaake!"*

Losing all control of her body, she jumped onto Doctor Visconti. She would faint—and then die!

"It will not harm you," he assured. "They only bite when threatened."

Clutched onto his arm, Erzsi looked up at him. "How do you know whether it feels threatened?"

"I just know," he said, ushering her along the crescent of the glassy pond. "Come."

Lush flora sprouted from the edge where they walked, blurring the threshold of land and water. Up ahead, heaps of globe-shaped cypresses and laurel bushes in tubs lined the serpentine path.

Erzsi's voice still shook a bit as she spoke. "I am the second of us you have saved today," she said.

"Then perhaps you should be the one thanking me, Highness."

"What I am trying to say, if you will just allow me to *speak,*" she said, annoyed, "is that I no longer believe you are a charlatan."

Doctor Visconti glanced at her; the corner of his mouth upturned in a smirk. "At least not completely."

"Not completely." Erzsi shrugged, fixating on the floundering bees ahead. "You are strange, but at least you are interesting. There is no worse sin than being dull."

"Thank you, for not thinking me dull, Highness."

"It is worth adding that you are the first person I have spoken to in months that is neither a servant, family member, nor my dog."

"Blitz," he said.

Erzsi didn't recall telling the doctor Blitz's name, but, finding his amusement encouraging, she went on.

"You will like Marmorschossl much more than Kaiservilla. My

grandfather thinks of it as a place to be exiled—but at least *here,* one is free to exist however one wishes."

"I take it you yourself have been exiled?"

Erzsi looked over at him, brows perked high. "I have asked to marry below my rank," she replied. "His Majesty hopes a summer away will change my mind."

"And has it?"

"I am more ready than ever to renounce any claim I have to the throne."

Doctor Visconti slowed his pace. "Who is this man who has captured your heart?"

"You assume me to be a romantic," she said with a laugh. "Prince Otto of Windisch-Graetz will make a fine husband, but it is not love that moves me."

"Yet, you would renounce your nobility," he said. "Why?"

Erzsi felt that familiar fire stoke within her chest. "Freedom!" she exclaimed. "Do you know what my grandmother's last words were, Doctor? When that man plunged a knife into her?"

"I do not, Highness."

"At last." Erzsi pursed her lips. "She was dead long before her death."

Doctor Visconti walked quietly beside her, listening with what seemed like his complete attention.

"Each time I step foot in the Viennese court, I come a day closer to sharing her fate," she added.

"Astra inclinant, sed non obligant."

Erzsi halted in front of the magnificent weeping beech, which stood in opposition to the marble cottage. A wrought iron bench sat beneath its swaying branches, fringed by a white, shedding spirea.

"What does that mean?" she asked.

"It means *the stars incline us, they do not bind us.* That we are the masters of our own chariots."

Latin. Erzsi cared for Latin no more than she did French, or any foreign language for that matter.

"What will you do when you are free?" asked the doctor.

"I will put myself to good use." Making her way toward the bench, Erzsi took a seat upon its summer snow. "I will march in the streets, and they shall call me *The Red Archduchess,*" she added, grabbing a sprig from the steeplebush. "Namesake be damned."

"You share a name with my daughter as well," Doctor Visconti added, joining her. "Elisabetta."

A *daughter?* As if wearing a ring was not enough, Philippa would be—

"She passed away before she could be born into this world," he added.

Erzsi awkwardly tore off a handful of petals. "It is an odd coincidence," she murmured. "That I should share her name."

Doctor Visconti smiled faintly. "A nice reminder."

"You may call me by my first name, then." Erzsi looked to the swaying tops of the spruce and juniper trees across the pond. "If you wish."

"May I?"

"If I may call you by yours," she said, plucking at the mangled blossom.

"Troilo."

"You should know, Troilo, that Doctor Bohm was quite generous with the laudanum, and that Philippa will surely ask you for it."

"I will keep that in mind."

"It was the same carelessness that killed my father. Perhaps he would not have died so shamefully if his brain was not so rotted from the inside out."

Troilo fell quiet. "We all remember where we were when the story broke about His Highness, The Crown Prince."

"I suppose Doctor Kerzl told you the truth about how he died," she murmured.

"There are no secrets at the Burghölzli," he replied, shifting toward her. "We study such cases to avoid making the same mistakes."

Hesitantly, Erzsi met the eye of her new friend. "You can tell me what was wrong, then? Why he..."

"In my time in the Orient, I saw many men lose themselves to opium, trying to numb themselves to a deeper pain," he said. "You must understand that your father was no longer himself, and you must find it in your heart to forgive him for it."

For as many condolences expressed over the years, and for all the words of wisdom imparted on Erzsi, none had ever felt so sincere.

"I never knew him, but people always remark on how alike we are," she admitted with a shrug.

"The stars incline us, they do not bind us." He offered a smile. "It also means that you are a star of your own, completely unique. Perhaps a red one, like Betelgeuse, for *The Red Archduchess.*"

Erzsi covered her laugh as she turned away. "You are a strange man."

"I have been told as much."

"Well, I for one am grateful that you will be replacing Doctor Bohm."

"I am afraid he will not be leaving us quite yet."

What?

Erzsi felt a stone drop in her stomach. Had her plea not been enough?

"You will stay though," she said, pivoting his direction. "You will stay and help her?"

"I will stay. I will try my very best to help her, I promise you."

"Then I will do anything I can to assist you! I can tell you anything you need to know about her. We share everything—even dresses!"

"Her Highness did say something rather peculiar to me today," he murmured. "When she came to."

"Pippa says a good many peculiar things."

Erzsi laughed under her breath, but the doctor seemed far away, lost in some thought.

"My knight," he added.

"Oh, her knight—?"

Erzsi had meant what she'd said. She could tell him of Philippa's favorite books and her favorite plays. She could tell him of her hopes and fears. But this?

"Would you have any idea who she is referring to?" he asked.

Erzsi opened her fist, releasing a handful of petals. Some stuck to the inside of her palm. "Yes, well. He is..."

It was hard not to question at times whether Philippa truly *believed* the stories she read. Stories of glass castles and animal bridegrooms that she'd gnawed to the bone, as though she were waiting for her own fairy king to whisk her away and take her home, to whatever otherworldly place she belonged. Speaking too openly to the wrong doctor about these fantasies could have Philippa landed in an asylum. But Doctor Visconti—*Troilo,* as she now knew him—Troilo with his dead child and his spiritualism wouldn't sentence Pippa to such a fate, would he?

"He is *what,* Erzsi?"

"Philippa believes that he is..." She gulped anxiously. "A *spirit.*"

FIVE

June 9, 1900
8:00 A.M.

Hot blooded and incarnate in a room just down the hall, with only a few physical walls of separation, Philippa's knight lay tangled within the sheets of his new bed, having hardly slept.

Telepathy is what they called it: the ability to connect beyond the five senses, mind to mind. Though it had not impressed contemporary psychologists when it was coined in 1882, it had given Troilo a revitalized framework on how Philippa might be experiencing him.

According to this idea—just like a medium in a séance may receive impressions from a *sender*—so too could any pair of entangled souls. Such souls might also be able to lend their eyes to one another or leave their bodies at night to fuse together in the dreamworld, only to return to their vessels in the morning. Even a relatively experienced medium might mistake such impressions and meetings as spirit-based in nature, when in all actuality, the soul on the other side of the line was embodied. Philippa *was* connecting with someone, but Troilo was no spirit.

Rather, he was something in between.

And now he knew that Philippa—having confided in Erzsi about it—was as consciously aware of their bond as he was.

Turning onto his side, Troilo imagined the pillow cloth to be the back of her neck. *Perhaps, Doctor,* she'd told him, *you may study me more efficiently in my bedroom.* Though he'd been caught off-guard, her meaningless kiss had awakened a raging sun of desire coiled inside of him, and if he wasn't careful, she might just feel it.

Troilo's eyes shot open as a knock permeated his door.

"It is Fräulein Coudenhove," said the voice on the other side. "May I come in?"

"Just a moment." Retracting the hand that had inadvertently dropped to his loins, Troilo climbed out of bed and readjusted himself under his freshly cleaned dressing gown. "Fräulein," he greeted, at last opening the door. "Good morning."

"I hope I did not wake you?"

"No, no." Troilo rubbed his eye with the back of his hand, glancing down at the tray of porcelain she held in her arms. "I have been awake for quite a while now."

"I thought you might like some coffee."

Very much needing it, Troilo stepped aside. "Thank you."

The governess smiled as she walked in, setting the tray on the desk between the two narrow windows. "No sugar?"

"On a usual day, I take one. Thank you."

A single sugar cube clinked against the bottom of his porcelain cup, quickly dissolving under the stream of coffee. "I hope your sleep was not a restless one?" she asked, reaching for the spoon.

"The first night in a new place is always an adjustment." His eyes followed her stirring, round and round the teacup. "The quiet of this place, it is both pleasant and unnerving."

Governess Coudenhove watched with eager eyes, waiting for him to take a sip as she handed him the cup.

"It is perfect," he assured, wiping his mustache.

"You would not be the first to find the cottage unnerving."

"I mean only that it brings attention to the noisiness of my own mind."

Governess Coudenhove nodded. Like the nuns Troilo had encountered in his wanderings, her smile was controlled and pious.

"I do hope you will join us for breakfast on the veranda this morning?" she asked.

Troilo walked to the window, finding the reflective waters of the pond on the other side of the glass panel. "I would like some time to get settled, perhaps see the library."

"Of course."

"I hope you will not be offended," he said, turning to meet the despairing tone.

"Oh—not at all." Her tawny eyes sparkled against the champagne paisley wallpaper of his room. "But please know you are always welcome."

"You will not be joining us for breakfast?"

Troilo's pressed lips upturned at the sight of Erzsi appearing in his doorway. "Good morning, Highness," he said.

Cheek resting against the frame, Erzsi glanced to Mellie, then to Troilo. Had she brought him coffee?

"Perhaps another day," Troilo added.

"Shame," Erzsi replied, sliding backward into the hall.

She'd been hoping for his company, but no one would be more disappointed than—

"Good morning, Pippa," Erzsi said, plopping down on Philippa's bed.

Nose buried in a book, Philippa nodded, but kept her eyes on the page. Despite the debacle of yesterday morning, she seemed to have bounced back completely, as if nothing had ever happened.

"I *said* good morning..."

"I am almost finished," Philippa replied, holding up one finger.

"Do not be stingy." Erzsi grabbed at the book. "What is so important that you must ignore your beloved cousin? Your only true family?"

"*Oh what hells would I endure to taste of thy heavens,*'" Philippa read from the page, fighting her off. "*To drink from thy fountains and pray at thy temples once more.*'" Lowering the book, she brought both knees to her chest. "Is that not beautiful?"

Erzsi tilted her head to read the blue cloth cover with gold lettering, fanned beside them to mark the spot. "*Ballads of the Starlight Menagerie.*"

"There are one-hundred-and-sixteen of them that I am trying my utmost to savor."

Erzsi used to think that *she* possessed a love of reading—and then Philippa came to live with them, devouring the Hofburg library in mere months. Considering the library at Marmorschossl was much smaller, it was probably for the best that she was taking her time.

"I found it peeking out from the shelf only two days ago," Philippa added.

"Will you be sitting with us for breakfast?"

Philippa sat her chin on top of her knee. "That would all depend on..."

"It is too early for your pestering," Erzsi warned.

"I only want to know if he plans to sit with us?"

That was *not* all she wanted to know. Perhaps now would be a good time to discuss his dead child?

"He is much too old for you, Erzsi," Philippa sighed, falling back onto her fluffy pillow.

Erzsi abandoned the bed. "I am not interested in your doctor," she replied, finding her powder blue saucers beneath the cloth covering Philippa's vanity mirror.

So large, they were. And her lips, so small. And her *nose,* so pointy.

"I have seen how you look at him," Philippa countered. "He is mesmerizing, is he not?"

"I look at him how everyone looks at him." Erzsi resituated the handkerchief over the mirror. "Rather rich of you to accuse *me* of such shallow attraction."

"If not attraction, then what?"

"He fascinates me. His strange, foreign ways."

Philippa combed at her net of hair, catching her fingers on the ends. "He is not a character from your mystery novels," she snickered.

"Nor is he a prince from your fairy tales," Erzsi countered, grabbing the silver brush from the vanity's top.

Philippa extended her hand for it, but Erzsi refused, climbing into bed next to her. "Let me."

"He is handsome enough to be a prince," Philippa said, scooting forward.

Situating herself against the headboard, Erzsi lifted the hair from her neck, and from the birthmark it covered. It had always looked like claw scratches to Erzsi, though she knew better to say so. Philippa was self conscious about it as it was.

"Will you tell me nothing of your walk with him yesterday?" Philippa asked.

"I will say only that he has endured far too much to be your plaything," Erzsi replied, gliding the brush down her locks.

"You speak as though I will bewitch him."

Erzsi paused her brushing. "If I had your beauty, I would flaunt it, too," she admitted. "It is for the best that you cover your mirrors, so you do not fall in love with yourself as Narcissus did."

"You are kind, cousin," Philippa said finally. "Some days, I hardly remember my own face. For all I know, I could look like a crone."

Erzsi again paused her brushing. "You are not *old,*" she murmured. "You have hardly aged in all the time I have known you!"

Philippa turned over her shoulder, meeting Erzsi with the glint of a smile.

"Highnesses."

Erzsi's eyes snapped upward to see Troilo standing outside Philippa's room.

"I do not mean to interrupt," he added. "I just wanted to say good morning."

Philippa shifted her heavy hair to one side. "We were just discussing you," she teased.

Troilo glanced at Erzsi with a playful suspicion.

"Will you be sitting with us for breakfast?" Philippa asked.

"I am afraid I require a great deal of solitude in the mornings," he replied.

His grin was slight, but his eyes shimmered as Philippa examined him from her seat in bed. How could she question whether she was desirable when *all* men looked at her this way?

"When will Pippa's first session take place?" Erzsi interjected.

"I was thinking ten o'clock if it suits you," Troilo said to Philippa.

"The library at ten?"

"If it suits you."

"It suits me fine," she said.

Erzsi watched, her eyes first on Troilo, then Philippa. Would he *ever* leave? What was he waiting for?

"Ten o'clock, then," Troilo said finally. "Highnesses."

10:00 A.M.

The ruby-striped library was the most ensouled room in the cottage, as libraries often were. Each title that lined the freshly dusted bookshelves had been penned by the voices of old friends long lost, whose deaths marked the many chapters of Troilo's life.

As he stood beneath the crystal chandelier, he could almost envision Empress Elisabeth lying across the gold chaise in the corner, glancing up from her French novel to watch the birds pick crumbs from the veranda outside. Even the focal point of her quaint sanctuary—a stained-glass centerpiece, set gracefully above the cushioned windowsill—had been crafted just for her. Hundreds of cathedral windows from Paris to St. Petersburg had never sparkled with such devotion.

Pulling an olive-green spine from its cove, Troilo opened to the title page.

"The Serpent Prince?"

He looked up from the woodcut illustration—a maiden wrapped within the coil of a serpentine dragon—to see Philippa in her nightgown, hair freshly brushed.

"One of my favorites as a child," she added, peering at the woodcut over his shoulder.

Troilo turned to her, one eyebrow raised. "A curious favorite."

"It is a story about a princess who is forced to marry a snake." Philippa reached for the open book, guiding his hand to lower it. "But she finds that beneath his snakeskin, he is a beautiful man."

"There is a name for that, where I am from," said Troilo.

Her expectant gaze was sharp as a knife's edge.

"Zmajeva nesteva."

"Is that..." She paused to think. "*Slavic* dialect?"

"Istria is old land."

"Hm." Leaning in closer, Philippa fixated on the page as she spoke. "Then you are well-acquainted with the creatures of old lands."

"Pardon, Your Highness?"

"Creatures of interest. Fairies, dragons..." Her eyes teased him. "Perhaps the dreaded Tazelworm?"

Suddenly enraptured by her nearness, Troilo felt himself tense, but she didn't seem to notice.

"This one was a gift from Ludwig," she added, flipping the title page to reveal a cursive inscription. "See?"

"To the Dove, from the Eagle."

"Their pet names for one another."

A coldness grazed Troilo's shoulder as Philippa pulled away.

"Did the King of Bavaria give your aunt many books?" he asked.

"They were both avid readers," she replied. "As am I."

Troilo looked down at the open book in his hand. "This is the tale where the maiden burns the serpent's skin in the stove, is it not?"

Halfway to the windows, Philippa halted. "It is," she replied over her shoulder. "His mother—"

"Meddling woman that she is."

She turned slowly, head cocked with a smile. "Indeed."

Satisfied with having impressed her, Troilo closed *The Serpent Prince,* sliding its spine back into place.

"The mother convinces the princess to burn his skin so that everyone will know his true form," Philippa added. "Do you read many fairy tales, Doctor?"

Troilo had spent the last few centuries observing the ebbs and flows of his own lore, watching it take root in folk tales. *The Serpent Prince* was one of many.

"Only ones with creatures of interest," he replied, glancing back at her.

Philippa laughed, then turned away. "I read only ones with happy endings."

"It would not be a true fairy tale if not for a happy ending." Pivoting toward her, he changed the subject. "Highness, is there a particular reason you do not like to dress or style your hair?"

"Is there a particular reason I *should* like to?"

"I have only noticed that you reject—"

"What is suitable for a woman?"

"For lack of a better term," Troilo murmured. "Yes."

"I dress when I have a good reason to." She shrugged as she floated over to the chaise. "As for my hair, wearing it loose conceals my dreadful birthmark..."

Crossing the room, Troilo pulled a chair from under a desk. "Does the chaise suit you, Your Highness?"

Philippa nodded, lowering herself onto the gold cushion. "My father always said it looked like gills," she murmured, reaching for her neck.

Troilo placed the chair in front of her, then pulled a small notebook from the inside of his jacket pocket.

"But never mind that," she added as he took a seat. "Shall we begin?"

"I will start by asking you some questions. Please answer them as honestly as you can."

"Yes, Doctor."

"When was your last menstrual cycle?"

Philippa shook her head. "I cannot remember."

"Have you ever been pregnant?"

"No."

"Do you ever engage intimately with the opposite sex?"

"Do you?"

Troilo kept his eyes on the paper as she shifted in front of him.

"When did your fits first begin?"

"They began when I was seventeen, but I have had night terrors since I can remember."

It felt strange for Troilo to be sitting in front of her now, with his own memories of how her nightmares used to wake him. No matter what bed or country he had found himself in, his skin would start to tingle and burn, and he would lie awake, delicately restringing the chords of her nervous system by sending visions of pink clouds and wind songs.

"When the fit has subsided," Troilo continued, "do you have any recollection of..."

"What has happened?"

Troilo glanced up. "Or where you have been."

"No."

"You do not have any recollection of Schonbrünn, then."

"It seems the more distance I gain from it, the more I forget even the simplest of details of that day."

"What kind of details?"

"Little things," she replied. "Like what the weather was like, or what I did that morning."

Troilo scribbled into the book. "Do you often experience lapses in time?"

"Yes..." She paused. "Time seems to move differently, sometimes."

"The footman who was present the morning of your most recent fit, Felix—"

"What did he say?"

The mention of Felix seemed to stir her considerably.

"Is he all right?"

"He was transferred to the villa," Troilo replied. "How long has he been visiting your quarters?"

Philippa tilted her cheek to the window, looking annoyed.

"Please try to answer honestly."

"I thought you wanted to talk," she said.

"We are talking, Highness," Troilo replied. "And it is not my business how you conduct your personal affairs. But—"

"There is always a *but* with men like you," she grumbled.

"Men like me?"

She turned back to him with a scowl. "Men who claim to know what is best for me."

"I understand you have seen many doctors," Troilo murmured.

"Countless."

And none of them had ever been able to help. Who could blame her for her lack of faith?

"To answer your question, only in the last month or so," she said at last. "I feel terrible about what happened to him."

"Why?"

"Why do I feel terrible that he was injured?"

"No—" Troilo swallowed hard, torn between the tension of blissful ignorance and the sickening need to know. "Why did you ask him to visit you?"

Philippa's eyes narrowed on him in that cat-like way. "Are you asking because you are my doctor, or because you are curious?"

"I only mean to ask if you love him."

"No," she said softly.

Troilo studied her as she stretched over the gold fabric of the chaise, resting her left arm behind her head.

"I understand you were engaged while in Vienna," he said.

"To Duke Sixten, yes," she replied. "He is a friend of my brother, Franz."

"Duke Sixten Siegfried. There is a Siegfried in the *Nibelungenlied.*"

"Indeed," Philippa replied.

It seemed she'd already made that connection.

"But he bears little likeness to Prince Siegfried."

"Why was your engagement broken?" Troilo asked knowingly.

"I was ignorant of his stormy antecedents when I agreed to be his wife."

Troilo knew everything there was to know about Duke Sixten Siegfried as it was, having researched him from his Zürich office after the announcement of their engagement broke in the newspapers. Accused of throwing a courtesan from a Munich balcony a few years prior, the duke had been well-covered in the media despite eventually being cleared. How relieved Troilo had been to see their separation a mere month later.

"I was not intimate with him," Philippa added, somewhat jeeringly. "If that is what you meant to ask me next."

Gripping the pen in his hand, Troilo looked up from his booklet. Philippa's eyes were sea foam again, wrapping themselves around him like a familiar blanket.

"Can I ask *you* a question, now?"

Troilo gave a wary nod, hoping he would not regret his decision.

"What is the ring you wear around your neck?"

"It is my wife's wedding band," he replied.

"You are married."

"I *was* married."

Philippa brought her fingers to her lips, looking equally curious as she was sad. "What happened to her?"

The stampede of horse's hooves sounded in Troilo's memory as he remembered racing as fast as he could to reach her under a darkening sky.

"Do you still have nightmares, Your Highness?" he deflected.

"No, but often I wake up crying, like I..." There was deep longing in her tone as she spoke. "The feeling of something lost lingers long after I wake." Philippa blinked rapidly, as if to banish the feeling. "It is rather stuffy in here—might I have something to take the edge off?"

"I am sorry, Highness." Troilo closed his notebook. "I cannot give you any."

"What? You have no right to refuse me!"

"On the contrary, I do."

"But why would you?" she demanded. "Why would you deny me comfort?"

"Do you know what is *in* laudanum, Highness?"

Philippa pouted as Troilo leaned closer.

"It is a tincture of opium, codeine and morphine, dissolved in alcohol. It is highly addictive, as you can see—and I have seen more than enough men destroy their lives for just another drop." He paused. "You may have some *wine* to calm your nerves, or take some air outside—"

"I shall take some air, then!" Philippa shot to her feet, then stormed off toward the door. *"Alone!"*

"We may take our sessions outside if you like," Troilo called, following her out. "At any point of day, whatever makes you most—"

She whipped around with a menacing glare.

"...comfortable."

Making her way toward the empty veranda, Troilo did the same. Birdsong echoed down from the tops of the evergreens as she barreled down the stairs.

"Let me be hysterical in peace, would you?" Philippa snapped her neck to look at him, half-concealed under the mass of blonde hair which tangled in the breeze. "Do not pretend you have anything to gain by getting to know me!"

"Gain?" Gripping the iron railing, Troilo shouted down to her. "You believe I am here to line my pockets?"

"That," she shouted back, "and the notoriety of having cured me!"

Craning his neck over the veranda's edge, he watched, tongue-tied, as she made her way down to the pond, where a stately pair of swans floated under the branches of the corkscrew willow. "God *damn* it," he cursed, shaking himself against the rail.

Having spent more time with the memory of her, Troilo had forgotten that her soul had always been this fiery. But no longer was he the young knight who might playfully pin her to the ground. He would have to earn her trust all over again.

Unmoved, Philippa stood at the edge of the pond as elegantly as a storybook maiden as he approached.

"Your Royal and Imperial Highness," Troilo said, loosening his cravat under the summer rays. "It is not notoriety that I seek."

"Perhaps you have enough of it already." She turned to look at him, their proximity close enough for him to spot the dimples on the corners of her smile. *"Conjurer."*

The larger swan glided over, peeking around the willow branches as Troilo stepped closer.

"Perhaps I misjudged you, but I do not like being spoken to as if I am invalid who cannot make her own choices," Philippa added, taking a knee. "Even if you believe that is the case."

"Then you misjudge me again because I think no such thing."

Philippa narrowed her gaze on him. "Is it true that the dead speak through your patients when you put them to sleep?"

"Well—"

"What if someone does not *want* to be rid of the spirits attached to them?"

She was speaking of her knight, surely. But something told Troilo she would not tell him as much.

"Then I would ask them why not," he replied, extending his hand to the male swan. "Why they would not wish to be free."

"What if the spirit is benevolent, like an angel?"

Troilo raised an inquisitive brow as he glanced up at her. Is *that* what she thought he was—an angel?

"I am speaking in hypotheticals, of course," she backtracked. "Not every attachment must be negative."

"No, certainly not." Troilo turned his attention to the female swan, who had followed her mate. "*Love* is the chain of chains. It is the strongest bond of all."

Philippa rested her chin on her kneecap. "Lohengrin is the more sociable of the two. It is Elsa who..."

Reaching out, Troilo pet the soft white feathers of the female's wing.

"She is suspicious of most people..."

"Elsa and Lohengrin," he murmured.

"*Lohengrin* was Ludwig's favorite of Wagner's plays."

Troilo turned to Philippa. "Was it you who named them?"

She nodded. "Would you know, the two of them just appeared one day, shortly after my aunt was killed? I like to think they are Her Majesty and Ludwig, that they were reborn as swans."

Troilo lowered his hand, the twinge in his heart, one a hundred years could not soften. "Have you studied much Eastern philosophy, Highness?"

"It only feels natural to me that we would come back. Though..." Philippa ran her fingers over the top of the water. "I have yet to understand why I did."

After *centuries* of near silence from her spirit, Troilo had wondered the same.

"I wish I would have come back as a swan." The reflection of the water glistened on Philippa's cheeks as she smiled down at the lily pads. "I cannot help but prefer the company of animals to people. They do not care that I am haunted by a world I cannot see."

Muffled chatter from the veranda rode on a gentle wind, which blew rings over the glass reflection of the Salzkammergut peaks.

"I was eighteen the first time I saw my name plastered across the tabloids. *Emperor Franz Josef's Niece: Dwindling Hope for the Mad Archduchess.*" Philippa dangled her fingers, allowing the water to trickle onto the lily pads below. "No one ever treated me the same again."

"No species is crueler to one another than man," said Troilo.

"Why, then, have you dedicated your life to helping people?"

"Because, Highness," he replied. "We must embody the change we want to see."

Her brow crinkled a bit as she turned back to the water, as though she might be pondering his words.

The irony of Troilo's profession had never been lost on him. Closer to a monster than man, he'd fallen to this world with an all-too-trusting heart. A heart that—despite having eroded over time like a battered oceanside cliff—still sought to reflect goodness back into the world, no matter how minuscule.

"I often wonder..." One drop of water fell from Philippa's

fingers, then two. Three. "...who of us are *inside* of the menagerie, and who of us are looking in."

Reminded of the star emblem he'd seen gazing into the pond, Troilo studied the way the droplets sputtered and danced across the lily pad until suddenly, they stopped.

"They say you have serpents inked on both of your arms," Philippa said, looking up at him.

"From my time in the Orient, yes."

She dropped her gaze to his hands, then lifted it again. "May I see them?"

Hot under her stare, Troilo unbuttoned the cuffs of his sleeves and rolled them up his forearm, revealing the faded red dragons that spiraled from his elbow to his wrist.

"Creatures of interest," Philippa breathed.

"*Kālkubi.*" Troilo assessed the pinprick scales, which had held up quite well for being nearly a century old. "On my way from Istanbul to China, I stopped in Tehran, which is a city in Persia."

"I have never seen copper ink before," she said, leaning closer. "Only black and blue."

Troilo grinned, recalling how the elderly gypsy woman pricking him had been startled to see red, too. Having been convinced that Troilo was something special, she had taken extra care.

"The technique has not changed for centuries," he went on. "They begin by rubbing jadwar and tanzu, two Chinese herbs known for their healing properties, over the area before painting the design. Then, they prick it into the skin with a needle." Troilo looked up to see Philippa gaping, which made him smile. "I sat for almost three days," he added, staring into the pupil of one of the dragons. "They are an homage to my ancestors."

Grabbing hold of his wrist, Philippa gently turned it over. "What is—?"

Troilo glanced down with a hard swallow. Even the dragons

could not *completely* conceal the vertical scars that rivaled the length of his forearm.

She spoke in a tender whisper. "And how did you get these?"

Troilo remembered it clearly. The way the blood had run from his wrists in watery rivers, dying the ecru fabric of Costanza's collar and Mesjec's white fur. The moment he'd decided that if he would not be permitted to die alongside her, then none would be spared from the furnace of his anguish.

An ear-splitting scream ruptured the air, bringing Troilo back to the present.

"*Erzsi!*" Snapping to her feet, Philippa took off through the swaying wildflowers. "Erzsi, what—!"

Troilo took only a second to roll his sleeves back down before bolting after her. Around the front of the cottage, Erzsi huddled against Governess Coudenhove's chest like a baby chick.

"Herr Visconti!" Erzsi shouted, stumbling into Troilo's arms. "It is Doctor Bohm! He..."

Troilo glanced at the governess, who looked as though she might throw up if she spoke.

"Where?" he asked, turning back to Erzsi.

"Over there!" Philippa pointed to the row of bushes lining the oak path, and to the hand that, judging by its color, had been lying there for some time.

Pulling his handkerchief from his pocket, Troilo covered his nose as the women found his side, one by one.

"Should you check for his pulse?" Governess Coudenhove stuttered.

Troilo took a knee next to the blue-veined Doctor Bohm, whose eyes were iced over in fright. "We must send word for a coroner."

"What happened to him?" Philippa asked.

They watched in harrowing silence as Troilo searched the body for a puncture wound, lifting each sleeve to inspect. The viper would be long gone by now.

"As I thought," said Troilo, peeling back Bohm's blood-soaked sock. "He has been bitten by a venomous snake."

The fleshy bite mark staring up at them elicited a gasp, then a shriek from behind.

"Mellie!"

Troilo reached for the fainting governess, whom Erzsi had managed to catch. "Have someone phone the house," he directed, steadying her head on his shoulder. "Tell them Doctor Bohm is dead."

If the sweat running down Troilo's temple was any indication of the day to come, the body would be rotted by midday.

Servants gawked with worried eyes as he followed Philippa and Erzsi through the cottage door with Governess Coudenhove limp against him. "Fetch me some cold water and a rag," he called out as he pivoted into the library.

"You said they would not bite."

Troilo turned to see Erzsi picking at the skin around her nail as he lay the governess on the chaise. "I said they would not bite unless threatened," he replied, waving the maid in.

Erzsi stepped closer as he reached for the cloth on the neighboring tray, soaking it with chilled water. "He threatened it, then? Doctor Bohm?"

Troilo dabbed Governess Coudenhove's forehead with the cloth, knowing the viper must have been listening as he and Bohm conversed by the pond. "He must have," he replied finally.

As Troilo spoke, the eyes of his patient shot open with the hazy look of attraction.

"*Easy,* Fräulein," he hushed.

"You fainted, Mellie," Erzsi added, taking a seat next to her on the floor.

Governess Coudenhove delicately massaged the bridge of her nose. "I find snakes most dreadful," she mumbled.

"The coroner is on his way." Philippa hung in the doorway, catching her breath. "They asked that you meet them outside."

"I will be right there." Troilo turned his attention back to Governess Coudenhove. "Do not overexert yourself," he directed, pressing the cold cloth to her forehead. "You have had quite a fright."

"Yes, Doctor."

Philippa was waiting on the staircase when Troilo emerged, eyes shining in a most particular kind of way.

"Your Highness, are you well?" he asked.

As if she were trying to blink away a thought, she glanced to the parquet floor. "It is a strange feeling with no name."

Troilo knew the strange feeling she spoke of. He had felt it himself the day he'd first seen her picture in the paper. *Philippa Annunziata of Austria*—a seventeen-year-old Habsburg arch-duchess, reborn to the same family line who had seen to her demise.

The door to Marmorschossl opened behind him, and in came Doctor Kerzl.

"I am here, what has happened?"

Troilo glanced up at Philippa again. "Have some water," he directed, rebuttoning his cuffed sleeves.

In the forty minutes it took for the coroner to arrive, the heat had claimed the body, and the flies swarmed the ankle wound as if it were another melting teacake in the sun.

"*This!* On the morning I leave for Vienna," said the emperor, pinching his nose with a handkerchief. "How long has he been out here?"

Troilo shut the panicked eyes of his dead colleague with his thumb and forefinger.

Poor Doctor Bohm.

"Judging by the looks of his body," replied the coroner, "since early this morning."

"I hope it was quick, God willing."

"The reaction to venom is rapid, Your Majesty." Troilo turned to the emperor. "Five minutes or less."

He looked surprised. "Do you have much experience with snake bites, Doctor Visconti?"

"In the lands I have visited, such things are inherent knowledge."

"*Morocco,* yes." The emperor stepped away, removing his handkerchief. "Until further notice, the young ladies staying in the cottage are not to leave the veranda without your accompaniment."

Troilo looked to the marble teahouse, imagining them peering from the windows. "Yes, Your Majesty."

"I will return within a few days," the emperor replied, signaling to the coroner.

"Herr Visconti," Kerzl mumbled, finding his side against a nearby tree. "I know you and Doctor Bohm did not quite see eye to eye."

"Doctor Bohm and I had, in fact, put aside our differences." Troilo stroked his mustache, keeping his eyes straight ahead. "He was on his way to meet with me."

"*Was* he?"

Troilo nodded, watching from the sidelines as the coroner's men lifted Bohm's burly corpse into the creaking carriage. "It is a shame he did not live to see our collaboration," he replied.

In the library, Erzsi stood watch at the window, enticed by the circus outside. It was an interesting development on the heels of yesterday's conversation with her doctor friend, who was now walking back to them.

"It could have been any one of us," Mellie lamented from the chaise.

Philippa let out a long, nervous sigh as she paced from one side of the room to the other. She was getting antsy—in clear need of a drop of laudanum, and regretting that she hadn't thought to search Doctor Bohm's pockets for the small brown bottle.

Erzsi let go of the tasseled curtain as the front door shut, sending an echo through the ruby halls.

"His Majesty the Emperor is leaving for Vienna as planned," said Troilo as he walked into the library. "He has asked that in the meantime, no one leave the veranda without my supervision."

Erzsi's gaze found both Philippa and Mellie, whose expressions couldn't have been more opposing.

"If you would like to go outdoors," he continued, wiping his forehead, "then I must accompany you."

Mellie struggled to an upright position. "Your supervision?"

"Am I not already prisoner enough?" Philippa demanded.

"I am sorry, Highness. It was not my decision."

"But you are glad to enforce it."

This fiery exchange between them felt quite *personal* from where Erzsi stood. What had their session been like, out there by the pond?

Philippa rubbed both her arms with a shiver, then looked away. She was really fiending now, and Troilo could see it, too.

"The cravings will subside," he said. "But you must work through them."

"Certainly, you would not deny me now?" Philippa held out her trembling hands. "After all I have seen today?"

"I am sorry, Your Highness."

Her eyes alight with fury, she shoved past Troilo. "It should have been *you*," she seethed.

He bit his tongue as she stormed up the stairs, slamming her bedroom door hard enough to shake the cottage walls.

"She does not mean it," Erzsi interjected.

Troilo managed a wan smile, but something leaked from the sides. He had taken her words to heart. He *cared* what she thought.

"I will take some air on the veranda," he said quietly.

Erzsi raced to the window, watching him find a wicker chair

outside. Whatever this flammability between him and Philippa, it needed to be smothered, or her treatment would surely suffer.

If only Erzsi could find him a *safer* distraction…

"What do you think of him, Mellie?" she asked, turning back to her governess as if it weren't dreadfully apparent.

Mellie inhaled sharply. "Doctor Bohm?"

"No, not Doctor Bohm!" Erzsi rolled her eyes. *"Doctor Visconti."*

"Oh. Well, I think he's well spoken, well mannered…"

"That is not what I mean, Mellie," Erzsi went on, calling her over. *"I mean* do you fancy him?"

Huddled at the window, the two of them watched as Troilo pulled out a little green journal, folding it over his knee. Mellie only stared out the glass, pondering what it might be like to be the pencil between his fingers.

"Perhaps with a bit of time together, he could fancy you, too," Erzsi added.

12:27 A.M.

The shadow of an oil lantern danced over his open journal as Troilo sat hunched at the desk. There had been no picture charades that night, none received nor sent. As the woman of his fantasies lay one room over, her heart hot and resentful, Troilo's rattled like an empty shell with the thunder outside.

It had been a similar night in Geneva, the summer of 1816, when Troilo first got a glimpse of his future as a poet. While a storm raged outside the villa Diodati, he had sat by the fire with physician John Polidori and his poet friend, Lord Byron as they welcomed some friends from England who were renting a house nearby: another poet by the name of Percy Shelley—who would later become a dear friend of Troilo's—and a pair of sisters, one of whom Shelley was romantically involved with.

Eighteen-year-old Mary Godwin was the first Troilo had befriended that night. Having fled England with Shelley, and her stepsister, Claire, she had recently suffered the death of her infant daughter the year prior. When a friendly competition was floated by Byron to see who could write the best ghost story, young Mary had been the first to jump.

Troilo hadn't known at the time that this stormy evening would usher in one of the most prominent chapters of his life, because without Shelley, he would have never met John Keats. And without Keats, Troilo would have never written his gift for Costanza.

A gift that would become his only published work.

Keats had taught him that much like jumping in a lake and feeling its chill, there was no *working out* a poem. Inspiration could dry up for days, then all at once, it would come. Stanzas would flow into his mind, like the vertical rivers that ran down Troilo's glass window, blurring the white fire bolts that pierced the sky. And if the poet failed to capture them, the words would never return in the same combination again.

As Troilo meditated on the sputtering flame of his candle, he could almost feel Keats' ghostly hand on his shoulder. He thought back to that night in Geneva with Mary Godwin, as they had talked on the floor of one of the villa's vacant rooms, pondering how much love it might take to resurrect someone from the dead.

I speak to the storm cloud, I say—

A spot of ink bled over the paper as Troilo began to write.

How do you choose between destruction and deliverance?
I ask him how he holds his sorrow

I ask him how he carries his grief.

He tells me only that he comes to cleanse.
And I envy his ability to swell and burst,
For I, too, am black and brewing,
But with no hope of relief.

Shadows crept over his writing until Troilo saw only darkness, aside from the candlelit glint of a brass doorknob in his mind's eye. Withdrawing his pen, he slowly turned to his bedroom door.

Philippa meditated on the flicker of her flame in the door-knob's reflection as she stood outside, a book tucked under her arm. She'd noticed the dim glow beneath Doctor Visconti's door on her way to the library, and like a moth to a flame, her conscience had pulled her toward it.

He was rigid, yes—but her new doctor was many other things, too. He was progressive and exotic, having seen more of the world than Philippa could ever dream of. The self-inflicted scars on his wrists; marks of profound suffering. And *maybe,* just maybe—

Unlike the others, Doctor Visconti actually did care what happened to her.

Broken from her reverie by the sound of his chair scraping across the hardwood, Philippa skipped quietly to the staircase. Embarrassed as she was, she took comfort in the notion that even if he had caught sight of her candelabra, he wouldn't bother seeking her out. Not after witnessing the venomous words that had spit from her mouth earlier.

Words that had—in addition to her nervous condition—kept her from finding sleep.

There was no indication of footsteps down the stairs behind her as Philippa drifted into the dark library and took a seat beneath the stained glass. Rain outside scratched at the tall windows, begging to be let in as she lifted her knees onto the window cushion and opened to her bookmarked page.

The pain of this life is agony,
But the beauty is almost too much to bear.
The sunlight mocks me,
The green spring spurs my jealousy,
All of nature dares go on without thee.

O that it were night forever!
Would that it were eternal winter,
That I might sleep away the hours
In silent oblivion.
But nay, I recant!
For this bed, without thy warmth, is the cruelest
tormenter of all

Philippa traced the words with a shaky fingertip. She had known it from the first page—that *Ballads of the Starlight Menagerie,* this constellation of words—somehow belonged to *him.* The faceless man of her dreams.

Where had he been all night, her beloved spirit?

Seized by the sudden feeling of being watched, Philippa's gaze snapped upward as a flash of lightning penetrated the library, spattering the colors of the stained glass across the face of her observer.

"You are indeed light on your feet, Doctor Visconti," she said.

His grin was offset in a charming way, almost boyish as he stood before her in his dressing gown. In his hand was a tiny glass of what looked like wine.

"A peace offering," he said, motioning to it. "May I join you?"

Philippa looked him over. If he had no interest in taking her to bed, what did he want at this hour?

"It is I who should be offering *you* a token of peace," she replied as he walked in. "I find it hard to believe that you still think me good company after today."

"You misjudge me again, Highness." Doctor Visconti took a

seat on the inlay cushion next to her. "Here," he said, offering the glass. "It will help."

Philippa reached for the wine with a trembling hand, keeping the other clasped over her open book. "You did not poison this, did you?" she teased, taking a sip.

His smile brought as much relief as the alcohol's warmth.

"I took it from the kitchen," he admitted. "I meant it when I asked if there was anything I could fetch you."

Perhaps he *did* intend on taking her to bed.

"Why did you do it?" Philippa shifted to face him on the sill. "The scars on your wrists, I have thought of them all day."

Doctor Visconti dropped his gaze, turning his forearm upward. "I wanted to be with her," he murmured, fiddling with his sleeve. "Perhaps trade my life for hers."

His words wrapped around her heart like barbed wire, squeezing tight. Only when he looked up did Philippa realize how closely she'd leaned in.

"I did not mean what I said to you," she whispered shamefully. "It was unkind, and no way to treat the man who saved me."

Nodding, he offered another smile, more wistful. "Please, do not trouble yourself over things said when you are not yourself."

"I do not ever feel that I am myself."

The words had bubbled to the surface without warning, and unnerved by them, Philippa took another sip, forcing the wine down her tight throat.

"You enjoy poetry, do you not?" she asked.

"I do, Highness."

"Perhaps you would like what I am reading." Philippa turned her attention to the open book in her lap. "It is a compilation of ballads."

"By whom?"

"I do not know," she replied, closing the pages over her fingers. "The author wrote under a peculiar pseudonym."

Doctor Visconti smirked. "An obscure title?"

"Ludwig was a collector of obscure titles," she said, handing it to him. "But this poet, *Belarius* as he calls himself—he is as gifted as Byron and Shelley and all the rest."

The life seemed to drain from Doctor Visconti as he took the book into his hands and opened to the title page, lightly rubbing his thumb over the 1818 publication date. "Where did you find this?" he asked in a hushed whisper.

"Here, at Marmoschossl."

"Here—in the library?" he demanded. "Have you read it in its entirety?"

"No, not yet," she replied, taken aback by his interest. "When I found it, it was as though the world stopped turning, as if it were waiting for me."

Doctor Visconti flipped the title page over, to the handwritten inscription.

To the Dove, From the Eagle

"That is a silly thing to say, I realize," Philippa added nervously. "It is no wonder people say I am mad."

But he did not laugh, nor speak. It was as if *Ballads of the Starlight Menagerie* had stopped time for him, too.

"Doctor?"

"Yes." Closing the book, he stumbled dizzily to his feet. "I apologize, Your Highness," he said, setting it on the cushion. "I do need to get to bed."

Philippa sprung up with equal haste. "Must you?"

"You should consider the same." Doctor Visconti paused, as if to draw attention to the quieted thunder. The cheer in his voice had faded, along with his interest. "It seems the gods have called their truce," he added.

"Very well," she said, huffing past him.

Philippa lit the way in her draping, spectral nightgown. What had she done to make him flatten? What had she said wrong?

Perhaps he thought it pathetic, the way she'd floundered on and on shamelessly, the colorful creations of a kept princess.

"Highness."

Turning around outside of Erzsi's door, Philippa shielded the glow of the candle with her hand.

"Forgive me for being so abrupt," said Doctor Visconti. "For making you believe you have done something wrong."

She frowned. "I do not—"

"You see, I am a collector of obscure titles myself." His irises brightened in the candlelight. "And that one, it…"

"You know it?"

"By heart," he said, pinning his gaze to the floor. "Seeing it again exhumes difficult feelings from me."

Could it be that Philippa's poet—her spirit—had found *him,* too?

Overcome with a sudden endearment, she stepped closer, pressing her cheek to Doctor Visconti's chest in a soft embrace. "There is a servant's passage that connects all the bedrooms," she whispered, steady against his beating heart. "If you would rather not be alone tonight."

He stood so still that at first it seemed like he might be considering. And then, his nose found the crook of Philippa's bare neck as he snaked both arms around her tight.

Never before had her skin prickled in rapture at the touch of another person. Not when her heart belonged to a man whose love could be found only in the warmth of the sunshine, or between the words on a page. A man that, to the rest of the world, did not exist.

"Come," she urged with another whisper.

"You are…*so* lovely."

A crimson flush overtook Philippa as he retracted.

"But I *cannot*—"

"Very well, Doctor. It seems I have misjudged you again." Philippa blew out the candle, plunging the hall into darkness. "I shall see you at ten o'clock tomorrow," she added, leaving him.

"Yes, Highness," he whispered back.

SIX

June 10, 1900
8:00 A.M.

The Hungarian china shook with each step as Mellie climbed the
stairs with her tray. Having taken Erzsi's words to heart, she had
tossed and turned all night in disbelief. Doctor Visconti fancying
her? She was so ordinary, no more interesting than a common
wren, or so she'd always thought. The notion that he may see past
her plain looks and appreciate her many other virtues—namely
her honest, loyal disposition—was enough to stir a smile and
stomachache all at once.

Gathering a breath of courage, Mellie knocked gently on his
bedroom door.

Laughter erupted from the room down the hall, and Mellie
craned her neck. Philippa's liaisons with servants and the like
were nothing new, but where the rest of the cottage reveled in
the gossip, Mellie hated being privy to it. Perhaps because *she*
was a woman with dignity—another one of her undervalued
virtues.

Redirecting her attention, she again knocked on the doctor's bedroom door. "Herr Visconti," she called, turning the knob. "Are you well?"

Greeted only by a crisply made bed, there was no sign of him in the room. Mellie's palms became slippery against the handles of the tray as she stood in the doorway, listening to the sounds of the archduchess and her lover penetrate the walls.

No—it couldn't be.

Yet Mellie had seen the way Philippa had eyed him when he first arrived, the way a cat plays with its food before devouring it. Could it be *him* that she was shamelessly flaunting? Aware that the walls were paper thin? The thought was appalling. Worse than appalling. From Philippa, she could have expected such a thing, but from *him?*

Unable to bear it a second longer, Mellie retreated for the stairs, eyes blazing with angry tears.

"Fräulein?"

Charging past the well-meaning maid at the bottom of the staircase, Mellie made a beeline for the veranda. She would never speak of this to anybody, least of all Erzsi, who—

"Mellie, are you all right?"

More violently than intended, the glass door slammed behind her. "Oh," Mellie gasped as she stepped onto the veranda, where Erzsi sat with her new friend at one of the wicker tables.

Doctor Visconti withdrew his lips from the rim of his teacup, mid-sip. "Good morning, Fräulein," he said, shuffling the ears of Blitz, who sat in his lap.

"Yes," Mellie squeaked, imagining her face, red and splotchy. "Good morning. I was just..."

Doctor Visconti's gaze fell to the tray in her arms. "I hope you were not looking for me?"

"Oh! No, I was..."

Erzsi tapped the outer edges of her teacup with her long, boney fingers. "Herr Visconti and I were just enjoying the veranda before the heat returns."

"The storm seems to have chased it off, for the time being," he added.

"And you see, Blitz has made a new friend!"

Mellie willed a smile, again finding the dog seated in Doctor Visconti's lap.

"Would you like some coffee?" he asked.

"No, thank you," Mellie replied, setting the tray on their table. "I am quite well."

"Perhaps a walk, then?"

Mellie glanced at Erzsi, who urged her with wide eyes to accept. Had Erzsi convinced him to ask her? What had they been discussing?

"The morning is fine," Doctor Visconti added.

"As long as I am not imposing."

"Nonsense, Mellie," Erzsi replied, reaching for Blitz as the doctor stood up. "It is no imposition at all."

The tension in Mellie's cheeks softened, and she smiled. "Your offer is most kind, Herr Visconti," she said, taking his arm.

It was relatively cool out, but damp and dewy. Crystal droplets fell from the needles of the evergreens, mimicking the sound of rain as they walked under the cover of the oak trees.

"Archduchess Erzsi mentioned that you may need a bit of fresh air to recover from your spell yesterday."

"I feel better already," Mellie replied. "It was the least the storm could do, to bring us a cool morning. I have never seen such lightning as I did last night."

"Yes, it would have certainly woken me if I had not already been awake." The doctor seemed to hesitate. "You must understand, Fräulein," he added, turning to her. "I am not used to anyone looking after me."

"Oh, no. Please, pay no mind to my state this morning. I was flustered over what turned out to be nothing at all."

"May I inquire as to what flustered you so?"

Now it was Mellie who hesitated. "Forgive me for speaking so frankly..." She forced an awkward smile. "I do not mean to assign judgment, but..."

Doctor Visconti raised his brows in anticipation.

"I heard someone in the room of Archduchess Philippa this morning. Someone else."

He mouthed only a simple "*oh,*" as he turned forward, looking pensively upon the path ahead.

"Such liaisons are nothing new," Mellie added. "But she used to take more care in hiding them."

"It would seem she is attracted to a certain type of man."

"Commoners, yes." She glanced at him for a reaction, but none came. "It all started on her nineteenth birthday, when she was found in the stable with one of the grooms."

The doctor's energy seemed to shift, and when Mellie turned to him, he was staring inquisitively at her.

"What did he look like?"

Mellie tried to think. The young man had been quite comely from what she could remember. "He had dark hair. Light eyes—greenish, or perhaps blue. It has been some years."

"Thank you, Fräulein."

"I do not mean to bother you with gossip," she said. "I try my best to ignore it, but..."

"Some things are difficult to ignore," Doctor Visconti murmured.

His body language seemed to stiffen, signaling a deep discomfort.

"And do you..." Shifting her eyes to the ground, Mellie took note of each pebble and blade of grass she stepped over. "Do you have anyone back home to miss you?"

"I have not had anyone to miss me in a very long time."

"What about siblings? Or parents? Have you any family at all?"

"I was raised by my sister, fifteen years my senior," Doctor Visconti replied. "Her son—my nephew—was a duke. They took me in."

It was clear by the way that he spoke that his adoptive family was no more. How alone he must feel.

"If you ever find yourself in need of companionship while you are staying here at Marmoschossl, I would be…"

His gaze fell away, and the knot welling in Mellie's throat made it hard to find her voice.

"Have I spoken out of turn?"

"Your offer is a kind one, Fräulein, and I do enjoy your company," he said. "But it is only right that I be forthcoming with you."

Oh, what she wouldn't have given to take back what she'd said as Doctor Visconti unbuttoned his collar.

"You see," he went on, revealing the wedding band hanging on the end of a chain around his neck, "I have lived my happiness already."

Mellie cupped her hand over her mouth. She'd heard of this ring that he wore, though she would never admit to indulging the hearsay of the house servants.

"But you are so young," was all she could manage. "Would your wife not want you to—?"

"I could live a thousand years and it would make no difference," he said, tucking the ring back into his collar. "A heart of ash cannot love."

The words stung, the very bluntness of them. Could he be so certain? How could *anyone* be so certain?

"Do you not think it is a disservice to yourself?" she asked.

Doctor Visconti smiled as he turned over his shoulder, back toward the pink cottage, where Philippa stood in her white night-gown. "My *work* is what guides my heart's compass now," he said.

Philippa fiddled with the ends of her hair as she leaned against one of the wrought iron columns, eyes fixated on Mellie and Doctor Visconti as they walked the oak path. A rainbow hue seemed to surround him in particular, as though he reflected the sun.

"He will be right back, Blitz." Erzsi struggled to keep the

writing dog on her lap as she sat on the top stair. "Do not interrupt them!"

"What would a man like him possibly have to talk about with Mellie?" Philippa sneered.

Erzsi peeked tauntingly over her shoulder. "Perhaps he likes her, Pippa."

"It is a preposterous notion," Philippa mumbled, shading her brow. "She does not suit him at all."

The more she focused on Doctor Visconti, the more pearlescent he appeared. She had not slept much, but was she tired enough to be seeing things?

A sharp whistle split through the air as he and Mellie neared the veranda, causing the dog to bolt from Erzsi's arms.

"Blitz!"

The terrier took an obedient seat in front of the doctor, as though awaiting further direction.

"Herr Visconti!" Erzsi called. "How did you manage to get him to do that?"

"Perhaps someone taught him," he shouted back.

Erzsi let out a confused laugh. "Blitz does not know *whistle commands,*" she said, turning back to Philippa in disbelief.

Arms crossed, Philippa eyed Doctor Visconti stoically as he rose to his feet with Blitz in his arms, at last meeting her gaze.

She had sought out Felix's replacement—was *Hermann* his name?—to ease the sting of his rejection, and perhaps to punish him for it. But the truth was, even as Philippa had acted out her vengeful liaison, she'd thought of nothing but Doctor Visconti's lingering touch. The resemblance between them had made it all the easier.

Blinking back at him, Philippa abandoned the column as he climbed the veranda stairs.

"A word, Highness?" he called, opening the glass door to the cottage behind her.

"It would seem you have plenty of them, Doctor Visconti,"

Philippa remarked over her shoulder. "Though you looked quite bored from where I stood!"

Ducking into the library, Philippa halted in the center of the room, then turned to the doorway.

"Yes, and you look quite tired this morning," said the doctor, appearing in frame. "Highness."

"Well, I hardly slept at all."

Closing the library doors, Doctor Visconti pinned her to the wall with his gaze as he stripped down to his vest.

"Have you met our new house servant, Hermann?"

Philippa crossed her arms as he stepped closer with all the muster he'd lacked last night, as though he might take her against the library shelves right then and there.

"Are you quite finished?" he asked, looking down on her.

Circling his face, she smiled up at him. "Not quite."

The green eyes of the doctor flickered like ancient peridot, and the muscles in his jaw flinched, in spite of the smirk he wore. "His name is *Helmut,* Highness. Please take your seat."

Leaving him, Philippa walked over to the chaise. Doctor Visconti paused, but only momentarily before pulling out his notebook and placing a chair in front of her.

"Do you still find me lovely?" she asked, stretching across the golden fabric.

Philippa could imagine where his eyes might wander—where his thoughts might roam—when he noticed the peaked satin of her nightgown.

"I may share a likeness with them but I will not be one of your meaningless toys," he replied, eyes on his notebook. "Nor another knight for your guard."

How had he—?

"Who told you!" Philippa demanded, shooting upright in horror.

Doctor Visconti halted the movement of his pen, at last

yielding to her. *"You did,"* he replied with a smile. "Who is he? Your knight."

How could she ever convey the space that her spirit held in her heart? How he'd held vigil over her bedside as a child, warding off her nightmares? The fantasy she'd constructed around him—her poet, her protector.

"Highness?"

"My knight is not of this world."

"Ah." Doctor Visconti smirked. "You believe you are being visited by a spirit."

Philippa's stare hardened. Surely *this man,* with his rumors and his occultist friends, was not being facetious with her.

"Your docile pet. A familiar to do your bidding..." He leaned inward. "Do you feel him here with us now?"

A shiver crawled up the back of Philippa's neck. "Yes," she admitted.

"How can you be certain?"

"My skin prickles when he is near..." Her voice trailed off, and when she spoke again, it was barely a whisper. "It is like a cold chill without being cold."

"And the identity of this so-called spirit, do you know it?"

Philippa looked past him to *Ballads of the Starlight Menagerie,* still sitting on the windowsill from last night. "I do not," she replied.

Doctor Visconti let out a wicked laugh as he shook his head.

"What?" she stuttered.

He motioned with his eyes to the window. "You believe your spirit is the author. *Belarius,* was it?"

It sounded even sillier coming from someone else.

"A remarkable coincidence finding his work, wouldn't you say?"

"I suppose so, if you believe in coincidence," Philippa replied.

His eyes seemed to soften, though his brow remained knitted.

"And what would you call it, Highness?" he asked. "What would you call stumbling upon something by coincidence?"

"I would call it a sign."

"A sign to where?"

Philippa watched in silence as Doctor Visconti pulled a prong and a coin-sized mirror with a long stem from the medical bag at his feet.

"To your destiny?" he asked, snapping the lock shut.

If he wasn't being facetious before, he certainly was now.

"It seems to me, Highness…" Doctor Visconti took a knee before her, tools in hand. "That you are in love with this dead poet of yours."

"Do you believe in spirits, Doctor Visconti?"

He laughed a bit. "You are asking me if I believe in spirits?"

"You have never stated explicitly one way or the other, but if in fact you *do*, you should know that it is not unheard of for them to take humans as lovers."

"Not unheard of, no. But not common."

"I believe it is more common than you want to admit—John Keats writes of such an experience in his *Endymion*. Her Majesty herself swore she was connected to Heinrich Heine!"

"Do not lecture me on Keats, Highness—I assure you no one knows his works better than I."

Leaning in closer, Philippa traced his face with a gentle regard. "That is a rather bold claim for a man who shows no other signs of boldness."

"You are plenty bold for both of us."

If only he *would* just take her against the bookshelves and be done with it—then perhaps they could move on with her session!

"You give your body but never your heart, because that is reserved for *him*." Doctor Visconti blinked; his serious gaze locked on hers. "It is a half-life."

Turning away, Philippa retracted with a scowl.

"I would know," he added.

"My life will always be halved as long as he is dead," she countered.

"And if he were alive?"

Philippa studied the coves of the irises gazing up at her, crests crashing against a dark green perimeter. Such an unsettling familiarity in them.

"He is not," she whispered.

Doctor Visconti nodded solemnly. "So each night, you set a glass of water by your bedside, hoping that—"

"Do not speak of things you know nothing about!"

"You forget this is my wheelhouse, Highness," he whispered. "It is the oldest conjuration trick in the book." Knowing he'd cornered her, an infuriating smirk took hold of him. "You wish your spirit lover to appear to you, but he *never* has."

"And your dear wife?" The fire rising in Philippa's throat threatened to burn her insides. "How many times has she manifested for you? You accuse me of living a half-life but you are no different, *are you?*"

Doctor Visconti glared at her as though he'd been pierced with a dozen arrows. The game had been won, but it was a pyrrhic victory.

"She has never once come to me," he said. "Not even as a dream."

Philippa could not believe it. Not with all the mediums he had sat with! How many nights had he spent with strangers around tables, waiting, waiting, *waiting*—like a dog begging for scraps—for any indication that his love had not been lost to him forever, floating adrift in a dark, cosmic sea?

Overwhelmed by the desire to touch him, Philippa drew back. "I am quite finished now, Doctor Visconti."

As though he'd been tempted to do the same, he looked up at her with glossy eyes. "As am I," he murmured. "Highness."

And just like that, Philippa was his patient again.

"Do you plan to hypnotize me?" she asked, glancing down nervously at the tools in his hand.

"I thought we might try it, yes."

"All right."

"I will guide you through it," he assured. "You only need to follow" —he pinged the metal fork— "my voice."

A buzzing chime filled her ears.

"Keep your eye on the glass," he murmured. "Very good."

Philippa's focus began to blur around her reflection in the slender mirror as he moved it side to side.

"Very good. Are you watching closely?"

She mouthed *"yes,"* her lashes heavy.

"Very good."

The mirror stilled, then moved toward her nose.

"Eye on it. Eye on it..."

"What is your name?"

Philippa looked to Lohengrin and Elsa in the pond.

"Your Highness, can you hear me?"

She turned left, then right, only to realize she was alone.

"Do you recognize my voice?"

So sweet it was it, like a melody caught in her head.

"Am I dreaming?" she asked.

"It is similar to a dream, but we can control when you wake."

Philippa looked to the pink cottage over her shoulder. That's right! Only moments ago, she'd been in the library with Doctor Visconti.

"Can you tell me where you are?"

"I am outside," she said, stepping onto the grass. "Outside by the water."

"Can you state your full name?"

"Philippa von Habsburg."

"What month is it?"

Philippa focused on the veranda creepers but could see no movement inside the library. "It is June," she answered. "Nearly my birthday."

"I would like to revisit your most recent stay at the Schonbrünn."

"But," she stuttered, "I..."

"You need only summon the intent to go there."

Suddenly her legs were wet, completely engulfed in warm, sudsy water. Then more toppled over her face. Wiping the drops from her eyes, Philippa reached for the edge of the porcelain tub with her other hand.

She was in the tub at Schonbrünn.

"I am here," she whispered. "Remarkable..."

"Can you describe your surroundings?"

Philippa looked around the decadent gold wallpaper of the bathroom with its French windows to the terrace that lay just outside, lined with rose bushes. Schonbrünn was the most beautiful of all the properties, and her personal favorite.

"Can you hear me, Highness?"

Philippa sat forward and hugged her knees. Oh, how she missed this lovely place! Its shined marble floors and vases of peacock feathers. She would like nothing more than to stay here.

"I am having my hair washed," she replied. "I think something is about to happen."

"Allow it to come."

Philippa turned to the doorway, where Mellie stood with a vase of crimson camellias. "Duke Sixten has sent me camellias," she said, waving her in. "Mellie is bringing them inside."

"They have been sent by your fiancé?"

Mellie entered the bathroom obediently, setting the vase on a white, baroque vanity.

"I..."

The room began to blur in visions of white and gold, fading in and out of the sunshine.

"Highness?"

"I...I feel strange," she gasped. "Like a current is pulling me elsewhere."

"Allow it to take you."

Philippa looked down at her feet as she stood on the edge of a dark water, rippled with starlight. "I am somewhere else now," she said.

"Do you know where?"

"It is a quarry of some sort," she answered. "I cannot recall how, but..."

"What do you see in the quarry?"

The narrator's voice seemed to shudder and echo against the cliff sides around her. At first, Philippa saw only what looked to be a small cottage across the water. But then, an expectant mother with long, sandy hair appeared.

"I know this place," Philippa whispered, focusing on the figure.

The young woman looked up and met Philippa's eye. It was clear by the shocked expression on her face that she hadn't expected to see her there.

"Can you hear me?"

Philippa tilted her head, and as if the woman were her mirror image, she did the same.

"Philippa, I would like you to return to Schonbrünn."

But Philippa could focus on nothing but the way her body involuntarily moved to mimic the girl, as though she were a puppet. "I cannot," she managed shakily. "I..."

The girl gagged on silent words as she opened her mouth to speak, seemingly choked by an invisible force. Philippa wanted to scream out, to help her, but found that her own voice had been taken. The girl scratched at her neck, desperate to breathe. To be set free.

Philippa plunged into the dark quarry after her, but her body sank like lead as she struggled to keep her head above the surface. The eyes of the apparition widened until blood ran from them like tears. And then there was water all around, stealing Philippa's every breath. Flooding her lungs with a dull, excruciating ache.

Philippa's eyes shot open; her back arched, pliant as a willow stem. "The water! All around me—!" she shouted between panicked breaths. "I have seen it. I..."

"What have you seen?"

Gathered in the arms of Doctor Visconti on the floor, she gaped at the fresh scratches across his forehead. "Did *I* do that?"

His sole focus seemed to be her heaving chest, so close to his, as though he might be investigating its rhythm.

Humiliated, Philippa tore herself away. "I am a feral creature," she whispered, resting her cheek against the edge of the gold chaise. "I can see it in your eyes, that way that people look at me."

Doctor Visconti lifted his hand slightly like he might reach for her. "Again," he said, splaying his fingers back across the floor, "you misjudge me."

Even his hands were beautiful, sunkissed from knuckle to nail bed. A sliver of red dragon peeked out from beneath the sleeve cuff of his white dress shirt. Rising to the surface was a longing in Philippa to be coiled within them. To crawl onto his lap like a house cat.

"I did not think you would sleep so deeply on the first try," Doctor Visconti added.

"Have your patients visited the quarry before?"

The way he straightened to attention made Philippa uneasy. "You recall it?"

"I..." She lifted her head.

The dream, clear as it had been, was already beginning to slip away.

"You must tell me all that you remember."

Taken aback by his intensity, a nervous smile tugged at Philippa's lips.

"Please," he said. "It is important."

Repositioning herself against the chaise's edge, she tried her best to recall. "I saw a young woman with long, wavy hair as I stood at the edge of the water at night. She could not have been much older than Erz—"

"Stansi."

"Pardon?"

Refusing her eye, Doctor Visconti rose to his feet, murmuring under his breath, "I have seen the face of Death..."

"She felt like kin," Philippa went on, "like a distant cousin that you only see every few years."

Visibly shaken, he paced to the window. "Did this young woman speak to you?" he asked, rubbing his forearms in an anxious manner.

"No," she replied. "She could not—what are you not telling me?"

Doctor Visconti met her eye, his gaze sickened and wary.

"Your wife," Philippa gasped. "But she..."

"We lived near a waterfall in Istria," he said, turning back to the window. "A region called the Sopat."

A chill spread from Philippa's neck, down her arms, covering her in goosebumps, and as though he felt them, too, Doctor Visconti began to rub at his arms again.

"Stansi..." Philippa said.

"Costanza." He focused on the treetops outside the window. "Costanza Visconti."

"But she has never come to you," she said, hesitantly finding his side. "Why would she come to *me?*"

Abandoning the window, Doctor Visconti slid past her, unwilling to share whatever he might be thinking.

"Tell me she did not drown?"

His eyes were teary, now, as he turned back. At last, Philippa understood what Erzsi had meant about all that he had endured.

"But she was..."

Doctor Visconti dropped his eyelids to the floor. "I once met an old traveler woman while passing through these parts. Magda Orsini," he said. "I shall never forget her name for as long as I live."

Philippa reached for her hair, and, pulling it to one side, began to comb it with her fingers.

"She spoke to me in riddles." The Adam's apple in his throat bobbed as he swallowed something back. *"You stand on the shore. She is one with the water."*

Philippa inhaled deeply, never more aware of her own breathing. "Costanza was with child..."

"Highness." With quivering lips, Doctor Visconti willed a smile. "I think we both have had enough for one day."

SEVEN

June 11, 1900
7:20 A.M.

Philippa stared at the glass of water by her bedside as she lay against her pillow. In this contained form, it was only water.

The hours of the night had been strung together with shallow dreams of places she had never been, and experiences she had never had. And each time she'd managed to drift off, visions of hollow eyes would startle her awake. The spirit of Costanza Visconti had followed her to bed, and she had yet to leave.

Philippa blinked sleepily, adjusting the pillow under her cheek.

What did this spirit possibly want with *her?*

The water in the glass began to whirl as she meditated on it, much like it had wrapped around her lungs in the vision.

Philippa had thought of Doctor Visconti, too, and the love he'd lost like a shipwreck to the sea. How cruelly she had toyed with him, trying to fan his jealousy and catch a spark from the burning funeral pyre of his heart.

He would not be her lover, but perhaps he could be her friend. Aside from Erzsi and her brother, Franz, Philippa had never had a real friend before. And she should like to have one so well-traveled and worldly.

Her lashes had finally begun to close when Philippa heard a voice, smooth and sensual, without being a voice at all.

Hello, it said.

Opening her eyes to an empty bedroom, she spoke out loud. "Hello?"

A cold breath teased the back of her neck like a frosty kiss, making its hairs stand on end.

How she'd missed her spirit!

Clutching her pillow, Philippa closed her eyes with a shiver and a smile. Beneath her cocoon of blankets, she could imagine the feeling of an arm around her waist, pulling her closer. Closer to the astonishing density of whatever lay behind her—whether man or mirage.

"Do you intend to seduce me, spirit? After days of silence?" she teased. "Without ever showing your face?"

A vision of the pond outside bled into her mind, as if painted in watercolor.

The doctor from Zürich has arrived. Mellie's words replayed as Philippa envisioned standing in the water, lily pads at her feet. The same iridescent halo she thought she'd seen yesterday surrounded Doctor Visconti as he waited on the bank, his eyes sparkling like gemstones. *It is an honor to finally meet you,* he'd said.

Philippa's eyes shot open. "Doctor Visconti?" she whispered.

Throwing off her covers, she leapt from the bed.

Since its discovery, Philippa had used the dusty, marble passageway to evade the prying eyes of servants. And so, unfastening the latch, she made her way to the doctor's bedroom.

"Doctor—!"

Doctor Visconti, still in bed, jumped back as she emerged from the door nestled within the wall next to him. Sitting shirtless against the chestnut headboard, his faded dragons were even more magnificent to behold on full display, their red ink especially vibrant against the champagne wallpaper of the room, and the white sheets on the bed.

"I had to see you right away," said Philippa, trying not to gawk at them.

His lips parted but the doctor did not move to cover himself, nor did he speak, as if he were waiting for her to say something more. As though he were *expecting* her to.

"Your Highness," he said finally. "Are you...?"

"I am well," Philippa replied. "Well enough, but..." Nervous under his stare, she willed herself to explain. "But *she* has not left me. Costanza."

He blinked. A hard swallow followed.

"I apologize for intruding unannounced," she added, shutting the passage door behind her. "But I hardly slept, her presence was so strong."

"I see."

"And my spirit, he..." Philippa crossed the room, wringing her hands. "He showed me a vision of *you* by the pond."

Keeping his eyes on her, Doctor Visconti reached for the paisley dressing gown which hung from his bed post.

"Do you believe it is possible that my spirit and your wife have conspired our very meeting from beyond the grave?"

"Respectfully, Your Highness," he murmured sheepishly, "if we are to continue this conversation in my private quarters—"

"Yes?"

"Would you mind turning around so that I can get dressed?"

"*Oh*, yes—of course. I..."

Doctor Visconti motioned across the room. "If you would not mind just..."

Philippa made her way to his desk, where she faced herself toward the window. "Is this better?" she asked, fixating her gaze on the items strewn across the top.

"Yes, thank you."

An oriental black box sat among the pile of books and papers. Red dragons, too, covered this miniature antique chest.

The bedsheets rustled, and the frame creaked behind her. "If I may..." he said.

"You may," Philippa replied absently.

"I have noticed that you seem to avoid your own reflection."

Glancing up, she found the bronzed skin and back dimples of Doctor Visconti in the reflection of his desk mirror. "Since I was a girl it has felt like someone else is looking back at me through my own eyes," she murmured.

As though he could feel her admiration, the doctor seemed to linger in view.

"What is this?" Philippa asked, turning her attention back to the box. "Did you bring it back from your time in the Orient?"

"It is from China," he replied, climbing back into bed. "You may turn around now."

But Philippa had been seized by something else on his desk. A little green journal, its leather well-worn and well-loved. Picking it up, she spread its pages.

"Highness?"

Philippa scanned the cursive stanzas, each one dated in the upper right hand corner.

"Doctor Visconti..." she said, pivoting toward him. "You failed to tell me that you yourself write poetry."

Crossing his arms tightly over his chest, he curled his shoulders away from the headboard. "For her, yes."

"It is no wonder my spirit has taken a liking to you," Philippa added, needing no further confirmation that their meeting had been divinely orchestrated. "You and he are kindred souls. May I read your poetry?"

"I would rather you did not."

He seemed to be withdrawing again, in the same manner he had that night in the library.

"I understand." Philippa returned the journal to his desk with a hopeful smile. "Perhaps your words will find her, one day."

"Perhaps they already have," he whispered.

A sudden fist cracked against his door, followed by Mellie's voice.

What was *she* doing there?

"Herr Visconti, may I come in?"

"Ah—yes, Fräulein," he called back, glancing at Philippa. "Just a—!"

The knob turned. "Good morning," Mellie greeted, a full tray of china in hand.

Philippa stood quietly by the desk, assessing the morning offering of biscuits and coffee with a freshly plucked pink rose.

"Oh." Mellie's smile dropped at the sight of her. "I did not..."

"Her Highness was just discussing with me a dream that she had."

"Oh."

"You may leave it, Mellie," said Philippa.

Mellie looked down at the tray, then back to Doctor Visconti.

"Right there is fine."

The china sang as Mellie set the tray down on the bed.

"Thank you," Philippa added, in as friendly a tone.

The governess walked to the door, nodding once at the doctor before closing it behind her.

"Does she bring you coffee every morning?" Philippa asked, taking a seat opposite him on the bed.

"Every morning so far."

"Mmm," she said, pouring some coffee into the teacup. "Sweet Mellie. I for one am surprised she would have any interest in befriending you."

Doctor Visconti laughed under his breath. "Why is that, Highness?"

"Your reputation is nothing if not scandalous—you with your dragon tattoos and your mesmerism."

"*You* do not seem bothered by these things," he said.

"Why should I be?" Philippa shrugged. "I am a madwoman."

He watched silently as she dipped a biscuit into the coffee, then took a bite.

"Would you like some?"

"No, thank you."

"You must tell me, then," she continued, sipping from the rim of the teacup. "Am I anything like your Costanza?"

His eyes seemed to protest the question.

"I am only wondering if I have things in common with your spirit in the same way you do mine," she added.

Doctor Visconti reached for a biscuit on the tray. "The short answer is yes."

"And the long one?"

He smirked but looked away from her. "It is not one thing I can pinpoint," he said, biting the biscuit.

"I feel as though I owe you an apology for the way I..." Philippa jumped a little as the door once again creaked open. "*Yes?*" she snapped.

"I am sorry to interrupt," said Mellie. "But I just received word that His Highness, Archduke Franz, will be here at noon."

"*Franz?*" Philippa returned the teacup to its saucer with a laugh. "My brother is coming to Kaiservilla, and this is the first I am hearing of it?"

Doctor Visconti brushed the crumbs from his fingers, and Mellie looked to the floorboards with a forced smile.

"I suppose he has caused quite a stir," she added. "The whole court is likely after him by now."

Between Philippa and her brother, they had given Vienna plenty to talk about over the last five years. She, the "Mad Niece of the Emperor," and Franz Ferdinand, the heir presumptive of the Austro-Hungarian throne who had fallen in love with the lady-in-waiting of Archduchess Isabella, and refused to marry anyone else.

"There is something else, Highness," Mellie added.

"What?"

She pursed her lips, clasping her hands across her abdomen. "Duke Sixten is accompanying him."

Duke Sixten?

There at noon?

The thought made Philippa's throat constrict. He had not taken their broken engagement well, sending flowers to Schonbrünn both day and night, and letters that—with Erzsi's encouragement—she had eventually stopped responding to.

"What brings the duke to Marmorschossl?" asked Doctor Visconti.

"Well, they are great friends, after all." Philippa tried to sound unbothered, despite knowing that his accompanying Franz could only mean one thing: he had come to make amends with her. "It is no bother." She reached for another biscuit.

A silent conversation seemed to be happening between Doctor Visconti and Mellie, though neither dared to ask any questions.

"Right, well." Philippa shot to her feet, mouth full. "I must dress."

11:50 A.M.

"You know, in another world, Franz might have married my mother."

Troilo lifted his chin from a knot of laced fingers, casting his gaze across the library to where Erzsi paged aimlessly through a book.

"Had he not fallen in love with Sophie, that is. He kept her likeness in a locket, which was discovered by Archduchess Isabella—who was thinking it was *her daughter* inside."

Erzsi cackled under her breath, and Troilo wondered if she were actually reading as she flipped another page. From the pillowed bench, he had a perfect view of the pond, where Elsa and Lohengrin circled each other without a care in the world.

To be so blissful.

"Do you believe His Majesty will grant them permission to marry?" Troilo asked absently.

"It is only a formality that Franz grovels. In truth, he is too tenacious to take no for an answer, and my grandfather cares too little to refuse him." Erzsi flipped another page. "Whether he is heir presumptive or not, His Majesty will never name him Crown Prince, regardless of who he marries."

"I see."

If Troilo had learned one thing from living parallel to the world of nobility, it was that human beings loved to live in cages of their own making.

Standing at attention, Blitz began to bark, which called Erzsi to the east window.

"There they are," she said, urging Troilo to her side.

Outside, a pair of men in Austrian cavalry uniforms dallied in the yard.

"That is Franz," said Erzsi. "My cousin. You have seen his picture, surely."

Troilo's eyes glazed over the archduke to the man at his side with courtly posture and flaxen hair. *Duke Sixten Siegfried.* Scorned fiancé, bringer of camellias, friend to Archduke Franz Ferdinand. Murderer.

His resurfacing was another snagged bobbin Troilo hadn't foreseen.

"And him," he said, turning to Erzsi. "What are your thoughts on him?"

Her icy blue eyes flickered.

"They're here!"

Footsteps thundered down the foyer staircase, following Philippa's voice.

Erzsi offered the book she'd been reading to Troilo. "I am afraid we lack the time to share my feelings," she said, urging him to take it. "Come, Blitz."

As she made her way to the foyer, Troilo read the title, indented in brown leather.

The Strange Case of Doctor Jekyll and Mr. Hyde

He grinned as Erzsi glanced back over her shoulder, motioning to him to come along.

Glad to see her brother, Philippa rushed to the middle of the parquet floor to meet him in a dizzying yellow sundress, her lustrous head of hair styled in an elegant French braid. "Franzi!!"

Lifting her in a burly embrace, the stocky archduke spun her round until she was sick with laughter.

"Are things so terrible in Vienna that you chose to join us in exile?" she asked, securing her straw hat with the back of her palm.

A smile emerged beneath her brother's thick, curled mustache.

"Quite the scandal, indeed, you and Sophie," Philippa teased. "I thank you both for giving those vicious society hounds something to focus on other than me!"

"We will wed on the first of July, if His Majesty allows it."

Maids and footmen hugging the parlor walls made room for Troilo as he stepped out of the library, joining them on the sidelines.

"But Franz," said Philippa. "He is away on business in Vienna."

"Is he?" Archduke Franz shot a look across the room to Duke Sixten, who lingered in the doorway. "I suppose that gives us more time to visit."

Troilo studied the duke from where he stood, watching him measure every inch of the room with full lips resting in a confident pout above a cleft dimple. His eyes, as dark and glassy as the game that lined the halls of the Kaiservilla. There was something familiar about him, something Troilo couldn't quite place.

Duke Sixten met Troilo's eye in mutual acknowledgement, then he stepped toward Philippa. "Your Royal and Imperial Highness," he said, nodding to her. "It pleases me to see you again."

A shy smirk emerged beneath the shadows of Philippa's straw hat. "Duke Sixten," she said.

Troilo looked to Erzsi, who held Blitz tight against her chest as Philippa walked over. Beneath the shadow of her hat, he could spot the peculiar birthmark on her neck.

"You remember our cousin, Archduchess Erzsébet Marie and her governess, Fräulein Mellie Coudenhove," said Philippa.

The servants stepped aside as the duke crossed in front of Troilo.

"Hello again, Your Grace," said Mellie.

"Fräulein." The duke cocked his head as he centered his attention on Erzsi. "You look well, Your Highness."

Erzsi smiled, but her stare was baleful.

"And you." Duke Sixten turned on his heel to Troilo. "You must be the doctor from Zürich. Visconti, is it?"

Philippa shot her brother a disapproving look.

"I hope you will not be cross with Franz for telling me," Duke Sixten added.

"Doctor Visconti, our aunt counts herself among your many admirers," said Archduke Franz.

Troilo assessed Philippa's brother with his tight haircut and eyes the color of silver mist. "Your Royal and Imperial Highness, I am honored to make your acquaintance."

"Forgive me, Doctor, but you look incredibly familiar."

Turning slowly back toward the duke, Troilo felt his body go cold.

"'*Vipereos moreos non violabo,*'" Duke Sixten proclaimed in a stately voice. "'*I will not violate the customs of the serpent.*' That is your family's motto, is it not? The Visconti of Milan?"

Troilo's mind slid backward in horror to the courtyard overlook at the Pazin castle, and the things spoken within its stone walls.

Let us settle this as men.

And if you win?

Against you, Troilo?

Duke Sixten smiled, his gaze grinding against Troilo's like cold metal. Like clamoring swords.

I do not imagine I will.

"I am a far cry from any noble birth," Troilo murmured. "My father was only kind enough to give me his name."

"Still, I..." Duke Sixten looked him over. "I cannot shake the feeling that our paths have crossed before."

Troilo reached for the ring around his neck, which suddenly felt as heavy as an anvil. "Your face is not one I would forget, Your Grace."

Your Grace.

He nearly choked on the words.

Was he still such a subservient dog?

"Are you well, Herr Visconti?" asked Governess Coudenhove.

Troilo could hardly catch his breath against the incessant thumping of his heart. "Yes, thank you, Fräulein."

"Shall we take a walk before lunch?" Philippa asked suddenly. "Doctor, perhaps you can join us and tell us of your travels. Franz has spent his fair share of time in the Orient as well, isn't that true, Franzi?"

"I fear I must decline," Troilo replied, still collecting himself. "I have much work to do."

"Perhaps tomorrow would be better," Archduke Franz suggested. "I thought we might all go on a hunt."

Troilo nodded, feeling Philippa's eyes on him. "I look forward to it, Your Highness."

He stood aside as Philippa led the emptying of the room. Erzsi peeled herself from the wall, and the last out the door, she stuck her tongue out at him playfully.

"Would you like lunch brought up to you?" Governess Coudenhove asked.

"No, thank you, Fräulein."

"Are you certain you are not ill?"

"Not ill in a physical manner," he replied, watching Duke Sixten disappear from sight. "Sometimes it just...finds me."

"What?" she asked timidly.

"The past." Troilo turned toward the staircase. "Excuse me, Fräulein. I need a moment alone."

"Yes, of course."

Whether or not she was *trying* to garner his attention by sulking, Troilo couldn't say.

"I will join you for lunch in the parlor when I am finished, if you do not mind the company," he added.

Her cheeks rounded with glee. "I should love the company."

The air seemed thicker upstairs since he'd left it, as if the sunshine had sealed the humidity into the walls. Troilo scanned the pond from his bedroom window, spotting Philippa between the two men as they walked its edge. Such a strange, tangled web was fate.

Troilo pocketed his shaky hands as he peered through the wavy glass. *"Matthias,"* he sighed, watching the duke walk Philippa out of view.

His brother, his killer. Lord of cruelty.

Could it really be that *he,* too, had found her again?

The assortment of dresses stacked upon Philippa's bed was the first thing Troilo noted when he walked into her room, further evidence that Duke Sixten Siegfried was much more than a snagged bobbin.

He was a *knot.*

Troilo walked the perimeter of Philippa's gilded cage, meandering over to the covered mirror, where a miscellany of well-loved jewelry, open fragrance bottles, and a pair of delicate silver shears scattered the surface of her vanity. He recognized many of the more sentimental trinkets from visions of her childhood—a turret shell she'd found on the Mediterranean coast with her father, a glass quill, and her mother's music box.

Ever since that stifling July afternoon in 1876, when she entered the world with the umbilical cord wrapped around her neck twice over, Troilo had witnessed snippets of Philippa's life through her eyes. Even as she had taken her first breath, coming to life like Pygmalion's Galatea, a *knowing* had shot through him as he'd sat seven hundred miles away in a Paris lecture hall.

Costanza had been reborn.

Troilo shifted his attention to the paper cranes that stood watch on her windowsill, where *Ballads of the Starlight Menagerie* waited patiently for the return of its muse.

There had been only one hundred copies made at the time of publication, and if it had been up to him, there would have been even fewer. But his English friends—with their drunken escapades and hedonistic ways—were nothing if not persuasive. Now, face to face with one of those copies almost a century later, Troilo felt their absence acutely.

Reluctantly, he picked up the book and opened to a random page, where a single piece of long, blonde hair glistened in the sunlight. Pulling it free, he held it between his fingers like a golden thread.

I found you in the water,
And I lost you to the water,
Sea-born and sea-bedded.
If I drown, will you come back to me?
If I founder, will you rescue me?

If I sail my ship, and listen for your song,
Will you take me under?
Or is it only my hope I see ahead—
Dashed against the rocks,
And washed up on the shore.

Troilo turned to the last page, to ballad number one-hundred-and-sixteen, where Costanza's name was spelled out.

Would Philippa think it a sign that her spirit lover and Troilo both lost someone named Costanza?

Would she connect the dots like a constellation?

Troilo had tried to show her earlier that morning who he was. And when she'd burst into his room so abruptly, he had hoped that she might whisper, *"My knight, is it really you?"* And Troilo, losing himself in a revere of marzipan and honey, would say, *"I am alive! I have searched for you in every sunset, from one corner of the world to another, hoping I might find you there,"* as he ran his fingers through her hair.

"Oh."

Troilo jumped at the sight of Erzsi standing guard outside of Philippa's bedroom.

"I was sent to fetch her gloves," she said, waltzing in with a sly grin. "What were *you* sent to fetch?"

"I…"

Erzsi hugged the wooden bedpost, leaning her temple against it with an expectant look.

"I have a stray thread on my jacket," Troilo said, claiming the shears from her vanity. "I was looking for some sewing scissors."

Erzsi's smile grew, and her arms fell to her sides. "Those were a gift from His Majesty. I have an identical pair," she said, joining his side. "I might find your story more believable if" —she peeked out the window— "this room was not the perfect vantage point."

Troilo grinned without meaning to. "You take me for a spy?"

"Better to be taken for a spy than a *fool*." Erzsi cocked a dubious eyebrow before turning back to the glass.

"I do not think you a fool," he replied. "Far from it."

But her stare was fixed on the party, standing at the edge of the glittering pond below.

"Would Archduke Franz really allow such a man to court his sister?" Troilo asked, watching the hand of Duke Sixten find Philippa's back.

"I *said* Franz was tenacious—not that he was a good judge of character." Erzsi turned to him, looking unsurprised. "You have read about him, then. How he strangled a woman with his bare hands and was acquitted?"

Troilo nodded.

"I told Pippa not to accept his proposal, but she saw what she wanted to see." Erzsi swiped the pair of lace gloves from Philippa's vanity. "The duke's family insisted that he was not the perpetrator, rather that it was one of his men, because surely a handsome, *upstanding* man would never be caught dead with a courtesan in the first place."

"What of the witnesses that saw the body thrown from the balcony?"

"It was dark." Erzsi shrugged. "Their testimony did not hold."

Troilo studied the tall, broad-shouldered duke. "Why did she decide to break the engagement?"

"He began showing his true colors once they were betrothed," Erzsi murmured, wringing the gloves. "He was possessive, and his moods swung from one side of the pendulum to the other. He would fly off the handle over nothing at all. Eventually, Pippa had enough."

An uncomfortable silence fell over the room.

"He has come to try and repair the engagement," said Troilo at last.

"It certainly wasn't the *pheasant hunting* that brought him here," Erzsi sneered. "His interest is money, of course. Pippa, even with her damaged reputation, is still sister to the heir presumptive. He wants to tame and polish her into his own little society doll."

"A spirit like hers," Troilo murmured under his breath, "it is not so easily tamed."

"*Tell me*, have I convinced you to join us for lunch?"

Troilo pivoted toward her. "I have promised my company to your governess."

"Oh?" Erzsi hung back in the doorway with eager eyes. "Shall I let her know you will be right down?"

Troilo loosened his cravat, watching her eyes pinpoint the shears he held at his side.

"Now that you have found your..."

"Yes," he said hastily. "I am quite finished."

Erzsi smirked. "Perhaps she can help you repair your jacket."

Clever girl.

"I will not tell anyone that I found you in her room," she added.

"Erzsi?"

She peeked back around the corner. "Yes?"

"You are no fool."

"And standing so plainly in the window, *you* are no spy, Troilo."

Erzsi slapped the satin gloves against her hand, rounding the staircase with a snicker. A funny thing, catching him in the act. But she was grateful for the opportunity to talk, for the devil himself had come to Marmorschlossl, and she would need Troilo's help to exorcise him.

"What has gotten into you?" Mellie asked from the bottom of the stairs. "Is something funny?"

"I have just heard about your lunch with Herr Visconti," Erzsi replied, stretching the gloves.

"Oh." Mellie moved to tuck a stray hair behind her ear. "Yes."

"He said he will be down in a moment to join you," she added, jumping from the second stair onto the hardwood.

With Mellie to distract him, Philippa's spell over Troilo would surely lose its momentum. Troilo could then focus on curing her. Especially now that Duke Sixten had resurfaced again, like a wart that wouldn't go away.

This time it would be different. He wouldn't dare harass Philippa as he had at Schonbrünn, because as long as she was in treatment, Philippa had a man to speak on her behalf. And not just any man—a doctor. If Duke Sixten had indeed come to win back Philippa's affections, they would block his every path.

Erzsi could hear the discussion of family politics down by the pond as she examined the finger sandwiches that had been set out for lunch. On a sunny day like this, their demise was inevitable.

"Erzsi!" Philippa called. "Did you fetch my gloves?"

"Coming!" she yelled back, mouth full of cream cheese and cucumber.

She could've done without them watching in unison as she ungracefully made her way down to the water, trying to pick the dill between her teeth with her tongue. Duke Sixten wore a smug smile as she approached. The kind of smile that evaded murder charges.

"Do watch your step, little one," he teased. "You do not know what could be lurking underfoot."

Little one.

Who did he think he was to address her in such a manner?

Erzsi wanted to laugh as she extended the gloves to Philippa with a flop. "Thank you for your concern, but I need not worry," she said, meeting his eye with a piercing stare. "For *I* am the snake in the grass."

"What held you?" Philippa asked.

"The dread of this heat," Erzsi replied.

"I thought perhaps you had abandoned us for more worldly company." Philippa laughed, picking at her gloves as she turned to Franz. "You see, Erzsi has made a great friend of our doctor."

"He is taking lunch with Fräulein Coudenhove."

Philippa turned to her, brow knitted in question, but Erzsi was more focused on Franz and Duke Sixten.

"I see Pippa has told you about Doctor Bohm?"

"Indeed," Franz replied. "An exciting summer it has been, I hear."

"I thought Herr Visconti had work to do?"

Only Duke Sixten seemed to notice Philippa's interest.

"Well, he must eat," Erzsi replied nonchalantly.

"How is your mother, Erzsi?" asked Franz.

"She wed this past March. I did not attend."

He nodded awkwardly, washed over by her chill. He should have known better than to mention her mother.

"Franz, tell me why when *you* request to marry beneath you, your wish is granted," Erzsi teased, "but when I do the same, I am locked away for the summer?"

"His Majesty wants to see if you will change your mind," Franz replied knowingly. "Have you?"

"I have not changed my mind. And to prove my point, I *will* not."

"You believe you will be happy with Prince Otto?"

"As long as whom I marry is my own choice, I will be happy."

"I know you scoff at such comparisons, but you *are* your father's daughter."

"So I have been told." Erzsi smirked as her eyes floundered between the three of them.

"Tell us of your new friend," said Duke Sixten.

Erzsi followed his stare to the parlor window, where Troilo and Mellie paced inside. "What of him?"

"Is he married?"

"Widowed."

Duke Sixten squinted at the cottage. "That explains it, then."

"Explains what?" Philippa asked.

He glanced at her as though she should know better. "His strangeness."

"Strangeness?" Philippa let out a nervous laugh. "I do not find him strange. I find him—his *life,* quite fascinating really."

"Do you?"

Philippa met Duke Sixten's eye with an uneasy smile. An uneasiness Erzsi could feel in the pit of her stomach.

"We should ask Fräulein Coudenhove to come along on the hunt tomorrow," Erzsi said.

Philippa let out a strained laugh. "She has no interest in hunting..."

"Come now, Pippa," Franz chimed in. "Do you dislike her so?"

Her lips pursed in annoyance as she turned to Erzsi.

"The more the merrier," Franz declared.

EIGHT

June 12, 1900
1:45 P.M.

From her grassy spot beneath the tree, Erzsi squinted up from the open pages of *The Strange Case of Doctor Jekyll and Mr. Hyde*. "Tiresome bunch, they are," she mumbled.

Troilo let out a subtle laugh as he stretched his leg under the shade next to her.

Ahead of them, Philippa stood tall against the vibrant summer landscape—Archduke Franz on one side of her and Duke Sixten on the other—holding her rifle steady to a cloudless sky. It had been many years since Troilo had gone hunting for sport, though his marksmanship had not suffered for it.

He watched as Philippa tracked the brindle feathers of a pheasant down her barrel, teasing the trigger of the shotgun.

"Almost," Archduke Franz coached. "Almost..."

A shot rang out, startling Governess Coudenhove nearby.

"Well done, Pippa!"

Philippa took a bow before her applauding spectators,

lowering the Witten Excelsior to her side as the archduke whistled for the dogs.

Troilo turned to Erzsi. "Your cousin is an exceptional shot."

"It drives men absolutely *mad.*"

"Excellent!" Archduke Franz exclaimed. "Someone has at last caught up with Herr Visconti..."

Philippa glanced to Troilo from under her suede hat, cheeks pink from the heat, and eyes a lemony green. "Do you hear that?" she called. "We are tied."

Her smile was lovelier than any of Troilo's imaginings. It was impossible not to smile back at her as she swiveled in place.

"He does not know which is worse..." Erzsi smirked as she motioned subtly to Duke Sixten. "The fact that he lost to her, or to *you.*"

"Look there," the archduke hushed, drawing his rifle.

Troilo rose to his feet and stepped forward, spotting the chamois that had emerged from the wood line about thirty yards away.

"Time to break your tie." Archduke Franz nudged his sister. "Take the Werndl."

Lifting the rifle, Philippa straightened her back, her golden braid assuming center.

Troilo could envision the faint shape of the chamois' antlers down her barrel. It was the perfect shot, but she wouldn't take it.

"It is no different than a pheasant," Archduke Franz assured.

Philippa lowered the barrel with a heavy sigh.

"Here," said Duke Sixten, lifting it for her.

Troilo studied the duke's other hand as it found the cinched waist of her striped, brown dress, the throbbing pulse in his veins a tart reminder of his own humanness.

"Oh, Franzi." Philippa dropped the rifle, tearing herself away. "I cannot!"

"It is the easiest shot in the world!"

Duke Sixten grinned haughtily. "Her Highness has a soft spot for goats, it would seem."

"Doctor, would you like to break our tie?" Philippa asked, turning to him.

"I will take this one," said Duke Sixten, intercepting the rifle.

As he took aim, Troilo focused on the chamois with one, loud thought.

Run.

The tail of the chamois disappeared into the woods faster than Duke Sixten could fire.

"Redemption is not in the cards today." A grin stretched beneath the mustache of Archduke Franz. "How did it know?"

"Chamois are remarkably intuitive."

"Oh?" Duke Sixten turned to Troilo. "I was not aware there were chamois in Italy."

"Istria."

"I do not recall asking," he rebuffed.

His imposing stare, his lofty tone. The duke had always hated to lose.

"Herr Visconti!" Erzsi called from the shade. "Will you accompany me to the horses so I may retrieve my parasol? I am dreadfully hot."

"Certainly, Highness."

"I shall join you, Herr Visconti," said Governess Coudenhove, practically leaping to his side. "I need to stretch my legs."

At last, her chance had arrived. Incapable of loving or not, Doctor Visconti had been vulnerable enough to express such a thing to her on their walk together, and with time and patience, perhaps he would see that starting over was possible. And when he did, *she* would be there waiting.

"Not leaving just yet, are you, Doctor?" Philippa asked. "We have not broken our tie."

Duke Sixten seemed to laugh under his breath, more annoyed than he was already.

"The victory is yours, Highness," Doctor Visconti replied, turning his back to her.

"Be mindful of the tall grass," Archduke Franz reminded.

"Do not worry, Mellie," Erzsi called over. "Herr Visconti will protect you if they come near."

"A serpent charmer, are you, Doctor?" asked the duke.

"It is only a byproduct of my travels, Your Grace."

"Hm." Duke Sixten erected himself. "It is in your blood, I suppose."

What had Doctor Visconti done to warrant such a comment?

"Come, Fräulein," he urged. "Watch your step, there."

Mellie looked back as they disappeared over the grassy hill. "I believe Duke Sixten is envious of your score," she said, stumbling a bit. "I hope you are not offended."

"He was merely referencing the *biscione* on my heraldry."

"Pardon? I do not..."

"The grass snake on the Visconti crest is depicted with a human in its mouth. It is a common misinterpretation that the biscione is devouring it, when in fact, it is giving birth to it."

"Well." Mellie took a deep breath. "It is Duke Sixten it reflects badly on. His behavior does nothing to help those terrible rumors."

"I have known men like the duke." Pushing his hair from his forehead, Doctor Visconti turned to her with a smirk. "We study them in my profession."

Mellie looked to her feet. "I myself was quite surprised by your marksmanship."

He laughed a bit. "Archery was an integral part of my upbringing. My sister's son and I would hunt together often."

"Oh, yes—your nephew?"

"He was..." Doctor Visconti's expression seemed to harden as he cast his gaze to the wood line, where the horses flicked their tails. "More like a brother. We were so close in age."

"Do you ever find that you miss Istria?"

"It was only home because *she* was there." He shook his head, appearing deep in thought. "Without her, I have no reason to ever return."

"Your wife..."

"Yes."

A breeze whispered the grass around them, loudly enough that Mellie had to make an effort to talk over it.

"It seems a lonely way to live, to belong to no banner or country," she said.

"On the contrary, Fräulein," he replied. "I am a citizen of the world. And I have seen more of its virtues than most can claim."

"When you are finished treating Her Highness, will you return to Switzerland?"

Met by his smile, she could have melted.

"That is the plan, yes," he replied, holding her gaze.

"Doctor! Fräulein Coudenhove!" Erzsi shouted, running through the sea of emerald grass. "We are finished!"

"Already?" Mellie asked.

She'd hardly had ten minutes with him!

"I am not one to protest," Erzsi replied, the rest of them in tow behind her.

"But..." Mellie squinted into the sun, finding Duke Sixten. "The day is still young."

"Her Highness is tired."

"I am easily winded," Philippa added, hanging on his arm. "I spend far too much time in bed these days. Doctor, I cannot shake the feeling that you let me win..."

"I did nothing of the sort," he replied. "Your Highness."

Frowning, Erzsi studied Troilo, whose demeanor had changed from reticent to playful in the blink of an eye.

Some distraction Mellie was! It had only taken a simple remark from Philippa to eclipse her presence entirely.

"I will send the huntsman to retrieve the game," Archduke Franz called over. "Come along, everyone!"

Philippa tipped her hat with a smirk as Duke Sixten pulled her away. And as though he'd only just remembered she was standing there, Troilo turned to see Mellie finding her horse.

Perhaps Erzsi had underestimated the allure Philippa had over him. But Troilo was a professional, and certainly he would know the dangers of entangling himself with a patient. No, Troilo wouldn't let his attraction to her interfere with finding a cure.

He had promised to help, after all.

Light spots trickled through the crown of leaves, falling over the party as Franz led the way through the woods.

"You said you were from Istria," he called back to Troilo, who rode adjacent to Erzsi and Mellie at the back. "Where about?"

"Pićan," Troilo replied. "A tiny village right outside of Pazin."

"Pićan!"

"You have been, Your Highness?"

"Oh yes, Fräulein. Pićan has the most wondrous overlook in all of Istria." Franz glanced at the duke, riding next to him. "They are known for their wine, which Duke Sixten and I spent many a night sampling."

"What is it like?" asked Philippa.

Duke Sixten slowed his pace to match her. "When you are cured, I will take you there and you will see for yourself," he replied.

Erzsi rolled her eyes. Only two days he'd been at Kaiservilla, and he was already offering her the world on a platter.

"Perhaps we will all take a trip to the heart of old Imperial Istria." Franz turned his cheek to Philippa. "You and I have ancestors who lived in the Pazin Castle."

"This is the first I've heard of an Imperial Istria," said Philippa.

"The Habsburg monarchy reigned over Pazin territory in the 1430s after a long fight with the Venetians," Franz replied. "In fact, if I am not mistaken, I believe one of them was a daughter of Bernabò Visconti." He tugged the reins, causing his horse to snort in retaliation. "If what they say about Bernabò is true, I am certain we have a common ancestor, Herr Visconti!"

Philippa laughed. "What do they say about Bernabò? Do tell, brother."

"He had upwards of thirty children. Half of them illegitimate."

"Thirty?"

"Let me be the first to tell you, there is a legend regarding our ancestors..."

Erzsi groaned under her breath at the oncoming history lesson.

"A great fire nearly destroyed the castle in 1433 when lightning struck the tower." Franz chuckled. "It was said that destruction was brought upon the castle by malefic forces."

Erzsi glanced at Troilo next to her, only to see that his knuckles had drained of color from holding the reins so tight. *"Troilo,"* she whispered.

But he seemed not to hear her.

"According to the proprietor of the vineyard—I will try my best to recall this properly, as I was a bit incoherent at the time—there was a great betrayal that occurred between the Duke of Pazin and one of his fellow knights, when the knight abducted the duke's mistress."

A windsong swept through the treetops, so strong that it beckoned Erzsi to look up.

"It is said the knight was the son of a dragon," Franz went on. "The duke sent a party to retrieve his mistress, without knowing that she was a seductress and witch, who had pitted the two men against each other. When they arrived, the wolves of the forest shredded his men to pieces."

"Troilo," Erzsi whispered again.

The party slowed to a halt as each rider met the eyes of their neighbor, taking notice of the stillness. All but Troilo, who was transfixed forward.

"Do you hear that?" Erzsi asked.

"Hear what?" he breathed.

The wind had stopped blowing. The birds had stopped chirping. Aside from the horses' hooves, the forest had fallen deadly quiet, as if all its inhabitants were listening.

"What happened then?" Philippa asked.

"Some say that before she was slain, the witch summoned a great storm," Franz replied, picking up the pace. "Others say it was the knight taking his dragon form to avenge the death of his lover."

"What a terribly sad story," she protested.

"You do not believe the duke escaping the fire was a happy ending?" Duke Sixten countered. "He was the one betrayed, after all, from what I can understand."

Franz relaxed into a laugh. "It is merely local folklore, an intriguing tale nonetheless."

Philippa seemed to tense considerably as they emerged from the wooded trail with the steeples of Marmorschlossl in view.

"Are you well, Pippa?"

"It is the heat, Franzi," she replied, laying her palm across the front of her corset. "I have exhausted myself."

"We will soon be back inside and out of the sun."

Something was wrong—and Erzsi knew Troilo could feel it, too. Directing his horse to Philippa's left side, he trotted alongside her.

"Take my hand, Highness." Duke Sixten moved closer, bumping Philippa's horse with his. "There is no reason to be nervous."

Now sandwiched between them, she smiled down at her shaky fingers, then mouthed something to Troilo—something Erzsi could not quite make out. Whatever it was, though, he seemed to understand it.

"Sweet sister—you have lost all color in your face," Franz added.

Philippa let out a sharp sigh, clutching her abdomen. "Have I?"

Troilo reached over, lowering his voice. "Highness, may I—?"

"*You may not,*" Duke Sixten snapped back. "Here. Take my hand."

"Stop it, both of—!" Furiously, Philippa began to tear at the top of her dress, as though she'd been overtaken by a malefic force herself. "I cannot breathe," she whimpered. "The corset—I cannot *breathe!*"

"What is happening?" Franz demanded.

"*It is her,*" Philippa gasped.

"What—?"

The porkpie hat tumbled from her head, releasing Philippa's braid like the tail of a wild stallion as she took off in full gallop toward the marble cottage.

"Pippa, wait!" Erzsi called, taking off after her.

She'd witnessed enough of Philippa's fits to know she could not safely ride during one. If she lost control of her limbs, as she often did, she could fall off—and at such a speed?

Erzsi glanced back over her shoulder, to the sound of thundering hooves behind her. Duke Sixten was leading, and by the time Erzsi turned forward again, he'd surpassed her. Even from a distance, she could see that Philippa's body was starting to succumb to the tremors as she slipped down from her horse, and clawed her way up the veranda stairs.

Skidding to a halt, Erzsi jumped to the ground.

"Doctor Visconti!" a maid called from the door.

Over Erzsi's shoulder, Troilo leapt down from his horse.

"You must come quick—Her Highness has locked herself in her room!"

Troilo lifted his gaze to the second floor.

As the air settled, Erzsi heard it, too—faint shouting. "Troilo, wait!" she shouted, chasing him through the cottage doors, where the servants wore their discomfort plainly as banging rattled down the staircase.

Erzsi rushed for Philippa's room, but Troilo stopped her.

"Stay," he ordered, stepping ahead.

"What is—?" Franz, now at Erzsi's side, had only just begun to speak when Troilo snapped at him.

"Highness! I suggest you take control of your subordinate *before I am forced to do it myself!*"

Erzsi had never seen her cousin tremble—not before men, or beasts he hunted—but as his lips parted in awe beneath his thick mustache, she could see that Franz was afraid.

"Philippa, let me in!"

Brought back to reality by the shouts of the duke, Franz blinked, then nodded.

The sound of Duke Sixten's fist striking her wooden door grated every chord of Troilo's nervous system as they climbed the stairs.

"Please, darling, just..."

"For Christ's sake, man!" yelled the archduke. "Control yourself!"

It was Troilo's eye that the duke met first when he looked down the hall, pushing the stray blond hair from his brow as he wiped his forehead.

As if he'd just woken from a dream, he straggled away from the door. "I do not know what came over me."

"God knows I go mad, too—seeing her in the grasp of this illness. But you must control your passions."

Troilo bit his tongue as Duke Sixten halted momentarily in front of him.

"Come," the archduke urged. "We must leave Doctor Visconti to his treatment."

The hallway felt cold as Troilo turned back to Philippa's room, now quiet.

Part of her had recognized the Istrian legend, now skewed by history. The version of their story that had villainized the innocent—the blame for which lay partially at Troilo's feet.

He had known it as he'd sat perched atop Mesjec at the highest point, watching the flames of the Pazin tower reach heavenward under a crimson sky, that Costanza's name would be lost to history, but this tragedy would be remembered for decades to come. As steadily as the rain that fell upon the ruins that night, Troilo had stood by as witness to the incineration of all those he'd once called family. And when the screams of their wives and children had erupted from the valley below, he knew he had tainted Costanza's memory for the purpose of vengeance.

Please, will you come to me?

The voice in Troilo's head was so clear he could have sworn Philippa had spoken out loud, and, exorcising the smell of burning flesh from his nostrils, he turned his attention once again to her bedroom down the hall.

Please, spirit, she begged. *I do not know if my thoughts are my own, or...*

"Highness," he said, knocking softly on her door. "It is Doctor Visconti. May I come in?"

Met by silence, he knocked again, but still there was nothing. Even the voice in his head had faded.

Abandoning her door, Troilo stepped into his bedroom and looked to the fault line in the wallpaper. The master key.

The marble passageway smelled of old wood, and Troilo noted the single window as he walked through a cloud of dust, lit by its rays. She had suggested he use this route to visit her the night of the storm, and as he reached the other side, Troilo wondered how many of her lovers had touched the same latch.

Stripped down to her underdress, Philippa scrambled to her feet in a half-unlaced corset as he emerged from the wall next to her vanity.

Her eyes, which seemed a darker shade, swirled with recognition. Something was—

"*Troilo,*" she gasped.

For all the many words he'd written for her, it was the hundreds of unspoken ones that overtook him now. "*Costanza?*"

"Why did you—?"

Troilo seized her. "Five hundred years, Stanzi—*five hundred years!*" he exclaimed. "I have waited without so much as a word, did you hate me so much?"

Tears streamed down Philippa's cheeks faster than he could wipe them away.

"Why did you not come?" she whimpered.

"*I did come for you,*" Troilo countered, feeling his mind slip backward, to a past he never wished to revisit. "I..."

"Your presence is greatly missed here. By me, most of all."

Troilo had not expected his welcome to be so warm when he'd arrived at the castle in his armor, and certainly he hadn't expected for the duke to receive him at the gate.

"I am still your loyal subject," he had replied. "As is Luka Indrigo."

"You have come to ask for his job?"

"I have come to take responsibility, Your Grace." Troilo halted in front of the courtyard, squaring his shoulders. "The fault is mine and mine alone."

As though the entirety of the court sought a glimpse of the exiled knight, the halls of the castle swarmed with nobles. Yet, as they looked upon Troilo, it was something closer to pity than disdain.

"Is there nothing I can do to mend this betrayal?"

Resting both hands on the courtyard's stone ledge, the duke turned to him with lively eyes. "I will tell you this, Troilo—let us settle this as men."

"A duel, Your Grace?"

"For old time's sake," he'd coaxed. "If you win, I will reenlist Indrigo as the goldsmith."

"And if you win?"

"Against you, Troilo? I do not imagine I will."

"I tried to reach you," Troilo whispered.

It was Philippa's body he held in an embrace, but Costanza that trembled beneath his touch.

"But I was..."

"It seems we have an audience," the duke had remarked, pointing his sword at the ledge.

By the time he had emerged ready and armored in the courtyard, all the stairwells had been blocked by spectators there to watch the duel.

"We both know you are the better swordsman, so it is only fair that I strike first!" the duke exclaimed, throwing his sword against Troilo's in a fit of fury.

Crossing his blade, Troilo pushed him back, then swung himself.

"You may see I have become better in your absence," added the duke, motioning for him to throw another.

Troilo swung his sword right, then left, blocked both times. "Compliments to you, Your Grace."

"While I have your ear," he replied, sliding the edge of his blade against Troilo's, "may I be honest with you?"

Troilo!

An anxious plea slid down the bond from Costanza, seizing Troilo's attention.

The duke threw a strike, knocking him off balance. "There is something you should know about your bride," he said, circling him. "I have intercepted the most dreadful gossip about her..."

"What are you——?"

"Witchcraft in Pazin! They say that the child in her belly is the devil's seed."

Turning his attention on Costanza's sight, Troilo could see a battery of soldiers outside their cottage, but the duke quickly threw another strike at him, forcing him out of it.

"Show us!"

"What—?"

"Show us the power you wield," the duke commanded.

"We fight as men!"

"You are no man, Troilo." His tone was an eerie calm, his smile sinister. "Summon a storm large enough for my men to see, and she is safe!"

Troilo stumbled back, gripping his sword. Veins pulsating, he closed his eyes. He tried with all his might, but only clouds came.

"Come—is this the best you can do?" the duke taunted. "Call the wind!"

"I cannot," Troilo breathed.

The duke laughed, raising his chin to the crowd on the balcony. "This is what you have all been waiting for!"

Troilo again closed his eyes, but there was no connection to the sky.

"Behold, your zmaj! Castrated from his power!"

With all his human strength, Troilo rammed the duke against the stone wall. "I will still spill your blood, with everyone as witness!"

A flicker of satisfaction flashed across his dark eyes as he leaned in closer, between the blades. "Then I shall send your regards to Costanza, brother," he scorned through his teeth.

Through her sight, Troilo could see that she was on her back, a soldier spreading her legs forcefully as another pinned her to the table.

"She is rather plain. With distance I have seen that my affections were merely circumstantial," he added. "I told the soldiers to take what they like from her."

Troilo charged for the stairs, his vision blinded by flashes of white fur and bloodshed.

"Do not stop him!" the duke had called as Troilo barreled his way through the crowd. "Let him run to her!"

"I was too late." Troilo closed his eyes, breathing deep into her braided hair. "I should have listened to you. When you begged me not to go, I should have..."

The smell of honey and marzipan tickled his senses, reminding him of where he stood, and who he held. Philippa, who, despite the way she reflected Costanza's likeness like a diamond—was a woman all her own.

Troilo drew back, his own face now streaked with tears.

"Come with me," Philippa whispered absently, running her fingers across her neck. "Come with me and there will be no pain..."

Lifting her chin, Troilo could see the birthmark, four lines all in a row. Just like gills.

Troilo's mind again slipped backward to the quarry.

"Come back," he'd sobbed, kneeling in the water. "Please, give her back to me—I will do anything you ask, anything of any God..."

The she-wolf howled from the shore, surrounded by bodies of slain soldiers, her fur now pink with blood.

Clutching Costanza's lifeless body, Troilo pleaded for her return. He begged to be taken instead.

She had died for him.

Because of him.

"What do the legends say?" His sobs turned to near hysterical laughs as he called out to the darkening sky above. "That to wed a dragon destines one to an unfortunate fate?"

Troilo brought her cold cheek to his. "Please," he whispered, removing the wedding band from her finger, "I cannot bear another day of this life without you..."

As he spoke to her, a flash of light had rippled beneath the surface of the crimson water, as quick and sudden as a strike of lightning.

.   .   .

"You stand on the shore," Troilo murmured to himself, studying the birthmark closer. "She is one with the water…"

The meaning of the old woman's riddle had been literal.

"Rusalka."

On the verge of death, Costanza had made a pact with one of these mermaid-like spirits, known for their beguiling beauty.

"As sweet as a siren's song," Troilo whispered, echoing what Felix had told him.

At last, he understood the piece of the equation that had always managed to elude him—Costanza's silence from beyond the grave. She had been taken by the rusulki and remade in the Otherworld, where no human medium could reach her.

Gathering her face in his hands again, Troilo spoke a steady command. "Philippa, you must *come back.*"

Philippa blinked, then looked around the room as if she'd just woken up.

"Come back to me," Troilo hushed. "It is all right."

He could imagine what alarm might set in when she realized she was stripped down to her undergarments, eyes burning with tears she would not remember crying.

Instead of panicking as she lifted her wet lashes to Troilo, Philippa reached out to touch his cheek, grazing her fingers against the wet streaks tenderly.

Coiling his arms around her, he nearly lifted her off the ground. As much as Troilo had wanted to hold onto Costanza's essence a little longer, his heart had anchored itself here now.

"I felt her again," Philippa whispered into his shoulder, "your Stanzi."

"I know," he whispered back.

Arms still around him, she drew back with a scrutinizing look. "*Why* am I half-dressed?"

What happiness it was to be teased by her. Troilo couldn't help but grin in response.

"Would you, please." Turning her back to him, she clutched her stomach, still restricted beneath the corset.

Troilo reached for the remaining laces, unstringing them one by one.

"What happened to me?" Philippa asked, watching him over her shoulder.

Troilo swallowed hard as he focused on the corset. Instead of recognizing Costanza as part of *herself,* Philippa was experiencing her as an external spirit. Between this life and the last, her soul had been fractured. And given that the traumatized fragment could take over Philippa's conscious faculties on a whim, this was especially dangerous.

"You slipped into an altered state," Troilo said, pulling the last lace.

Philippa lifted the corset over her head, slinging it to the floor. "I *am* mad," she said, finding the edge of her bed.

"In ancient times you might have been a great priestess," said Troilo. "Just because it is one of the many notions this modern world has left behind, does not mean it no longer exists."

Undoing her braid, Philippa combed the ends of her hair with her fingers until its length flowed down in a golden stream, pooling onto the bed.

"The waters of madness are the same in which mystics swim," Troilo added. "What makes it *madness,* is that the person does not realize they have fallen through a puddle."

Philippa brought both knees to her chest. "Is that what happened to me, just now?"

"Yes." Crossing the distance of the room, Troilo took a seat on the edge of her bed. "And we must never allow it to happen again."

Her coruscant gaze brimmed over with curiosity.

"There are ways to control these things," he went on. "You can train yourself to summon it at will, so that it does not overtake you."

"But why *me?* Why does she choose me as her vessel?"

Abandoning his seat, Troilo walked to her vanity, noting its covered mirror. "There is something that connects the two of you," he murmured. "Something I cannot explain."

Scanning the artifacts across the top, he picked up the glass quill.

"Then what will you have me do?" Philippa asked behind him.

Studying the curvature of the quill, Troilo was struck with an idea. "Highness, are you familiar with the term 'automatic writing?'" he asked, turning to her.

She shook her head.

"It is when a medium goes into a trance and channels messages through written word."

"You want me to..."

"For one week, you will set aside time each day to sit at your vanity," said Troilo, handing her the quill. "You will begin by focusing on a pinprick of light in your chest...then, relinquishing all thought, you will invite her to speak through your pen."

"Your *wife.*"

So many nights Troilo had spent alone, making love to the remembrance of her, offering his climax in the hope it may draw her spirit to him. All the times he wished himself dead, he could have never foreseen that he might live long enough to meet her again.

Philippa tugged on the quill, reminding him to let go.

"Yes," Troilo said, releasing his grip. "This will ensure you do not slip into an altered state again unexpectedly."

"Herr Visconti, are you up here?"

"If I do as you suggest," Philippa went on, ignoring the call of Governess Coudenhove, "if I allow her to speak through my pen—"

Troilo moved for the door, but Philippa slid down from the bed, blocking his exit.

"How do you know I will not drown in her memories?"

He looked her over, their faces a mere inch apart. It was a controlled experiment at best—the hope that if Philippa could tell herself the story of her past life, then perhaps her soul could at last integrate it.

"Your silence is concerning," she added.

"I do not know," Troilo admitted. "But—"

"Oh, what a very comforting thought..."

"I promise that if the need arises," Troilo whispered, leaning in, "I will bring you back myself."

Philippa lifted her gaze to his, her back pressed against the hollow wood. "That is what they say about you," she murmured. "That you have a knack for finding what is lost."

"Herr Visconti...?"

"There is one more condition, Highness," he added.

She eyed him with a subtle squint.

"You must not read back what you have written," he said, reaching for the doorknob behind her. "I will read it myself at the end of the week."

Governess Coudenhove was nowhere to be found when Troilo emerged from Philippa's room. He paced the hall, checking each room for any sign of motion, and then—

"Fräulein."

The governess clasped both hands in front, standing at attention in the center of his bedroom. "Ah, there you are."

"I thought I heard you calling for me," he said, eyes circling the room.

Foolishly, he'd left the corridor door cracked open.

"How is Her Highness?"

Troilo did not budge from his place in the doorway. "The fit has subsided," he replied, pocketing both hands.

"Wonderful," said Governess Coudenhove. "That is wonderful news." But the words were tart on her tongue, sounding anything but wonderful. "Archduke Franz and Duke Sixten have retired to the villa for the remainder of the day."

"That is for the best," said Troilo.

She turned to the window. "It is a shame the day was cut short."

The day—meaning their time together. Either he hadn't been clear enough, or she had chosen to ignore his boundary.

Troilo glanced again to the cracked corridor door.

"I shall leave you, then," the governess said suddenly.

"Fräulein," he protested, stopping her on the way out, "did you need something from me?"

Smiling sweetly, she shook her head.

NINE

June 21, 1900 — *present day*
11:15 A.M.

Leaving Inspector Ziegler in the parlor, Rudolf dragged his feet to the veranda, rehearsing what he would say with each lingering step. Surely, Archduchess Erzsi would not still be upset with him, would she? He hadn't meant to antagonize her. And how was he supposed to know she would be so indignant?

Rudolf halted outside of the glass door. Reading beneath the canopy of luxuriant creepers that hung from the veranda's tin roof, she looked peaceful enough. Perhaps she had cooled.

"Stay objective," Rudolf whispered, pushing the door open.

Archduchess Erzsi looked up from her book as he stepped outside. "Oh," she sighed. "It is *you.*"

"Your Royal and Imperial Highness." He tried to smile, but all that would come was a tight, thin line. "Would you mind if I join you?"

Her wintry eyes—despite how they shimmered like crown jewels—studied him as a wolf might study prey. "In fact, I would," she replied. *"Mind,* that is."

"Yes, well..." Rudolf motioned subtly to the parlor window, where Inspector Ziegler paced inside, awaiting information. "You see, I find myself in a predicament."

"Hm." Archduchess Erzsi seemed to follow. "Inspector Ziegler has asked you to speak with me."

A grin found Rudolf more easily this time, though he could imagine how awkward he looked.

"Well, I have told him everything I know, and I have nothing left to say."

"Perhaps then, you will allow me to sit with you, so it appears that I have done my job?"

Archduchess Erzsi shut her book, looking almost entertained.

"I do need to impress him."

"Very well," she said, motioning to the wicker chair across from her.

"Thank you, Your Highness."

"Do you find him ornery?"

"Inspector Ziegler?"

"He is much grumpier than I remember."

"Well, his meticulous nature is what makes him so good at his job."

"And in time you will prove yourself to be worthy of his praise?"

Rudolf rubbed the back of his neck, unsure if she was teasing him. "Yes, Your Highness. That is the hope."

"You may call me Erzsi, if you like."

Rudolf opened his mouth to speak, but nothing came out. She wanted him to address her by her first name?

Erzsi's brows raised in anticipation. "And you, *Herr Kaspar,* are—?"

"Uh, Rudolf," he sputtered. "Highness."

"*Rudolf.*" She looked him over with exaggerated suspicion. "You share a name with my father."

Whether that was a good thing or a bad thing, her mannerisms did not indicate.

Rudolf glanced at the window, imagining Inspector Ziegler watching him through the glass.

Stay objective!

"What are you reading, if I may ask?" Rudolf asked, dropping his gaze to the blue book in her lap.

Erzsi slid it to him across the wicker table.

"Ballads of the Starlight Menagerie." He read the gold inscribed letters aloud. "By Belarius."

"The author is unknown."

"Though a reader of Shakespeare, I'd venture to guess," Rudolf said, examining the woodcut of a shooting star on its title page. "And Shelley's publisher, no less."

He had studied both Jacobian playwrights and the Romantic poets at the University of Vienna. *Cymbeline* and *The Tempest* had been among his favorites of Shakespeare's plays.

"What?" Erzsi asked.

"Belarius. It is the name of one of the characters in *Cymbeline,*" said Rudolf, paging through. "I read it in school, before joining the force."

"And why did you join the force?"

"To touch a great mystery." He looked up, grinning. "Do you often read poetry?"

"I prefer mystery novels, myself," Erzsi replied, holding his eye. "But this was dear to Philippa—perhaps one of my only links to her, now."

Rudolf, reminding himself yet again to focus on the objective at hand, looked up at Erzsi with full attention. "Chief Inspector has told me of your concerns. Have you no hope at all that your cousin might still be alive?"

"Hope is a sister to denial, and both, more blinding than the sun." Erzsi set her sights past the oak trees. "How old are you, Rudolf Kaspar?"

"I am twenty."

"I am seventeen. The same age as my father's late mistress." Her breathy laugh was tinged with judgement and disdain. "I thought that when I reached the same age, I might understand what would have possessed her to agree to die by his side."

"Love, perhaps."

As Erzsi turned slowly toward him, Rudolf knew he'd said the wrong thing.

"Stupidity," she murmured. "A waste of a perfectly good life."

Rudolf had spent much of his boyhood wondering about the daughter the Crown Prince had left behind that fateful winter day. Complicated grief was perhaps the only thing he and Erzsi had in common.

"Inspector Ziegler told me he was on the scene at..."

"Mayerling?" Erzsi finished.

"Yes," Rudolf murmured.

"And am I what you expected?"

"I must admit I have not given it much thought," he admitted. "I could not have imagined a world where you would one day be sitting across from me."

That made her smile again, but barely.

"Archduchess—?"

"Erzsi."

"Erzsi." Rudolf paused. "May I speak frankly?"

"Nothing has stopped you so far."

"Inspector Ziegler has always spoken highly of your father."

Crossing her arms, she leaned back in her chair. "Everyone speaks highly of the dead."

"The Crown Prince wanted to reform the country, make it more progressive, did he not?"

"Certainly *that* is not what your Inspector speaks highly about."

"Well, no, but—"

"Leaving my family to scrounge for an heir was a funny way to do it."

"Right."

Apparently, sharing a name with her father was *not* a positive association, after all.

"Do not think me bitter," she added. "I have forgiven him. Besides, his death taught me more about life than he ever could have."

"There is no teacher quite like death."

"You do not say?"

Rudolf looked to the window, which was now free of Inspector Ziegler's prying eyes. "My own father's passing was a great relief to me," he said, turning back to Erzsi. "I have yet to forgive him for his cruelty toward my mother."

"Then you know *his kind*." Erzsi motioned to the body bag of Duke Sixten, being threaded by constables. "And why I am glad he is dead."

"Your Highness...erm, *Erzsi*." Rudolf lowered his voice, adopting a more serious tone. "What do *you* believe happened last night?"

"Is it not clear to you?"

"No," he murmured. "Not immediately."

"I believe the duke tried to have his way with her," Erzsi sighed. "And that she defended herself out of necessity, but..."

Rudolf leaned in closer, and she met his eye.

"He would have given her a terrible beating in the process."

There was fear in her eyes, as though Erzsi had witnessed this violence firsthand. Rudolf, well acquainted with that look, could not bring himself to hold her gaze.

"Is it true what they say about her?" he asked, changing the subject. "That she is..."

"Mad?" Erzsi laughed to herself. "I encourage you not to believe everything you read, Rudolf."

Relaxing a bit, he let out a quiet chuckle.

"Pippa was a romantic," she went on. "She lived with one foot in another world. No one ever tried to understand her."

"Except you. You understood her, yes?"

"She was a sister to me," Erzsi replied earnestly.

"And Doctor Visconti," Rudolf poked. *He* understood her?"

"In a way not even I could."

"Fräulein Coudenhove has suggested that you are in possession of a collection of poems that he wrote for her."

"I am not."

Rudolf inhaled deeply, then released the air from his lungs.

"But if you are looking for Troilo's little green journal, then I am certain you would find it in his desk, among everything else he left behind."

"In his desk," Rudolf stuttered as he moved to hand *Ballads of the Starlight Menagerie* back. "Thank you."

"Read it at your leisure," she said, hopping up from her seat. "I just finished."

Holding the book in his hand, he looked as though he didn't know if he should accept it.

"Are you allowed?" Erzsi taunted over her shoulder.

"Uh—" Rudolf stuttered, pulling the book to his chest. "Of course I am allowed."

"Good!"

He blinked, then Erzsi blinked. Something in her wanted to laugh.

"Enjoy it then," she added, opening the cottage door.

On the other side of the glass, Erzsi exhaled. The foyer had never been dirtier, and its parquet floors never so tarnished. It had also never felt so empty. All at once, Erzsi felt like a little girl again, orphaned in the wake of another loss.

The sound of nails clicked across the wood, drawing her attention to the hall, where Blitz stood in front of the parlor doorway.

"There you are, Blitz." Walking over, it took only a minute for Erzsi to notice Inspector Ziegler standing in the parlor with his smoking pipe, open book in hand. "Inspector," she said, picking up the dog. "You are still here."

"I need quiet to think." Meeting her gaze, it seemed as though the book was suddenly hot in his hands. "My apologies, Your Highness," he said, extending it to her. "I believe this belongs to you."

"Oh no," Erzsi sighed, almost playfully, as she eyed Philippa's diary. "It is not my story."

Ziegler retracted the book.

"Do you like to read, Inspector?"

"Once in a while," he admitted gruffly.

"Yes, well. I suppose you and Herr Kasper differ in that way." Erzsi's fingers circled the fluffy tuff of Blitz's cheek. "You may return it to the library if you do not wish to read it. Though..."

The pipe stem found Ziegler's lips.

"My cousin was a gifted storyteller." Erzsi smirked as she slid out of view and back into the hallway. "A gifted storyteller indeed."

The Sky Flower's Bride

PART II

When Costanza arrived in Pazin that winter with her father, she found neither Troilo nor the duke waiting at the castle gate to retrieve her from the cold. Instead, she was greeted by the usual guard, who eyed her in a similar manner as the duke each time her father turned his head.

"Mistress," he greeted as another guard took Mjesec's reins.

Costanza glanced up to the loupe hole above them, wondering if Troilo might be watching from the other side of the castle wall. "Where is His Grace?" she asked, taking her father's hand as he helped her down.

"He is in the courtyard," said the guard. "Come with me."

Costanza's father coaxed her to follow when she glanced back at him.

Even he had seemed to notice how her complexion had paled in her months away, and soft bags hung beneath her green eyes, as though she might be pining for someone all hours of the night.

A fire roared in the hearth of the great hall, which smelled of winter spruce.

"Please remain here," the guard ordered, leaving her in the company of the crackling flame. "I will alert His Grace of your arrival."

Costanza nodded, craning her neck as he disappeared around the corner. Then, knowing where Troilo could be found, she made a quiet rush for the door.

Hit with the chill of the outside, as well as the stares of the ladies in waiting who watched from the courtyard ledge, Costanza shrunk back around the stone corner.

"You do me no favors to let me win," the duke jested among the echoes of clashing swords below.

Peering down, Costanza smiled at the sight of Troilo.

"I do no such thing," he swore, reaching up to wipe the sweat from his brow.

"It would be a shame to embarrass you." The duke motioned to the ladies on the ledge. "We have an audience."

Troilo smiled handsomely up at them, straightening his shoulders. "Then we must give them a show," he taunted back.

Costanza swallowed hard as the duke threw his sword, which Troilo blocked.

"When are you going to tell me which one is keeping you up all hours of the night?" the duke asked as he circled him.

"I will never tell," Troilo teased, running his blade along the edge of the duke's.

Costanza bit her bottom lip. It was hard not to grin at the thought of him retiring early to bed to meet her in his dreams.

"Indeed, seduction takes time," the duke replied. "In my experience."

Troilo dropped his sword. "May I be honest with you, Your Grace?"

"You have my ear."

"I do not see the appeal of your peasant girl," he said. "She is rather plain."

Feeling the eyes of the ladies on her, Costanza's stomach dropped as they giggled amongst themselves.

Troilo had told her it was an act—was he still acting?

"She is a *ripe apple,* ready for picking." The duke flashed him a grin, urging him to swing. "You would not understand."

Troilo threw his sword, hard and fast.

"You will see," the duke grunted, holding the crossed swords. "She will warm my bed, and once she does, you will be green with envy!"

Costanza turned her back flush to the stone, nauseated.

"It is foolish to waste your affections when the fruits of the court are so plentiful."

"I presume you speak from experience," said the duke, pinging the end of his sword.

"Your Grace," called the guard from the other side of the ledge. "The goldsmith and his daughter have arrived."

Looking down upon the courtyard one last time, Costanza watched the duke toss Troilo a sly grin as he handed off his sword.

"Now, go and do what you do best," he said, nodding to Lady Melisande on the ledge.

By the time Costanza reached the great hall, she was perspiring and out of breath. The Troilo she had just witnessed was a different man than the one she had come to know, talking about her in such a way, and so openly!

"Costanza."

The duke was smiling when she turned to him, holding an arrangement of camellias in one hand.

"Forgive me, Your Grace," she said, clutching her stomach. "But I feel as though I may..." Costanza sighed as she fell back, mentally preparing herself to hit the floor.

"Ah!" Catching her, the duke motioned for her to take his arm. "I will take you to rest at once."

The red flowers seemed only to mock her from the mantle as Costanza lay her head on the pillow. She had feigned fainting to avoid the duke, but had Troilo heard that she was ill? She had hoped he might come to her once the South Wing was quiet, but well into the night there was still no sign of him, in either body or mind.

When his voice finally stirred her from sleep, Costanza thought herself dreaming.

"At last."

She turned in his arms, met with the density of his flesh.

"I am sorry I did not come sooner," he whispered, leaning in to kiss her. "Are you ill?"

Shooting upright, Costanza hugged her knees. "You said you were not like him, but you are a matchless pair!" she countered. "I overheard you both in the courtyard, talking about me as though I were a common wench—"

"As an illegitimate son, I am free to ask your hand." Troilo traced her face with a gentle smile. "His Grace is the only barrier. What I say to him is merely a ploy to shift his interest elsewhere."

"It is an act, then, as you say," she scorned, turning toward the dying embers. "That is what I would expect you to say if you were here to bed me."

"I will not bed you until you are my wife," he said. "You have my word. I will not so much as attempt it."

"Even if you *were* successful in discouraging the duke, I have not agreed to be your bride," Costanza reminded. "The legends say that to wed a dragon destines a woman to an unfortunate fate."

The light of the dwindling hearth reflected in Troilo's eyes as he pulled her closer. "That cannot be true," he said, running his finger over her lips. "It is my fate that yields to yours."

"There are no longer seers," said Costanza. "There are only witches."

Surrendering to his kiss, she slid her hand over the muscles of his chest, expanding between breaths.

"Without my skin, I am as human as you," he said, laying his hand over hers.

Costanza could not fight it. If her fate would be unfortunate, she saw no reason not to kiss him fiercely, and revel in his every touch.

"Take me now," she gasped.

Laying her on her back, Troilo only shook his head as he lowered his lips to her navel. "Not until you are my wife."

Costanza awoke with the rising sun in an empty bed, feeling much more of a woman than she had the day before. Completely rejuvenated, she leapt out of bed and readied herself for breakfast with the duke in the banquet hall.

"My dear girl, you have risen with the sun!" he exclaimed as she entered.

Costanza took a seat at the end of his table, set with fish and fresh fruit. "Thank you, Your Grace," she said. "I am feeling much better."

"I trust you slept well?"

The chamber door closed, seizing his attention before she could answer.

"Ah, Sir Troilo," he remarked. "Fair morning to you."

The sight of him over her shoulder made Costanza go weak in the knees.

"Pardon my intrusion, Your Grace." From the platters of fruits, Troilo picked up an apple, fresh from the orchard. "I do not wish to interrupt," he said, tossing it in the air.

"Stay," said the duke, nodding to Costanza. "Honor us with your presence."

Troilo looked to her, then turned back to the duke, who eyed him with a coy smile.

"If it pleases you," Troilo replied, taking a seat at the halfway point between them.

"Join us for our ride today," the duke declared, taking a bite of fish. "I would like the two of you to become more acquainted."

Troilo's eyes taunted Costanza as he bit into the golden apple. *You are ravishing.*

She watched as he licked his lip, wet with fresh apple juice.

"Mistress," he greeted.

Costanza nodded, looking at him as though she hadn't slept against his chest in a state of pleasured bliss. "Sir Troilo."

"It is settled, then," the duke added cheerily.

For the remainder of her stay, Costanza tagged along on their hunts, and watched them sword fight from the courtyard ledge. Stolen glances and knowing smirks passed the days until nightfall, when Troilo would sneak off to her room while the castle slept. There, they would read the *Nibelungenlied* and learn the landscapes of one another in secret. He would sleep with Costanza wrapped in his arms until sunrise, then leave her with a kiss before returning to his own quarters. The Duke of Pazin sat with them at breakfast each morning, blissfully unaware of the affair happening under his nose.

Troilo had kept his promise to Costanza, even as the hunger to consummate their love grew greater. It was not until her final night in Pazin, when they faced the certainty of separation, did they finally give way to desire.

"A ring," said Troilo, holding the gold band to the firelight. "For a lady."

Costanza had never been so happy than when he slipped it onto her finger. A ring that Troilo had forged himself, away from the curious eyes of her father.

"Lady Costanza." Troilo ran his thumb over the engraved floral pattern. "We shall marry, and soon."

"What of His Grace?"

"Ever since I assured him that Lady Melisande is not my mistress, he seems to be taking more interest in her."

"You have done it, my love," said Costanza, kissing him. "I am yours."

"I shall find us a priest," he murmured.

Costanza brushed his bottom lip with hers, whispering only, "Let us be our own priest tonight."

Her grandmother was the first to notice the food aversions and fatigue over the weeks that followed. Costanza could feel that her body no longer belonged to her alone, but whether or not Troilo could sense the life teeming inside of her through their bond, she knew not.

"You must send word to him," her grandmother said, urging Costanza to eat a piece of bread. "Soon, you will start to show."

"It is far too dangerous a letter to send with Tata..."

"No, not a letter." The old woman dropped her gaze to the wooden table, indented with cuts from butchering. "Send word through your *bond*. Go to him in a dream, and tell him to send his response with your father."

Costanza felt sick, and not just because of the baby. The thought of her father knowing about her and Troilo troubled her deeply.

"You must be brave, child," said her grandmother, reading her mind. "For you are to be a mother."

That night when Costanza lay down, she envisioned Troilo as she did each night, only this time, she placed his hand on her belly. *Come to me,* she told him, drifting off to sleep. *Tell my father of our plan to marry.*

Word came three days later when Costanza's father returned from the castle.

"Sir Troilo has located a priest outside of Pazin," he said, avoiding eye contact with her as he walked in. "Costanza will travel there by moonlight tonight. He has asked that she meet him at the forest's edge just after midnight."

"I will accompany her," her grandmother declared.

Costanza's father eyed his mother with an uneasy stare.

"Tata."

Hesitantly, he turned to Costanza.

"I am sorry, Tata," she whispered.

He nodded to himself, steadying his balance with one hand on the wooden table.

"He is a *knight,* Luka," her grandmother hushed, wrapping both arms around her son's shoulders. "Sir Troilo will be a good provider, and our Costanza will be a lady. She will still be able to care for us as we always planned. It will more than make up for..."

Constanza could sense his disappointment, his fear. She knew that Troilo providing for her was the least of her father's worries.

"What is done is done," was all he said.

Costanza passed the time that day by pondering what life might look like for her once she was elevated to a lady. She thought of living at the castle with Troilo, in the company of the duke, who was likely already courting his new interest. Lady Melisande was a far better match for him, just as Costanza was for Troilo. She would even forgive Lady Melisande for her past slights, since they would now be equals.

Soon enough, nightfall came. Sitting atop Noć in a black cape, Troilo's armor glinted in the moonlight against the dark forest.

"Troilo!" Costanza gasped.

Sliding from his mount, he ran to greet her. "It is true, then?" he asked, bringing her forehead to his lips.

Costanza nodded as his fingers trailed the length of her hair, finding her stomach.

"I felt her presence," he said. "As though we were no longer alone in our bond."

"Her?"

Despite the dark, Costanza knew that he was smiling. Then, feeling her grandmother's quiet observation, they both turned to her.

"Thank you," said Troilo.

The old woman nodded, and Costanza thought for a moment he saw a smile among her wrinkles, filled with the wash of the full moon.

Troilo's thumb grazed her knuckles as she rode with her cheek to his back.

"Have you spoken with His Grace?" Costanza asked.

Troilo hesitated. "We will ride to the castle in the morning," he replied, squeezing her hand with reassurance. "I will tell him of our marriage then."

Costanza lifted her head. "Troilo, he will be angry!"

"He will be, at first. But Matthias is my friend—he would not want bad blood between brothers any more than I would, I am certain of it."

The moon shifted in the sky as they rode, drowning out the echoes of stars long dead. Rays of moonlight shimmered over the fields, illuminating the way, until at last, they came to a quaint stone bridge. Tying his Noć to a nearby trunk, Troilo helped Costanza down from the mount. She looked around, noting the family of trees with white petals that hung over the overpass. Only the sound of a gurgling creek was present.

Costanza peered over the bridge as Troilo led her across, tossing a bag of coins to the mysterious figure waiting for them in the shadows. Hastily, the priest motioned for them to join hands. Standing tall like a prince of night, Troilo grinned at her.

The priest chanted over them both in Latin, then asked them to repeat vows, but the real exchange between them was mind-to-mind.

Love of mine, divine star, Troilo thought, *I seek to make all your wishes come true.*

Costanza smiled back at him. *Dear Troilo, you are my greatest wish.*

The priest laid his hands on theirs, declaring them man and wife in the eyes of God.

Troilo drew back from their kiss, wiping away the single tear that had fallen down his cheek. "A mortal affliction," he whispered.

Noć snorted by the tree as Troilo untied him, offering Costanza a hand up.

Arms wrapped around his waist, she rode quietly, trying to soak in every detail of him before their inevitable parting. So lost in his scent, she did not realize that Troilo had veered toward the Sopat until she could hear the rushing of the waterfall.

"Where are you taking me?" she asked.

Troilo let out a low laugh as they halted near the rocks.

Holding her steady, he helped Costanza step from rock to rock, until they reached the quarry. It seemed ages since she had found him there the day of his falling.

Illuminated in the moonlight, a small unfinished cottage awaited them. For months, Troilo had labored away in his limited time, all for her.

"My Lady," he said. "Welcome home."

Their first night as newlyweds was blissful indeed, so much so that Costanza was sad to see the sun rise. Feeling more swollen than she had the day before, she mounted Noć with Troilo and they made their way to Pazin under an August sky. For as much as Costanza had pondered her future as a lady of the court, she could not envision it, as though something in her *knew* that they may no longer be welcome at the castle.

"Where is His Grace?" Troilo shouted to the guard as he dismounted.

"In the banquet hall, Sir Troilo."

Taking her by the hand, Troilo did not seem to notice the way the ladies and lords turned their heads as he and Costanza walked past.

"Please," he whispered, halting outside of the banquet hall. "Wait here, my love."

Costanza's stomach began to knot as she resigned herself to the door.

"Where have *you* been all night?" the duke jeered from inside. "Sit, have a drink with me!"

"I cannot, Your Grace. Perhaps another time."

Peeking around the corner, Costanza could see the brow of the duke twitching in question. "What has happened?" he asked, resting both hands on the table.

"I have taken a wife."

"A wife!" the duke exclaimed. "How could you keep such a thing from me? Well, who is she!"

"Costanza Indrigo."

"You astonish me! Only a few months ago you expressed disdain at her name, and now you steal her away in the night?" The duke laughed, but then his expression turned deadly serious. "Has she enchanted you with her charms?"

"Enchanted me?"

"Has she *bewitched* you?" he demanded. "Everyone has always said she is a peculiar girl. Solitary and strange."

A bolt of fear shot through Costanza as her thoughts slid back to her grandmother's warnings. How quickly her nature could be turned against her.

"No, Your Grace. I have married her on my own free will."

"Then you have betrayed me of your own free will."

"I..."

"Do not deny it," the duke warned.

"Your Grace, what of Lady Melisande?"

"What of her!"

Costanza covered her mouth to stifle her gasp as the wine glass went flying.

"Do you know what the peasants said of you when you first arrived? The ridiculous rumors I had to dispel? *All that you are* is because of me! Everything you have—your skills, your title, your money—is because of me!"

"I am eternally grateful for your patronage. You are like a brother to me, Matthias, which is why you must *hear* me..."

"Do not address me in such a manner!" the duke shouted, shoving the food off the table and onto the floor. "You have lost the right to address me by name!"

"Please," Troilo replied weakly. "She is carrying my child."

The duke glared long and hard, then walked to the hearth. *"Vipereos mores non violabo,"* he said, resting his hand on the mantle. "You are no brother of mine."

Emerging from the banquet hall, Troilo nearly knocked Costanza over. "We must leave," he whispered hastily.

"What of your things?" Costanza asked.

"I arrived with nothing, and I will leave with nothing."

He was noticeably flustered, which worried Costanza, but she would not ask questions until the castle was long behind them. Standing at the courtyard's ledge, Lady Elisabetta met Troilo with concerned violent eyes as she lifted her veil.

"Your Ladyship," he said, voice shaking as he kissed her hand.

For the first time Costanza could recall, Lady Elisabetta looked directly at her.

"May I introduce my wife," Troilo added. "Lady Costanza Visconti."

The lady nodded to Costanza. "Send word when the child arrives," she said, turning back to Troilo. "When he or she comes of age, I will take the child under my patronage."

Whether or not Lady Elisabetta believed fully that Troilo was her blood brother, the love between them did not suffer for it.

"Then we shall name her after you, My Lady," said Costanza.

"I thank you for your generosity." Troilo dropped his gaze. "I will cherish it always."

Lady Elisabetta looked past him, to where her son resided down the hall. "Troilo," she said, lifting his chin gently. "You must not look back."

Managing a solemn nod, he released her. "Farewell, dear sister."

Months passed and Costanza's belly grew, as did the widening gap between Troilo and the Duke of Pazin. Rumors spread that without Troilo there to manage him, the duke had become increasingly withdrawn and paranoid. Costanza's father, guilty by association, had been stripped of his role as the royal goldsmith and told never to return.

Freed from a life of courtship and duty, Troilo seemed happy enough to labor on the cottage and hunt during the day, though Costanza could sense that he missed his old life. He had never planned to live in exile, and still Troilo held onto the notion that his friend might one day forgive him and all would be well, which is why he jumped at the opportunity when word finally came from the castle.

Hearing a foreign voice, Costanza stepped outside to see that Troilo had hacked his axe into a tree stump and was talking with a page boy.

Troilo scanned the words of the letter quickly as Costanza peered over his shoulder, wrapping herself in a shawl.

"The Duke of Pazin requests my presence," he said. "To speak of the Ottoman campaign."

"What shall I tell His Grace, Sir Troilo?" asked the page.

"Tell him I accept."

Costanza gripped Troilo's sleeve in protest.

"Stanzi, I must." He looked again at the page boy. "Tell His Grace that I accept his offer."

The page nodded, taking his leave.

"I cannot allow your father nor the court to suffer any longer," Troilo went on. "His quarrel is with me."

"He will not look past this!" Costanza argued. "His own mother all but said so."

"I am still one of his knights," he said softly. "It is the honorable thing..."

"Are you certain it is not the *zmaj* in you, who still craves glory and adventure?" she asked, turning away. "Perhaps our life is not enough for you."

"No." Laying both hands on her shoulder, he turned her to face him. "Our life is more than enough."

"Yet, still you answer when he calls? You are not his loyal dog!"

Troilo sighed. "I know him."

"You *believe* you know him."

"*Stanzi,*" he whispered, "you have heard the same rumors as I. He used to listen to me. If there is any chance he may listen to me still...I must try."

Costanza found herself unable to sleep that night. Leaving Troilo on the straw bed, she wandered outside to the edge of the quarry, which reflected a crisp, starry night at her feet. She ran her fingers across the water, rippling the pools of starlight that gazed up at her like portals to another world.

Feeling the presence of another, she was certain Troilo had followed her out, but it was not he Costanza saw when she looked up. Across the pond, a woman stood in a gown as white as Mjesec, with soft blonde hair that flowed down her back.

Costanza had grown more and more accustomed to visions since becoming pregnant, but none had ever felt so foreboding.

Gripping Troilo's arm, Costanza roused him from sleep. "You must not leave tomorrow," she wept hysterically. "I have seen the face of Death!"

"*Costanza,*" he hushed. "What is it, my love?"

"If you leave tomorrow, you will not return," she sobbed.

Gathering her in his arms, Troilo pulled her into bed with him. "What is it you saw?" he asked, wrapping her tight.

"A spirit woman dressed in white."

Troilo slipped out of bed and made his way to the door, but upon opening it, he saw no such thing. "My Lady," he said, climbing back into bed. "Though we cannot always see them with our human sight, you know these woods are filled with spirits aplenty."

Costanza nodded as she snuggled against him. "Why did the spirit reveal herself to me, if not in warning?"

"I will take Mjesec tomorrow," Troilo murmured in her ear. "If I find myself in trouble, I will have the faster horse...you need not worry."

Costanza had never clutched him as tightly as she did that night. For all of his reassurance, she could not shake the feeling that she may never see Troilo again, and that thought was more than she could bear. He had told her he could only be killed in his true form, but that did not mean he could not be imprisoned and tortured. Troilo was not immune to the cruelty of man.

"Promise me," Costanza pleaded the next morning. "Promise me that you will return."

Kneeling before her, Troilo kissed her belly. "I will return before nightfall," he said.

Wrapped in her shawl, Costanza hugged herself as Troilo mounted Mjesec.

"Until this evening, My Lady," he added gently. "You are the only star in my sky."

"Be brave, child," Costanza whispered to herself as he rode off. "For you will be a mother now."

As she busied herself feeding Noć, her nerves began to fade. Perhaps she thought too ill of the duke, and he really did call upon Troilo for military matters. At the very least, Lady Elisabetta would not let her son imprison him.

"He will return this evening," she assured Noć.

Knowing the chill that would come with nightfall, Costanza decided that she would make a stew for them to share. That, along with some freshly baked bread, would be enough to warm his bones again.

She had only just begun to knead the dough when Costanza thought she heard Noć rear up outside. Wiping her hands across her skirt, she opened the cottage door to see seven soldiers standing outside.

Troilo, she thought as terror gripped her insides.

"Lady Costanza?"

Closing the door behind her, she ran to them. "I am she," she said. "Has something happened?"

The soldier in the front removed his helmet, a makeshift guise of cloth and chainmail.

"Oh," Costanza sighed, comforted by the familiar face of the guard who had received her at the gate so many times before. "Do you bring me news of my husband?" she asked. "Has he been injured?"

"Your husband is at the castle with His Grace as we speak."

Costanza smiled as she scanned the group of men, confused. If there was no news of Troilo, why were they there?

The guard pulled out a decree from his satchel, then read out loud. "Lady Costanza Visconti, you have been accused by your neighbors of witchcraft."

"Witchcraft?" she stuttered with a nervous laugh. "I am no witch. I am baking a loaf of bread that **I** am happy to share, and if

you will be kind enough to wait for my husband's return, you will see that this is a grave—"

"You and your husband stand accused of consorting with the Devil to plot against His Grace with black magic, a crime punishable by death," the guard read over her. "Therefore your execution has been determined for this day, the eighth of November in the year of our Lord and Savior, 1433."

"On what *grounds?*" she demanded.

Rolling up the decree, the guard then removed something from his satchel. "Does this belong to you, Lady?" he asked, stepping toward her.

In his hand lay the grass star Costanza had woven for Troilo.

"This magical poppet was found in Sir Troilo's room," he said. "Villagers claim they have seen you weaving them before."

"It is only a star," she countered. "A token of affection from one lover to another!"

The soldiers were unmoved.

"We have been given the orders by His Grace himself, Lady."

"Orders for my execution?" she choked.

"If your husband may call in a storm large enough for us to see, you will both be spared."

The words were silent on her lips. "He cannot..."

Costanza stepped back as the group of soldiers began to close in on her. The Woman in White had come to warn her, but it was not Troilo who was in danger.

Glancing once to Noć, Costanza did not think as she lunged for the sword in the guard's belt. Rushing for the horse, she had nearly hoisted herself up before two soldiers pulled her off. "Go!" she shouted, cutting Noć loose.

Struggling for the sword, she was knocked to the ground by one of the soldiers, while another snatched her up by her hair. "My child is kin to Lady Elisabetta!" she shouted as the soldier made her kneel before the guard. "Do I not have the right to a trial?"

"The Duke of Pazin has sent Lady Elisabetta back to Milan," the guard snapped. "This *is* your trial."

A sense of panic overcame Costanza as she knelt before this man she had interacted with so many times before. Without Lady Elisabetta, neither she nor her child had protection. She looked to the skies of Pazin with a desperate plea, but Troilo was silent through their bond.

"Come along," the soldier ordered, clutching Costanza's hair and shoving her forward. "Your trial awaits."

The distant howling of a wolf pierced through the laughter of the men as the guard barged through the cottage door, clearing the wooden table.

"I will have her first," he announced as the men threw her onto it. "Close the door!"

"*I am a witch,* in allyship with the Devil himself!" she screamed at the top of her lungs. "I curse every one of you who touches me —may you all be bitten by venomous snakes!"

"*Hold her down!*"

Two soldiers pinned her arms to the table as the guard lifted her skirt to her neck. "Finery indeed, you have, Lady," he grunted, adjusting himself.

Troilo! Screwing her eyes shut, Costanza called out to him through their bond. *Troilo, help!*

One of the soldiers holding her arms chuckled. "I will have her secon—"

The door burst open, and faster than Costanza could open her eyes, the warm sensation of blood splattered over her opened legs and pregnant belly. The white she-wolf growled ferociously with the neck of the guard in her jaws, nearly decapitating him as she pulled him off.

"She is a witch!" one of the men shouted.

Ducking under the table, Costanza watched the she-wolf tear the head completely off of her attacker, then turn her snarling fangs on the remaining men.

"Look at what she just commanded!"

Hugging her knees and soaked in blood, Costanza was too terrified to move. Then at last, a command from Troilo shot down the bond.

Run!

As though he were flying to her, she saw only a vision of shifting trees.

Costanza met the eye of the she-wolf for a brief second as she tore off the limb of another soldier. *"Thank you,"* she whispered, dashing for the door.

A few mangled bodies lay outside of the cottage, but Costanza did not stop to observe them. Thinking she could swim across and hide behind the waterfall until Troilo arrived, she ran into the quarry.

"Witch!"

Tackled, Costanza fell into the shallow water.

"Costanza Visconti, having been found guilty of witchcraft, sorcery, promiscuity, divination and appearing in the form of a succubus—" The soldier held onto her by the waist as Costanza struggled to free herself. "Does the condemned woman have any last words?"

"May you burn! May you burn for all the innocents you have—"

Grabbing her by the hair, the faceless soldier dunked her underwater.

"The death of innocents is on your hands!" she screamed, gasping as she resurfaced. "The death of my child is on your hands! May you all bur—"

Costanza fought for air, but the soldier's hold was relentless as he held her under. And as the water overtook her, she reached for Troilo in her mind, for any shred of his essence.

Come.

Beneath the quarry, Costanza opened her eyes to see a pale woman with silver hair and iridescent skin hovering in front of her. **A** serpent-like fish tail replaced her legs, and long claws tipped her skinny fingers.

Rusalka! Songstress of the seas, seducer of men!

Costanza wanted to speak, or even to gasp, but her life was dimming. Through blurred vision, she saw the creature reach for her.

Come with me and you will feel no pain, the rusalka sang, slicing four delicate slits into Costanza's neck.

The pressure in her lungs released, and Costanza felt her spirit pull away from her body, which now floated limply above them.

Blood overtook the water's surface like a red ink as Troilo charged into the quarry, plunging his sword through the heart of the soldier holding Costanza. She tried to reach for him as he gathered her body in his arms, but she was no longer solid, and the surface of the water, like glass to the touch. Even grasping for their bond, she found little trace of it, extinguished like the last remnants of a candle flame.

Costanza turned to the rusalka, her maker. *I must return to him!*

You may, one day, she hummed. *But know that time passes differently here, and he will likely be dead by the time you are able.*

What of our child?

She has returned to whence she came, the rusalka replied. *In time, you will forget this life.*

Costanza would not forget! She could not!

Turning back to her body, she watched as Troilo pulled the gold ring from her finger. *I will find you again,* she thought. *In the next life, I will find you again.*

But condemned to the mortal world, Troilo could no longer hear her, for the water was as Otherworldly as the stars he had fallen from.

TEN

June 16, 1900 — *four days before the murder*
12:01 P.M.

Leaning forward in his chair, Doctor Visconti blinked at Philippa as she sat on the gold chaise. Between them, a glass of water rested on top of a table.

"I would like you to move the water without touching the glass," he said.

His eyebrow perked up as Philippa opened her mouth to protest.

"I *know* you can."

Their session had begun in the same manner they usually did, with Philippa wandering downstairs, dressed for a day of hunting and socializing, to have coffee with him on the veranda. There, Doctor Visconti would ask her about her dreams, and Philippa would ask him about his travels. Eager to hear more of the world, she reveled in the stories he told of the Orient, and the cultures of these ancient lands.

He told her of the djinn—the spirits that inhabited the desert sands of the Holy Land—and watching sunsets on the Nile. He spoke of China and its Great Wall that stretched from the mountains to the Yellow Sea, where junket ships with red sails trailed the coast. And the colorful halls of Tangier, where he had served as a physician in the sultan's court before finally returning to Europe.

Philippa learned that Doctor Visconti could speak *nine* languages fluently, or so he claimed. He could write in both Mandarin and Arabic, which he'd demonstrated for her. Most days, their conversations would span the entirety of her session, and before Philippa knew it, she would be called upon by her brother and Duke Sixten for the afternoon.

Today, though, Doctor Visconti had brought her back inside the library.

Concentrating hard on the glass of water, Philippa let out a frustrated sigh. "I cannot," she said. "I cannot command it to move, it is always…"

"Accidental," he finished. "Or is it?"

She grinned, having grown accustomed to his trick questions.

"It is not so much about *commanding* the spirit of a thing as it is inviting it in. Merging and becoming one with it, just as you do when you sit down to write."

"Become one with the water?" Philippa teased. "That would imply that water has a spirit of its own."

"Eastern religion teaches that all things have a spirit," Doctor Visconti explained. "Try again, and this time, quiet your mind."

Philippa looked down at the glass of water. Closing her eyes, she focused on the pinprick of light in the center of her chest.

"There you have it," said Doctor Visconti, snapping her out of the trance.

Philippa gaped at the subtle whirl within the glass. "What makes me possess this capability?"

"Simply speaking, you have a special connection to water," he replied. "Therefore you are more attuned to its frequency than others."

It was clear from the way he spoke that this was not the first time Doctor Visconti had seen such phenomena.

"And did you learn this in the Orient as well?" Philippa asked.

"No." He grinned. "Not quite."

Philippa regarded him: at thirty-four years old, he seemed so much wiser than she, as though he'd drunk from the fountain of youth and wandered the globe for a hundred years.

"One day soon, I shall conquer my fear and learn to swim," Philippa declared. "Perhaps you may teach me as part of our next experiment."

"Perhaps."

"I will have you know I wrote nine pages or so this morning," she added, glancing down to her ink stained hand.

"That is two more than yesterday."

"I suppose Costanza has much she wants to say to you."

Doctor Visconti nodded to himself as he turned to face the window, where another hot day awaited. "And you have not read them back?"

"I have not."

To her own surprise, Philippa had abided by his request. Perhaps it felt too private of a thing between him and Costanza, a bearing of heart and soul that she should not be privy to.

"Pippa!" Erzsi called, banging on the library door. "Pippa, they are—"

Philippa straightened up on the chaise as she barged in, then immediately halted in front of them.

"Oh dear," Erzsi mumbled. "Am I interrupting?"

"We are just finishing up," Doctor Visconti replied, loosening the cravat around his neck.

"Pippa," she sighed, cocking her head. "The *hounds* are here."

For three days now, they had followed the same routine. After Philippa's session, Franz would show up and rouse them for another hunt. Mellie would pack them a picnic basket, and they would be on their way, dressed in all white. Philippa assumed this afternoon would follow the same trajectory, only with an added star fall in the forecast for that evening.

"Tell them I will be right out, Erzsi."

"Take all the time you need," she replied, disappearing back into the hall as she closed the door.

Turning her attention back to Doctor Visconti, Philippa clasped her hands in her lap with a smirk.

Clearing his throat, he glanced up at the clock behind her. "I apologize, Highness, but I must go as well."

"Do you have *plans,* Doctor?" Philippa teased. "You are normally so solitary."

"Fräulein Coudenhove has asked me to accompany her on a walk."

"Oh..." Philippa rose to her feet, straightening her sundress.

Was that really the kind of woman that he wanted? Someone devout and uptight like *Mellie?*

"Well, have a lovely time," she said, averting her eyes.

"Wait," Doctor Visconti said. "Are you certain you feel well enough to go along?"

Looking him up and down, Philippa crossed her arms over her chest. "Quite," she snapped.

"If you do not feel that you can withstand the heat, I can tell His Highness that it would be better if you did not go."

"No, Doctor, it is quite all right," Philippa insisted. *"You* shall take your walk with Fräulein Coudenhove and *I* shall go hunting with my brother and Duke Sixten."

He pursed his lips in annoyance, an expression she had come to know well.

"Good afternoon," Philippa added, leaving him in the library.

3:50 P.M.

. . .

Erzsi plucked a grape from the bunch hanging over the corner of the picnic basket. The sun had finally lowered enough to kiss the treetops, and the remnants of the light washed over Philippa's straw hat, illuminating her stray, golden hairs in the honeyed light of the June afternoon.

Erzsi tilted her chin to the sky. "You are quite moody today," she said, tossing the grape in her mouth.

Met with silence, she looked past the basket full of cheese and bread to Philippa, who was staring across the lawn. Lost in her own world, a permanent line had seared itself into her brow.

Erzsi forced a cough. "Any particular reason?"

"None that I would like to discuss," Philippa answered absently.

Leaning back onto her elbow, Erzsi craned her neck. "It is Doctor Visconti, no?"

Philippa eyed her reluctantly.

"You cannot help but bicker with him," Erzsi relented, flopping onto her stomach. "Can you?"

"It is *he* who insists on bickering with me."

"Well, how am I supposed to know? Your opinion of him changes constantly from one hour to the next. Either he is so very" —Erzsi widened her eyes dramatically— "*fascinating,* or you cannot bear to be in the same room with him."

"He is equal parts interesting and arrogant," Philippa mumbled.

"How angry can you really be, Pippa? Whatever treatment he has you under seems to be working. It has been over a week since your last fit!" Erzsi reached for another grape. "What *does* he have you doing?"

Philippa lifted her hand, stained with dark ink. "My treatment," she added, spreading her thumb and forefinger.

"Writing?"

"Of sorts."

"Writing what?" Erzsi asked, flicking the grape into her mouth. "A story?"

"No...it is not a story. I do not actually know what it is."

Erzsi eyed Philippa flatly as she broke off a piece of bread. "You do not know what you are writing...?"

"Well, Herr Visconti..." Philippa pursed her lips, visibly hesitant. "He believes the basis of my madness is spirit-inflicted."

"Spirit-inflicted!"

"I might have been a great mystic if only I had been born in another time," she went on. "So he is teaching me to control my channeling through the means of automatic writing."

"What on earth is that?"

"It is when a medium allows a spirit to speak through their pen while under trance."

"Who is it that guides your hand?" Erzsi choked.

Philippa only shook her head.

"Is it your knight?" Questions started tumbling out of Erzsi's mouth. "Is it Her Majesty the Empress? My father? *Who?*"

"We do not know," Philippa said hastily. "And I do not remember what I write."

"Wouldn't you be able to pinpoint the spirit's identity by reading the messages back?"

"Doctor Visconti has asked me not to. He said he will read them at the end of the week."

Erzsi sat back with a stunned blink. All this time, *this* is what Troilo and Philippa had been doing?

"I did not think you believed in such things," Philippa added.

"Are you *certain* it is not my father?"

"It is not the Crown Prince. Though, I believe..."

A shot echoed through the treetops, and Erzsi jumped, knocking over a nearby glass of red wine. *"Ah,"* she groaned.

Philippa reached into the basket for a napkin.

"Must we tag along at their beck and call?" Erzsi grimaced at the splotches on her cream dress as Philippa tried to blot them. "Men! I despise them!"

Howls of laughter erupted from the wood line as Franz and Duke Sixten emerged, carrying shotguns over their shoulders.

"*My,*" the duke sneered. "Who have you gutted, little one?"

Erzsi rolled her eyes to Philippa. "*As I was saying,*" she scorned.

"Did you drink my wine, Erzsi?" Franz added. "I swore I left my glass half full."

Philippa grinned up at them. "Do not tease her," she ordered. "Is it not enough that her dress is ruined?"

"We are finished," Franz replied. "It is a shame you did not come along, Pippa. Though" —he nudged his friend— "I am certain the duke appreciated your absence."

Erzsi looked at Duke Sixten and his wounded smile. "Do not despair," she added cheerily. "Her marksmanship would humble anyone."

"Come now." Franz adjusted the rifle over his shoulder with a friendly wave. "We could all use some freshening up."

Philippa rose to her feet and Erzsi did the same, assessing the maroon spattering across her chest. The smell of hot grapes made her stomach curdle.

"Do not fret," Philippa assured, squinting skyward. "You have plenty of dresses."

"It is not the dress I care about." Erzsi shot a glare toward the horses, where the men were mounting up. "It is that everyone insists on talking to me as though I am a child."

"You know Franzi, he..."

"I am not talking about Franz."

Philippa bit her bottom lip, dragging her teeth over it. "I know you do not like him," she said quietly.

"His redeeming qualities are few and far between."

She motioned for Erzsi to grab the other side of the blanket. "I expect that he will ask me to reconsider our engagement tonight under the star fall."

Erzsi felt her expression droop like a melted candle. "It is why he is here, after all," she said, meeting Philippa with the corner of the blanket. "He wears his intentions plainly."

Philippa fell silent as she folded the blanket smaller, then smaller.

"You *are* going to decline him, yes?"

"Well..."

Erzsi threw her hands together in a patronizing clap, her smirk brimming with disapproval. It was idiotic. Worse than idiotic, it was—

"I have not thought it through," Philippa argued, snatching the basket from the ground. "But I know I want to have a life of my own, just as you do. I want to travel and see things!"

"You will have no such life with him!"

"You do not know that. Once I am cured—"

"What does Doctor Visconti say?"

The way Philippa halted in her tracks told Erzsi that she had yet to tell him.

"He will disapprove as I do."

Philippa's eyes turned to the color of moss agate. "Then it is good that he has as little say in my marriage arrangements as you."

"I am parched!" Franz called to them from his horse. "Shall we?"

"He is too preoccupied with his own endeavors to take notice of mine," Philippa added.

Erzsi picked up the basket as Philippa began to walk. "Pippa," she urged, hustling to her side. "You cannot marry him!"

"It is foolish to go around throwing away perfectly good proposals."

"It is even more foolish to *settle*," Erzsi countered, blocking her.

"Are you not doing the very same with Prince Otto?"

"Argh! Otto is not a—!"

"A *what?*"

Erzsi stilled, then lowered her voice. "I *know* he did it," she said.

"It is slander," Philippa replied, plowing past. "I know better than anyone what it is like to be the subject of rumors."

"What of Troilo?"

"What *of* him?" Philippa countered, turning back.

"If you will not listen to me that you deserve better, then listen to him."

Philippa's gaze found the horses behind Erzsi.

"Are you coming?" Franz called.

"Or," Erzsi hissed as Philippa slid by, *"you may tell Duke Sixten that your dowry includes spirits!"*

The men led the way back over the rolling hills, where the town of Ischl could be seen past the evergreen firs in the distance. Philippa rode silently by Erzsi's side, avoiding each glare she cast her direction, until eventually the pink glow of Marmorschossl came into view.

Soon enough, she'd be subjected to gathering with the lot of them under the star fall, knowing Duke Sixten would pull her cousin away to propose. It was an opportunity Erzsi couldn't allow.

"Do you think we should invite Herr Visconti to watch the star fall with us tonight?" she asked, twisting the reins around her finger. "The more the merrier, I say."

"He has work to do, certainly," Duke Sixten replied offhandedly. "Books to read."

"I was asking *Franz,*" said Erzsi. "Franz?"

"If you would like to extend the invitation, certainly."

Erzsi stared at the back of the duke's head, ready to gloat a vindictive smile if he dared to look back. "Pippa," she said, turning to her cousin, "what say you?"

But Philippa was looking toward the pond behind her.

"Do look at the two of them," Franz said with a chuckle.

Over her shoulder, Erzsi spotted Troilo sitting with Mellie under the weeping beech. Perhaps all hope wasn't lost for the two of them, after all?

"Indeed, he is plenty occupied," Duke Sixten added as they trotted closer. "See?"

Mellie, taking notice of them, rose and began her walk down the curved pathway, leaving Troilo on the bench. "A nice picnic, I hope?" she called.

"A glorious day," Franz shouted back.

Erzsi watched Philippa closely as they slowed to a halt. Erzsi could feel she did not want to take Duke Sixten's hand as she dismounted, but for the sake of being polite, Philippa yielded.

"I have had lunch prepared in the parlor," said Mellie. "Highness, what happened to your dress?"

Stained with wine, Erzsi slipped down from her horse. "I would rather not discuss it," she groaned.

Amongst talk of the picnic, the hunt, and her ruined dress, Erzsi's ears perked up at the sound of Philippa's voice nearby.

"No, no—go ahead without me."

Duke Sixten's face contorted in a distrustful grin as she stepped back onto the path.

"Erzsi needs to change so I shall invite Herr Visconti," Philippa added. "I will join you in a moment."

"If you insist," the duke muttered under his breath.

Erzsi grinned as she watched Philippa walk away, knowing that whatever Troilo's trespass had been, she'd forgiven him. And if he could manage to stay on her good side until tonight, he might be able to convince her to decline Duke Sixten's proposal.

"Come, Highness," Mellie said, ushering her away. "Let us find you some new clothes."

A light wind tumbled Philippa's hair as she walked toward the spirea topped bench, where Doctor Visconti flipped through the pages of a book in such a melancholic way that she could have sworn he was searching for something within them.

"Hello," she announced.

"Highness." Closing his book, he looked up from his shady seat. "I must admit, I did not expect to see any more of you today."

"Yes, well." Philippa swept a handful of white petals to the ground, finding a seat next to him. "In comparison to sultans and pyramids, most topics fall flat."

Doctor Visconti began to smile as she continued.

"Do you plan to watch the star fall tonight?" she said, looking across the pond. Unlike the other side, it was much too deep to see the bottom. "They predict it will be quite a show."

"Are you inviting me so that you do not have to suffer in dull company alone, Highness?"

Philippa grinned ahead, refusing to look at him. "It is Erzsi who insisted on your presence."

"You do not wish me to enrich you with conversation, then?" he asked, straightening himself on the bench.

"No, please do enrich me." Meeting his eye, she nudged his leg with her knee. "I am starved for stimulation."

"Devises heroïques by Claude Paradin," he said, glancing down at the closed book. "It is a collection of woodcut emblems and mottos."

"An emblem book? It would seem you *are* quite the collector."

"They were widely popular during the Renaissance. This one in particular was given to me by a dear friend while I was visiting him in England."

"It looks very old."

"It was published in 1557," said Doctor Visconti as he opened the book. "He told me it belonged to one of his ancestors."

Dropping her gaze to the discolored pages, Philippa wrinkled her brow at the woodcut emblem of a shooting star staring back up at her.

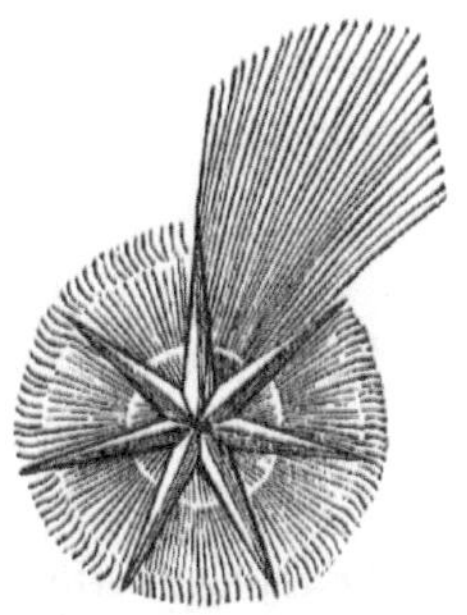

ASTRA INCLINANT, SED
NON OBLIGANT

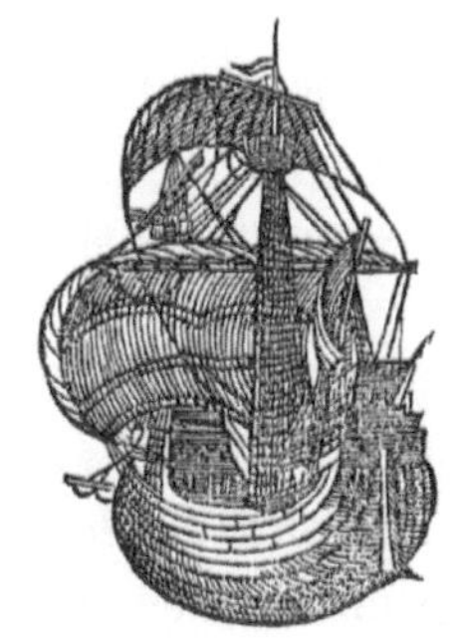

EN ALTERA QUE VEHAT ARGO

ORDO EQUESTRIS FORTIS ET
MAGNIFICUS

LATET ANGUIS IN HERBA

FESTINA LENTE

SIMUL ET AETERNUM

"*I know this,*" she whispered, running her finger over it. "I have seen it somewhere before."

Doctor Visconti was quiet, yet amusement danced in his eyes as if he knew something she didn't.

"There was a comet in the sky the day I was born," Philippa added, meditating on the emblem. "According to certain regions, such an omen predestines a child for *otherworldly talents*. At least, that is what my father told me."

"The peninsula is among such regions," he replied softly.

"Istria?"

Doctor Visconti nodded.

"You never speak of it," said Philippa. "Your homeland is the only place you do not tell stories of."

"It is not a place I wish to revisit," he said, lifting his gaze to the pond. "Not in the world, nor in my mind."

"Then tell me of your generous friend," she insisted, tapping the book. "The Englishman."

"He was a poet like myself, though much more successful."

Relaxing against the hardback bench, Philippa turned to him with full attention.

"I was vacationing in Geneva—living in Venice at the time— when I met him." The reminiscence in his eyes flickered as a faint smile overtook him. "There was a group of them I spent the summer with, sleeping on the floor of an old chateau. I had never been so drunk on *enriching conversation,* or on wine." Doctor Visconti laughed a bit, nodding to himself. "I visited him and his wife in London that fall, and I found myself in such good company that I did not leave."

"The company of women, certainly," Philippa added cheekily. "With these wild friends of yours."

"*Women,* no. And only in Venice."

Philippa's eyes widened.

When he spoke, it was deliberate and slow, with a smile. "Are you shocked?"

Holding his gaze, she leaned in. "Herr Visconti, I do not believe you could say anything that truly shocks me."

A static charge threaded the air between them, as though they were inside a thunderhead.

"Time will tell, Highness," he whispered, almost tauntingly. "There is much you do not know about me."

"Tell me, then" —Philippa drew back, laying both hands over her crossed knee— "have you visited your English friend recently?"

Doctor Visconti shook his head. "No."

Feeling her smile drop, Philippa watched as he shut the emblem book. "What happened to him?" she asked.

"He was sailing, and his boat got caught in a storm." Doctor Visconti bit his lower lip. "It was the second death of a friend in the span of a year. When they found him on the shore...I left England after that."

"And you traveled down to Istanbul."

It was no wonder Doctor Visconti armoured himself so heavily. He'd spent seemingly his whole life running from grief.

"Does a simple invitation take so long?" Duke Sixten called from the path.

Troilo's pulse surged as Philippa rose to her feet like an elegant flower.

"I have hardly had a chance to ask him," she chastised, reaching for a piece of hair that had broken free from her braid.

Duke Sixten turned his attention to Troilo. "Well?"

How Troilo hated him, wanted him dead. It didn't matter that *lifetimes* had passed. His fortified heart was blind to lifetimes.

"Thank you for the invitation but I am occupied already."

"There you have it," said Duke Sixten to Philippa.

Suddenly, an obsidian black snake slithering through the snowy spirea seized the duke's attention.

"Get back!" he barked.

"It is a harmless black snake," Troilo assured, having known all along it was sharing the shade with them.

Duke Sixten removed the knife from his belt. "Adam would say otherwise."

"It is harmless?"

Troilo glanced over at Philippa, who had dropped to her knees.

"Yes," he replied in a near whisper. "Completely."

Reaching her hand across the grass, Philippa did not tear her gaze from Troilo's as the snake crawled into her palm.

Zmajeva nesteva.

Rising with the snake in both hands, Philippa bounced a smirk between both men.

"Must you befriend every repulsive creature?" Duke Sixten scolded. "Release it at once!"

"I will be right in." Philippa looked to the beady eyes of the serpent, coiled comfortably around her ring finger. "After I take *you* somewhere safe," she added playfully.

"*Your Highness*," Troilo added, turning his attention to Duke Sixten as she walked away. "Would be the proper way to address her."

"I do not know what game you are trying to play," the duke snarled, lunging at him like a rabid dog. "But I am telling you, *stay away from her.* Archduchess Philippa and I have far too much history—"

"Oh?"

"To be derailed by a lowly common man such as yourself," he spat. "Least one who claims he is a miracle worker."

Troilo blinked, unyielding.

"I may play nice with you for the sake of appearances," the duke said in an eerie calm. "But I assure you, Herr Visconti, I am watching you closely."

"As I am *you,* Your Grace."

Duke Sixten's forehead crinkled as Troilo stepped closer to him.

"Only one of us has thrown a woman from a balcony," he murmured.

The duke was the first to break their stalemate and walk away, leaving Troilo alone under the beech. Up ahead, Philippa trailed the wood line, looking for the perfect patch of ivy in which to lay the snake.

"Herr Visconti!" she called, waving him over. "Do you think—?"

"You have an audience waiting," Troilo reminded her.

Philippa pursed her lips in a smile, showcasing the miniature dimples that constellated the corners of her mouth. His words caught in his throat as he dropped his gaze to her fluctuating chest, then to her dewy lips as she spoke.

"So eager to rid yourself of me?"

A breeze swept up through the grass, unleashing a flurry of dandelion seeds into the air.

"Erzsi will be disappointed," Philippa added, waving her hand through them. "That you will not join us tonight."

Troilo cast his sights across the pond to the cottage, to the unseen eyes that lined its windows. "Please extend my apologies."

"Have I done something to offend you?" she asked suddenly.

"Pardon?"

"You are acting as though we are strangers again."

Troilo reached for the dandelion seed caught in her hair. "Forgive me," he said, pulling it gracefully from her temple.

Philippa lifted her chin, just slightly. "I forgive you," she said softly. "Troilo."

Never had he felt such desire for another breathing soul. But faster than Troilo could utter a response, Philippa averted her gaze to the ground as though she were the one who was guilty.

"Is there something you wish to tell me?" he asked.

"They are waiting, I really must go," she replied, stepping back onto the path, clumsily. "Perhaps you will change your mind and we will meet tonight under the stars!" she called back. "You and Fräulein Coudenhove!"

Troilo watched Philippa's braid trail behind her as she retreated up the veranda stairs. "Perhaps, Highness," he replied under his breath.

9:45 P.M.

Erzsi pouted as they lounged on the slopes. Entranced completely with the counting of stars, Philippa didn't seem to notice the way Duke Sixten's presence sapped the magic, nor the way Erzsi glared each time he spoke. Each time he shifted closer to them.

With the way he'd stormed out of the parlor to retrieve Philippa earlier, it was no wonder Troilo refused to join them.

"You have to look up if you want to see one, Erzsi," she teased.

Erzsi leaned back in the grass, her nose tickled by the fragrant breeze blowing Philippa's loose hair. "My neck hurts," she mumbled, unwilling to admit how small and inconsequential she felt looking up, and how much she hated that feeling.

They'd ventured out around nine under a mostly clear sky, and what little remained of the cirrus clouds had dissipated as they walked under the enchanting darkness of the new moon. The last glimpse Erzsi had gotten of Troilo was through the lamp-lit library window from her place in the yard, and the image of his lonely silhouette had yet to leave her.

"There is one," said Franz. "To the south."

"How many is that now?" Philippa asked Duke Sixten over her shoulder. "Ten? Eleven?"

"We should move to the other side of the wood line where there is a clearer view of the horizon."

Flipping onto her stomach, Erzsi closed her eyes and

stretched her arm across the grass. Another warm breeze brushed a strand of hair from her face. Even she could not deny the beauty of such a night. Duke Sixten would have no better opportunity to propose.

Lifting her eyelids, Erzsi gazed out into the open field, filled with shadowed valleys. And, realizing that two figures were walking towards them, she perked up like a watered flower. "Troilo!" she exclaimed.

"Who is that, out there in the field?" the duke inquired.

"Oh," Franz replied. "It looks like—"

Philippa leaned over, whispering gleefully into Erzsi's ear, *"He came!"*

"Up here!" Erzsi called, cupping her hands around her mouth.

Troilo and Mellie halted in the valley, but faster than he could lift a hand to wave, she was sprinting down the shallow slope. When asked what they had discussed under the weeping beech earlier, Philippa had refused to say.

"I must speak with you at once," Erzsi huffed. "Duke Six—!"

"Good evening, Doctor." Philippa's voice floated on the wind over Erzsi's shoulder. "You changed your mind, I see."

Troilo nodded. "More a change of heart than mind."

Erzsi had never heard him speak so softly. Looking from Troilo to Philippa, she could not help but feel like she was interrupting something.

Mellie must've felt it, too. When she spoke, her voice was a mere squeak. "Thank you for the invitation," she said to Philippa. "Your Highness."

"Fräulein! Doctor Visconti!" Franz exclaimed, finding Erzsi's side. "You are just in time! We were just about to walk to the best view in all of Ischl."

"You will join us, won't you?" Philippa asked.

Troilo looked to Mellie, who gave a reluctant assent.

"Come, then," said Franz. "We are moving south to avoid the tree line."

Erzsi fell in behind Franz but kept her attention on Philippa, and how she seemed to slow her step.

Duke Sixten greeted them from the top of the slope. "Doctor. Fräulein," he said, extending his arm to Philippa. "How very fortunate that you could join us."

"I could not bear to disappoint Her Highness, Archduchess Erzsi," Troilo replied.

Of course, he'd turned to *Philippa* as he said it.

"Yes," the duke mumbled, pulling her away. "Of course."

Erzsi watched Philippa turn back to look at Troilo, who grew quiet in her absence. What was this tenderness that had so clearly blossomed between them?

Could it be that *he*—and *she?*

Perhaps keeping Philippa from Duke Sixten would not be so difficult, after all.

The darkness of the night seemed luminous compared to the wood line. Converging into a mass of black, the trunks and leaves and bristles were inseparable from one another. Only a handful of fireflies dared to venture beyond the threshold of the forest.

"Is it wise to traverse the grounds with snakes afoot?" Mellie asked.

"They have much more reason to be wary of us," Troilo assured.

"Indeed, Fräulein. You are in safe company," said Franz, stepping back to offer Erzsi his arm. "Cousin?"

The ground crunched beneath their feet as they walked beneath the summer firs. Even knowing exactly where they were, Erzsi felt as though they'd left Ischl altogether.

"I, for one, am not afraid," Philippa announced.

Duke Sixten laughed under his breath.

"You do not believe me?"

"One encounter with a black snake does not make you a serpent charmer."

Erzsi looked ahead to the spotty parts of sky, caged by countless pine needles. Philippa and the duke had fallen behind, and their voices, lost in the brush.

"Philippa!"

Erzsi felt a hook under her other arm as Duke Sixten's shout rang out from behind.

"Come with me," Philippa demanded, pulling her from Franz.

Unable to gauge her footsteps in the dark, Erzsi held tightly to Philippa's arm as they plowed through the remaining undergrowth until the woods spat them out into a clearing. All was deadly calm on the other side of the hedge.

"What is so urgent that you must drag me through the forest?" Erzsi asked, picking a stick out of her sock.

"I have thought about what you said," Philippa sighed. "About Troilo."

"Troilo?"

"Doctor Visconti," she corrected.

"Did you tell him you planned to consider the duke's proposal?"

"I wanted to today, but a part of me cannot bear the thought of it..." Philippa tilted her chin to the nebulas that swept across the black sea above them, as though she were searching for a prince among their stars. "I must confess, I—"

"Shh," Erzsi shushed, hearing a twig snap underfoot.

The wart had returned.

"Darling," Duke Sixten chastised, "were you in such a rush to leave us all behind?"

"I was excited." Philippa's laugh was rigid and forced. "I do not know what came over me."

Erzsi took a step back as everyone gathered outside of the pines. Situating herself next to Troilo and Mellie, she watched Duke Sixten snake his arm around Philippa's waist in front of them.

It would happen any time, now.

"You are a wonderful guide," said Mellie to Troilo.

"It is my pleasure," he replied absently.

His attention lingered on Philippa, but in a way that seemed more ill than carnal. Erzsi had read about such stares in novels.

Were they even *aware?* That they were falling in love?

As if to answer her, a star shot diagonally across the horizon, causing everyone to *ooh* and *aah* in unison.

"I must go," Philippa said, breaking free from Duke Sixten's side. "I must go at once!"

Erzsi snapped her attention to the debacle in front of her.

Had he proposed? Had she declined him?

"Pippa!" Franz called after her. "Do not go into the woods alone—what is she doing?"

Turning to Troilo, Erzsi could see he had already abandoned Mellie.

"Surely she just needs some air!" Mellie protested. "She will not go far, will she?"

"We must find her." Troilo reached for Erzsi's hand. "Quickly."

The ironed satin of Philippa's dress snagged on cobwebs of branches as she ran. Duke Sixten had only begun to state his intentions when she felt herself *slipping* into dark waters of the mind, and wanting only to escape this unrelenting fear, she'd bolted for the safety of the trees like a spear in the dark.

"What is it you want from me, Costanza?" she whimpered, stumbling over fractured branches. "What purpose does it serve you to impart your horrors on me?"

The answer came in the form of a vision which, in the dark, was impossible to separate from her immediate reality. A splintery, wooden fence, a moonlit landscape, and a cacophony of voices.

I do not have the time to help you realize your destiny, I have my own! Love of mine, divine star...

Philippa combed the air until her fingers touched bark and, grabbing onto a tree, she slid down its trunk to the soft, moss-covered ground. A warm, dark crypt.

You have made your choice, zmajeva nesteva.

"Enough," Philippa pleaded, covering her ears. "Enough!"

My soul? It is yours! I lay it at your feet!

"Spirit, my dear knight—if you are listening," she pleaded tearfully. "Please, make it stop. Make them stop..."

Time passed differently in the dark under the pine needled canopy, where Philippa lay with her cheek on her knee, picking at the moss as the voices grew dimmer and dimmer, until there was nothing but the cicada song of the forest.

"Pippa?" Erzsi squeaked at last. "Is that you?"

Philippa extended her hands out to the crunching footsteps but was lifted to her feet by a hold much too strong to be her cousin.

"The madness has taken me!" she cried into Troilo's chest. "I can no longer tell what is real, and what is a dream!"

"Philippa." His hands cupped her cheeks, dried with salt water, and the stirring within her quieted. "You are *here*, with me," he said.

"You..."

Philippa tightened her grip around his waist as he brought her in closer. Eyes closed, she was deaf to everything but his steady heartbeat.

"May we leave the forest?" Erzsi asked. "I feel things crawling on me."

Loosening his hold, Troilo seemed to wake from their shared reverie. "Follow close," he directed. "The way is not far."

Guided back by a whispering breeze, they found dozens of stars shooting slantways across the sky as they stepped onto the plains.

"There are so many!" Erzsi yelled, running out into the field. "Too many to count!"

Philippa and Troilo watched as she twirled as gleefully as a child in the snow—her laughter unrestrained.

"I do believe this is the happiest I have ever seen her," he said.

"She has not been afforded much opportunity for childlike

wonder," Philippa replied, lifting her chin to the void of the starlight menagerie.

Troilo stood quietly at her side as Erzsi cackled in the distance. It felt to Philippa that he was watching her more than the celestial shower.

"*'Oh what hells would I endure, to taste of thy heavens, to drink from thy fountains...'*" she recited by heart. "*'To pray at thy temples...'*"

"*'Once more,'*" he breathed.

Philippa turned to see Troilo staring, astonished. Was he thinking of Costanza still? Or was it possible he was thinking of...

"I know now," Philippa whispered, "what your Stanzi and I have in common."

Troilo's hand opened as she laced her fingers with his.

"It is *you,*" she said, meeting his gaze.

"Philippa." Taking her other hand, Troilo squared his shoulders. "Will you meet me by the pond just after midnight? There is something I must tell—"

"*There! Over there in the field!*"

Troilo retracted as company rushed at them from the wood line.

"Did you not hear us calling?" Duke Sixten demanded. "Was it too much to include us—your brother and me—in your adventures?"

Philippa glanced to Troilo, feeling herself deflated. She hadn't even had a chance to tell him *yes*—that she would meet him!

"Her Highness felt a fit coming on," Troilo said.

"Well, she seems perfectly well, now," Duke Sixten countered.

"It is a blessing Herr Visconti chose to join us tonight," Erzsi chimed in. "It is lucky he was near."

"Lucky," the duke scoffed, turning to Troilo. "She does not seem to have fits *without* him nearby."

"Now, now, that is enough," said Franz. "There is no need for hostility in the wake of such good new—"

"Nor without you nearby, Duke Sixten." Erzsi's words bared

teeth, and the sheer magnitude of their bite was enough to quiet everyone. "And need I remind you," she snapped, "you are not her husband, nor her family, *nor* her doctor."

"Erzsi!" Mellie scolded, seemingly appearing from thin air. "Hold your tongue!"

"It is quite all right, Fräulein." Sixten let out a relaxed laugh. "Her Highness has yet to hear."

Hear what?

"Tell them, darling," he added, looking to Philippa.

Confused, she combed at her hair. "Tell them what?"

"Oh..." Concern reverberated through his voice. "That is right, the memory lapse..."

"Pippa," Franz urged. "You do not remember accepting Duke Sixten's proposal?"

Her heart shattered in her chest as her gaze snapped to Troilo's. *"No,"* she mouthed, "I did not—!"

"You did," the duke assured. "It may have even been the excitement that frightened you, so."

Philippa swore she had not accepted nor declined his offer— she didn't even remember him *asking* her, but how could she trust her own memory to recall anything correctly?

"Did you, Pippa?" Erzsi pleaded, her eyes glazed over in disappointment.

"I do not know," she admitted timidly. "Herr Visconti—?"

But halfway disappeared under the cover of night, Philippa watched helplessly with strained vocal cords as Troilo walked back to Marmorschossl alone.

ELEVEN

June 17, 1900
Just after midnight

Erzsi scanned the perimeter of her bedroom, draped in shades of midnight. If it were any other night, she would have long been fast asleep, especially after a day with so much socializing. But the way Philippa had looked at Troilo under the star fall scratched at Erzsi's brain, and she couldn't understand why she would have accepted Duke Sixten's proposal.

Could such a look have only been one of her games?

As she pulled the blanket to her chin, Erzsi pondered the way she'd mocked Philippa's claim over sharing a connection with Troilo. If they hadn't had one then, they definitely did now, and what had grown between them was more than mere lust. It was *friendship.* The perfect foundation for love. And yet, Philippa had still given herself away to a man who she neither loved nor liked.

Why?

For money? For status?

If it weren't for the candlelight that accompanied the foot-steps outside of Erzsi's door, she might have thought them imaginary. Propping herself onto her elbow, she watched the flame draw near, then vanish.

"Pippa?"

Sliding from her bed, Erzsi skipped to her window, where below, Troilo sat in the grass just beyond the corkscrew willow. Fireflies frolicked like summer sprites, huddling on the corner of his journal as if to light the path of his pencil. His gaze, though, seemed to be on the pond and the sparks of light that twinkled across it, as though he were scrying its reflection like a black mirror.

He was waiting—for her!

Erzsi pushed against the bottom of her windowpane, doing her best to stifle the sound of it cracking open as Philippa's blonde locks appeared below. Walking toward Troilo in her plum robe, she combed her way through the breezy branches of the willow.

The fireflies took flight in succession as Troilo moved to stand, pocketing his journal.

"Were you going to tell me?" he demanded.

"I do not remember it," Philippa replied. "I swear, I..."

Clutching the windowsill, Erzsi held her breath.

"If you do not remember..." Troilo's voice was faint but decipherable. "Then perhaps you did not."

Cricket chirping filled the air until at last, Philippa spoke. "I was considering accepting his proposal," she admitted. "I told Erzsi as much."

Troilo shook his head as he pivoted toward the pond, where an orchestra of lights danced over the water.

"I was going to tell you," she pleaded.

"When?" he asked, turning to face her. "At the wedding?"

Philippa cast her gaze to the other side of the pond, where the white petals of the spirea glowed under the beech, its weeping branches, too, adorned with fireflies. "It is easy to judge me from where you stand," she said. "As a *man* perfectly content to be alone forever."

"Rest assured, twenty-four is plenty young to still find love," Troilo countered. "And old enough not to settle."

Losing her composure, Philippa whipped around to face him. "I will receive no other offers of marriage!" she shouted. "There will be no other opportunities."

"And will he be the father of your children?"

Erzsi shrunk down to the floor, splaying her fingers across the cool hardwood.

She remembered the day Doctor Kerzl had told Philippa that she would likely never bear children, the cause of her infertility unknown. She had cried for two days straight.

"As I was saying, no one else would want something so damaged," said Philippa.

Erzsi peered back down through the open crack of the window to see that she and Troilo were now facing each other, separated by only a couple inches. He seemed to search her eyes as both of them stood shrouded in shadow.

"A poor choice of word if you are describing yourself," he said, just loud enough for Erzsi to make out.

Philippa lifted her chin to him. "What word would you suggest, Doctor Visconti?"

Reminiscent of that day in the woods, the same silence fell over them; the crickets had stopped their chirping, and the frogs had stopped croaking.

"Exquisite," Troilo murmured.

Erzsi inhaled sharply, imagining the invisible threads between them as he brushed the strands of silken hair from Philippa's cheek.

"If I were not your only link to *her*," Philippa whispered back, her teeth losing their grip on her bottom lip in a nervous laugh, "would you care so much for my fate?"

Erzsi gasped over her shoulder.

It was too blasphemous to say out loud—the notion that it

was Troilo's *late wife* who Philippa had been channeling in her writings?

When Erzsi looked back out the window, she saw that Philippa had left Troilo in a lush tangle of green darkness. Abandoning the sill, she ran to her bedroom door and into the hall.

Philippa seemed neither surprised nor distressed to see her standing at the top of the staircase.

"Either you are conniving, or you are mad," Erzsi whispered sharply. "I am not sure which is worse."

Shielding the dancing flame of her candelabra, a fiery glow illuminated Philippa's face as she stared ahead.

"Will you even bother to deny it?" Erzsi demanded. "What an unbearably cruel way to get close to someone, Pippa!"

"Even you do not know everything, Erzsi," Philippa murmured, nudging past her absently.

9:21 A.M.

Sulking in his wingback chair, Troilo watched from the parlor window as the sun burned off the morning fog.

How he'd wanted to tell her. To break out his oriental box and confess to her that her ghost was no ghost at all, but the *man* standing in front of her. A man with no record of ever having been born, who had been forever condemned to wander the earth in a human coil.

How would Philippa feel once she knew he had sought her out from the beginning? Would he claim it had been for *love?*

Troilo had committed atrocities in the name of love.

And all the while she had been reaching for his hand under the star fall, Philippa had been considering Duke Sixten's proposal.

Dropping his eyes to *The Serpent Prince*, laid open across his lap, Troilo slammed it shut. The entire morning he'd meditated on its woodcut imagery, but was still no closer to a solution.

The doorknob turned, and Erzsi peeked in with a stern brow. "Come quickly," she urged.

Troilo followed in quick steps down the hall, careful to avoid the eye of Governess Coudenhove as he rounded the staircase bannister.

"I found it this way," Erzsi said, waving him into the library. *"Look."*

Troilo felt a cold sweat as he scanned the library shelves, from which a section of books had gone missing.

"I will ask you this only once, Troilo." Erzsi wandered over to the shelves, adjusting one of the spines that had fallen over. "Who is the spirit my cousin claims to be in communion with?"

Troilo traced his jawline with his thumb and forefinger. Something told him that Erzsi already knew the answer.

"She has told me of her automatic writing," she went on, turning to him. "Do you believe she is mad?"

"I believe she is the furthest thing from mad," Troilo admitted.

Erzsi locked onto him with an icy, unwavering gaze, which was broken by the sudden *crash* of something upstairs.

"Pippa," she whispered.

Troilo bolted for the second floor, rushing past Governess Coudenhove at the bottom of the staircase.

"Herr Visconti—?"

"Please, Fräulein," he called back to her. "I have things under control."

Erzsi flew down the hall ahead of him, finding Philippa's bedroom door unlocked at the end. Catching himself in the door frame, Troilo halted.

Seated at her vanity, Philippa scribbled away with her glass pen among a collection of candlesticks melted down to the wick, the uncovered mirror in front of her completely broken out.

Turning back to Troilo with eyes wider than a full moon, Erzsi hesitantly stepped over the slivers of cut paper and mutilated books scattering the wood floor.

"Pippa, have you slept at all?" Erzsi asked.

Closing the door softly behind him, Troilo's gaze caught on the silver shears resting on the bed, among a cushion of paper stars.

Each star, Costanza had once said to him, *is but a flower of the sky...*

He could still envision the grass star in the center of his palm as he ran his hand over the paper carnage.

"'And the night, a heavenly garden,'" Troilo whispered to himself.

"She is bleeding!" Erzsi exclaimed.

Troilo found his reflection in Philippa's shattered vanity mirror as he steadied himself on the back of her chair. Staring straight ahead, eyes open, her right hand moved in messy cursive strokes, trailing blood over the paper.

"Pippa." Erzsi fell to the floor, demanding Philippa's attention to no avail. "I hate the way I spoke to you—what is wrong with her?"

"She is in an altered state."

Gently, Troilo reached for her hand, imbedded with mirror shards. "Philippa," he murmured, halting her writing. "Enough."

Turning to him, her hazy stare was as infinite as it was empty.

Removing the quill from between her fingers, Troilo took a knee. "Erzsi," he whispered, "would you fetch my medical bag?"

Shooting to her feet, Erzsi was gone in a flash.

"Troilo," Philippa whimpered, seemingly to herself. "I did not mean to make a mess..."

"No more of this," he said, closing her diary.

"But the week has not finished. I have not—"

"I do not care."

"All right," Philippa whispered.

Troilo pinched the bridge of his nose, where a single tear had fallen. "Please forgive me," he pleaded, laying his head in her lap. "I am a coward."

Feeling Philippa's fingers stroke the top of his hair, a vision bled into Troilo's mind of her uninjured hand tangled in his dark locks. Only then did he realize the seemingly random nature of his visions, and why he saw some things through her sight and not others. She loved cream puffs and swans, and her trinkets. *Love* was the bridge.

"You may speak with authority on many things," Philippa said softly from above. "But cowardice is not among them."

Lifting his head from her thigh, Troilo looked into Philippa's eyes to see a vision of his own looking back at him.

"Here!" Erzsi said, dropping the leather bag at his side.

He cleared his throat, wiping the remaining tear from his eye. "Thank you."

Erzsi, unsurprisingly, did not budge.

"Would you leave us, please," Troilo added, glancing at her.

Obeying with a reluctant nod, Erzsi backed up one step at a time, until she reached the bedroom door, which she slithered around, then closed.

"I know Costanza's life was taken from her," Philippa said as Troilo reached for her bloodied hand.

He clenched his jaw, listening as he began to extract the mirror shards with a pair of tweezers.

"I cannot tell you how, but I saw it," she went on. "The last I remember, I was looking into the mirror and something completely possessed me. It would not let go."

"This will sting," Troilo warned, preparing a cloth gauze with alcohol.

"How archaic of a homeland you have" —Philippa winced— "to condemn a woman to such a fate."

Troilo's heart caught in his throat as he spoke. "It was I who was her ill fate."

"I do not believe that."

Glancing up at her, he watched Philippa's lips quiver into a smile. "There is much about me you do not know, Highness," he said, reaching for a bandage.

"Perhaps you might tell me."

Troilo focused on wrapping her hand.

Even without knowing what Philippa had channeled in her writings, he knew it was only a matter of time before she might concede to her curiosity and read them back. And what would he do, then? Would he flip to page one-hundred-and-sixteen of *Ballads of the Starlight Menagerie* and point to Costanza's name? Break out his box of travel papers?

Philippa wanted the truth, but what if she couldn't fathom it?

"There," Troilo said, laying the bandaged hand on her lap.

"Would you take me swimming?"

So caught off guard by the question, he almost laughed. "Pardon?"

"Swimming," Philippa said cheerily. "I would like to learn to swim."

Rising to his feet, Troilo helped her do the same. "Perhaps another day," he said, steadying her. "I think you should try and sleep now."

"Tomorrow, then?"

"Perhaps tomorrow," he replied, walking her to bed.

"I am quite tired," Philippa murmured, watching him clear the paper stars from the bed. "But..."

"Here you are," he whispered, pulling down her covers.

Leaning onto his arm, Philippa climbed beneath the blankets. "Would you stay?" she asked, situating herself.

A tinge of shameful desire rippled through Troilo's chest.

"It is just that I—" She pursed her lips. "I am afraid to fall asleep."

Nodding, Troilo took a seat on the edge of her bed. "I will stay until you fall asleep," he assured.

Philippa's smile fell as she took in the state of the bedroom, which lay in shambles around them. "Should we call someone to clean the room?" she asked warily.

"I think it would be better if we did not call upon anyone," Troilo replied. "I will straighten things myself."

Slinking beneath her covers, Philippa pulled them to her chin.

"It is all right," he whispered to her. "I do not mind."

"Would you fetch me my book?" she asked, pointing to her vanity.

Troilo didn't need to ask which book as he scanned the surface, scattered with leftover mirror glass. Picking up *Ballads of the Starlight Menagerie,* he brought it to her.

"Thank you," she said, turning onto her side.

Troilo tidied the room as best as he could, hiding the shreds of paper and gutted books in the corridor. Philippa had glanced up from her pages intermittently as she read, until finally, she drifted off to sleep with his book in her hand.

She didn't move as he removed it from her bandaged grip, bookmarking her place at ballad one-hundred-and-eleven. The sand in the hourglass was running out—and the window of opportunity for him to tell Philippa of his identity was closing.

Holding the book in his hands, Troilo studied the rise, then fall, of her chest. For so long, he had energetically watched over her as she slept, trying to imagine how peaceful she might look. How her lashes might flutter with dreams.

Troilo slid the book onto her nightstand, then leaned over her, pressing his lips to her forehead. Philippa flinched only a little, letting out a soft sigh as he pulled away.

Not expecting to find anyone waiting outside her bedroom door, Troilo startled back as he stepped into the hallway, where Erzsi and Governess Coudenhove had been sitting on the sofa with Blitz.

"She is asleep," he announced as they rose to their feet in unison. "It will likely take all day to recover, so I ask that no one disturb her in the meantime."

"Of course," Governess Coudenhove replied. "Is there anything I can do?"

Arms crossed tight over her chest, Erzsi narrowed her gaze on him and tapped her foot. She had questions, understandably, but Troilo could not answer them here.

"No, thank you," he replied, splitting a nod between them. "Rest is all."

TWELVE

June 18, 1900
5:20 A.M.

"Troilo," whispered a voice.

Deep in an unshakeable slumber, he stirred as chilly fingers grazed his bare shoulder.

"*Troilo.* It is tomorrow."

So sweet it was, he wanted to turn—to follow the voice at his bedside as though it were the sun, and he was a sunflower.

Troilo awoke suddenly on his back to find himself alone. The hour of morning was beginning to take shape, washing the bedroom in a soft glow. Erecting himself in bed, he rubbed his eyes. Having taken his own advice, he'd slept all through the afternoon and night without waking, which left him feeling groggy.

Forcing himself out of bed, Troilo began to dress. He needed coffee, and to stretch. Then he would check on—

He paused the buttoning of his sleeve cuff, noting that the corridor door was cracked open about an inch.

"*It is tomorrow,*" he whispered, darting to the window.

Down below, Philippa had bunched up her nightgown and was wading through the flora and into the pond.

Erzsi startled awake as Troilo ran past her door, but he paid no mind, his feet hardly touching the ground as he flew down the stairs.

"Philippa!" he called, leaping from the veranda. "Do not go any further!"

Rays of sunrise pierced a cluster of stray rainclouds over the mountain range behind her as she turned back to see Troilo on the shore.

"I tried to wake you!" she called.

"Please," Troilo pleaded, short of breath. "Do not wade out any further."

"But I am not afraid anymore!" she exclaimed. "I am a new woman!"

Troilo braced as she wobbled a bit.

"Is it not wonderful?"

"It is wonderful, indeed, Highness," he replied, tearing off his vest. "I am overjoyed that you are no longer afraid—but *you still cannot swim!*"

Philippa unfurled her bandaged fist as she looked down at the water, now up to her hips. "Oh dear," she said. "I see."

"Do not move," he directed. "I will come to you."

Warm water soaked through his pants as he waded in to meet her, sending a tidal wave among the lily pads.

"I did try to wake you," she reminded him.

"I know." Troilo pushed his hair back and out of his face as he sloughed through water. "Take my hand—"

Losing her footing, Philippa fell into the water. "Ah!" she shouted, digging her fingers into his shoulder as Troilo lifted her.

"You mustn't fight it," he said, keeping her level. "The more you thrash, the heavier you become."

Settling in his hold, she relaxed her wounded hand as it lay across his shoulder.

"The first lesson of swimming is not to swim," Troilo said, taking her deeper. "It is to float."

"I am..."

"Weightless," Troilo said, noting the buoyancy of her lower half. "As light as..."

"A feather," she whispered, lying back.

Lighter and lighter on his fingertips, she floated only just above their touch, outstretching her arms like angel wings across a bed of watery florals. Beads of pond water speckled her lashes, reminding Troilo of the way the rain had once trickled over Costanza's blue lips, washing her glazed, waxy skin free of any blood.

Might he ferry her away, now? Somewhere safe and undisturbed?

She who had been reborn, even stronger, even more radiant than before?

For all the wonders Troilo had glimpsed—the snow-capped pines of a Russian winter, blue waves of the Aegean, desert sunsets over the pyramids—the sight of her, glistening like a pearl, eclipsed them all.

Lifting her head, Philippa readjusted herself in his arms with a laugh. "Is *this* what I have been so afraid of?"

"There is something I must confess to you," Troilo whispered suddenly.

Mirroring his serious expression, her lips parted in anticipation and the air around them suddenly cooled.

"You might be a conjurer after all," Philippa whispered, as a curtain of mist, shimmering in the sun like a thousand rainbows, began to fall all around them.

It fell as quietly as snow, leaving the two of them untouched in the center.

"Perhaps that is why..."

The tips of her fingers found the back of Troilo's neck, making the hairs stand on end.

"...each time I call out to my spirit, it is *you* who comes."

Troilo swallowed hard, pulling her even closer. "You cannot marry Duke Sixten," he said.

"How could I?" Smirking slightly, her green eyes rounded his face. "How could I marry him, when fate has sent you to me?"

For centuries, Troilo had trekked stormy sea after stormy sea, void of any lighthouse, on an infinite odyssey of nothingness. And here she clung to him, having fallen in love with the zmaj all over again.

"It was not fate, nor your spirit that brought us together," Troilo whispered, teary-eyed. "It was me."

Philippa squinted at him as she drew back.

"I stitched the threads of fate myself."

"What do you...you *sought me out?*"

"I did," he admitted.

"Why would you..." Philippa's voice cracked, and her eyes widened with dilated pupils. "You needed a channeler. Someone to speak to Cost—"

"No!"

"Is that all I ever was to you?" she asked. "A *placeholder* for your wife so you could feel her again?"

Jumping from his hold, Philippa stumbled through the floral debris. The misting rain came to a sudden halt as she emerged onto land like a princess of the sea, her transparent nightgown sticking to her like a second skin.

"*Do you not find yourself so very cruel?*" she demanded, ringing her long rope of hair. "To have ensorcelled me this way? And to think that I questioned if your" —she let out a vexed laugh— "*feelings* for me were anything more than remnants of..."

"Philippa," Troilo pleaded. "I love you."

"You *used* me!" she snapped back. "You love what I remind you of!"

Climbing out of the murky pond water, Troilo reached for his vest sprinkled with dew, shuffling through the pockets until he found his green journal. "You wanted to read my poetry—" On all fours, he held up the offering, urging her to take it. "Please."

Philippa grabbed it. Then, flipping furiously through the pages, she halted somewhere in the center.

"They are all for you."

Her brow flexed as she read, softening with each word, until finally, she looked up.

"Every word I have ever written," Troilo breathed, "I have written for *you.*"

Philippa took a step back, swallowing as though there were a stick caught in her throat. "You have only just met me."

"Is that how you feel?"

As if Troilo were the dangerous outsider he'd been painted to be, her eyes darkened further into alarm.

"That we have only just met?"

Philippa tore the page, crumpling it in her fist. "There is much I do not know about you, indeed," she said, dropping his journal to the ground.

Erzsi, who had been watching from the window of the parlor, loosened her grip on the curtain just as Philippa burst through the door.

"Pippa, what—?"

Dripping water all over the freshly waxed parquet, Philippa grabbed onto the hard chestnut of the railing. *"Not now, Erzsi!"* she shouted, charging up the stairs.

Erzsi gathered her skirt, careful to avoid the puddles she left behind. "Wait!" Racing ahead, she skidded to a halt in front of Philippa's bedroom door. "What is it, in your hand?"

"Leave me," Philippa ordered, trying to nudge her way past.

Erzsi disregarded the command. "I want to know what is happening," she said, clasping the doorknob in both hands. "And if you do not tell me, I will—!"

"You will what?" Angrily, Philippa brought her wet hair to one side. "Tell everyone that I am a fickle enchantress?"

"I *said* I was sorry," Erzsi murmured. "*You* were too busy channeling to hear me."

Philippa sighed an unconvincing sigh, an indicator that she was tired, and Erzsi had almost won.

"It is *Troilo* I do not trust," she hissed. "Now, let me see it."

Straightening out the paper, Philippa reluctantly handed it off to Erzsi, who uncrumpled it further as she followed her into her room.

How many times have I thought upon it,
When I should see your face again?
In what ways altered but ever-constant,
My Star of the Sea,
Let your name prove true
As my love for you.

I have grown accustomed to my nightly wanderings,
In my tearful dreams,
Parting lips, entering into
Your silken and velvety wedlock.
My thoughts drift to bed, but your eyes don't lie—
They keep me awake, in the twilight gray,
Where there is no day.

My dear, my heart,
Quarry of my life—
Your starry beams I track in strife.
But a golden net doth me enrapture,
And in your locks am I thus captured.

"He said every word he has ever written has been for me," Philippa said at last.

Erzsi's arm dropped to her side. "How can that be?"

"He must have known a great deal about me before he

arrived," she replied, taking a seat on the bed, which had been discreetly restored to its original state. "I do not know whether to feel afraid or flattered."

"Perhaps he was not being literal."

"No..." Philippa looked as though she might cry. "I believed that perhaps something divine had brought us together. Now I see it was something much more calculated."

"But what motive would he have for such a thing?"

Philippa combed at the tangled ends of her wet hair with her injured hand. She would be needing a new bandage.

"It is because I remind him of Costanza," she murmured. "To him, I am just a vessel his wife may speak through."

Leaning back on the bed, Erzsi massaged her temples. There was something Troilo was not telling them.

"It is not so simple as him falling in love with your likeness in the paper," she murmured, handing the poem back. "Aunt Valerie is the one who found him. We would not even know him, if not for her."

Philippa seemed to be thinking, but she didn't share her thoughts. "I cannot send him away," she said finally.

"Of course not," Erzsi replied, hopping down from the bed. "There is a mystery to be solved."

"What are you doing?"

Ignoring her, Erzsi made her way to Philippa's vanity, where her diary lay closed. "You are channeling his wife, yes?" she asked, whipping around with the book in hand.

"Yes, but I..." Philippa blinked rapidly as she glanced down at her lap. "It is personal, Erzsi. You should not..."

"Troilo found the banner of serpent heraldry he had seen outside," Erzsi read out loud from a random page. *"And with a single point...sealed his destiny."*

Philippa seemed to liven as Erzsi's gaze flicked upward from across the room.

"Perhaps *she* can tell you what he will not."

A sudden knock rattled the bedroom door, and Mellie entered.

"Mellie!" Erzsi darted over to meet her, slipping the diary to Philippa on the way. "To what do we owe the pleasure?"

"Duke Sixten has come with a message," she said.

Oh—in all the trouble with Troilo, Erzsi had almost forgotten about the wart!

"His Majesty has allowed Archduke Franz to marry Sophie. We are to celebrate his engagement tonight at the villa. We are all to attend..." Mellie at last located Philippa, who had wandered over to the vanity in her wet nightgown. "Even Doctor Visconti. Your Highness, you are..."

Erzsi made an awkward face as she swiveled away from her governess, just in time to see Philippa tuck the poem in between the pages of her diary.

"Herr Visconti is teaching me how to swim," Philippa said, setting the diary on her vanity's top. "I suppose I should wash my hair."

"Duke Sixten is downstairs," Mellie reminded her.

"She cannot see him this way," Erzsi chimed in. "Not smelling of pond water! Come, come, Pippa—I will help you wash up!"

Philippa found Mellie's side as they made their way to the door. "Please pass on to Duke Sixten that I am in no state to see him without a proper hair washing," she directed.

Alone in the doorway, Mellie looked to Philippa's vanity as their voices vanished down the hall.

The royal pair were not as sly as they believed. Having long decoded their unspoken language, it was clear to Mellie immediately that she'd intruded on a private meeting upon entering. Since the star fall, everyone's already suspicious behavior had only worsened.

Whatever Philippa had hidden within that book, Mellie knew it would likely hurt. Still, she walked over and fanned its pages, written in messy cursive, until she landed on the bookmark.

It was better to know the truth. At least that's what Mellie reminded herself as she neared the bottom of the stairs, tearfully clutching the poem in her hand.

"There you are, Fräulein." Duke Sixten stood tall and strong, grinning in the empty foyer. "I was beginning to worry."

"Forgive my tardiness."

He looked upward to the second floor in obvious anticipation.

"Your Grace, Her Highness has gone to bathe," Mellie added.

"You told her I was waiting?"

"She has been swimming."

The duke stepped forward. "Swimming?"

Mellie's finger brushed across her brow.

"Swimming where?"

"In the pond," she stuttered.

"*The pond!* How absolutely—"

Mellie would surely burst into tears, but they wouldn't be caused by him. Duke Sixten had been just as fooled as she had.

"Fräulein..." His voice softened as she stood before him. "Is something the matter?"

"I just have a slight headache," Mellie replied.

"Look at me."

Obliging his command, she met his eye through blurry vision.

"What has..."

No sooner did he reach for her, Mellie collapsed into sobs.

"What is the matter?"

"I cannot," she wept.

"*Of course,* you can."

Mellie averted her eyes, already spilling over.

"Mhm." Duke Sixten nodded. "The good doctor has broken your heart."

"He loves another." The words came more easily than expected. "Right under my nose, no less. Right under *all* our—" Mellie caught her tongue, meeting the now stony expression of the duke.

He'd always seemed to dislike Doctor Visconti, always seemed to distrust him, and now Mellie understood why.

"I must admit to you, Fräulein," said the duke. "I have always found him suspicious in character."

"Surely, he..." Mellie crossed her arms in annoyance.

"He has serpents inked on his arms, for God's sake," said Duke Sixten, leaning in. "This love you speak of. Has it been consummated?"

"I cannot say," she replied. "The cottage is so small; I cannot fathom where..."

A slow, dismissive nod followed. "Then there is no proof," he said.

Mellie looked down at the crumpled note she clutched at her side. "I found this," she murmured. "In Her Highness' room."

"May I?"

Reluctantly, she handed it over, watching as the duke unfolded the poem. He read slowly, digesting each word.

"You have done the right thing by showing me," he said at last.

Panic raced through Mellie's chest as he pocketed the poem, pivoting toward the door. "Your Grace—?"

"Yes, Fräulein?"

"What...what do you intend to do?"

"Everything in my power."

Mellie stepped hastily after him. "You intend to tell His Majesty?"

"Personally, Fräulein," he replied, lowering his voice, "I could do without the embarrassment of such a thing going public. I have enough gossip attached to my name already." He brought his fist to his mouth, then cleared his throat. "It is merely a whim. Is it worth igniting the plans we have made over a whim?"

"I suppose not."

"Then allow me to put an end to it quietly." His grin was lighthearted. Much *too* lighthearted for such a thing. "Their senses will return once they see the error of their ways."

Mellie felt a curdling in her stomach. "Put an end to it quietly, *how?*" she asked timidly.

Duke Sixten smiled again, this time with teeth. "Fräulein!" he teased. "I am no *monster.*"

"No! I would never suggest—!"

"I will simply see to it that Philippa is never within a hundred yards of your doctor," he added, folding a crisp crease in the note. "You need only place your faith in me."

THIRTEEN

5:30 P.M.

Erzsi's eyes narrowed knowingly as she took Troilo's hand to hop down from the carriage platform. "Thank you," she said, looking ahead to the spitting water of the marble fountain.

She had watched Philippa step out first in her dark blue evening dress, their hands merely brushing as he'd helped her down.

He had replaced her bandage in painful silence after her bath, and the short ride from Marmorschlossl had been no better. Troilo had sat stiffly next to Mellie, watching the hazy thunderheads that floated over the mountains out the window, while Philippa reached for her hair out of nervous habit every few minutes, only to find it pinned up with the empress' diamond stars. Neither dared to look in the other's direction.

"Watch your step, Fräulein."

Erzsi turned back to Troilo, imagining the clamminess of Mellie's hand as he helped her out. Her face was splotchy, as though she'd been crying.

"My darling brother," Philippa gushed up ahead. "Congratulations to you!"

"His Majesty will be pleased to see you wearing Her Majesty's jewels," Franz remarked. "They suit you wonderfully."

Erzsi looked up to the gray sky, watching Troilo in her periphery.

Dinners with Franz and her grandfather had always been a bit fiddly. Now, in addition to the layers of tension, Erzsi would have to watch two lovesick pigeons pine for each other across the table.

Love was a disease, truly. God willing, such a thing would never happen to her.

"I am overjoyed you could join us, Herr Visconti," Franz exclaimed.

"The pleasure is all mine, Your Highness," Troilo replied, at last closing the carriage door.

"There she is."

Erzsi wrinkled her nose as Duke Sixten approached, his grating footsteps a worse harbinger than the hovering storm clouds.

"My dear Highness, what happened to your hand?" he asked.

"Oh." Philippa glanced down at her bandage. "I was trying to adjust the mirror on my vanity when it broke."

"Broke?"

"Poor sister," Franz interjected. "You have never had much luck with mirrors."

"Still, you look marvelous." Duke Sixten jauntily kissed Philippa's cheek. "A remarkable creature, is she not, Doctor?"

Erzsi turned to Duke Sixten.

What was he doing?

"It is fine to agree," he added.

"Enough," Philippa begged.

The way Troilo looked at her, with her downcast eyes and dazzling stars, was enough to make Erzsi's chest hurt.

"Am I not a very fortunate man?" the duke went on.

"It will rain," Erzsi interjected. "Any moment now, the sky is sure to open up."

"Then let us go *inside*," Philippa added, tearing herself away.

"She does not know her own beauty," Duke Sixten added as he crossed in front of Mellie.

The way her gaze met his in silent communion—it was a look exchanged between *allies*. Mellie with her false niceties! How carelessly they'd left her alone in Philippa's bedroom.

"Highness," Troilo said, appearing at Erzsi's side. "Accompany me, would you?"

"You have made an enemy of him." Taking his arm, she motioned first to Duke Sixten, then to Mellie. "And of her."

"It was never my intention to make enemies."

"I am not the only one rather confused by your intentions as of late," Erzsi countered. "Whatever it is you have done to my cousin—"

"I have not *done* anything to her, Erzsi." Troilo lowered his voice to a whisper. "I have only brought something already within her to the forefront."

"We do not have much time, so let me make myself clear," she hushed. "I will help you because I believe she loves you."

It was clear by the look on his face—the way his eyes softened in that silly, romantic manner—that Philippa had not told him as much.

"Now you know," Erzsi added. "And so do *they*."

She motioned ahead, where Duke Sixten was pulling Philippa under the creeper-wrapped columns, out of sight.

"My hair!" Philippa scolded. "I mustn't ruin it."

"His Majesty will receive us in the drawing room for champagne," said Franz, nodding at the footman who waited to greet them. "I saw to it that all the rooms were decorated in lilies."

"Sophie's favorite," Erzsi clarified, urging Troilo forward and through the door.

"I heard about your little sunrise swim." Duke Sixten spoke just loud enough to hear as they started up the bifurcated stairs. "There are much better places to swim in Ischl, Doctor," he added over his shoulder.

"It was not his idea," Philippa reminded. "It was mine."

Erzsi tightened her grip on Troilo's arm. She thought she heard a faint scoff from Mellie next to them, who up until that point had kept to herself.

"Right," Duke Sixten conceded. "Of course it was."

In the drawing room, several servants distributed fresh pours of French champagne from silver trays. It was the most ostentatious the room had ever looked, at least since Erzsi could remember. Philippa seemed not to notice, appearing as somber as Troilo. A remark from the duke or Mellie at the dinner table would be more than enough to expose them.

And what then?

Troilo would return to Zürich with a ruined reputation, and *Philippa!* If she refused to marry Duke Sixten, who knew where she'd be sent off to.

"Pippa, I must steal you," Erzsi said, appearing at her side. "I am dreadfully upset."

"Is it about Prince Otto?"

"I am happy for Franz, I really am! But..."

Philippa turned to Duke Sixten. "You must excuse me for a moment."

He sized them up with his beady blue eyes. "I will fetch you a glass of champagne," he said.

Erzsi pulled Philippa to the left, finding sanctuary near the decorated fireplace mantle.

"Thank you," Philippa said, shielding the room with her back.

"You must listen to me," Erzsi warned. "Duke Sixten knows."

Philippa appeared to stop breathing.

"Mellie found the poem Troilo wrote for you. I have not worked out what they have done with it, but..." Erzsi could see that the duke was watching them as he talked. "If you want to be with Troilo, he must grovel before His Majesty as Franz did for Sophie, and he must do it soon."

Philippa spotted Troilo over her shoulder, across the room.

"You must speak with him," Erzsi urged, reading her mind. "Once the second course comes, feign illness and have him take you back to the cottage."

"What of Duke Sixten?"

"He will not dare stop you in front of everyone," she whispered hastily.

"I feel as though I am being talked about," Duke Sixten announced, arriving with Philippa's champagne. "My ears are ringing like mad."

Erzsi willed her thin grimace into a smile. "Good things only," she said.

"Sister," Franz called over. "Come, stand with me."

Philippa nodded to Erzsi and Duke Sixten, then crossed the room to meet her brother, leaving the two of them alone.

"It is good that you and I should have some time together, Highness."

"I could not disagree more," Erzsi replied, pretending to watch the room.

"Do not think I am unaware," he said, leaning in, "of what liaisons you might be encouraging."

Erzsi turned slowly to meet his gaze, then rolled her eyes forward. She knew better than to take the bait.

"You are unkind to tease a man so viciously." Duke Sixten let out a soft, unbothered chuckle, lowering his voice further. "Especially looking as lovely as you do this evening."

Lovely?

Erzsi clenched her jaw as she turned back to him.

"Of course, you lack Philippa's figure, but some men prefer to conquer..." He circled her face, then her chest, stripping her naked with his eyes. "...women of a feistier demeanor."

It was as close to a threat as he could manage. A reminder that he could take what he wanted, when and how he wanted it.

"Yes." Erzsi blinked. "Well."

She must have looked as revolted as she felt, because Troilo was already headed in her direction.

"Men are despicable creatures. Are they not?"

"Highness," said Troilo. "Are you well?"

She only nodded as the duke took a sip of champagne.

"His Royal and Imperial Majesty, Emperor Franz Josef."

Erzsi stepped to Troilo's side as the emperor made his way to Franz and Philippa.

"My dear niece." A bittersweet smile glowed beneath the wintery beard of the emperor as Philippa bowed her head, showcasing her hairpins. "Come," he said, extending his arm. "I shall escort you."

A footman announced each guest by name as they trickled into the dining room, which smelled richly of lilies. It only took Erzsi a moment to find her place at the small table, bedecked with floral centerpieces so large that she could almost hide behind them. Troilo took his place beside her, and Mellie next to him, with Franz, Philippa and Duke Sixten claiming their respective chairs across the table. The emperor was the last to find his place at the head, and the party followed as he took a seat.

Philippa's diamonds sparkled beneath the light of the chandelier as she looked past Erzsi to her reflection in the credenza mirror, framed by lit candelabras.

"As per our conversation the other day," began Franz as two footmen entered the room and began filling everyone's glass with a crimson wine, "I thought this would be most complimentary."

Erzsi balled her fists in her lap, unable to quell her hands from shaking. The sight of the duke across the table—his pearly, predatory smile—was more than enough to make her lose her appetite.

"Wine from the heart of Istria." Franz nodded across the table to Troilo. "You must tell us if it tastes of home."

Philippa reached for her glass, waiting patiently for the emperor to make his toast.

"To my nephew and his future bride," he said, with as much civility as he could muster. "A life of great happiness."

"Thank you, Your Majesty."

Franz and Duke Sixten carried the conversation through the first course, engaging the emperor on everything from the unpredictable Ischl climate to various hunting techniques to the local game. Erzsi sipped her wine delicately as she played mental chess, studying the duke's every move from across the table.

"The *only* reason that chamois escaped was because of her gentle heart—how many pheasants did you count, Pippa?"

Philippa outstretched her empty wine glass, focusing on the pour as another footman removed her hardly touched soup. "Nine," she replied.

"Rivaled only by Doctor Visconti," Franz added.

The emperor paused long enough for the valet to set a plate of Tafelspitz in front of him. "Is that true, Doctor?" he asked. "That our Philippa surpassed you?"

"It is the highest compliment to place second to Her Highness," Troilo replied. "Majesty."

Erzsi halted all motion of her fork as she turned to Philippa, who nervously reached for the heavy diamond stars with her bandaged hand.

"You are too kind, Herr Visconti," she said, focusing on the fast-emptying wine.

"One of these days," Duke Sixten interjected, swiping his glass from the table, *"one of these days,* Doctor Visconti, I will recall where I have seen you before."

"I have a familiar face," Troilo replied, glancing up from his knife and fork. "I have been told as much."

"You do have that way about you," Franz chimed in. "A certain mystique."

"Yes." Duke Sixten nodded. "Indeed, we shall be missing you."

Philippa looked up in alarm, catching Erzsi mid-chew.

"You see," he went on, wiping his mouth with his napkin, "Her Highness and I have some news—if it pleases His Majesty to hear, of course."

"You may proceed, Duke Sixten."

Philippa froze, looking as though she wanted nothing more than to dissolve into the patterned gold wallpaper as the men talked over her.

"Darling," said the duke, "would you like to tell them, or should I?"

Erzsi felt the grip of her fork grow slippery. Her eyes screamed at her cousin across the table—*now!* Act madder than a rabid dog! Surely, they will still see you are unwell!

But Philippa did not move.

"Her Highness, Archduchess Philippa and I have decided to resume our engagement," Duke Sixten announced.

"Splendid news!"

Philippa's eyes found Troilo. *"No,"* she mouthed, "I did not—!"

"We would like to be married by fall."

Franz turned his attention to Troilo. "What do you have to say about her progress, Doctor?"

"I have not accepted," Philippa interrupted.

The table went ghostly silent, and the emperor lowered his fork as everyone turned to look at her.

"What?" asked Franz.

"I said" —Philippa threw her napkin onto her untouched Tafelspitz— "I have not accepted Duke Sixten's proposal."

He laughed. "Why, of course you did!"

Erzsi glanced down at her glass of water to see a ripple expanding to the edges, as though someone had dropped a pebble in the center.

"You do not *remember* because of your illness. Majesty, she—"

"Even if I did accept your hand, I have changed my mind!"

Duke Sixten leaned in, grabbing Philippa's wrist beneath the table. "Now is not the time for a display of your hysterics," he scolded sharply.

The way Troilo sprung to his feet, Erzsi thought he might lunge across the table for the duke's throat.

"Unhand me!" A glass of water cracked, sending a shockwave over the table as Philippa tore herself from Duke Sixten's grip. "Unhand me or you will *see* hysterical."

Erzsi stood, exchanging a look with Troilo as Philippa blasted past the footman and through the dining room doors.

"My deepest, sincerest apologies, Your Majesty," the duke seethed, maneuvering himself out from the table.

"What is the meaning of this?" Franz called after him. "Duke Sixten!"

Philippa ripped through the villa halls, turning the head of every servant along the way. She'd sooner find herself in the nunnery than married to a man like the duke.

"You will apologize for storming out!" Duke Sixten chased her into the parlor, hot in pursuit. "We will sit down and enjoy the rest of this dinner," he warned, "and they will see that it is only a lovers' quarrel."

"It is not a lovers' quarrel."

He was close enough that she could see the sweat seeping from his pores, count the whiskers on his face.

"I do not love you," Philippa declared. "And I will *not* marry you."

"Because you prefer men of a more simple variety—who ink their forearms and sell snake oil," he spat. "Isn't that right?"

Philippa stepped back only to realize that he'd cornered her.

"I am certain he loves you well, with all of his charms and travels—"

Philippa's gaze slipped past Duke Sixten's shoulder to the parlor entry, where Troilo was walking toward them like a knight in shining armor.

"Herr Visconti!" Philippa pleaded, unable to push past the duke. "I would like to—!"

Blocking her, Duke Sixten held her in place.

"I would like to leave!" she shouted.

"You will not leave and humiliate me!"

Blown by a huge gust of wind, the French doors to the terrace flew open, sending a whirlwind of sticks and leaves into the parlor. The very ground seemed to quake as debris ricocheted off the walls.

When Philippa opened her eyes, she saw that Troilo had caught Duke Sixten's hand in midair.

"You were right, Your Grace," he said, constricting his fingers around his arm like a cobra. *"We have met before."*

Low thunder rumbled the walls of the parlor, shaking the hanging crystals of the mantle's candelabras.

Philippa looked to the doors, one nearly off of its hinges. Had *he—?*

Duke Sixten blinked, visibly in pain, as though Troilo might snap the very bone.

"Troilo," Philippa breathed, lightly touching his back.

Releasing his hold, the firestorm in his eyes dissolved as he turned to her.

"I will not tolerate this in the home of His Royal and Imperial Majesty!"

They turned in unison to the entryway, where Franz stood with Erzsi at his side.

"Highness," Duke Sixten stuttered, clutching his wrist. "Thank God—!"

"Duke Sixten, I suggest you collect your belongings at once."

"You." The duke turned his attention onto Erzsi. "You maniacal little—! Do not believe a word she has told you!"

"She need not tell me a thing. I have seen it for myself."

"Franz! You cannot..."

"I *cannot?"*

Philippa ran to Erzsi, who was studying one of the many sticks the wind had blown in.

"Did you—?" she asked, gaping at the doors.

Philippa only looked to Troilo across the room, who seemed equally stunned as he stood there, rubbing his arms.

"Sister," Franz said, turning to Philippa. "Are you all right?"

Avoiding Duke Sixten's glare, she nodded weakly.

"Take the carriage back to Marmoschossl," he ordered quietly. "Herr Visconti?"

Troilo perked up from across the room.

"Please accompany my sister back to rest."

"Come, Pippa," Erzsi added, pulling her into the hall.

Troilo nodded to Franz as he followed them out. "Please relay our sincerest apologies to His Majesty for the disruption."

On the other side of the wall, Erzsi pulled Philippa close. "You must go at once," she warned softly, looking to Troilo. "I will distract Mellie as long as I can."

"Darling cousin," Philippa hushed, squeezing her cheeks. "Thank you."

"*Go,*" she mouthed. "There is not much time."

Philippa did not look back as Troilo grabbed her hand.

"What happened just now?" she asked as they ran through the corridor. "That was no ordinary wind!"

Rounding a corner, he hushed her. "You are not the only one who is followed by strange phenomena," he murmured, pulling her close.

What?

Philippa tried to pull back, but he wouldn't allow it. "All this time and you have not told me?"

Though it was still daylight when they reached the carriage, dark clouds had plunged the courtyard into shadow.

Troilo first ushered Philippa onto the platform before joining her inside. "As you know, it is not so easily explainable," he said, slamming the door.

Her eyes found the curtained window as they pulled away. "You become more and more a stranger to me."

Troilo lifted his gaze. The space between them in the carriage, suddenly an ocean of distance.

"I know so much of your life, but nothing of your heart. Nothing of its—"

Taking her face in both hands, he swallowed her words in a slow and steady rapture. It was unlike any kiss she'd ever been given, like something she'd tasted in a dream, to only dissipate upon waking when he pulled away.

"Reasonings." Philippa spoke in a broken whisper. "Who *are* you?"

Troilo blinked, his green irises resembling an oasis in the middle of a drought. So many times, she had lost herself in eyes the color of his, as though her heart had always known the face it was searching for.

"It is as if I..." She bit down on her lower lip, letting it slide from her teeth. "As if we have somehow..."

Troilo's shoulders tensed along with his stare. "As if we have *what?*"

Philippa wouldn't say it—what she felt he wanted her to say. She would not dare speak it out loud. The possibility that they had known each other before, in some other life entirely.

The carriage came to an abrupt halt, sending Troilo further into her lap. "What?" he asked again, more urgently.

"Excuse me," she said, reaching for the handle. "My courage has gone with the wine."

Troilo stepped out behind her as she scurried through the falling raindrops. Ignoring his calls, she hustled through the cottage foyer.

"We have!" he shouted, bursting through the doors behind her.

From the staircase landing, Philippa turned back to see Troilo standing in the middle of the room.

"We have met before."

Reaching for the bannister to steady herself, Philippa cocked her head. His stare was cautious, wary. Brimming over with a promise of safety, as though she were a wild horse, and he was trying to gain her trust.

"Your heart and mine," he breathed, "are very old friends."

As she stood there, part of her wanted to cry—or maybe laugh? Whatever game this was, Philippa no longer wanted any part in it.

"You frighten me," she whispered as a low rumble of thunder enveloped the room.

Leaving him downstairs, she retreated to the second floor.

Philippa was afraid, though it was not *him* she was afraid of. Never had she felt unsafe in his presence. Not before his confession, nor after. Perhaps it was this feeling of safety itself that scared her. And perhaps that is why she took shelter in his room instead of her own.

Philippa took a seat on the edge of his bed as raindrops began to erratically hit the windowpane. Unused to her hair being pinned up, her scalp was notably sore.

She had every right to be angry. Every right to feel manipulated. But as Philippa began to unfasten her heavy locks, the overarching emotion was a sadness she could not place.

Dearest knight, hear my plea, she thought to herself as she laid her head on Troilo's pillow. *Who is this man that haunts me so?*

The answer seemed to come in a vision of her curled on the bed, facing the wall. Philippa could see the few diamond stars scattering Troilo's pillow as she rummaged through her hair with her bandaged hand, struggling to pull them out.

Then, she felt the weight of the bed shift as someone sat down behind her.

"How long had you been following my life in the papers before you became my doctor?" Philippa asked, keeping her eyes on the gold wallpaper.

"Quite some time," Troilo admitted.

"Why have you come here?" The diamonds only caught further as Philippa resumed her search for hair pins. "If you were not seeking a channeler for Costanza, as you claim..." She turned her cheek to him on the pillow. "Why are you here?" she asked, meeting his eyes.

"I had to meet you," he replied, gently untangling a star from her crown. "I had to see for myself you were not a dream."

Tears ran from the corners of her eyes as a wellspring of longing bubbled up, its true origin unknown to her.

"For so long you lived only in my imaginings. To never meet..." Troilo dropped his gaze shamefully. "You only need to say the word and I will disappear, and never return for as long as I live."

"You have made me fall in love with you." Philippa managed a sad laugh as she slipped her fingers around his neck. "And now you want to *leave?*"

"No." Taking her other hand in his, Troilo pressed her palm to his chest, and to his heart, which pumped brilliantly beneath her touch. "I do not wish to leave."

Philippa could imagine this vibrant pulse against her back on a cold winter night.

"At least, not alone," Troilo added, releasing her.

Sitting upright, Philippa watched as he walked to his desk and dragged the black oriental box to the edge of its surface. "My entire life is in this box," he said, extracting the key from his jacket.

Just as she heard the lock unlatch, the staircase creaked, causing them both to snap their attention toward the door, where a maid walked by.

Whatever Troilo wished to show her, it could wait.

Slipping down from the bed, Philippa took hold of his hand. "Come with me," she said, pulling him toward the passageway door.

He followed her into the dimly lit corridor like one might follow a lantern on a dark shore.

Philippa turned her back to the window as he sealed the door behind them. "You have yet to tell me what you want of me," she whispered, lifting her fingers to her mouth.

"*Your Royal and Imperial Highness,*" he said, approaching her, "there is little I do not want of you."

Philippa stumbled back, grabbing at his clothes as he lifted her into the window sill. A startled gasp found his ear as he yanked her to the edge of the windowsill, his lips worshipping every place that had ever tempted him.

"You wish me to be your wife?"

"Not only my wife," he said, snaking his hands up her dress. "I wish you to be my true equal in every way—" Troilo leaned in, pressing his lips to hers. In his fantasies, he would have let such a feeling linger, building and budding for all eternity, but in *this* life, he had waited long enough.

A warm honey welcomed him as his fingers found her split bloomers, and she pulled him further onto the windowsill.

There was no substitute for consecrated love, no amount of dreams or ghostly kisses that could have ever satisfied him. Because perhaps, thought Troilo, in a world full of so much pain and suffering, *this* was humanity's true redemption, achievable only between two human beings with beating hearts.

Philippa sighed hot against his ear as the last diamond star lost its hold from her hair, and she reached beneath her layers of dress to unbutton his pants.

Seized by a voice, Troilo halted, and the corridor went silent in all but the sound of panting and rain against the glass.

"What?" she gasped.

"*Herr Visconti?*"

Their eyes met like a broken spell.

"No," Philippa begged, clutching onto him. "Please."

"She cannot find us this way," he whispered back.

Her lips met his in a desperate plea as he pulled away.

"I will come to your room at midnight," he promised, buttoning his pants. "Once everyone is asleep."

Her voice seemed to tremble between despair and anger. "And *what* then?"

"If you still feel the same way," Troilo replied, kissing her again, "then we will leave this place."

She grabbed his shoulder. "Take me back to Zürich with you! I can recover there as your patient."

"I have no intention of returning to the Burghölzli."

"Herr Visconti, are you up here?"

"Midnight," Troilo said again.

"Midnight, then," she replied, stepping down from the windowsill.

Troilo turned back as he swiped his jacket from the ground. "Philippa?"

She spun around with a sigh, and he met her with another kiss. "I love you," he whispered, releasing her.

His bedroom was just as they'd left it as he stepped out of the corridor, including the diamond stars on the pillow.

"Hello?"

"Fräulein," he called back, scooping them out of sight.

Dripping wet, Governess Coudenhove at last rounded the corner.

"You got caught in the rain," said Troilo, shoving his hand deeper into his pocket.

"So I did," she replied.

Philippa had looked beautiful soaked to the bone with pond-water. Mellie knew she could not compare. And Doctor Visconti would never know the way she'd sat at that dinner table watching the clock, knowing he and Philippa had come back to the cottage together.

"How is Her Highness?" Mellie asked, unsure what else to say.

"She has come down with a fever."

"A fever?" she asked, taking in his lopsided cravat and flushed face. "What kind of fever?"

"The body is known to overheat in times of great stress."

Mellie glanced at the indented pillows on the bed, where surely Philippa's marzipan perfume still lingered. To think that she could have ever competed with the Austrian princess for his affections—no thought had ever been so foolish.

"Fräulein, may I fetch you a towel to dry off?"

"Yes," she replied, swallowing her humiliation. "That would be most helpful."

Doctor Visconti slipped past her without another word.

Dropping her fingers onto his bed, Mellie followed its perimeter, trying to imagine what might have taken place there, even trying to imagine herself in Philippa's place. But the bed itself seemed too neat.

Fearful that she might find the archduchess on the other side, Mellie's hand hovered above the latch to the passage door, as she pressed her ear to the wall.

Nothing.

Gently, she opened it and walked inside. The corridor felt *lived in*—drenched in an elixir of honey and salt—and on the ledge of the window, a diamond star glittered beneath silver shadows.

Mellie's heart sank in her chest.

As badly as she wanted to believe that Doctor Visconti wanted Philippa only for carnal desires, the poem he had written for her was proof that he didn't. It was a proclamation of *love*—something he'd told Mellie he was incapable of.

Philippa had been the exception to his rule. But why? Aside from her royal name, her beauty would one day fade, and her mind was fading already.

What virtue had *she* possessed to reawaken his heart?

Was it merely the allure of a woman he could not have?

Mellie took a seat on the sill, next to the diamond hairpiece.

How badly she'd wanted such words of devotion to have been addressed to her.

A vicious envy took hold as she eyed the diamond hairpiece. Where there was one poem, there had to be more.

Abandoning the corridor, Mellie walked back into his bedroom. Doctor Visconti had yet to return, and knowing she didn't have much time, she scanned the contents lying across his desk. Sitting next to a little black box with red-painted dragons was his green journal—which looked to be about the same dimensions as the singular poem Mellie had discovered.

Pocketing it in her skirt, she stepped away just as he returned with her towel.

"Here you are, Fräulein," said Doctor Visconti.

Mellie willed the happiest smile she could muster. "Thank you, Doctor. You are very thoughtful."

FOURTEEN

9:23 P.M.

Philippa brushed her hair in long, thoughtful strokes as she watched the clouds outside her window part for a crescent moon, sharp and silver. She'd been sitting there for quite some time meditating on the cold, milky glow of dusk that had overtaken her room.

The cuts on her hand were beginning to heal, leaving only cat-scratch marks behind. In front of her sat her mauve diary.

Only hours earlier, Philippa had been content to accept the gaps in Troilo's story and live out the rest of her life anonymously by his side, tending the garden of a small white house with honeysuckle and blackberries growing over the fence. But an unsettling thought had begun to creep over her as the sun fell behind the trees. Where Troilo felt handpicked by Philippa's spirit, Costanza's influence was a mystery.

If she chose to live out a life with Troilo, would it always be the *three* of them?

Troilo, Philippa and her?

The flame of her candle stretched high, then shook, illuminating the top of the diary's cover in a golden hue. *Perhaps she can tell you what he will not,* echoed Erzsi's words in her mind.

Abandoning the brush, Philippa hesitantly opened the book and began to read. There was no introduction or mention of Troilo on the first page; rather, it seemed to describe a setting similar to one of her fairy tales, opening with Costanza sitting under a pear tree.

"It *is* a story," Philippa whispered, skipping forward. *"Costanza stumbled to her feet, just in time to see a fiery, green tail stretch across the celestial plains overhead."*

She hadn't channeled messages at all.

Philippa had written a *story*—one that she had no recollection of writing.

But why?

Drawing the candlelight closer, she read on, finding herself further captivated with each turn of the page.

"Hair darker than a new moon," she murmured, taking note of the dragon boy at the quarry. "Troilo?"

Frantically, Philippa skimmed the next few pages to see that her hunch had been confirmed.

"Troilo, a..."

Dragon?

Her hair fell over the lit pages as she leaned in closer, following each word with her finger until she landed upon a familiar word.

There is a name for that where I am from, Troilo had told Philippa while they'd discussed *The Serpent Prince.*

"Zmajeva nesteva," she whispered.

The more Philippa read, the more uncomfortable she began to feel. From Costanza's connection to the *Nibelungenlied,* to the Duke of Pazin's resemblance to Duke Sixten, the parallels were uncanny. Most of all, Philippa could imagine the real Troilo as a reckless, romantic youth, too pure for this world. All the young knight was missing were the doctor's dragon tattoos, his own version of a *skin*.

Wax splashed across the brass candelabra as Philippa reached the page she had written the day she smashed the mirror.

I have seen the face of Death.

Tears fell upon the blood-smeared words as a vision of the Istrian quarry summoned itself to the forefront of Philippa's mind. "It was *me*," she breathed. "I am the woman in white."

But how?

Racing through the final pages, she cried silently to herself as the characters were severed from each other most violently.

"*I will find you again,*" she read in a whisper. "*In the next life, I will find you again.*"

Philippa shivered with adrenaline as she slammed the book shut. She had no words for what she'd just read—at least none that would satisfy this numbing cold that whipped at her cheeks like a winter wind.

It only feels natural to me that we would come back, she'd once told Troilo, outside near the pond. *Though, I have yet to understand why I did.*

Leaning back in her wooden chair, Philippa gazed into the broken mirror as she pulled her hair from her neck. Her breath stilled as she ran her fingers over the faded birthmark.

There is something that connects the two of you, Troilo had said as he'd assessed her covered mirror. *Something I cannot explain.*

"No," Philippa gasped in disbelief.

Had she fallen through the puddle at last, just as her ancestors before her?

The idea that Philippa could be the reincarnation of Costanza was an impossibility. Considering Troilo was only ten years Philippa's senior, she and his wife would have both walked the earth at the same time.

"Oh God," Philippa whispered, burying her face in her hands. "I have lost all sense of..." Glancing up at the waning candle flame, she paused. "Every word I have ever written has been for you."

That is what Troilo had told her.

And as she sat there at her vanity, crouched over this fantastical account, Philippa felt mad enough to actually believe it.

Ballads of the Starlight Menagerie's gold letters glimmered to her left, and for a reason unknown to her, she reached for it and flipped decisively to the last page.

> *Costanza,*
> *My tempest, my treasure—*
> *I will give you a proper burial,*
> *I will be your chief mourner,*
> *Carry you on my shoulder,*
> *To the ground of your keeping.*
> *O fortunate, hallowed ground,*
> *How I hate and envy you!*
>
> *And deep in that rich earth,*
> *I will make you a nuptial chamber.*
> *Death to anyone that disturbs your sleep,*
> *Or tries to prize you from my hold,*
> *My prize you are,*
> *My bride you will always be.*

Philippa shot to her feet.

You believe your spirit is the author of these ballads, Troilo had teased. *A remarkable coincidence finding his work, wouldn't you say?*

Flipping back to the title page, Philippa's blood ran cold at the sight of the shooting star woodcut emblem.

I know this, she'd said that day under the weeping beech. *I have seen it somewhere before.*

Staring at the page in disbelief, she remembered standing in Troilo's bedroom. *Perhaps your words will find her one day,* she'd said with his green journal in hand.

"Perhaps they already have," Philippa whispered to herself.

11:57 P.M.

Slipping her pair of silver sheers beneath her pillow, Philippa eyed the passageway door from her bed with a scrutinous gaze. In mere minutes, Troilo would walk through and see her waiting for him on the bed in her white nightgown.

And she would soon know how serious he was about her being his equal.

Philippa slipped down from the mattress as the sound of footsteps drew nearer, and the door cracked open. Before she could speak, his lips found hers in the glow of candlelight.

"Hello again," Troilo said softly.

Philippa blinked, seeing him clearly for the first time for what he was. "Hello," she replied, running her hand down the lining of his dressing gown.

His smirk reminded her of the knight in the story, as though the boy from the quarry had come back to life.

Reaching for the ring that hung against his chest, Philippa felt his stare as she examined its faint marking, still visible. "Would you like to take it off?" she whispered, meeting his gaze.

Troilo nodded as he reached around his neck and unfastened the chain, dropping it into his paisley pocket.

Their lips met again as Philippa slipped her hands beneath his housecoat, circling his ribs with her fingers.

"I have locked my door," he whispered, pushing her back to the edge of the bed. "No coffee, no morning interruptions—"

Philippa pulled him on top of her, unstringing the front of her nightgown faster than he could tear it from her shoulders. As she lay back—her full, round breasts peeking beneath waterfalls of golden hair—Troilo bit down in a quiet groan.

"You are real," he whispered, more to himself than to her.

Beautiful, wandering hands. Her nipple hardened under his touch as he leaned over and kissed her delicately.

"In what world am I not real, Troilo?" Philippa asked, tracing the red dragon on his left forearm.

"None that I have ever known," he said, drawing back to look at her again.

Hard against her, Philippa flipped him onto his back, where he admired her as she sat astride him.

Having Troilo right where she wanted him, she leaned into his ear. *"Costanza—!"* Pressing the sharp point of her scissors to his neck, Philippa drew back to meet his gaze. *"I will give you a proper burial, I will be your chief mourner."*

Troilo lifted his chin, exposing himself to her blade.

"What year were you born, Troilo Visconti?" In the flicker of the candlelight, she detected a slight smile. "I want to hear you *say it,*" she said, holding the point steady.

"1432," he said, raising his hands in surrender.

"Your soul is not human."

"Neither is yours," he said. "Not completely."

Philippa inhaled sharply, angling the point toward his jaw.

Troilo's eyes became glossy in the low light as he looked up at her. "Everyone falls from grace when they are born into this world," he added. "It does not matter how."

"Who are you?" she whispered.

Lifting himself to her, Troilo pressed further into the tip of her scissors as he guided Philippa onto his lap. He pushed her hair behind her neck, grasping it in handfuls.

"I am but your docile pet," he said, laying her on her back. "A familiar to do your bidding."

Arms pinned above her head, Philippa lay beneath him in awe. "It *is* you," she murmured, loosening her grip on the scissors. "You are him, and I..."

Troilo's lips grazed hers again, soft enough to elicit a whimper. "I am *her.*"

Closing her eyes, Philippa felt the tips of his fingers run over her temples, brushing away any stray hairs. His lips brushed the skin under her eye, then her jawline, sending ripples of warmth throughout her body.

"You said it was not fate," she breathed, grabbing a headful of his hair. "You said it was not fate but you were wrong..."

His skin felt so hot under her touch, like a pulsating star was burning beneath.

"Your words found me long before you did."

Philippa could not recall who shed their clothing first, as they now shared an essence, beating within each other like a second heart. Troilo nudged her legs open with his knee as she pulled him back down for a kiss.

Her knight, her poet—he was *alive.*

She bit down on his shoulder as he stilled inside of her, and as Philippa felt his dragons coil around her back, and the burn of his stubble against her cheek, she understood why she had never before been satisfied with anyone else.

Her breath found Troilo's neck as he lifted her back onto his lap. "A part of me never forgot you," she whispered.

Visions tore through her mind of herself through his eyes, where they connected with each sweeping stroke, until in a zenith of rapture, they collapsed on a bed of stars.

Philippa opened her eyes to see him on the pillow as they lay entwined like a caduceus, their bond surging with the radiance of the brightest sun.

"I have waited four-hundred and sixty-six years to do that

again," Troilo murmured, grazing the top of her knuckles with his thumb.

"Is that...?"

His large, teary eyes seemed to possess entire worlds within their crystal vision.

"How old you are?"

He smirked, pulling her closer. "Four-hundred and sixty-*seven*."

Philippa ran her fingers over the faded scales of his forearm.

"I have kept most of my travel papers," Troilo added. "In case I ever needed to prove it to you."

So *that* was what he'd tried to show her, locked securely in his Chinese box. Looking back, she could see all the ways in which he'd tried to tell her the truth.

"I do not need proof," Philippa said at last. "Your word is enough."

"Then whatever you would like to know," he promised. "Whatever questions you may have..."

The story Philippa had written were mere fragments of a dream. Only by hearing Troilo's side would she know how closely the account aligned.

"I want to know everything, from the beginning," she said.

Bringing her onto his chest, he settled in. "I do not remember anything before I fell," he began. "I do not remember anything before her." He shifted. "Before *you*."

Philippa snuggled against his chest.

"I fell into the Sopat quarry, which is where you found me. Not knowing much about the world yet, I was a bit crude. But you fed me and clothed me, and took me back to your village with your father. He was a goldsmith at the castle, and offered to keep me there as his apprentice.

"When zmajevi fall, they are attracted to things like lakes and serpents...anything that resembles their true form, which is why I pointed to the Visconti heraldry in the Pazin banner hall. I did not know the language to communicate anything else when asked who I was. By coincidence or *fate*, the Duke of Pazin's mother was a Visconti. The relation afforded me privileges I would have otherwise had living in the castle, and..."

"The duke and you became great friends," Philippa added.

"We were inseparable." Troilo sighed. "Just as you and Erzsi. He was interested in you as well...it did not matter that he was already married. He knew you before I did, and so he had claimed you. But you were bonded to *me*, and so..."

"We could not stay away from one another."

"I was naive," he said. "I believed the duke valued his relationship with me, and that would be enough to save us from his wrath. I was wrong."

As Philippa lay there on Troilo's chest, lingering on the taste of love and sea salt, she felt no spirits present between them.

"When you were four months pregnant, he called me to the castle. You begged me not to go...you told me of your vision for fear I would not return, but I did not listen." Troilo removed his hand from her shoulder to wipe his eyes. "It was a trap to lure me away from you."

"Troilo," Philippa whispered, sitting up.

"He cornered me in the courtyard for a duel and challenged me to call the wind but I could not..." Troilo buried his face in his hands. "By the time I reached you I was too late."

Her heart sank as he began to cry, soft as a child.

"I *begged* on my knees for the Fates to take me instead that day," he whispered. "I tried to trade my life for yours, without understanding that when humans die, there is no bargain to be made." His lashes webbed with tears, Troilo met her eye. "That was enough to call the wind."

"The storm." Philippa allowed a few tears to fall. "It was you who summoned the storm."

"It was the volatility of my emotions...my anger, my anguish, that summoned it, but I did not try to taper it. I could not—not when I was glad to watch the castle burn. It was years before I found out that Matthias made it out alive. The following morning, I returned your body to your father and grandmother so you could be properly laid to rest. I pounded on their door in the pouring rain...news of the fire had already reached the village." Troilo grew silent. "I told them to leave Pićan and never return, for they would be in grave danger for as long as I lived."

"Where did you go afterward?"

"At first, I went into exile. For years, the only company I kept were the horses, but they eventually died. In 1494, when I was confident everyone who might remember me was gone, I made my way to Milan to find that the city had been taken by the Sforzas, so I changed my surname to Albizzi and moved south to Florence where I became an ambassador for the Medicis." Troilo wiped his eyes, smiling a bit. "Eventually, people started to notice that I hardly aged."

"What did you do?" Philippa asked, resting her chin on his chest.

"I faked my death and left for Prague," he said. "The name I took there was Rhys Reimer. I lived off the money I had kept for almost a year until finally, it began to run out, and I answered an advertisement for a magician's assistant. His name was John Dee."

"John Dee?"

"He was very close to the Queen of England, so he convinced me to continue to assist him with his projects in London. England was bursting with playwrights and plague, in equal measure. Someone you had just seen one day might have a red cross painted on their door the next. I found myself untouched by death, yet surrounded by it...one day it became too much, so I left in the middle of the night and boarded a ship in Marseille headed for the West Indies. They had promised a New World there, but what I found was worse than England's plague. The most abhorrent thing I have ever seen humans do to one another..."

Philippa watched Troilo's brow knit.

"People—men, women, even children—bound in chains. In

Haiti, my own grief meant nothing. Not as families were severed every day, sold like cattle to sugar plantations. The enslaved were a people still connected to their culture—they had their own version of what I am. I learned their language and formulated a plan.

"I slit the throat of every trader in the port while they slept and took their gold. Then, posing as one of them, I purchased one hundred and fifty people from neighboring plantations, as many as I could load onto a ship. No one dared ask why a slave trader might want to leave so quickly—not after six of them had been found dead the prior morning. We left for Marseille that afternoon."

"And you granted their freedom upon your return to France?"

"They were free the moment they boarded the ship," Troilo replied. "When we docked, I purchased a smaller ship in hopes of working as a merchant—some of them chose to stay on and become part of my crew. I refused to transport sugar, coffee or indigo, because of their ties to the slave trade."

"Then what did you transport?"

"Soap." He grinned. "I sailed the world selling Marseille soap."

Philippa brushed his hair from his forehead with a smile. "And then?"

"By 1710, I found myself in Prussia living under the alias Andrei Sidorova. Russia was at war with Sweden, and another outbreak of plague had traveled up from the Baltic Sea. To curb the spread of the disease, they quarantined the city of Königsberg. I chose to stay.

"Day in and day out, I sat with the infected in fever houses. Most died within days of their symptoms appearing—all I could do was ensure they were comfortable. It was here that I first began to question if my curse was a gift in disguise. Sitting with the dying, I realized there is only one thing people truly wish for in this life."

"What is that?"

"More time," Troilo murmured, meeting her eye. "In 1715 I enrolled in the University of Leiden in Amsterdam. I opened my first practice there, and settled for as long as I could. I even met a woman there. She wanted to marry, but…" He shook his head. "I could neither offer her love nor honesty. So I packed up and left for France as *Laurent Valicourt*. The class divide had only grown more tense since I had last been there, and my doctoring was called upon for a different purpose when war finally broke out."

"You acted as a medic to the Jacobins," Philippa gasped. She'd heard the stories of Marie Antoinette as a girl, always told as a cautionary tale of rulership gone sour. "They executed their queen by *guillotine*. It was barbaric."

"Men do barbaric things when they are hungry," Troilo added. "When they are deemed as less than."

"No one chooses to be born royalty any more than they choose to be born a peasant," she argued.

"There is a cost for *every* fate," he whispered. "Highness."

The way he cocked his eyebrow told her this would not be the first time she would disagree with things of his past.

"What happened next?"

"By 1805 I was desperate to leave the madness of war and sickness behind. So, I changed my name back to Troilo Visconti, and left Paris for Venice."

"And did you find peace there? In Venice?"

"I would not say it was *peace* I found." Troilo grinned as he relaxed into better memories. "I first encountered Byron at the San Lazzaro degli Armeni, a small island in the Venetian lagoon where he saw me writing in the courtyard of the Armenian monaster—"

"Byron? *Lord* Byron?" Philippa demanded. "What was he like?"

"As mythical as they say. He was living at the Palazzo Mocenigo on the Grand Canal, hiding from English debtors and working on an English-Armenian dictionary when we encountered each other at the monastery. I had grown so accustomed to a solitary life that at first I rejected his offer of camaraderie, which only made him try harder to befriend me. He asked me each time he saw me what I was writing, and each time, I told him the truth—that it was nothing but my own thoughts. In the end, he won."

Imagining Troilo's reticence brought a smile to Philippa's face as she listened.

"My life changed in every possible way from that day forward. I found myself surrounded by people constantly, staying up well into the night talking and...well. Many other things." Troilo laughed to himself, shaking his head. "It was the first time in perhaps all of my life that I truly understood what it was to touch a life of leisure, and pleasure. A life of adventure. We were inseparable, and that summer, I traveled with him to Geneva."

"Where you met your English friend," said Philippa, remembering their conversation. "Who died at sea."

Troilo nodded. His chest rose, then fell as he held her gaze.

"Percy Bysshe Shelley."

"Nicely done, Highness," he praised. "Without him and Mary, *Ballads* would have never found publication. But if not for my time in England with John Keats, I would have never written it at all."

"You have lived a thousand lives, Troilo," Philippa said softly.

"So devastated was I by their consecutive deaths, I ran as far as one could run, seeking peoples and cultures completely foreign. Feeling as though I belonged nowhere at all, I sought to disappear in the Orient, and never return."

"Why did you?" Philippa said, tracing the dragon tattoo on his arm. "Return?"

"While working in the sultan's court, I befriended a fellow by the name of Eugène Delacroix, a painter who had come along with the French ambassador. I showed him all around Tangier, and watched him paint scenes in watercolor. It was the nostalgia of speaking with him that called me home again, back to France.

"Those were quiet years, though Eugène and I kept in touch until his death. When claims about being able to connect with the dead began to surface, I was so possessed by the idea of speaking with you that I traveled all over Europe, sitting with any medium who would have me. I did not know you had been taken to the Otherworld, though now, I do not know how I missed it."

"I was one with the water," Philippa whispered, reaching for her neck. "You were on the shore."

"Though my own attempts at contact failed, what I witnessed in the séances changed me. I became fascinated with the human mind."

"That is why you chose to study it at the Salpêtrière?"

"It is."

"What happened then?"

"You," he said.

"Me?"

"You were born."

Philippa laid her cheek to his chest. "You *felt* me?"

"Like a strike of lightning," he said, hugging her to him.

"If you have felt me all this time, why did you not come sooner?"

"You were just a child." Troilo sighed, running his finger over her shoulder. "I told myself that whoever you were, you were better off never knowing me. But the bond carried over regardless of how I felt. Your nightmares would wake me all the time."

Philippa was silent as she thought back to all the times she'd felt lulled back to sleep in her own mind.

"You were my guardian angel," she said.

"When I realized you were ill, I knew I could help you. But... not all of my motives were so selfless. I wanted to live *in* your world. To look into your eyes instead of looking through them." He paused. "In the end, I could not stay away."

Sitting upright, Philippa hugged the covers around her. "I am not Costanza," she said. "She only lives within me."

Troilo reached over, grabbing the necklace from the dressing gown of his pocket. Philippa watched as he sat up beside her, and reached for her left hand.

"It is not Costanza who binds me," he said, slipping the ring onto her finger.

Philippa looked down at the ring on her finger. A perfect fit.

FIFTEEN

June 20, 1900
5:37 A.M.

When hints of morning began to trickle through the window, Troilo still lay awake, too preoccupied by Philippa's soft and steady breaths against his chest and her sleepy laughs as she lay cocooned in his arms.

"Let us leave right now," she murmured, turning back to look at him. "Before anyone wakes."

"I arrived here thinking you were alone," he sighed, stroking the length of her hair. "But Erzsi and Franz, they care deeply for you. Disappearing without a trace would cause them great pain."

Philippa held his knuckles to her lips in a contemplative kiss.

"I do not intend to make the same mistake twice," he added.

"Then what shall we do?"

"I will ask for your hand properly."

Philippa sat up in bed. "You will ask His Majesty?"

"I will speak with your brother first," Troilo replied. "I will request his audience this afternoon."

"And then?" she asked, grinning ear to ear.

"We will marry here, among your family, and leave on our own accord."

"Must we leave at all?" she asked, bringing her knees to her chest.

Troilo propped himself up on his elbow. "People will begin to question why I hardly age."

"What of me?"

"Only time will tell how long we have together." Troilo shifted in bed toward the locked bedroom door, watching the golden doorknob with serpentine eyes. "I heard something."

Philippa moved to leap out of bed, but Troilo held her in place. "Let me speak to her," he said.

Breathless, Erzsi caught herself on the railway bannister. "This is a dream," she gasped. *"This is a dream!"*

Her chest burned as the events of the last few weeks began to align chaotically in her mind. Had *he* caused Philippa's illness, having haunted her all her life like some sort of vampiric specter?

"Think, Erzsi," she exhaled. "Think."

Whatever Troilo really was, no one would believe her without proof. Erzsi reached for her silver shears, still hanging from her belt from her sewing that morning and then, straightening her back, she glanced over her shoulder at the doctor's bedroom door, knowing the answers lay behind it.

He'd locked his door—*predictably*—but Erzsi was prepared. Retrieving a hairpin from her braid, she began to pick at the lock, breaking it in record time.

Burghölzli correspondence and doctorly notes filled the crevices of Troilo's desk, which lay behind haphazard stacks of books on anatomy, physiology and medicine. Erzsi tore through drawer after drawer, desperate to find anything that might indicate that he was not who he claimed. Such evidence would at least be enough to put an end to his plan to abduct Philippa.

"Rubbish," she panted, throwing her disheveled braid over her shoulder. *"Where* is..."

Erzsi was not sure how she'd missed it, the oriental black box, painted with clouds and dragons. In the crevice of the desk lay a small, black key. Erzsi opened the top of the box and peered inside at the thick coil of papers. Slipping off the twine, she began to sift through them, noting how the paper began to look discolored, and significantly *older*.

"Andrei Sidorova," she read. "Kingdom of Prussia, 1712..."

She flipped it over, revealing a Paris travel paper behind it, with a different name from 1798. Then another from London, and another from Venice.

"This will do," she declared, gathering them up.

"Erzsi."

Whipping around, she clutched the travel papers to her stonewalled heart.

In the doorframe stood Troilo, looking neither surprised nor vexed as he shut the door behind them. "Erzsi," he said, "give them to me."

"I know your secret and I will no longer be your unwilling accomplice." Her eyes widened as she stepped back against the window, gripping the papers with white knuckles. "Do not come any closer," she warned. "I do not know *what* you are, but I have my shears at my waist, and I will not hesitate to *drive this silver into your heart.*"

"You, my friend" —Troilo stepped closer— "have been reading too much Bram Stoker."

"I am not your friend," she fired back. "You have *played me* since the very beginning. You are a liar and manipulator."

"And you, Erzsi? Are you not guilty of meddling?"

She swallowed hard, edging her back up against the window. "We are *not* the same," she breathed. "You told that viper to bite Doctor Bohm, I do not know how you did it but I know you did!"

"The viper helped me on his own accord." Troilo's tone was gentle enough, but his eyes were hard as a glacier. "Just as you did."

"I did not know any better." Erzsi coiled her arms around the evidence. "You have made a fool of me."

Troilo shook his head. "You are no fool, Erzsi."

"Who are you, Troilo Visconti?" she asked, whipping out her scissors. "Who are you and what do you intend to do with my cousin?"

"I intend only to love—"

"Stay where you are!"

Troilo halted, raising both hands in the air.

"What of your wife's spirit, inhabiting Pippa as though she were a doll?"

"That is a complicated matter that would be best explained by Philippa," Troilo said, inching toward her.

"All the better," Erzsi argued, backing up. "Since I cannot trust a thing *you* say."

"If you cannot trust me, trust your instinct. If you truly believe I intend to act maliciously against Philippa, or you..." Troilo motioned to the exit. "I will not stop you from walking out that door."

Erzsi gritted her teeth as she looked into his eyes, which glimmered with an irritating sincerity. He was the closest thing she had ever had to a brother, or even a father. "Damn you," she cursed, dropping the shears to her side.

"I do not intend to take her from you," Troilo said, at last stepping forward. "Not without your blessing."

"My blessing!" Erzsi gaped in astonishment. "And if I say no?"

"You will not."

"If you are so certain, then why ask at all?"

"Because," he said, "of everyone, it is your blessing that matters most to me."

Feeling her cheeks rise, Erzsi wiped away the smile, turning her attention back to the evidence in her hand.

"And I believe you know that to be true."

"If you are not the undead," she said, reluctantly dropping the papers back in the box, "then what *are* you?"

Troilo only smiled with a subtle shake of the head.

"You are right." Glancing up at him, she cocked one eyebrow. "I would not believe you anyway."

"I am a human being," said Troilo. "I have lived a human life, same as you."

Inspecting him more closely, Erzsi crossed his path. "Why did you come here?"

"I came for her."

"That is obvious. I am asking *why*."

Troilo's eyes sparkled in the morning light. "We knew each other once before," he said. "A very long time ago."

"What year?" she prodded hesitantly.

"1432."

Erzsi froze. In the span of one morning, everything she once believed about the world had turned a varying shade of gray.

"You knew Pippa when she was...*someone else?*" she stuttered.

Troilo lowered his voice. "I knew her when she was my wife."

Turning her back to him, Erzsi walked back over to the desk. Philippa had said it from the beginning as they'd sat on the veranda together after meeting him for the first time.

They had a connection.

Every word he had ever written *had* been for her.

"Erzsi..."

"Yes, Troilo," she whispered, closing the lid of his oriental box.

"Have you taken my green journal?" he asked, finding her side.

Erzsi looked up at him. "I did not see it here."

"It was sitting right here on top," Troilo replied, shuffling through the papers.

"I did not see a green journal, I swear it. What is in it?"

"My writing."

"Your poems..."

Only someone with a vendetta against Troilo would take it,

and considering Duke Sixten had been banished, that left only one other suspect.

"If you intend to speak to Franz, I suggest you leave at once," Erzsi said, locking the dragon box. "Mellie has your journal."

"She must have taken it yesterday evening."

Turning back to Troilo, Erzsi dropped the tiny key into his palm. "I will take care of it," she said, rounding the box under her arm. "But this is coming with me."

11:40 A.M.

Mellie had lost track of how many pastry puffs Philippa had eaten, watching with sickened eyes from the dark corner of the parlor as she bit into the flaky dough, then licked the excess cream that oozed over her finger. After finding Doctor Visconti's bedroom door locked that morning, Mellie had retreated downstairs. Philippa had not noticed her sitting in the parlor when she floated down the staircase an hour later, regenerated with new life, nor had she seemed to feel Mellie's blazing stare through the window as she lounged on the veranda in the high noon sun.

With each indulgent bite Philippa took, Mellie descended further into jealousy as she clutched the written devotional that sat in her lap. She had read each page, meditating on every word, trying to imagine herself in Philippa's place. Even perspiring in the heat with her hair unbrushed, Philippa was more beautiful than she could ever hope to be.

The sound of knuckles across the parlor door caused Mellie to jump. "Erzsi," she sighed, catching her breath. "You startled me."

Hugging the corner, Erzsi scanned the room. "Have you seen Blitz?"

"I believe—"

"What are you doing?" she asked, slipping around the parlor door.

Mellie could feel her cheeks flushing as she spread her palm over the green journal. "Just enjoying the morning."

"Hm." Erzsi closed the door lightly behind her, throwing a quick glance toward the window where Philippa sat unknowingly on the other side. "What is that?"

"What is what?"

Erzsi walked in, circling her like a jaguar. "That right there. What are you holding?"

Mellie slowly rose to her feet, keeping the booklet clutched in her fingers.

"Oh, I have seen that somewhere before..." Erzsi pondered playfully. "I do not believe it belongs to you."

"It..." Mellie paused nervously. "It is..."

"Just what I am looking for."

Confused, Mellie's eyes darted over Erzsi's head to Philippa.

"You see, I wanted to discuss this very thing with you," Erzsi said. "I have reason to suspect Doctor Visconti is not who he claims."

"Not who he claims?"

Erzsi blinked. "A decent man."

"*Oh,*" Mellie mouthed.

"He has been indecent with Philippa, as you know already." Erzsi dropped her gaze to the journal in Mellie's hands. "But now I fear he plans to take her away and I cannot allow that."

"Take her away?" Mellie's chest fluttered as she spoke. "He wants to...*marry* her?"

"She is the only family I have."

It wasn't his indecency that had prompted Erzsi to turn, rather it was the threat of Doctor Visconti taking Philippa away from her.

"I must tell someone before it is too late," Erzsi added, extending her open palm.

Mellie's hand moved independently of her brain as she handed the journal off without a beat. Erzsi exposing them was the best of all outcomes, and now, her hands would stay clean.

"I plan to act discreetly so as to stay in the good graces of my cousin," Erzsi said, tucking the booklet under her arm. "This conversation never happened. Understood?"

She seemed so much older than seventeen as she stood before Mellie, waiting expectantly for an answer.

"Yes," Mellie said at last.

Willing the most convincing smile, Erzsi made a beeline for the exit before turning back on her heel. "Thank you, Mellie."

Evidence in hand, Erzsi made her way to the foyer, where Troilo was rushing down the stairs.

"Your Highness," he greeted. "I have a meeting with Archduke Franz, and I shall be back by evening."

Troilo was a good actor, having acted all his life.

Aware of Mellie watching from the parlor, Erzsi smirked at him, unveiling the green journal with a flick of the wrist. "Do take care, Herr Visconti. It is rather warm out."

Halting at the door, he opened it for Philippa who was returning inside from the veranda.

"Good morning, Doctor Visconti," she said.

"*Highness,*" he said. "I have an audience with His Highness, Archduke Franz. We will resume our sessions tomorrow."

"Please tell my brother hello," Philippa replied, refusing to linger too long on him.

Her eyes shot to Erzsi as Troilo left her at the door.

"Let us play a game of cards, Pippa," said Erzsi.

"Yes." Philippa nodded slowly. "Let's."

Once on the second floor and out of sight, they scrambled into Philippa's room, where Erzsi shut them in and locked the door.

"Troilo spoke to you?" Philippa asked.

Erzsi found it all at once hard to answer, having hardly processed any of it. "Yes," she managed.

Philippa paced to the window, fingers to her brow. "And you will not" —she swallowed hard, turning back to Erzsi— "tell anyone? Of his nature?"

She tracked Philippa's gaze to the green journal. "No one would believe such a fairy tale," Erzsi said, tossing it onto the bed.

"He explained it to you then," said Philippa. "Who I used to be."

"Does she still speak to you?" Erzsi asked, crossing the room to meet her.

Shaking her head, Philippa traced the eroded engravings of the golden ring on her finger. "No."

Silence found them as they stood side by side, watching Troilo disappear beneath the shadow of the oak trees on the other side of the window.

"Then perhaps you are cured, after all."

SIXTEEN

June 21, 1900 —*present day*
12:32 P.M.

"To leave everything behind..." The pipe clicked against his teeth as Inspector Ziegler shifted it in his mouth. "I suppose he does not plan on doctoring, wherever he went."

Rudolf knelt before Doctor Visconti's desk, now completely disemboweled. They had searched his bedroom all morning to no avail, sifting through his correspondence and antiquarian books, for *any* inkling of where he'd gone.

"Either he is innocent, or the most cunning man alive," Inspector Ziegler added, pacing to the other side of the room.

"Could someone be both?"

Rudolf felt the inspector pause as he stared defeatedly at the gutted desk in front of him. If Doctor Visconti had taken *anything* with him, it was that green journal. Perhaps Inspector Ziegler had been right about—

"What did she give you, hm?"

"Pardon, sir?" Rudolf glanced over his shoulder to see

Inspector Ziegler picking up the book of ballads from the bed. "Oh, it is..."

"*Ballads of the Starlight Menagerie,*" he read. "What is a *starlight menagerie?*"

"I believe it is referring to the constellations, sir. It was Archduchess Philippa's favorite poetry compilation."

"Right," he grunted, turning the book over in his hands. "Wild about poets, this family."

Rudolf turned forward, hoping that if he looked busy enough, he could avoid further prodding.

"What was your impression of Archduchess Erzsi when you spoke to her?"

"Well, sir," Rudolf replied, rummaging absently through the desk, "what is there to say?"

"Hopefully something more insightful than her pleasant company," countered the inspector.

"I do believe much of the way she presents herself is a facade. After all, she *has* dealt with much..." Rudolf paused, his gaze catching on a pigeonhole he'd somehow missed. "Tragedy..."

"What?"

"Eureka," he whispered, feeling a thin spine among the papers.

"What is it, lad?"

Rudolf pulled the tiny, green journal from its hidden compartment. "Doctor Visconti's poetry," he said, turning to his superior with a half-smile. "A green book—in the desk, just as she said."

"I was not aware that Her Highness confided its whereabouts to you."

"It was more of a guess, I think." Rudolf stumbled over his words as Inspector Ziegler walked over to examine the journal. "That it would be in his desk."

"Give it here."

As he watched the inspector flip through the booklet, a thought occurred to Rudolf. Whereas Inspector Ziegler did not speak this language, *he* did.

"Poetry is always confessional, sir," he said.

"Is it now?" Inspector Ziegler mumbled, fiddling with torn edges in the center.

Rudolf stepped forward, craning his neck for a better look. "There is a page torn out?"

"Perhaps our doctor was not happy with whatever he had written."

"*Or,*" Rudolf said, eyeing him, "it was a gift."

"Inspector Ziegler?"

Rudolf lifted his gaze from the pages to the constable in the doorway, whose face was plastered with urgency.

Did they at last have news?

"Go on, man," Inspector Ziegler snapped. "Out with it."

The tall, lanky figure walked in, handing him a damp paper, torn at the edges. "This was found on the body of Duke Sixten, sir."

"The missing page!" Rudolf exclaimed, snatching it.

The constable idled, withdrawing his hand. "It seems to be a..."

Ziegler watched as Rudolf held the bleeding words against the green journal. "A gift," he mumbled.

The lad had been right.

Rudolf began to pace, sliding his finger across each line as Ziegler and the constable stood by, confused.

"*'A golden net doth me enrapture, and in thy locks am I thus captured'*—It is a declaration of love," Rudolf said, turning to Ziegler.

The son of a blacksmith, Ziegler lacked a formal education—a fact that aggravated him like a papercut that would not heal.

"The golden net is a metaphor for her hair," Rudolf added.

Ziegler's voice softened as he lowered his pipe. "So it is." Now it was he who was pacing. "And this was found on the body of the duke?" he asked, pivoting to the constable.

"Yes, Inspector."

Combing the whiskers of his beard, Ziegler turned his attention to the cutout of the servant's corridor in the wall.

"Herr Kaspar," he murmured, walking toward it, "keep reading."

The passageway was dusty and grim, holding little remnants of this illicit love affair. Duke Sixten being in possession of the doctor's poem would have been more than enough to incite a quarrel, but how had he obtained it?

Stepping to the center of the indented window sill, Ziegler looked to the end of the hall, where Archduchess Philippa's door was cracked just enough to let in a sliver of light. Near the entrance sat a pile of books stacked haphazardly, surrounded by bits and pieces of what looked to be cut up paper.

Her room, like all the others, had been thoroughly searched, but he had been so caught up in the whereabouts of the doctor, Ziegler had yet to investigate it himself.

He walked over to the tower of books and picked one off the top, opening it to find that most of the pages had been torn out.

Peculiar.

Ziegler tried to imagine himself in the shoes of Troilo Visconti as he gently nudged the door open, emerging from the wall next to the archduchess' vanity. The mirror had been mostly broken out, the sight of which unnerved Ziegler enough to keep his distance. A glass quill with dried ink sat plainly on the vanity's surface.

Meditating on the quill, he thought about Philippa's story, and about how strangely *realistic* it had felt—ravings of a madwoman or not.

"*Inspector, come quick!*" Rudolf yelled down the corridor.

Ziegler burst through the passage door to find him glued to the window next to the desk. "Make room, lad!"

Across the pond, a few of their men worked to untangle a bloodied white gown from the bank.

"Inspector..." Rudolf turned to him with a soured expression.

"Come," Ziegler ordered. "There is no time to waste."

House servants flocked to the veranda to watch—many with tears in their eyes—as the inspector and his protégé made their way to assess the evidence.

"This is no longer just a missing person's case," said Rudolf, keeping Ziegler's step.

"Get everyone inside!" Ziegler shouted to his men. "This is a crime scene, not a circus!"

"You have read about the Munich incident," Rudolf went on. "Duke Sixten has a record as an aggressor."

"Without a body, we cannot say whose blood it is on that dress."

"The writing is on the walls, Inspector." Rudolf halted, out of breath. "If you just—!"

"Whether he was the aggressor or *not*, the duke is still the only victim we can confirm," he snapped. "Let me do my job, Herr Kaspar. When there is another poem to decipher, *then* I will ask for your assistance."

Met with a blank, dispirited stare, Ziegler turned to the constabulary. The group of men parted as he looked the gown over, its white and shredded threads now a watery, blood-soaked pink.

"We found these not far off from the embankment," one of his subordinates added, opening his palm.

There, in the center, sat a decorative pair of silver sheers engraved with a *P*.

"You were *saying*, sir?"

Ziegler met Rudolf's eye, conceding. "Do not get ahead of yourself, Herr Kaspar." Glazing over his understudy, he noticed Archduchess Erzsi standing like a doll in the library window. "Get Zürich on the line."

"Yes, Inspector."

If the scene had not been such a somber one, Rudolf might

have skipped to the cottage. Not only had he been right about the poem, but now, the murder weapon.

"Herr Rudolf Kaspar!"

Rudolf paused mid-step on his way up the veranda stairs.

"Over here."

To his left, above a budding rose bush, Erzsi leaned out the first-story windowsill, chin seated in both palms.

"Your Highness," he stuttered. "You should not be out here."

She then motioned to the fact that she was *not* outside.

Rudolf looked over his shoulder. Inspector Ziegler, who was intently paging through an open book, seemed distracted enough.

"What did you find down at the pond?" Erzsi asked.

He eyed her as she hugged her elbows, leaning further over. "I am not at liberty to tell you that."

"Is my cousin dead?"

Rudolf struggled for his words, unprepared for such a question.

"You found a body."

"We found a dress covered in blood," he replied, paranoid that Inspector Ziegler might appear behind him at any moment. "You mustn't say anything."

"Is that all they found?"

"That and a pair of sewing shears."

"Philippa and I both have a pair," Erzsi replied. "They were a Christmas gift from His Majesty."

Rudolf pocketed both hands, and an awkward silence befell them both until Erzsi finally spoke again.

"Do you believe me *now,* Rudolf?"

"We have one more testimony to collect," Rudolf replied, glancing at his watch. "Inspector Ziegler will question His Highness, Archduke Franz, once he arrives."

"He thinks I am hiding something. Your Inspector."

"He thinks you are protecting Visconti," he admitted, reluctantly meeting her eye. "Are you?"

At first, gauging her movements, Rudolf was certain Erzsi would retreat back through the window.

"Would you still like to touch a great mystery, Rudolf?" she asked.

He glanced over his shoulder, then back to her. "If it is one to solve then yes," he managed. "It is my job to find the truth."

"I *am* protecting Doctor Visconti." Erzsi's expression went blank. "But not because he is a guilty man."

"Then, why—?"

Before Rudolf could finish his sentence, Erzsi tossed him a bundle of rolled papers twice as thick as a man's wrist, tied together by a thin piece of thread.

"Because," she said, withdrawing back through the window, "Troilo Visconti is no *man* at all."

"Wait!" Rudolf urged. "Why are you doing this?"

But Erzsi had vanished as quickly as she'd appeared.

Rudolf walked up onto the veranda, craning his neck for one last look at the pond. The men had mostly cleared out, leaving only Inspector Ziegler behind. And whatever he was reading, he was more engulfed in it than he'd been five minutes ago.

His back against the pink marble, Rudolf gently slipped the thread from the roll. Some of the papers were fragile to the touch, nearly falling apart as he unraveled them. Only when he began to page through them did he realize they were...

"Travel papers?" he whispered.

SEVENTEEN

3:45 P.M.

Rudolf halted outside of the library, which was so quiet, he would have thought it empty if not for the wisps of pipe smoke that hung in the air. Outlined by a late afternoon glow, Inspector Ziegler sat beneath the stained glass, looking in a deep contemplation as he tapped the open book on his lap. The same one Rudolf had seen him reading outside by the pond.

"Sir?"

The inspector closed the mauve cover delicately, as though it belonged to someone he loved. "Shut the door, lad," he said.

Rudolf crossed the distance of the room, sliding his own books onto a table. He had come prepared with *Ballads of the Starlight Menagerie*, as well as Visconti's green journal.

"I just got off the line with Zürich," Rudolf began. "I spoke with Doctor Visconti's assistant who accompanied him here. Herr Jung."

"Yes." Inspector Ziegler puffed on his pipe as he slid the mysterious book from his lap to the window seat cushion. "What did he have to say?"

"Just that Visconti studied in Paris with Charcot at the Salpêtrière, dabbled in mesmerism, then obtained his doctorate at the Burghölzli and has been there ever since. Both his assistant and the Doctor Bleuler were more than willing to vouch for his character, although Herr Jung did not seem terribly surprised that he had turned up missing."

Rudolf glanced at the nameless, spineless novel sitting next to Ziegler. What had he been reading that had affected him so?

"Other than what the hospital has on record," he continued, "Visconti's paper trail is nearly nonexistent. It is like he is..."

"What?" Inspector Ziegler pressed. "What is he?"

Rudolf met his eager tone sheepishly. "A *phantom,* sir."

The word seemed to unsettle him, as he snapped quickly to his feet.

"Inspector, I know we do not have time to be chasing phantoms..."

The inspector puffed his pipe and shook his head erratically, as though he were trying to dispel a thought, or work out a plot hole.

"But there is something else."

"Out with it, then," he ordered, circling Rudolf with dark eyes.

Reaching into his pocket, Rudolf pulled out the roll of travel papers. "I found these under his bed," he said, handing them off.

Inspector Ziegler's reach was, once again, uncharacteristically gentle, and Rudolf studied his superior as he paged through the travel papers of Andrei Sidorova, Laurent Valicourt, multiple Troilo Viscontis, and a list of others—his hand becoming less steady with each one.

"Kaspar..."

"At first, I did not know what I was looking at because of the dates..."

Inspector Ziegler looked up, appearing just as perplexed. "There are enough aliases here for five lifetimes," he whispered hoarsely.

A part of Rudolf had hoped Inspector Ziegler would discredit the papers. Slice through the fog with his sword of mental clarity.

"Is it possible they could be counterfeit?" Rudolf asked meekly.

"Anything is *possible,* lad."

Rudolf gulped. "You believe they are legitimate."

Inspector Ziegler met his eye through the dust in the sunbeams, then turned away, toward the mysterious book. "I am a man of facts," he said, pipe clenched in his teeth. "But today, intuition is what speaks to me."

It spoke to Rudolf, too. It had spoken to him upstairs on the floor of Doctor Visconti's room as he'd knelt before the travel papers, laid out by date.

"I have a theory, sir," he sighed. "But it is only a theory."

"A theory," said the inspector, removing his pipe.

Rudolf grabbed *Ballads of the Starlight Menagerie* from the pile of books he'd carried in. "There are patterns in the aliases," he said, opening to the title page.

Inspector Ziegler wandered to his side. "Show me."

"This book here, Philippa's favorite, was penned in 1818 by someone called *Belarius,*" he began, meeting the eye of the stony inspector. "In William Shakespeare's *Cymbeline*, Belarius is the alias of an exiled nobleman. The author choosing this pseudonym is a play on his anonymity." Carefully, Rudolf reached for the stack of travel papers and slipped one off the top. "London, 1818. Troilo Visconti," he read out loud.

"The date is the same."

"Yes, but there is more..." Rudolf opened to the title page of *Ballads of the Starlight Menagerie,* then pointed to the publisher at the bottom. "Stylistically, the author's ballads are reminiscent of the Romantic poets of that time. Shelley, Keats, Byron..."

"I will take your word for it, lad," Inspector Ziegler whispered.

"And," Rudolf added, pulling the little green book from his

pocket, "the ones written by Doctor Visconti resemble this same style."

"What are you saying?"

Rudolf inhaled, big and deep. "If I did not know any better, Inspector...I would say the author of this compilation and Doctor Visconti are the same man."

Rudolf met the eye of the chief inspector, whose forehead dripped with beads of perspiration as he drew back in a slow daze.

"What is it, sir?"

"You have read the book," Ziegler mumbled, feeling the sweat drip down his temple. "These...ballads, yes?"

Rudolf nodded.

"What do you glean from them?"

"Well." Rudolf shrugged. "They are written by a griever, sometimes addressed to his beloved—"

"Who?" Ziegler demanded. "Who do you mean when you say his beloved?"

"There was one poem that included her name." Picking up the book, Rudolf flipped to the back. "The last one, I believe. Ballad one-hundred-and-sixteen," he added, handing it off.

"'Costanza,'" Ziegler read in a hoarse whisper. "'*My tempest, my treasure...*'"

"Yes, that is it. Costanza."

There it was, printed on paper—the same name of Philippa's unfortunate heroine. Had she merely reused the name for her story? Or—

"Even the poem found on Duke Sixten speaks of *constancy*," Rudolf sputtered. "See, it is merely wordplay on her name— Inspector? Inspector!"

Ziegler barreled through the library door into the hall, rupturing the peace of a few nearby servants.

Whatever Troilo Visconti was, he was not entirely human— and the story Archduchess Philippa had written, though allegedly fictional, held kernels of truth.

How could that be?

"Inspector Ziegler!" Rudolf called, running after him. "You dropped your pipe!"

By the cottage door, Archduchess Erzsi stood like a gargoyle, terrier in arm.

Did she know the nature of Troilo Visconti? What he *was?*

"Are you well, Chief Inspector?" she asked.

Averting his eyes, Ziegler didn't know how to answer. "Excuse me, Highness," he said. "I need some air."

The sun was low now, just visible over the treetops when he reached the veranda with Rudolf close behind.

"Inspector!" he yelled. "What is—?"

"Her story," Ziegler replied, at last whipping around. "It is her story."

"What story—Inspector, wait!" Rudolf crossed in front of him. "What *story?*"

"Archduchess Philippa." Ziegler exhaled a deep sigh as he pivoted toward the edge of the pond, where the pair of swans floated. "She wrote a story—Archduchess Erzsi left it in the parlor this morning. I started reading it, and..."

"And?" Rudolf coaxed. "What kind of story?"

"It was..." Ziegler grunted. "A story about a woman named Costanza, who lived in the 1400s."

The Adam's apple in Rudolf's throat bobbed as he swept his floppy curls out of his face. "And Doctor Visconti, is he in this...story?"

Ziegler only nodded. "I cannot explain to you how," he added, unable to say it out loud, "but her story is somehow true."

The swans seemed to watch from the shore. The only sound between the men, the tranquil water.

"He came back for her," Ziegler said.

"Came back," Rudolf repeated, "came back from where?"

"Perhaps it is more appropriate to say she came back for him..." Zeigler was losing Rudolf now, talking like a madman himself. "It is the night of June twentieth," he began, casting his gaze across the water to the weeping beech. "Tipped off by our scorned governess, Duke Sixten has discovered that Philippa and her doctor are lovers. The duke is banned from the villa premises, but that does not stop him from returning to confront Philippa in the night while Visconti is away, evidence in hand. The altercation turns violent, and if we have learned anything about the duke's history, it is that he has little regard for the fairer sex..."

Rudolf stood next to him in silent anticipation.

"Philippa kills him out of self-defense. Then, when Visconti returns, he helps her frame it as a double homicide. She strips her dress and they throw it in the water, planting her scissors nearby."

"Then Visconti does what he does best," Rudolf added.

Ziegler turned to him with approval.

"He secures travel papers under new aliases."

Time seemed to slow around the two of them as they teetered on the edge of a mystery near solved.

"Chief Inspector," a constable called down, "His Highness, Archduke Franz Ferdinand has arrived."

Ziegler turned back to Rudolf, pulling his handkerchief from his pocket.

"Do you think he knows?" Rudolf asked, lowering his voice.

Glancing over his shoulder, Ziegler caught a glimpse of Archduchess Erzsi, ever watchful in the window. "*She* knows Philippa is alive," he replied, dabbing his forehead. "But she wants us to presume otherwise."

Rudolf's hesitant gaze found the cottage behind them as the sound of carriage wheels rattled in the distance. "Because if she is dead, we have no reason to hunt for her."

"Precisely, lad."

Rudolf led the way back up the slope, brushing the tops of a few tall wildflowers with his palm. As they approached the carriage, Ziegler spotted Archduchess Erzsi behind the doors of the cottage, one hand pressed up against the glass. The turn of

Rudolf's cheek toward the veranda was so subtle that he would've missed it had he not been looking.

They would need to make this cross examination quick. The archduke couldn't tell them anything they didn't already know, and time was of the essence if they stood any chance of catching up with Philippa and her lover.

"Watch your step, Chief Inspector," said the footman as he opened the door.

Ziegler stepped onto the platform and into the stuffy car, managing a stifled "thank you" as Rudolf took his seat across from him.

"Are we losing our heads, Inspector?" he asked, turning his attention to the shifting landscape out the window. "What we have uncovered cannot equate to mere coincidence, yet...how can such a thing be?"

Ziegler understood wholeheartedly, though he could offer little comfort. As a devout Catholic, he was just as unsettled by the notion of Visconti being something not quite human.

"We must focus only on the facts at hand," he reminded. "The real murderer is at large, likely on her way to a boat right this instant."

"Chief Inspector," Rudolf stuttered. "You are not considering..."

It was clear by the look on his face he did not agree.

"I implore you to reconsider—!"

Ziegler grimaced as the carriage hit a bump. "I am aware you have stakes of a personal nature in this outcome, Herr Kaspar, but your little romance is not my concern."

Rudolf shook his head. "It is not nearly so shallow."

"You mean to tell me that you have not developed feelings for the girl?"

"Duke Sixten threw a woman from a balcony in Munich," Rudolf countered, more sternly than he'd ever spoken to him. "Women like Philippa, like my mother who suffered at the hands of my father for years—*these* are the people I took an oath to protect, Inspector."

Ziegler glared across the carriage. "You are suggesting that we aid a murderer, lad. For the sake of your job, I will choose to forget—"

"You know as well as I that the law rarely protects those most vulnerable!"

"Justice is justice," Ziegler berated.

"If we claim to be men of justice, then—!"

"Murder is murder! It is not up to me to create the laws, it is my duty to see to it they are enforced. The world is not gray as you would like to believe, Herr Kaspar. Justice is not contestable!"

Rudolf stared back, jaw clenched in visible frustration. "If we *truly* claim to be men of justice," he murmured, "we cannot in good conscience pursue her."

The carriage slowed to a stop, stilling the tension between them.

"You are overstepping," Ziegler warned, reaching for the handle.

The inspector dabbed his forehead as the butler led them through the maze of furred trophies. It seemed like days had passed since the emperor had received him that morning and he'd walked the very same halls. The curtains were still drawn, giving the inside of the villa a hazy appearance.

Rudolf lagged behind him, simmering in an angry obedience.

"Chief Inspector Alois Ziegler," a footman announced, showing them to the parlor doors.

Inside, Archduke Franz sat facing the hearth, a patient audience.

"Your Royal and Imperial Highness," Ziegler said, turning to Rudolf, "this is Herr Kaspar. He will be assisting me."

The archduke nodded to them both, expelling cigar smoke from both nostrils. "Chief Inspector, come in."

"May I begin by offering my condolences," Ziegler said, claiming one side of the velvet sofa.

The face of the archduke went pale. "Have you…"

"We have not located a body, Your Highness," Ziegler replied. "Only the gown." His fingers found the wiry whiskers on his chin. "My condolences were regarding Duke Sixten. I understand that you were close."

Archduke Franz seemed to graze over him with ghostly eyes. "May he rest in peace."

"Her Highness, Archduchess Erzsi, claims you asked him to leave the premises on the night of June nineteenth."

"That is correct. He returned to Kaiservilla without my knowledge or my consent."

"Why did you ask him to leave?"

"I found his behavior toward my sister and cousin to be appalling."

Ziegler hummed, stroking his beard. "Yet, you called him a friend?"

"I did." The archduke paused to flick his cigar in the crystal ashtray, looking deep in contemplation. "Our friendship ended the minute he intended to lay a hand on my sister."

There was sincerity in his tone, that of a man who had failed in his brotherly duties.

"Archduchess Erzsi testified that Doctor Visconti was with you the night of the murder," he continued. "She claims he came to ask for your blessing."

"That is correct."

"And did he leave with it, Your Highness?" Rudolf chimed in.

Ziegler met his eye with a fierce warning.

"He did," Archduke Franz replied. "Albeit, in rather a hurry."

"Why?" asked Ziegler, tearing his gaze from Rudolf.

"I cannot say, Inspector."

"No, Your Highness. Why did you grant Doctor Visconti your

blessing to marry your sister?" Ziegler sat back. "What deemed him worthy of such a request?"

Archduke Franz took a gentle puff of his cigar. "I witnessed him intercede with Duke Sixten."

"At what lengths do you think he would go to keep her safe?"

"Chief Inspector." The archduke sat back with a blink. "Doctor Visconti is an odd man with an odd reputation, but he is no murderer. I am confident."

A regular poker player was the archduke. Still as a stone wall, the only movement from him was the coiling smoke from his cigar.

"I am not implying he is." A droplet of sweat ran down the back of Ziegler's neck as he spoke. "Highness."

Archduke Franz motioned for him to go ahead. "Then what *are* you implying, Chief Inspector?"

"Doctor Visconti is well-versed in the art of fraud and forgery. He left behind a collection of travel papers with various aliases."

Ziegler felt Rudolf shift in his seat next to him.

"If there were any chance your sister were alive," Ziegler warned, too quiet for anyone else to hear, "things would become very complicated, indeed."

The archduke seemed to follow, his eyes blazing beneath their stony exterior. "And in your opinion, Inspector?"

At last, they had reached the crux. The moment of truth. Yet, it was not the justice Ziegler had imagined.

What of Costanza Visconti?

What of *her* justice?

"I am inclined to believe she is dead," Ziegler replied. In his periphery, he could see Rudolf snap his neck to face him. "Unfortunately the gown was quite torn, which indicates that the body was likely taken by an animal."

"Dear God," the archduke whispered under his breath. "Have mercy. You feel confident that this is the case?"

Ziegler turned to Rudolf, who stared back in visible approval.

"I do, Highness," Ziegler replied. "I will file the report with your permission."

"It is for the best that I break the news to His Majesty myself." Archduke Franz nodded as he quietly rose to his feet. "And Erzsi, I..."

"I can tell her, Your Highness," Rudolf said. "Gently. If you would prefer it."

"Yes..." The archduke leaned over, extinguishing the cigar. "Your work here has been most valuable," he said. "Both of you. Thank you, Chief Inspector."

Watching him, Ziegler could not say if he actually *believed* that Philippa was dead. But regardless, this would ensure her safety.

Why had Ziegler done such a thing?

He couldn't leave the stagnant parlor quickly enough—

"What of Doctor Visconti?" the archduke asked suddenly, catching them at the door.

"He has fled back into the obscurity from which he came," Ziegler replied.

Eager to get back to the cottage, he made haste with Rudolf on his heels, the arrow of his moral compass spinning.

"Sir—!"

The carriage door shut, snapping him from his spiral.

"Why did you do it?" Rudolf was mere inches from him, demanding an answer that Ziegler didn't have. "Why did you let them go?"

He reached for his handkerchief, face pouring with sweat. "Because I cannot in good conscience pursue her," he whispered.

EIGHTEEN

8:01 P.M.

Rudolf fiddled with the curled edges of the travel papers as he stood in the window, watching the sun sink between the trees. It was the first clear evening since they'd arrived, and as if nature itself were seeing them off, the entire parlor had been swallowed in a bittersweet tangerine glow.

"Herr Kaspar?"

Rudolf turned over his shoulder to see Governess Coudenhove lagging in the doorway, curious about how the questioning of the archduke had gone. Inspector Ziegler's having retired to bed early was only more reason to inquire.

"Hello," he said.

"Can I fetch you anything?"

"No." Rudolf wrapped his fingers around the cluster of rolled papers. "No, thank you, Fräulein. I am perfectly glad to observe the sunset."

She nodded, her smile nothing short of forlorn. "They can be quite beautiful here," she replied, allowing her hand to slide down the length of the frame.

Rudolf turned his attention back to the veranda, and to Erzsi, gazing out onto the pond under a pink sky. "Yes, they are," he said.

"I shall be in the library if you find yourself in need of anything," the governess added, leaving him.

Leaning closer to the glass, Rudolf again found Erzsi's long, sandy braid as she leaned over the veranda railing.

They had sat her down in the parlor just before six to inform her of Philippa's death. Expecting a performance, Inspector Ziegler had been unmoved by her tears, but she'd cried so convincingly that Rudolf had been convinced they were real.

In fact, he knew they were.

Her cousin and best friend, whether dead or alive, had gone away forever, leaving Erzsi even more isolated than before. And soon, Rudolf would be on a train back to Vienna, and she would disappear back into whatever palace she had come from.

Clutching the papers, Rudolf willed himself forward, propelled by the prospect of things unsaid.

The orange rays were beginning to dissipate as he closed the glass door quietly behind him. Erzsi, illuminated by the last remnants of a sunset halo, did not move.

"Will you ever see them again?" Rudolf asked.

A lifetime seemed to pass before she finally turned on her heel. "No," Erzsi answered, leaning back against the iron rail. "I shall never see them again."

A firefly announced itself next to her as Rudolf approached.

"I have touched a great mystery," he said, offering up the roll of travel papers. "The first and possibly the last of my life."

Erzsi shook her head in refusal as she turned back to the dark pond. "Then keep what I have given you—store it away in an old chest for your children to find one day."

Rudolf retracted his hand, but the chilliness of her tone would not be enough to deter him. "I leave for Vienna tomorrow," he said. "As do you."

"And?"

Gripping the railing, Erzsi had been reduced to a defensive little girl, armoring herself at the first sign of closeness.

Still, Rudolf stepped closer. "I would like to—"

Her lips found his cheek.

"I would like to write to you," he murmured as they lingered together, temple to temple.

Erzsi pressed her nose to his jaw, then pulled away slowly. "Goodbye, Herr Kaspar," she whispered.

Her exit twinkled with fireflies as Rudolf watched her walk away.

"Your secret is safe with me," he said suddenly.

Erzsi halted in her tracks, her eyes glazed over in something close to fright as she turned slowly toward him.

"I know you helped them escape."

She did not so much as blink, as though she were trying to gauge whether or not he was threatening her.

"I do not know how, but I do," Rudolf added.

"Good night, Herr Kaspar," Erzsi said shakily.

Only the sound of cicadas remained as she made her way inside, leaving Rudolf alone on the veranda. The cottage seemed, at that moment, to be in the middle of a jungle with no humans for miles. Only the caws of crows, and the chirps of frogs.

It was all over now, this great adventure. Washed away like the transient tide.

Holding tightly to the papers, Rudolf made his way to the library, where Governess Coudenhove sat.

"Fräulein," he said, knocking against the door with his knuckle.

"Herr Kaspar." She seemed to wipe something from under her eye as she turned around. "Can I do something for you?"

"I was wondering if you might light the hearth in the parlor," he said. "I have got a terrible chill in my bones that will not leave me."

Governess Coudenhove did not question his strange request, only rose to her feet to fulfill it. Rudolf could not help but feel a certain sympathy for her, having found her all alone. This feeling lingered as he followed her to the parlor and watched her light the hearth from the edge of the golden chaise.

"Are you glad to be returning to Vienna?" he asked, unable to bear the silence.

"I will be taking the train south," she replied, eyes on the hearth. "To Eisenstadt."

Rudolf laced his fingers over the wad of travel papers. "Oh," he said. "You will not be returning to the Hofburg?"

Governess Coudenhove paused to stoke the growing flame. "No."

The governess was the opposite of Erzsi. Timid, without direction. And, as he fanned the corners of the travel papers, Rudolf again felt a surge of compassion arise within him.

In the end, Troilo and Philippa's romance had been no different than any other great love story. It had blown in like a storm and left just as quickly, leaving nothing but despair in its wake. And Rudolf knew that all too often, the collateral damage left behind were those with beating hearts of their own.

Brushing her hands across her skirt, Governess Coudenhove stood. "This should last you a while."

"I am sorry, Fräulein."

She straightened her shoulders, visibly struggling for her words. "I do not know what you have to be sorry about, Herr Kaspar," she whispered.

Rudolf blinked, glancing up at her earnestly from his seat on the chaise. "I hope you find happiness wherever you go."

"Thank you, Herr Kaspar," she said with a faint smile. "Good night."

"Good night, Fräulein."

Alone, Rudolf turned his attention on the fire, the papers damp in his grip, the closest things to a miracle he might ever hold. Even if he did keep them into old age, Troilo Visconti might still be alive even then, living out his life somewhere with Archduchess Philippa.

Rudolf walked over to the hearth and knelt before the crackling flames, and, pulling a paper from the stack, he threw it into the fire.

"You are free," he murmured.

On the other side of the door, Erzsi watched him with teary eyes as he incinerated paper after paper, burning all the evidence to a crisp.

"Hello?" Rudolf asked, rising to his feet.

She pressed her back flush to the crimson wallpaper, listening to his voice grow closer as he walked to the door.

"Is someone there?"

Refusing to speak, Erzsi shut her eyes violently, feeling multiple tears splash onto her chest.

A mere inches away, Rudolf retracted back into the library. "Goodbye, Rudolf," she whispered, slipping down the hall.

NINETEEN

10:47 P.M.
The night before

"Why could Troilo not call the wind?"

Tearing her gaze from the inky sketch of a castle, Philippa pivoted toward Erzsi, who lay sprawled across her bed with Blitz. "Because he was trapped in a mortal's body," she replied. "Costanza burned his skin."

"He called it the other day at the villa, did he not?"

"He has had four hundred years of practice."

"Could he find a new skin, somehow?"

Having read Philippa's story front to back, Erzsi had been asking questions all night as Philippa sketched away, trying her best to pass the time until Troilo returned from his meeting with Franz.

"Snails find new shells," Erzsi added.

Philippa laughed under her breath as she turned back to her vanity.

"Has he *tried,* Pippa?" Erzsi asked, slipping down from the bed. "I for one would like to see his true form. It is the least I am owed."

"He has lived as a human longer than any man," Philippa countered. "In that way he is more human than us both."

Erzsi waltzed over, laying her hand across the carved back of Philippa's chair.

"They certainly are taking their time about it," Philippa sighed.

"It is the only way Franz knows how to be."

Philippa wanted to ignore the knots in her stomach and nod along, but could it really be so easy?

"Franz and Sophie have set a new precedent," Erzsi reassured, as if reading her mind. "I have no doubts that Troilo will obtain His Majesty's blessing, and, lest you forget, I am almost always right."

Philippa lifted the open diary to her lips. "Then I pray this is not a rare shortcoming," she added, blowing lightly across the wet ink.

"Beautiful," Erzsi murmured, marveling at the illustrated page. "Will you publish it under a pseudonym as the Princess of Romania does?"

"This is just for me," Philippa replied. "And for him."

"Might I make *one* tiny suggestion regardless?" Erzsi hung onto the back of the chair. "It needs a name. It is still a story, after all."

Philippa dipped her glass quill into the inkwell with a smile. "Then I shall give it a name."

Erzsi leaned her elbows onto the vanity, chin seated in both palms as Philippa's hand moved in graceful strokes. *"The Sky Flower's Bride,* by Philippa—" Erzsi paused. "Look! He has returned!"

Philippa lifted her gaze to the curve of the path outside, just past the sparkling reflection of the lamp's hanging crystals.

"And by the look of it, he has had one too many brandies with Franz!"

Blitz let out a low, sleepy growl from the end of the bed.

"No." Philippa lowered her quill as the figure drew nearer, and his fair features and military garb came into view. "Duke Sixten…"

"How dare he show his face here again?" Erzsi hissed, drawing back. "We must alert the house."

"He has come for me," Philippa contested, jumping to her feet.

"You are not intending to go and meet him?" Erzsi scolded.

"I am not afraid of him, Erzsi."

"You should be."

Philippa could feel her cousin's gaze, hanging heavy as a fog as she wrapped herself in her dressing gown.

"Then I shall come with you."

"No—" Philippa reached for the pair of silver shears resting atop the covered vanity. "Keep watch from the window and call the house if necessary. Troilo will return soon."

"Why not just wait for him, then?" Erzsi called after her.

Philippa's stomach churned as she tip-toed down the stairs, passing Mellie's room. The metal scissors against her palm had turned slippery from her nerves, but her core burned hot with anger.

Only a dim beacon of light from Philippa's bedroom rippled across the vacant pond, where the duke paced the path with a drunken urgency. The entire forest seemed to fall into a watchful silence as Philippa walked toward the water.

"You dare to show your face here again?" she called to him.

"You are up late, Highness," he said, pushing the hair from his glistening forehead. "I figured you would be…tucked away, cozy in bed. Prostituting yourself to an Italian foreigner."

"You would speak to me in such a way, Sixten?" Philippa asked. "It seems you have forgotten who I am."

He pivoted toward her with a laugh. "I am more clear than ever about who you *are.*"

Overcome with a sudden and uneasy recognition, Philippa did not move as the duke sauntered closer.

"And I, you..." She blinked, seeing clearly for the first time as he stood in front of her. "Your very presence brought illness upon me."

With the barest of snickers, Duke Sixten reached into his pocket. "I believe this belongs to you," he replied, holding Troilo's poem in his hand.

"Give it to me."

"If only your doctor knew how little it took to get you into bed." The scent of brandy washed over Philippa as he reached for her cheek. "He could have saved his ink," he said, brushing her hair behind her shoulder.

Philippa stepped back, but he followed.

"Come now," he snarled, grabbing onto her arm. *"Star of the Sea."*

Gripping the scissors tight, she directed the point at him, only for him to catch her wrist.

"I will throw your body in the pond and have everyone believe you drowned yourself for love," he snarled, prying them from her fingers. "And with your history, do you think anyone would question it?"

Philippa lunged for them in the grass, but was struck with a hard blow across the face.

"I would have spoiled you like a doll!"

A viper reared up next to his foot as Philippa came to, feeling the taste of salt gush over her bottom lip.

"Instead, you choose that ghastly man," the duke added, stomping the serpent's head in.

Philippa glared up at him. *"I would rather be his prostitute than your wife,"* she spat, sending the blood across his face.

Grabbing her by the hair, he pinned her to a nearby tree. "Then it is good that it is no longer your love I want—"

Struggling against him, she clawed at his eyes with the ferocity of a tigress. "Then you may enjoy me as a corpse!"

Her head hit the trunk of the tree as Duke Sixten squeezed her neck. His voice taunted her as he rummaged through her robe with his other hand.

"I have lost everything because of you."

Philippa could see over his shoulder that the light of the beacon had been snuffed, cloaking the lawn in the shadow of night.

Where was Erzsi—?

Would she die here at the hands of this man, strangled to death for Troilo to find on his walk back from the villa?

This time, there would be no spirit of the water to bargain for her soul. But wherever it migrated, she would wait for him—and he would find her. Twenty years or twenty thousand, it made no difference.

"You can not admit that he has won," Philippa gasped with what remaining breath she could muster.

A breeze blew a wind song in the leaves above as her vision blurred, and her body weakened. Lightening ruptured the sky in the distance.

Troilo.

And then, something sprung from the bushes behind Duke Sixten, hooking an arm around his neck with the savagery of a wild animal. The sound of puncturing flesh and slicing tendons filled Philippa's ears, and she reached for her throat as the duke stumbled backward, revealing his assailant in a ghostly white sundress.

Erzsi lifted her chin to the sky, dropping the scissors in the grass next to her. She winced as a raindrop hit her cheek, then another.

"Erzsi…"

The pitter patter of raindrops picked up their frequency, drowning out the groans of Duke Sixten.

Dazed, Erzsi looked down at her dress, spattered with his blood. *"I am the snake in the grass,"* she whispered, meeting Philippa's eye.

Nearing the cottage, Troilo charged ahead through the dark forest.

He'd been sitting in the parlor with the archduke when the *feeling* began to creep over him, and, within minutes, a murder of crows descended onto the villa terrace. Scratching at the glass, they cawed in warning—that the duke had returned, and Philippa was in danger. To the bewilderment of Archduke Franz, and with no time to call a carriage, Troilo left in a hurry on foot.

"Philippa!" he shouted, scanning the path. "Where—!"

Her and Erzsi's white dresses seemed to glow in the dark as they huddled together on the ground, indistinguishable from one another.

Gathering them both, one in each arm, he had never felt such relief.

Troilo lifted Philippa's bloodied chin, now being washed clean by the rain. "Will I never learn?" he asked, nearly in tears.

"Troilo..."

He met Erzsi's gaze as she lifted her cheek from Philippa's shoulder. Never had she looked so pale, and her eyes spoke what she could not utter as they trailed left, to something over his shoulder.

There lay Duke Sixten on his back next to the pond, his voice nothing more than a wheeze. "Doctor..."

"I had to do it," Erzsi whispered sharply.

But Troilo hardly heard her. Just as the day the Pazin tower had burnt to the ground, he found himself entranced by a hatred so divine that it could only be grief in disguise.

"Doctor... have mercy on me..."

A viper twitched next to Troilo in the grass, extending his venom.

"Mercy, indeed," he murmured, allowing the snake to slither into his palm.

The exacting moment of his heart's revenge had come, and at last, there would be retribution. For Costanza, for his unborn child, and for him. Matthias would not escape his fate a second time.

The duke's face contorted in a smile as Troilo took a knee, viper wrapped within his fingers. Unbuttoning the blood-soaked collar, Troilo lifted it back and assessed the multiple stab wounds.

"I know...from where I recognize you," Duke Sixten coughed.

He was fading, and his wounds were extensive, but he could be saved.

"It is all the better you know I am," Troilo replied.

"You are bound by an oath to do no harm. My...brother...."

"Brother." Troilo recoiled. "I loved you as a brother, and you—!" His oath was not lost on him, nor the irony of the serpent coiled within his fingers like an Asclepion rod. "You condemned me to a fate worse than death!"

Duke Sixten tilted his head upward, to the falling rain. *"Vipereos moreos non violabo,"* he heaved. "Oath breaker..."

Troilo opened his mouth, but it was Erzsi's words that came out.

"This is for my cousin!" she shouted, plunging the point of the scissors into the duke's clavicle. *"This* is for that woman in Munich—" She struck him a second blow. "And this, *this is for me,"* she said, dragging the opened scissor blade across his exposed neck.

The duke choked and gurgled on the pooling blood as Erzsi threw her blade to the ground. "I will be the only one to answer for his death."

Troilo watched the eyes of Duke Sixten turn still as glass. "May we never meet again," he murmured, stunned.

Philippa found Troilo's side, next to the body of the slain duke.

"I could not do it," he said shamefully, "I..."

Grabbing onto him with all her might, she brought him in close. "Your human heart, Troilo," she sighed. "Its capacity for love, for mercy—it is the *best part* of you."

Erzsi watched as Philippa kissed him all over. They would be free, now—both of them. Free to marry without consequence, to do and live as they deserved.

"Erzsi..."

She looked down at Troilo, whose eyes had glossed over in an unspoken appreciation.

"When they come for me, I will sleep with no regrets," she declared, wiping her hands across her dress.

Philippa untucked her nose from Troilo's shoulder, and he slowly rose to his feet, pulling her up alongside him.

"It will not be you they come for." He turned to Philippa. "I know someone in Vienna who can help us obtain travel documents, but we must leave as soon as possible."

"If you flee, you will look guilty," Erzsi objected. "I do not understand."

"In the morning, when you discover—"

"*I?*"

"When *you* discover the body floating in the pond, you will scream for help." Picking up his poem, Troilo tucked it securely back into Duke Sixten's pocket. "The Chief Inspector will be here by noon."

"Yes," Erzsi stuttered, watching him roll the body into the pond. "Chief Inspector Ziegler, I know him—he investigated my father's death."

"Good," Troilo replied, glancing up at her. "You will tell him that Philippa acted in self-defence, and remind him of the duke's violent record. Be adamant that you believe she died from her wounds."

"A double homicide?" Philippa asked. "But there is no other body..."

"We will plant Erzsi's bloody dress in the pond as though it belongs to you," Troilo replied, turning to her. "We will tear it so it appears that—"

"An animal has taken it."

Philippa and Troilo both turned to Erzsi.

"Yes," he said.

"These are engraved." Dropping to her knees, Erzsi reached for the pair of slippery scissors. "Pippa?"

Philippa crossed in front of her, swiping her own pair from the lawn.

"What of Mellie?" Erzsi asked. "She will tell them everything."

"She will. Given the circumstances, and my history with the duke, I shall be the first suspect."

"An honor killing."

"Yes," Troilo replied. "And if indeed they determine Philippa is alive and we have run off together, it will not matter. Their suspects will be long gone across the Atlantic by then."

"But..." Erzsi's voice shook a bit.

Troilo walked over, and as he kneeled before her, covered in bloody handprints, she was hit with the sudden, indubitable knowing that this was goodbye.

"You must do everything in your power to throw them off course," he said. "Share anything you can to distract them from looking any closer at you."

"Anything?"

"Anything," Troilo replied, stern.

Erzsi's eyes began to water as he reached into his pocket, pulling out the tiny key to his dragon box.

"I will leave this in your safekeeping," he said, closing her fingers over it, dried with blood.

"And where will you go?" Erzsi demanded tearfully, turning to

Philippa. "Across the Atlantic, where will you go? You are all the family I have!"

"Sweet cousin," Philippa said softly, squeezing her tight. "You have been a true friend to me, closer than a sister."

Erzsi's lip trembled as she looked between them. "What shall I do without you both?"

"You will march in the streets as you always planned," said Troilo. "You shall make yourself useful."

TWENTY

June 22, 1900
8:21 A.M.

Footsteps and chatter echoed through the halls as servants toted baggage down the wooden staircase, and out to the carriage. All packed himself, Ziegler had wandered down to the library, which was the only room that had remained untouched that morning.

The dog days of summer had gone, leaving behind the grief of what was and what could have been. And as Ziegler stood before the shelves, he opened to the middle of *Ballads of the Starlight Menagerie.*

> *This ache of longing*
> *Doth never leave my side.*
> *It walks with me as a shadow,*
> *Marking time with endless steps.*
> *'Tis mine own heartbeat*
> *That keepeth thee alive in me,*
> *And thus, I cannot sever it.*
> *Checkmate, my miserable fate.*

Closing the book, Ziegler peeked at the mauve cover of Archduchess Philippa's diary under it. Never in his thirty years of investigating had the inspector borne witness to such a story. Likely, he never would again.

Ziegler scanned the catalogued titles until he reached the weathered spine of the *Nibelungenlied,* then pulled out two titles next to it. Sliding the *The Sky Flower's Bride* and *Ballads of the Starlight Menagerie* into place, he stood back to observe.

"Chief Inspector?"

Ziegler turned to see Archduchess Erzsi in a wide-brimmed straw hat, standing in the doorway.

"Your Highness," he greeted, retracting his hand from the bookshelf.

"You enjoyed it, then," she said. "Pippa's story."

Ziegler nodded with a subtle shrug. "Her Highness was a gifted storyteller, indeed."

"Yes..." The archduchess averted her large eyes to the floor. "I will miss her," she added, picking at the frilled sleeves of her white sundress.

"I do hope you may find peace in her absence."

Erzsi's gaze snapped back up at him like a slingshot. "There is no peace to be had for me, Inspector," she replied. "But I thank you for the thought."

"Goodbye, Your Highness," he said, turning toward her with a bow.

"Chief Inspector," she replied softly with a nod. "May our paths not cross again."

Ziegler turned back to the bookshelf, where the two books now sat together side by side. He as her muse, and she as his.

"May they not," he mumbled, tapping the spines with two fingers.

Ziegler fiddled with his pocket watch as he made his way up the stairs, dodging the maids with their armfuls of dresses. Soon, his and Rudolf's carriage would arrive, and he would need to have his luggage downstairs, ready to load.

What the inspector didn't intend to find in Visconti's bedroom was Governess Coudenhove gazing out the second-story window.

"Fräulein," Ziegler said, finding her side. "Is something the matter?"

"Forgive me, Chief Inspector," she sniffled.

Ziegler followed her gaze to where the carriage below was being loaded with Archduchess Erzsi's belongings. "Are you a religious woman, Fräulein?"

"Very much so."

"Then perhaps it would benefit you to confess that which is on your conscience," Ziegler replied.

"It was I who exposed them to Duke Sixten," she admitted. "I am the reason he is gone."

"Doctor Visconti."

The governess nodded hastily, as though she were on the edge of a full nervous breakdown. Of all the reasons to be upset in her position, it was still the doctor who still consumed her thoughts.

"I assure you, Fräulein, the reasoning is much more complicated than that."

"Perhaps you will find him, yet," she said, tears streaming.

Ziegler eyed her sternly. "I do not imagine any man ever will," he mumbled with a nod.

Averting her gaze to the floor, she pivoted. "Farewell, Chief Inspector," she whispered, walking past.

"Goodbye, Fräulein."

Ziegler sauntered closer to the windowsill, where doors clamored below as the maids loaded the carriage with Erzsi's belongings. Dresses and hat boxes, in addition to whatever she'd inherited from Philippa.

"Chief Inspector," said Rudolf, walking in behind him.

"Fräulein said I might find you up here. Did you speak with her? She looked quite upset."

"She was, yes," Ziegler grunted. "Moreso over Visconti being gone than what happened to Archduchess Philippa—who *has,* for the record, been pronounced dead."

Rudolf crossed his arms over his chest as he found his side.

"Not long now," said Ziegler. "We shall be home by sundown."

"Home by sundown," Rudolf hummed. "Will you attend the funeral?"

"I have seen enough funerals."

Beneath them, Archduchess Erzsi walked onto the veranda in her crisp, reflective sundress.

Ziegler could feel Rudolf clench up next to him. "Have you bid her a proper farewell, yet?"

"I, ah..."

He turned to his understudy, dressed smartly in a brown vest and patterned cravat. "Not all of us are lucky enough to live nine lives, lad," Ziegler murmured. "Every second counts."

Rudolf nodded to himself as he peered down at Archduchess Erzsi. "It is moot, but..." He nudged Ziegler with the edge of a book. "Here are the passenger records you requested."

"Have you looked at them?"

"I have not."

Ziegler took the log into his hands, opening to the center, where hundreds of cursive names decorated the pages. "Moot...yes."

Rudolf turned his attention back to the window.

"Herr Kaspar—you said that the character of *Belarius* adopted an alias in this Shakespeare play, did you not?"

"Yes, sir. *Morgan.*"

Ziegler nodded, patting Rudolf's shoulder. "Go on."

"Do you need me to take anything downstairs?"

"Quite all right, lad," Ziegler replied. "I will see you at the carriage."

Rudolf fidgeted in place, then nodded, leaving him with a boyish smirk.

Pivoting back to the window, Ziegler watched Archduchess Erzsi as she descended the veranda stairs, clutching a black oriental box in her hands. He couldn't help but wonder what it might have looked like for her and Rudolf, in another time, where their lives had not crossed like ships in the night without a moment longer to know each other.

Ziegler licked his thumb and turned the page of the log and its montage of names.

Sir Morgan & Constance Waugh

Filled with a most peculiar satisfaction, he laughed. "Well done, Visconti," Ziegler breathed, combing his whiskers. "Well done."

In the end, Troilo Visconti had been a man much like him—who would have done anything for a second chance at life with the woman he loved. And whether by fate or by will, that prayer had been answered.

When Ziegler's gaze was at last drawn back to the window, he found Archduchess Erzsi looking up at him. On her lips, the tiniest glint of a smile—but her *eyes*—those large frosty eyes...

Ziegler felt in his bones the famed chill that lay behind *Erzsi's saucers*.

Things always hide in plain sight, Inspector. Her voice tore through in his memory as she reached for the carriage door. *If only one has the eyes to see them.*

BALLADS

OF

THE STARLIGHT MENAGERIE

BY

BELARIUS.

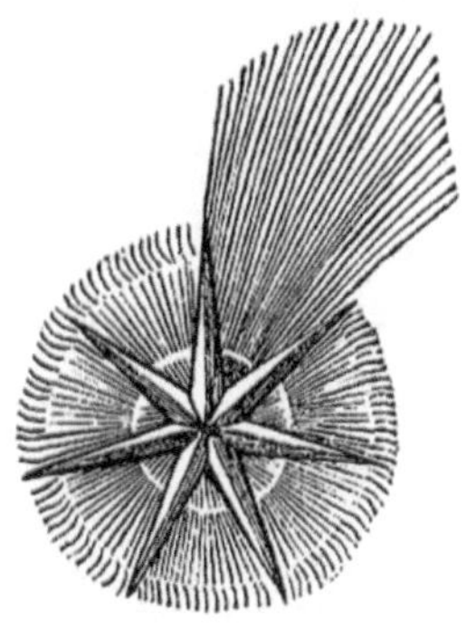

London :

PRINTED FOR
LACKINGTON, HUGHES, HARDING, MAVOR & JONES,
FINSBURY SQUARE.

1818.

I

Oh what hells would I endure
To taste of thy heavens,
To drink from thy fountains,
And pray at thy temples
Once more.

II

This ache of longing
Doth never leave my side.
It walks with me as a shadow,
Marking time with endless steps.
'Tis mine own heartbeat
That keepeth thee alive in me,
And thus, I cannot sever it.
Checkmate, my miserable fate.

III

The pain of this life is agony,
But the beauty is almost too much to bear.
The sunlight mocks me,
The green spring spurs my jealousy,
All of nature dares to go on without thee.

O that it were night forever!
Would that it were eternal winter,
That I might sleep away the hours
In silent oblivion.

But nay, I recant!
For this bed, without thy warmth, is the cruelest tormentor of all.

IV
How many times have I thought upon it,
When I should see thy face again?
In what ways altered but ever-constant,
My Star of the Sea,
Let thy name prove true
As my love for you.

I have grown accustomed to my nightly wanderings,
In my tearful dreams,
Parting lips, entering into
Thy silken and velvety wedlock.
My thoughts drift to bed, but thine eyes don't lie—
They keep me awake, in the twilight gray,
Where there is no day.

My dear, my heart,
Quarry of my life—
Thy starry beams I track in strife.
But a golden net doth me enrapture,
And in thy locks am I thus captured.

V
The time will come,
Our time will come!
When we will break from our bondage,

Free of our debts,
And take flight.
Where shall we go, my love?
What is your fancy?
What paradise awaits us?
O what Heaven awaits me,
In your eyes, and in your arms
At long last.

VI

I speak to the storm cloud, I say—
How do you choose between destruction and deliverance?
I ask him how he holds his sorrow,
I ask him how he carries his grief.

He tells me only that he comes to cleanse.
And I envy his ability to swell and burst,
For I, too, am black and brewing,
But with no hope of relief.

VII

I found you in the water,
And I lost you to the water,
Sea-born and sea-bedded.
If I drown, will you come back to me?
If I founder, will you rescue me?
If I sail my ship, and listen for your song,
Will you take me under?
Or is it only my hope I see ahead—
Dashed against the rocks,

And washed up on the shore.

VIII

I walk in your footsteps
To find where you have gone,
My dream phantom,
My waking nightmare,
I hear your echo and give chase—
Lead me onward!
I will follow!
I will follow.

I fall to my knees
A lonely pilgrim,
I pray for your love,
But I beg for your mercy—
How much longer must I sit here still, with your memory?

VIIII

Casket Song

Costanza
My tempest, my treasure—
I will give you a proper burial,
I will be your chief mourner,
Carry you on my shoulder,
To the ground of your keeping.
O fortunate, hallowed ground,
How I hate and envy you!

And deep in that rich earth,
I will make you a nuptial chamber.
Death to anyone that disturbs your sleep,
Or tries to prize you from my hold,
My prize you are,
My bride you will always be.

ACKNOWLEDGMENTS

There is always real-life magic that runs parallel to the creation of any book, at least for me, but I found writing *The Starlight Menagerie* to be especially so. I went through many major life shifts during its two year gestation process, and had many personal experiences that I may never be able to fully explain. *The Starlight Menagerie* touches on themes of grief, surrender, destiny and what it means to be a *human* vs. what it means to be a *soul.* I had my own gnosis around each of these things that I will not soon forget—yet, I could not have never written this story alone.

Firstly, I'd like to thank my co-author and best friend, Rory Sidney: not only for being Troilo's voice, but also a constant source of support and encouragement in my life. What first began as a "creative experiment" really blossomed into something so much bigger. Agape in all its beauty and complexity.

Secondly, I would like to thank my friend, Kat: whom, without her expertise, I would have never known about the zmajevi and their brides. If you are interested in the folklore that inspired this story, I implore you to check out her pamphlet, *Balkan Folk Magic: Zmaj* by Katarina Pejović.

To my sister, Ally, and the countless hours of childcare she gifted me: I would have never finished this book without you! To Sasha and all the folks on her discord: thank you for the safe space, the guidance, and shared experiences. To my cover artists Sarah and Shelby: thank you for bringing these characters to life. To my like-minded friends who inspired me so much in this period: thank you for encouraging me to "go to those places I have not been."